THE AGE OF
KALI

JOCELYN DAVIS

First published by Respondeo Books in 2021
respondeobooks.com

ISBN: 978-0-9993059-6-6 (paperback)
ISBN: 978-0-9993059-7-3 (ebook)

Book design by Adam Robinson
for GoodBookDevelopers.com

The epigraph is from *The Mahabharata of Krishna-Dwaipayana Vyasa Translated into English Prose*. Translated by Kisari Mohan Ganguli. Calcutta: Bharata Press, 1883-1896.

The "Hymn to the Origins of Sacred Speech" (Chapters 8 and 15) is Hymn 10:71 from the Rig Veda, a collection of Sanskrit hymns composed between 1700 and 1100 BCE. Translated by Ralph T.H. Griffith. Wikisource, 1896.

The "catechism" on page 2 is adapted from Hymn 10:90, the Rig Veda (various translations).

This is a work of fiction, inspired by characters and plot elements found in the Mahabharata. It is not a retelling of the Hindu epic; rather, a complete reimagining.

To my daughter, Emily

Afterward, [King] Janamejaya with all his sadasyas put a question to the eminent brahmin, with joined palms as follows:

"Oh brahmin, thou hast seen with thine own eyes the acts of the Kurus and the Pandavas. I am desirous of hearing thee recite their history. What was the cause of the disunion amongst them that was fruitful of such extraordinary deeds? Why also did that great battle, which caused the death of countless creatures, occur between all my grandfathers— their clear sense overclouded by fate? Oh excellent brahmin, tell me all this in full, for thou art the one who knows it."

—The Mahabharata, The Book of the Beginning

Contents

THE AGE OF
KALI

THE ROYAL FAMILY OF KURU
at the onset of the Great War

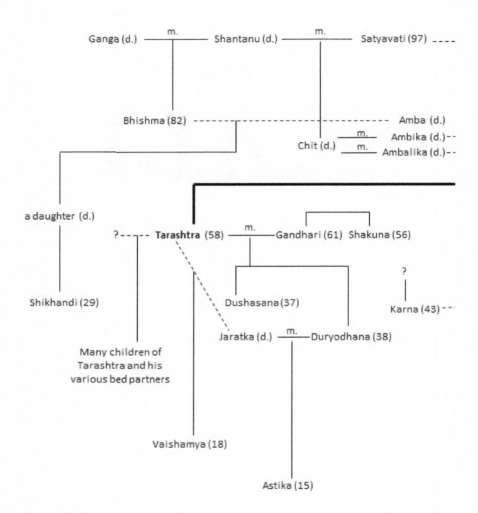

THE KAURAVA SIDE

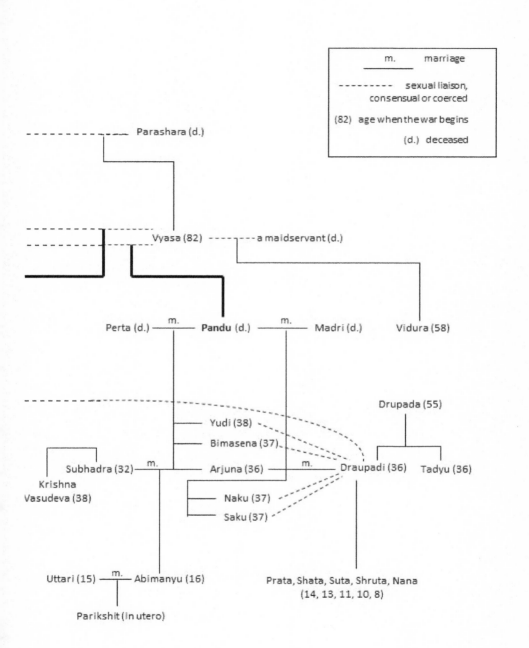

m.   marriage

- - - - - - - - - sexual liaison,
             consensual or coerced

(82)   age when the war begins

(d.)   deceased

Parashara (d.)

Vyasa (82) - - - - - - - a maidservant (d.)

Perta (d.) —— m. —— **Pandu** (d.) —— m. —— Madri (d.)   Vidura (58)

Drupada (55)

Yudi (38)

Bimasena (37)

Subhadra (32) — m. — Arjuna (36) — m. — Draupadi (36)   Tadyu (36)

Krishna
Vasudeva (38)

Naku (37)

Saku (37)

Uttari (15) —— m. —— Abimanyu (16)   Prata, Shata, Suta, Shruta, Nana
                                               (14, 13, 11, 10, 8)

Parikshit (in utero)

———— THE PANDAVA SIDE ————

List of Characters

FIRST GENERATION

Shantanu, king of the Kuru clan

Satyavati, daughter of Upa (a fisherman) and second wife of Shantanu; the "old queen" of Kuru

SECOND GENERATION

Bhishma, son of Shantanu and his first wife; removed from the succession in favor of Satyavati's offspring; regent of Kuru for many years

Vichitravirya (called *Chit*), son of Satyavati and Shantanu; king of Kuru for a short time

Amba, eldest daughter of the king of Kashi; purchased by Bishma to be Chit's wife, but sent back after she pleads a prior betrothal

Ambika and *Ambalika,* younger daughters of the king of Kashi; purchased by Bishma to be Chit's wives, married to Chit, and widowed soon after

Vyasa, son of Satyavati and the ascetic Parashara; high priest to the Kuru

Dhaumya, a priest from the land of Vrishni

THIRD GENERATION

SONS OF VYASA (by law, sons of Chit)

- *Tarashtra,* son of Vyasa and Ambika; the "blind king" of Kuru

- *Pandu,* son of Vyasa and Ambalika; a soma addict; king of Kuru for a time

- *Vidura,* son of Vyasa and a palace maidservant; chief counselor to Tarashtra

Perta, daughter of the king of Vrishni; senior wife of Pandu

Madri, daughter of the king of Madrasa; junior wife of Pandu

Gandhari, daughter of the king of Gandaram; wife of Tarashtra

Shakuna, brother of Gandhari; a prince of Gandaram but resident at the Kuru court

Drona, chief weapons master at the Kuru palace

Adiratu and *Radha,* husband and wife, a charioteer and corn-grinder of the town of Hastinapura

Ekalavya, a Naga tribesman turned stable-hand at the Kuru palace

Vasudeva, king of the neighboring land of Vrishni

Drupada, king of the neighboring land of Panchala

FOURTH GENERATION
THE KAURAVAS

- *Duryodhana,* elder son of Tarashtra and Gandhari

- *Dushasana,* younger son of Tarashtra and Gandhari

- *Vaishamya* (later known as *Vaishampayana*), illegitimate son of Tarashtra; Vyasa's adopted son and successor as high priest; nicknamed "Lopside" due to his missing arm

THE PANDAVAS

- *Yudishtira* (called *Yudi*), eldest son of Pandu and Perta

- *Bimasena* (often called *Bima*), second son of Pandu and Perta

- *Arjuna,* third son of Pandu and Perta (his biological father is Vidura)

- *Nakula* and *Sahadeva* (called *Naku* and *Saku*), twin sons of Pandu and Madri

Karna, an archer; son of Adiratu and Radha; Duryodhana's closest friend

Jaratka, a Naga girl, daughter of Ekalavya; Duryodhana's first wife

Krishna Vasudeva, crown prince of Vrishni, nephew of Perta, friend and advisor to the Pandavas

Subhadra, Krishna's sister; junior wife of Arjuna

Draupadi, daughter of King Drupada of Panchala; senior wife of Arjuna

Tadyu, twin brother of Draupadi

Shikhandi, a warrior woman; granddaughter of Bhishma and Amba

Ashwattama, son of Drona

Banumati, daughter of the king of Madrasa; Duryodhana's second wife

FIFTH GENERATION
Abimanyu, son of Arjuna and Subhadra

Astika, daughter of Duryodhana and Jaratka; narrator of the story

Prata, Shata, Suta, Shruta, and *Nana,* sons of Draupadi by the Pandava brothers

Uttari, daughter of the king of Matsya; Abimanyu's wife

SIXTH GENERATION
Parikshit (whom Astika calls *Parakeet*), son of Abimanyu and Uttari; king of Kuru for a time

SEVENTH GENERATION
Janamejaya, son of Parikshit; king of Kuru when the story opens

IMPORTANT GODS
Indra: God of Sky, Thunder, and Rain

Agni: God of Fire; transmitter of sacrifices and oblations

Yama: God of Death and Law

Brihaspati: God of Wisdom

Brahma: The Creator

Vishnu: The Sustainer

Shiva: The Destroyer

Kali: Goddess of Time, Change, Creation, Death, and Power; Great Mother of the Universe[*]

---

[*] Not to be confused with Kali the demon. In Sanskrit, the goddess's name is spelled with long *a* and long *i*.

Map of Kuru and Surrounding Lands

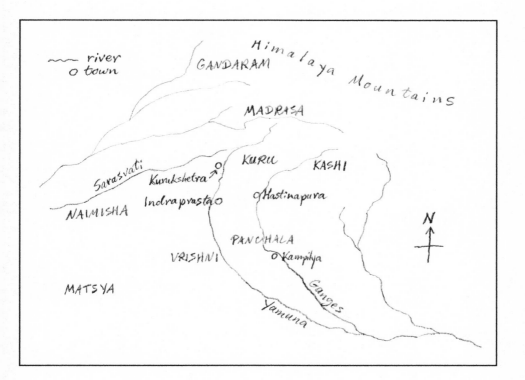

Author's Note: The story as I envision it takes place in what is today northern India, during the transition from Bronze Age to Iron Age, with the Kurukshetra war occurring circa 900 BCE. This was the time of the so-called Painted Grey Ware Culture that existed between the upper Ganges and Yamuna rivers. Archeologists have speculated that the central story of the Mahabharata, reimagined here, is based on actual people and events of the Painted Grey Ware region and period.

Prologue

ASTIKA

So, *Nephew: you have the Snakes.*

I heard you bringing them in last night. In the dark hour after moonset I awoke to a shriek in the distance, followed by—at first far off, but approaching north along the river—shouts and whip-cracks. It was still dark when human feet, horses' hooves, and chariot wheels began churning through the monsoon mud less than a stone's throw from my bedchamber window. There were dogs barking, babies wailing. I did not get up to watch. Torchlight flickered over my women as they lifted their heads from their mats, some fearful, some just sleepy and confused. I told them to keep quiet.

I knew it was the Naga. A whole tribe of six hundred or more were being driven through the south gate of the compound, around past the training grounds, and into the two larger horse barns. I lay with eyes open, and when at length the barn doors thudded shut, muffling the cries within, I closed my eyes and thought: "He didn't kill them."

Then I thought: "In the morning, he will ask me what to do with them."

And here you are now, Janamejaya, asking me what to do with them.

Others besides your Auntie Astika will be giving you advice, I'm sure. The high priest, I imagine, rushed to see you as soon as the sun was up, extolling your valor in defeating the snake-worshippers and your wisdom in taking them captive: the better to devise a fit punishment for them. Did he not? I can tell by your smile that he did.

When you told him you hadn't yet decided on their punishment—for the Law in this case is unclear—what did he say then? I imagine he launched into a paean of praise for the Kuru clan; and more specifically for the Pandava brothers; and *most* specifically for the most famous of those brothers, your great-grandfather Arjuna, who would be proud to see you avenge your royal father's murder with a bonfire of Snakes. The high priest is constantly reminding us of what we owe the Pandavas for saving the world from my father … my father, the evil Duryodhana, who instigated the great war in which thousands died and the Kuru line was nearly destroyed, all because he would not share power with his five noble cousins.

Or so the story goes.

"Not to mention," I can hear the high priest saying, "that by executing these Naga, you'll be ridding the land of one more pack of savages." He takes a harsh view of savages, does the priest, though he would be offended to hear me put it that way. "Indigenous tribes-people may join our society," he says, "provided they accept the Gods and submit to the Law." He likes to cite the opening lines of the catechism:

> Four are the castes of men, made from the parts of the First Man. His mouth was the brahmins, wise priests and teach-ers. His arms were the kshatriya, brave rulers and warriors. His thighs were the vaishya, shrewd merchants and artisans. And from his feet the shudra were made.

But since the Naga have refused to assimilate, he thinks leni-ency is pointless. That they eat fruit and roots and vermin rather than clean livestock and grain only increases the disgust he feels for them; "the disgust," he says, "that all Pure folk naturally feel for filthy dung-eaters." *Dung-eaters.* I must say, I do not like the term.

That hissing sound, coming from the barns. Do you hear it, Sire? Are they praying to their serpent god? It must be a tight fit in there, even though the horses, so few as we have these days, were long ago moved to the small barn. Are they able to move about? To lie down? It is not a pleasant sound. I think I will close the shutters.

Now, Nephew, if I am to advise you, you must first understand that our family history as told by the priests and bards is mostly lies, lies and omissions. I have never shared the truth with anyone (yes, I know the truth) but I will share it with you, if you're willing to hear it.

Oh, don't mistake me; I will say nothing against the Kuru. Everyone knows our clan is the best of all the Arya and our influence here in the doab is all for good. Before we came to this land between the rivers, the indigenes were scratching away on scrub-farms with no cattle, no horses, no sacraments, no one to intercede for them with the Gods, at constant risk of bandit attacks: wretched lives! In recent decades, happily, most have come to value our protection, and while it's true that many have had to give up their farms and go in service to an Arya household … well, their situation is so much improved, their children so much less likely to starve, that no reasonable person can feel sorry for them. I certainly don't.

And yes, you are right to remind me: it isn't as if they're stuck forever in the lowest caste. The Law says a shudra, if he lives lawfully and teaches his children the same, may one day see his grandchildren become vaishya, even kshatriya. Out west there are a few chiefs, you know, although I wouldn't exactly call them *kings,* whose ancestors were of indigenous stock. I've even heard of a few brahmins living hereabouts whose great-grandparents were shudra! No, Nephew, I won't tell you who they are. No, of course they aren't high priests; they are of that slightly disreputable type of holy man who wanders the countryside, offering his services to any householder who will give him a bed and a free meal—or a free hour with his daughter. Still, it all goes to show that the Law is not unduly rigid.

But the Naga, of course, do not see it that way. They've remained deep in their forest homes, refusing even to trade with us. Stubborn, they are. And we have let them alone, more or less, until recent events made it impossible to do so.

Ha! The high priest must be annoyed that you are not in the bath house right now, purifying yourself for that grand and fiery sacrifice of Snakes he has recommended. He'd be even more annoyed if he knew you were here in the women's quarters, talking with me. And if I were young (like you, Nephew), he'd be right: My counsel would be of little value. But I am old: the oldest lady of the royal house of Kuru, so it is really very sensible of you to come to me. In my fifty-six years, I have seen much. I know much. And there's no reason for me not to tell you what I know, given that I'll be dead soon.

Now, don't protest. You're just like my women; how they squawk when I speak of my death! "Oh, no, no, Lady Astika, you mustn't say such things! The Kuru are very long-lived, why, look at your great-great-grandmother Satyavati, she lived to be nearly a hundred!"

"Yes," say I, "but *she* was born of a fish and was a partial incarnation of the Goddess Kali. *I* am just an ordinary woman."

Then they go on fussing and saying, "No, no," and citing more examples—like Vyasa, the old high priest, or Bhishma, the venerable regent who at eighty-two commanded our armies in the Great War—until I feel I may die of irritation on the spot.

"Men's lifespans are beside the point," I say. "Women, unless they are part Goddess, simply don't live past sixty or sixty-five at the most."

Yes, women's lives are short … perhaps because we do know so much, yet are rarely permitted to speak of what we know, so the truth stays banked down inside us, burning like charcoal in a brazier. Heat like that is hard for mind and spirit to withstand. Well, and then there are all the ordinary hardships we must endure: being sent away from our families when we are married, submitting to the chastisement of our husbands and mothers-in-law, bearing children—of course I have been spared all this, but most women are not spared. Men, on the other hand, have easy lives! They have no real excuse for dying at all, unless they are shudra worn out with work or kshatriya killed in battle. No excuse whatsoever.

Oh, but … *tsk*. I am sorry. Your majesty, forgive me. That was tactless of me, what with your father so recently dead, and you so recently succeeded to his place. And you came to me for advice on how to deal with his murderers. I haven't been very helpful thus far, have I?

Also, you can't have eaten anything yet today. Wait now; let me call for some breakfast. No, no, you look pale. You must eat.

≈

There. You feel better now, don't you?

Dear nephew. You are so like your father (yes, I know I say it often); so like King Parikshit, Parakeet I always called him, with his beaky nose and hazel-green eyes. When he was a toddler he had a hard time with "Astika"; he called me "Tika" and stuck with it as he grew up, even after becoming king. He was always a lighthearted boy. Poor Parakeet …

It seems a long time since the day he set off for the forest-clearing works down in Vrishni, though I know it was, what, only two months past? Yes, it was the middle of the fourth month. You were with the stockmen that week, helping drive the herd upland in readiness for the monsoons. I stood in the palace yard in the hazy morning sun, and the king on his bay stallion smiled down at me and said, "Goodbye, Tika. Remember, you're in charge while I'm gone. Don't let Janamejaya suppose he is!" I laughed and waved as the twenty men, four carts, and two logging elephants, their mahouts swaying high on their necks, moved out the gate.

I never imagined it was the last time I'd see him. After all, there was little danger; Vrishni is rustic but civilized, as good an ally as ever, and the forest-clearing a joint project. It is a longish journey to the southwest; even so, quite safe, and they'd be gone only two weeks. When the messenger arrived with the news that the king was dead—"ambushed and killed, by Naga"—I could scarcely understand. He had to say it several times.

A week later I stood in the yard again, this time next to you in the pouring rain, as the cart with his corpse rolled up. The bay stallion was tied behind, walking with head low, mane dripping. Your father wouldn't have minded his warhorse being pressed into service to draw the wagon—as I say, he wasn't one for formalities—but the men wouldn't have liked it. The journey back had been slow, and the body, though decently covered, smelled already of decay.

The high priest managed the funeral well, I must say. Missing arm or not, no other holy man can match the precision with which he chants the hymns; he never misses a syllable. And you, Janamejaya: you were splendid, too. When you set the torch to the pyre by the river and the flames blazed up in the damp air, and just at that moment thunder rolled from the Himalaya—who then could have doubted your descent from Indra, God of the Sky?

Some of your friends, I know, wanted you to ride that very night with a dozen spearmen: "What need more," they said, "when it's only a few hundred wretched Snakes we have to kill?" But you declined and sent a small party to investigate, for (you said wisely) there are many ways to die in the forest: tigers, falls, actual snakes … And when the report came back confirming that the Naga had indeed done it, yet again you were patient, taking time to confer with your priests and counselors. When finally you gathered a chariot force drawn from our troops and the Pandavas' troops, those five old warriors (still living in their grand palace out west) being only too pleased to contribute to the mission, I felt little doubt you were doing the right thing. You had to kill the Naga.

But you didn't kill them. Instead you rounded them up and marched them back from the Vrishni forest: five days and nights in the rain and mud.

Now what will you do with them? What to do with that tribe of ...

No, Nephew. Do *not* say "dung-eaters."

No. Let me tell you something: My mother was a Naga. Yes, a Snake. And I won't have her memory besmirched with foul names; no matter what her people's crimes, I won't have it.

You are astonished, I see. I'll explain ... but there's the gong for this morning's oblation. You must go, and I'm sure the council will want to speak with you afterward, and then you'll want to rest. But come back this evening, Sire. Come back, and I'll tell you more.

≈

Your majesty; come in, come in. Did you have a nice rest? Would you like lassi or beer? ... Beer it is. I believe I will join you. Nagira, bring the jug and some cups. Quickly, girl.

Now: about my mother. You are astonished, but surely not because an Arya man lay with a Snake. That situation is common enough, what with the Snake hunts that many of our young men partake in to mark their coming of age. ("Snake hunt": there's another ugly term.) Naga women are skilled and eager in the bedchamber, it is said, and therefore good partners for a first foray, and often the boys keep the girl for a while before letting her loose to return to her folk, by which point she is pregnant. It was no different in the old days.

But you realize this was another thing altogether, for you know my mother's name—Jaratka—and you know she was not a bed slave, but my father's first wife. And you've never heard of an Arya man *marrying* a Naga.

He did marry her, though. You see, my father was a good man.

Don't look so skeptical! Yes of course I know the story, Nephew, everyone knows the story. It goes like this: Prince Duryodhana envied his cousins the Pandavas starting when they were all boys together. When they grew up, Duryodhana plotted to have them exiled on a trumped-up charge. Duryodhana lusted after the Princess Draupadi and couldn't bear to see her choose another; he brooded on her rejection for years, then at the great dice match took his revenge. When the Pandavas claimed their rightful portion of the kingdom, he went to war with them. Finally, in a blind fury at his side's defeat he did the unthinkable, thereby ushering in the Kali Yuga: this present age, the Age of Kali, polluted by sickness and crime and vice.

Yet the bards also say he went straight to paradise when he died. How could that be, Janamejaya, if he were evil?

It's generally accepted that my father was an incarnation of Kali—Kali the demon, that is, not Kali the Goddess—and the Pandavas incarnations of various Gods: Yama, Indra, I've forgotten the others. With such divine influences, you'd think those five brothers wouldn't have had any difficulty crushing their demonic cousin. But then they were always strangely limited, those Pandavas, each one renowned for just a single virtue: Yudi for wisdom, Bimasena for strength, Naku and Saku for beauty and learning, and Arjuna for valor. Each brother just one overwrought aspect of what a man should be. And indeed (I'll speak plainly, Sire, for it's just the two of us here) if we take Arjuna, all he ever *really* did in his life is roam around shooting at things with his ridiculously large bow and his peacock-fletched arrows.

I actually have a story about him and those arrows. Are you ready to hear a family story, my lord? One you won't hear from the bards? Just to whet your appetite for more.

Listen, then, and we'll go back half a hundred years: back to when the blind king and his veiled queen ruled here in Hastinapura, and the Pandavas were living in their palace on the Yamuna river, twenty kosa to the west. They had begun building that palace before I was born, naming it and the town that grew up around it *Indraprasta*: "For Indra lives in me," Arjuna would explain if anyone looked like asking. Twice a year we, the Kaurava side of the family, would travel out to visit them, and twice a year the Pandavas would come to us.

At the Pandavas' there would be other guests as well, and for an evening's entertainment everyone would be invited out back to the training grounds to watch Arjuna shoot flaming arrows at a target: a wicker hut, some pottery figures, or a jackal. He favored the jackal version, since it required precise technique. (He was never slapdash, I'll grant him that.) Earlier in the day he and his brother Bimasena would have snared a jackal out in the grasslands east of the river; golden jackals are plentiful there, and though wily, they can be lured with hunks of deer meat. Arjuna and Bima would trap and cage the beast and carry it back to the palace. Bima would stun it with his club. They'd wrap its body and legs in rags soaked in flaxseed oil. Then they'd tie it by the neck to a stake in the middle of the training grounds, ready for the evening show.

But I'm getting ahead of myself. Let me go back just a little further, Sire, so you'll be able to see it all as I saw it. Is your cup empty? Let me refill it. There now; listen.

≈

I was seven years old when my ayah, Deeba, told me I was old enough to go on the springtime visit to the Uncles Pandava and that I must be on my best behavior and make my father very proud. "Will we spend the night?" I asked as she was boosting me into the ox-drawn wagon that would carry the old ladies, servants, and children. The gentlemen and young ladies were already astride their horses, curvetting around us, calling to one another, eager to be off.

"Yes, Astika, of course we will," Deeba said. "It's a long way. It will take us two days to get there, and we'll stay for three days, then two days to get back." She laughed when she saw my face fall. "Don't worry, dearie. We have plenty to eat and drink along the way, plenty of honey cakes. It will be worth it once we get there. It's a palace of wonders, everyone says so."

As we drew up to Indraprasta on the third morning, it certainly did look big. The wall around the compound was higher than our wall, with a massive timber gate that groaned as the wardens swung it open. Once inside, I could see the buildings were made of mud brick with mud plaster, just like ours; the main house, however, was a good deal larger and had more windows. In the yard the horses tramped and snorted and the oxen stood with placid unconcern as we got down from the wagon. I gazed around, assessing, but I couldn't see anything so very special about the place. I remember feeling relieved that my new rose-pink costume—my first one like a grownup lady's, with draped dhoti, a chest-band, and a veil—which I had feared might be too plain for a palace of wonders—would surely be adequate.

Inside there was a great hall, again like ours with the roof supported by wooden pillars, but lighter and airier because of all the windows. The white plaster walls were decorated with paintings, some of which were designed to fool the eye by looking like doors giving onto other rooms or leading outside. I found the paintings interesting, but only for a minute. The thing that surprised me most was the floor: it was not packed dirt, but smooth stone, white with spidery dark lines. *Marble*, it was called—though I learned that only much later.

In the afternoon I played with the Pandava boys, particularly the two eldest, Prata and Shata, who were close to my age. There was a shallow indoor pool in the middle of the hall, its rim made of that same white stone. I remember running round it with Prata shouting, "Walk on it, Astika! Dare you, dare you!" The pool had a dark, flat stone bottom and so resembled a mirror I was almost going to try it, but then Aunt Draupadi, who was standing watching us with tiny Baby Nana in a sling, said, "Prata, stop it. Astika, it's just water, dip your hand in, you'll see." I poked the surface and laughed when my finger sank in, making ripples. Then Prata hit the water to splash me, and Aunt Draupadi told him again to stop it. She was wearing a light-blue sari and a delicate silver tiara with light-blue jewels in it; I thought she was so pretty.

I remember eating roti and dal for supper with the other children and the ayahs, sitting on sheepskins in another room, and afterwards my father coming to get me, waving Deeba away, and holding my hand as we went out back. Everyone filed along the path that led up to the long flat-topped hillock in front of the training grounds. Karna, my father's friend, came with us, walking behind; as we climbed the hill I looked back and saw his figure looming dark against the setting sun, his golden earrings glinting in its rays.

The training grounds were ringed by a tall fence made of bamboo stakes set a finger's width or two apart—I was impressed by this, for up until then I had only seen our own grounds, with their low brick border—but standing on the hillock, we could see the whole arena. Everyone spread out in loose rows: the young women in their colorful dhotis and veils, the older women in their embroidered saris, the men in dhotis and bare chests or vests, and everyone's jewelry clinking and clacking. The crowd seemed immense to me, but likely we didn't number more than fifty or sixty. At the center of the ring was the jackal, snarling and straining on its tether, its big ears laid flat. The pale rags that wrapped it looked, I thought, like priest's robes; its bushy tail had not been wrapped, but I could see the tail fur glistening with oil.

Uncle Arjuna came over the hill and down the path, thrust open the gate in the fence, and entered the arena. In his left fist was his enormous bow, unstrung, long and straight; in his right fist was one of those peacock-fletched arrows. A few paces in, he pivoted to face us, shook the hair out of his eyes, and cried, "Children up front so they can see! Come on, don't be shy!"

I felt a stab of panic as I saw some youngsters push their way forward, but my father kept hold of me and moved us over to where Uncle Yudi, the eldest Pandava, was standing a little apart from the crush. He had Aunt Draupadi next to him, his hand on her nape. (I remember thinking this a bit odd; husbands and wives were freer to touch in public back in those days, yet that brawny hand resting like a saddle on the slender neck gave me a strange feeling.) Her hands gripped the shoulders of her two little boys, Suta and Shruta, who were fussing and squirming against her legs. Baby Nana was still in his sling, asleep. As we approached I heard Uncle Yudi saying, "... there's no need, that's what the ayahs are for." Then he broke off, seeing us, and said, "Ah, Duryo! And little Astika—your first visit? That's right, get a good spot."

Aunt Draupadi looked straight ahead as we joined them. Karna had not come with us; I supposed he had stayed at the back. I clutched my father's hand and pressed my cheek against the copper armband he wore on his right bicep. The cool metal was comforting.

On the other side of my aunt and uncle, standing alone, was Prince Krishna. I knew he was the Pandavas' friend and often with them; the last time they had all visited us at Hastinapura he had come to the children's play-yard, called me over, and given me a string of— *seashells,* he had called them—to wear around my wrist. I was a little in love with him after that. I leaned forward now and peeked at him, standing very tall, dark, and slender with his blue cloak thrown back off his chest, his eyes on Arjuna down below. He seemed to sense my gaze, for suddenly he turned his head and winked. I gasped and pulled back behind my father.

Arjuna beckoned to one of the twins—Uncle Naku I think it was, with his beautiful long wavy hair. He entered the ring, bronze sword in hand, and crossed thirty paces to the stake. The jackal lunged, but the tether rope was short and Naku merely hopped back and wagged his finger *tsk-tsk*, raising chuckles from the crowd. Next, Uncle Saku (who did not look like Naku, but I knew twins didn't always look alike) came and stood by Arjuna, holding a lit torch.

Last to come was Aunt Subhadra, Arjuna's junior wife. She pulled her yellow dhoti up and tight around her rear as she minced giggling over to her husband, stacks of copper bangles jingling at her wrists and ankles. Upon reaching Arjuna she grabbed his arm and squealed as the bow, which was now strung and leaning upright on his shoulder, knocked her in the face. Arjuna grinned and gave her a kiss on the cheek, then peeled her off him and took her hand to lower her to the ground. Still giggling, she arranged herself in a dance pose: one leg deeply bent, the other extended behind, the hem of her yellow veil trailing in the dust. Saku stepped forward and placed the torch in her hands, whereupon she stopped giggling and bit her lip, teetering slightly. Then Saku went and shut the gate.

After one final glance around, Arjuna hoisted the bow in his left hand, raised right fist and arrow to the sky, and held the stance. The big ivory beads on his bare chest caught the torchlight; his black hair and white dhoti ruffled in the evening breeze. The crowd hushed.

"Watch now!" he said. "I will not shoot the beast. I'll barely graze it. Watch the arrow!" He turned to face the stake.

I don't remember him touching the arrow to the torch or putting it to the bow, but I remember the streak of light, the *poof* as the flames caught, and the *zing* of Naku's sword slashing down through the tether. The jackal took off screaming—not yelping, but screaming like a woman. It could not escape the arena; it could only run the fence, round and round with the fireball snapping and billowing. The crowd cheered.

I stood silent, rigid. I wanted to look away but could not. My father, too, stood silent, his big hand enveloping my small one; he was squeezing tightly, and it hurt, but I did not cry out. Most everyone else was whooping and yelling. Uncle Bima, at the back, was emitting bellows that made my ears throb. Uncle Yudi was applauding in a restrained way. Arjuna, Subhadra, and Saku had rushed to join Naku at the center of the field as soon as he'd cut the rope; now all four were turning on their heels to watch the jackal run, the men with expressions of concentration, Subhadra bouncing on her toes with squeals of glee.

After what seemed a long time the fireball dwindled and the

animal slowed, came to a halt on the left side of the ring, and began to jump about like a drop of fat in a hot skillet. A few flames still licked its head and body. It was denuded of rags and fur; its tail was a charred stick, its ears two black stubs, its eyes two glaring moons. Eventually it collapsed with limbs contracted, its convulsions raising a cloud of dust to mingle with wisps of smoke. With the audience grown quiet, I could hear wet pops and hisses. At last it ceased twitching and was still.

Naku and Saku pushed Arjuna forward and presented him to the audience, from which rose thunderous applause. Subhadra scampered over and flung her arms around him, plastering his face with kisses; Arjuna detached her, handed her off to Saku and his bow to Naku, then took a moment to stand erect, arms skyward in a V, before bringing his palms together at his forehead in namaste. I remember thinking him handsome in his white and ivory and recalling that his name in the common tongue was "White One." I wondered whether he always had to wear clothes and jewels that matched his name.

The sun was down, the twilight deepening as we waited for the other guests to shuffle their way onto the path back to the palace. I looked up at my father; he was still holding my hand, his eyes on the small black heap inside the fence. I heard Uncle Yudi ask, "Have you a handkerchief, my dear?" Aunt Draupadi was also looking at the small black heap, and she kept looking at it as she drew a square of light-blue cotton from her chest-band and handed it over. Yudi took it, coughed into it, and blew his nose.

"Fine show, eh, Duryo?" he said. He balled up the handkerchief and mopped the sweat on the back of his neck. It was a hot evening, the monsoons still a few months away.

My father turned his head and stared—not at Yudi, I thought, but at Draupadi, who was accepting the soiled cloth back from Yudi and tucking it away again without a word.

"Yes," my father said. "F-fine show."

I leaned over to see if Krishna might give me another wink. But he was gone.

≈

That, my lord, is one of only a few clear memories I have of Indraprasta. After that first visit my father was reluctant to let me go again; anyway, there weren't many more years before all the family visits came to an end as the threat of war loomed. Arjuna's jackal show stuck with me, however, and when the war was over—by then I was fifteen—I found myself wanting to know what life had been like in the palace of wonders.

I went to Aunt Draupadi and asked her. She was happy to tell me of her early life: how she had been the most desirable princess in twenty kingdoms; how her father had arranged the contest for her bridegroom choice, a contest my father won, but at the last minute she chose Arjuna instead; how she had returned to Hastinapura with the Pandavas, watched from afar as they built their new domain on the ashes of the Khandava Forest, and eventually moved out there with her sister-wife, Subhadra. But then she grew more reluctant, saying, "That palace, Astika ... it was not wonderful for me." And she would say nothing at all about the great dice match, when (it is said) she was so brutally mistreated by my father and his brother; nor would she discuss the origins of my family's conflicts. "If you want to understand that," she said, "you must go all the way back to your great-great-grandfather and his love for a fisher girl."

So I decided to go to the fisher girl herself: Satyavati. The old queen was by then ninety-seven years of age (remember, she was part Goddess), and her body was as round and wrinkled as an old apple but her mind still sharp as a broken plate. I spoke with her almost daily for half a year, right up to her death. She told me to speak also with her grandson Vidura, the royal counselor, because, she said, he knew more about the family than anyone except her. I went to him next. He was a quiet man, but he seemed touched by my interest in him and his stories.

I also spoke with Karna, my father's friend; he had survived the fighting but was badly maimed and did not live long. I spoke with my grandmother, Queen Gandhari—who, being my father's mother and none too fond of her five Pandava nephews, did not mince words. And I spoke with Krishna; after the war he was as tall and graceful as ever and still a good friend to the Pandavas, but his eyes had grown sad. He would lean on his teakwood staff as we walked and talked along the riverbank; if he saw me looking sidelong at him he would straighten his back and lighten his step. At the time, I still wore the little seashell bracelet.

Finally I went to ... I suppose I should properly say "Aunt

Shikhandi," but she always had me call her just "Shikhandi." She had been a warrior—she was granddaughter to the great regent Bhishma, you know—and when Uncle Yudi, or King Yudi as he was by then, made her put down weapons and return to womanly pursuits, the only way she could assert what she had been was to refuse to answer to "Aunt Shikhandi" or "Lady Shikhandi": just plain "Shikhandi." She told me about the progress of the war, which she had seen up close.

They are all long gone now, my seven storytellers (may their rebirths be fortunate). Gone, but not forgotten. For in the years afterward I took their many stories and forged them, day by day and night by night, into one story. Sometimes I used their words just as they'd spoken them; sometimes I used my mind's eye to picture events as they must have been. I beat and polished my story until it was sharp and shining, then I practiced it, saying each part to myself a thousand times just as a swordsman on the training grounds practices each attack and parry a thousand times. Now I have every word by heart.

Again you are astonished, I see. But why? Women can be bards, though it's not as common as it used to be. And it wasn't as if I had anything else to do. My chances of marriage were poor; yes, I was of a royal house, but the Kaurava side having lost the war was seen as disgraced, and what with so many kshatriya of nearby clans dead, the pickings were slim. A beauty might have attracted suitors nevertheless, but I was no beauty. And King Yudi was uninclined to bother about the plain daughter of his dead, despised cousin.

So I had plenty of time for my work. And now, Janamejaya, I want to tell you the truth: the truth about my father and the Pandavas, the truth about our family, the truth about the Snakes. If that fails to catch your interest, consider two more points.

First, you have said it yourself: What the Law prescribes in this case is unclear. The Law demands vengeance for your father's murder, which means execution of his murderers—so the high priest will argue. But what if the priest, infallible in the sacraments, is fallible in the Law? After all, the Law is greater than priests, greater than kings, greater even than Gods. It rules all beings, including those who don't acknowledge it—like those six hundred creatures locked up in your horse barns. That is the splendor of the Law, is it not? And the signs of the Law are subtle, the way easy to miss, especially when we live in an age so corrupt. Perhaps what I have to say will help you to discern the lawful path.

The second point? Yes, the second point.

Until the rains end, which will not be for some weeks, a fire big enough and hot enough to burn all those Snakes will be completely impractical.

So, Nephew: Will you hear my tale?

Good, good.

It begins with Karna: twenty-one years before the war.

PART ONE

THE LACQUER HOUSE

Chapter 1

KARNA

21 YEARS BEFORE THE WAR

Karna sat cross-legged on the sheepskin as his mother bustled about bringing bowls of rice, mutton, and lentils from hearth to floor mat. His father was talking; he had not stopped talking since Karna had arrived home half an hour ago, in time for supper.

"… and tomorrow at the tournament you'll show them what you can do. Everyone will see how you've risen, from sweeper to blades-boy to assistant weapons master—at the Panchala court, no less!" On the word *court* Adiratu gave a flourish with his spoon, sending a wet clump of lentils onto the floor.

"Assistant weapons master! Think of it!" said Radha, stooping to mop up the mess with a rag. She hurried to the door and flapped the cloth over the threshold—a couple of street dogs rushed snarling on the scraps—then hurried back and ladled more rice onto Karna's plate. "Though I must say I do worry, with you playing every day with those swords and spears and who knows what. So sharp; so *dangerous*. It's bad enough your father being a charioteer and having to drive the lords on their cattle raids and hunts and into battles and risk getting hit with an arrow or the chariot's tipping over and getting trampled by horses and even when it's just a forest-clearing expedition there are so many savages—well, anyway, it's bad enough, I say, that your father has to endure all that, and I don't see why you have to make it even worse by actually *fighting*."

She paused for breath and Adiratu seized his opportunity. "Radha, Radha, that's enough. Karna is a grown man, a warrior. He doesn't want to hear your bleats. You should be proud that your son, *our* son, has shown such ability. Why, he's not just a fighter, he's a teacher, a guru! He teaches princes the arts of war!" On *arts of war* he made another couple of jabs at the air with his spoon, which this time, fortunately, was empty.

Karna took a bite of rice. "Father, I've told you. I'm not a guru. I'm an assistant weapons master. I instruct the ordinary soldiers. I'm rarely allowed near the princes, and when I am, it's to set up their targets, carry their spears when we go hunting, bind up their scratches, things like that. Honestly, it's not that glamorous."

"My boy, you're being much too modest. I know your talent. You've stood on the west bank of the river here and hit a kingfisher on the east bank, and that at dawn with the sun smack in your eyes. You were twelve, with a homemade bow and arrows, when I first saw you do it. Now, granted, I haven't seen you do it since you went off to Panchala ten years ago, but my cousin who first got you the job there has told me how hard you practice and how well you've done. And each year when you've visited I've seen how you've grown taller, and stronger, and more assured in your manner, and what a ... what a ... what a fine young man you've become." Adiratu scratched the left side of his head with vigor, causing wisps of gray hair to stick out, and his eyes were moist as he beamed at his son across the dish-laden straw mat.

Karna, with his tall, muscular build, his clean-shaven jaw, his mop of dark-brown hair, and his wide brown eyes, was indeed a fine young man. He wore a saffron dhoti, an orange sash with saffron fringe, and a leather vest with spirals of copper studs that caught the fire's glow. The gold rings in his ears, from each of which dropped a gold charm in the shape of a sunburst, completed the radiant effect. His current manner, however, was not assured; with elbow on one knee, knuckles to cheek, he pushed a bit of mutton around his plate and avoided his father's smiling gaze.

"Father, about the tournament tomorrow ..."

"Yes, yes, let's talk about the tournament! It's going to be a marvelous show. King Tarashtra and Queen Gandhari will be watching—I mean to say, they won't be *watching*, of course not *watching*, but they'll be *present*. And Lord Bhishma will be there, and Lady Perta—she's the Pandavas' mother, you know, and no doubt she'll be giving out the garlands, because she loves to preside at these grand events ..."

Radha, who by now was seated on the floor with them, gave a snort. "Loves to have all eyes on her, you mean!"

Adiratu shot her a frown. "... loves to *preside* at these grand events, and all the court ladies will be there as well, and all the palace attendants and staff, like me. The whole town will come, of course, for the king has ordered two steers and twenty goats to be slaughtered for the feast afterward, which no one will want to miss, even those who don't care about the sport. And then in the arena we'll see—"

Karna put down his spoon and looked up. "Father ..."

"—we'll see all the kshatriya of the Kuru clan, competing for glory! Now, it will be a noble field, certainly, but I think Prince Arjuna is the only one you really need to worry about. All the smart bets are on him—not for the wrestling, no, Prince Bimasena will win that, but for the swordfights and archery. I had a chat with Drona the other day—he's chief weapons master at the palace, we're good friends, very good friends—and he told me that even though Arjuna is just fifteen, he already surpasses any student he's ever had. A natural, Drona says, an absolute natural. Ah, but Karna ..." the old man leaned across and tapped his son's chest with a knobby finger. "They aren't expecting *this* natural to show up and challenge them, are they? Heh, heh! No they are not! And so—"

"Father!" Karna slapped both hands hard on the mat, making the thin gray cups and bowls rattle. Adiratu froze with mouth open, arm and finger still extended.

Radha used a corner of her sari to absorb a spilled drop of lassi. "For heavens' sake, Karna, don't break the dishes, they're my good ones. Whatever's the matter?"

Karna pressed his palms together at his forehead. "I ... I'm sorry, Mother. I'm sorry, Father." He folded his hands in his lap and stared down at them. Adiratu sat back on his sheepskin, his expression mystified. There was silence for a long moment.

"Father, it's just that ... there's something I must ask you."

"Of course, my dear. What is it?"

"Well, you see ... only kshatriya may enter the tournament. Not vaishya."

"Oh, is that it? Well, yes, that's the official rule, but when I tell them you're my son, they'll not turn you away. No need to worry about that. I've been a Hastinapura charioteer for nearly thirty years, and as I say, Drona and I are good friends, very good friends. I've even mentioned you to him. Of course they'll let you compete!"

"Father, no."

"Karna, stop worrying. Everything will be fine."

"No, Father, I mean …" Karna looked up and met Adiratu's eyes. "I mean: I am not going to enter the tournament as your son."

Adiratu looked blank. "Not as my son? I don't understand."

Karna took a deep breath and spoke quickly: "I will enter the tournament as a kshatriya from Panchala. I've been away ten years, and on my few visits home I've come at nighttime, briefly, and only seen the two of you. No one at the palace knows me, and I don't think any of the townspeople will recognize me. And I have my own weapons. So I will announce myself as Karna of Panchala, and they will let me compete, and, and …" He took another breath, let it out, placing his palms on his knees. "And I will win."

Radha patted Karna's hand. "Of course you'll win, lovey."

Adiratu said, "Yes, of course you'll win. But then—when you win, what shall I do?"

Karna's eyes slid to the side. A flicker of pain crossed his face.

"Do nothing, Father. Don't greet me. Don't congratulate me. I need you to pretend you don't know me."

More silence as the hearth-fire crackled in the darkening room. Outside, the street dogs continued their quarrels.

≈

"Winner in archery: *Karna of Panchala.*"

Chief Weapons Master Drona pointed across the training grounds at Karna, who detached himself from the group of contestants standing at the southeast corner, stepped over the low brick border, and walked across the big square. Applause rose from the crowd: on the east side some forty lords and ladies, seated on stools and rugs, cooled by a canopy above and servants plying straw fans behind; under another canopy next to them, but without the stools, rugs, and fanners, some sixty senior palace staff; and on the other three sides of the grounds, standing and sweating in the heat of a late-spring afternoon, nearly a thousand townspeople. As Karna walked, the rays of the sinking sun lit his face and made his earrings shine. He wore his saffron dhoti, orange sash, and copper-studded vest; his bow and quiver, along with his bag of personal effects, had been left on one of the weapons stands, guarded (in theory) by two blades-boys who squatted in the dust, throwing dice and paying no attention to the ceremonies.

With the chief weapons master at the center of the field were four young men. They included the two kshatriya, both in the king's service, who had won the jousting and the steer-roping; the mountain-like Prince Bimasena, who had triumphed in both wrestling and spear-throwing; and Prince Duryodhana, a short and stocky youth who had, to the dismay of those in the crowd with bets on Arjuna, edged out his young cousin in the sword fights. Arjuna himself, though not a prizewinner, was also there, standing a pace or two back in the hosts' line along with his elder brothers Yudi, Naku, and Saku, none of whom were looking any too pleased as Karna approached— Arjuna least of all.

Karna's win in archery had been even more of a surprise than Duryodhana's in sword-fighting, and he had caused more bets to be lost by Arjuna's backers; nevertheless, the crowd's enthusiasm for him ran high. In the premier event of the tournament he had crushed the competition with ease, his arrows striking their targets with superhuman accuracy. His surprise victory made him an instant favorite. Arjuna had come in a solid second, but he couldn't match the newcomer—who was, moreover, very handsome. The women of the town stood tiptoe, waving and calling, "Kar-na! Kar-na!" as he took his place in the winners' line.

The hawk-faced Drona now gestured toward the nobility's tent and said: "Lady Perta will present the garlands."

A woman shaped like a bottle gourd rose from her seat and stepped over the border, broad hips swaying beneath a somewhat minimal scarlet sari, copious strings of beads swaying atop her large bosom and slender waist. Her face, framed by a scarlet veil, was heavily made up; her hair was a dark and lustrous brown, albeit with strands of gray, and fell to her knees. As she walked, the townswomen subsided from their tiptoes and the townsmen craned their necks for a better look. Behind her came an upper maidservant, also in scarlet but much more thickly covered, carrying a tray heaped with marigolds. The two paced slowly, gracefully, and stopped in front of the men in the middle.

As Drona re-announced each prize, the winner stepped forward and bowed to Perta, who took a garland from the maidservant's tray and placed it around his neck. She leaned close, smiling with chin tipped down and eyes looking up through her lashes, as she draped each loop of flowers: first on the two winners of the horse events, then her son Bima (to whose cheek she gave a little pinch), then Duryodhana (to whom her smile was a little cold). But when it was Karna's turn and she had the garland half-raised, she suddenly stopped. Her smile vanished, her chin came up, and she stared straight at him—brow creased, eyes flicking from side to side. Karna waited. For a few seconds, all on the training grounds was still.

Someone in the crowd sneezed, and Perta seemed to recall herself. She lifted the garland over Karna's head and stepped back, drawing her veil across her ample bosom. "Clearly we have saved the best for last," she said brightly. "You are from Panchala, sir, is that right?"

"Yes, my lady," said Karna, hands at his sides, eyes on a spot in the distance.

"And were you born there?"

"No ... no, my lady. I mean, I have lived there for many years."

"Ah. The Panchala court is magnificent, I hear. The Princess Draupadi—is she as lovely as everyone says?"

"Oh ... yes. I mean, I don't really know. I have seen her only from a distance."

"You don't spend much time at the palace, then? Well of course, you must have your own farmstead. Which side of the river is it on?"

Drona, the Pandava brothers, and the other prizewinners were still in their places, listening intently. Karna's feet shifted in the dust; his hands clenched and unclenched. Then he squared his shoulders and said, "Ma'am. I am assistant weapons master at the Panchala court."

Perta's puzzled look returned for a moment. Then with a tilt of her head and a brushing back of her veil, she recovered her smile. "I see! Well, that explains your skill with a bow, does it not? We must congratulate you, Karna of Panchala, for your performance today."

Karna's shoulders relaxed. "Yes, my lady. Thank you, my lady." He bowed deeply and stepped back to the winners' line.

The audience had become restless during this interlude, unable to hear what was being said between Lady Perta and the handsome stranger and growing distracted, in any case, by something more interesting: the aroma, wafting over the training grounds, of the two steers and twenty goats roasting in their pits away north of the horse barns. After glancing at Drona, who gave her a nod, Perta turned to the townspeople, flung out her arms as if to embrace them all, and cried: "The tournament is over! Let the feast begin!" The crowd roared with appreciation and broke up, heading for the food.

"Come," Perta said to the men, "the king and queen will greet you." She led them over to the central canopy. The royal couple, seated on wide flat stools draped with rugs, wore richly dyed clothing of crimson and purple. They were not old; King Tarashtra was ruddy and plump, Queen Gandhari tall and stately, and the skin on their neck and arms was smooth. But the king's eyes had a milky-white film, and the queen's face was covered by a veil of violet silk.

Seated just behind them were two older men. One was muscular, wearing an indigo dhoti and a bronze-studded leather belt: Bhishma, the former regent. The other was gaunt and shock-haired, in white robes, with charcoal-black eyes: Vyasa, the high priest.

The king and queen rose from their seats as the prizewinners approached, her hand lightly under his elbow. First and with obvious pleasure they embraced their son, Duryodhana; next and with considerably more restraint they greeted their nephew Bimasena, whose bulk as he knelt to touch their feet was like a baby elephant's. Next the two horse-event winners were presented and made their bows. Finally, Karna was ushered forward.

To the right, under the other canopy, stood a mass of stewards, upper maid- and manservants, horse masters, junior priests, and the like. Standing motionless at the front of this group, watching his son Karna take a knee before their majesties, was Adiratu. The old charioteer's hands were clasped tightly below a slim bronze neck-chain; his wispy gray eyebrows were raised so high they nearly disappeared into his wispy gray hair; his teeth were clamped on inward-folded lips, as if to keep those lips from making a sound.

Karna, as he stood up, glanced over at the staff tent and in so doing caught sight of his father. Their eyes met. Adiratu gave a tiny gasp, and his lips unfolded in a smile of such pride and pleasure he might have been receiving the king's felicitations himself. One hand, letting go of the other, jerked upward in what was almost a wave—then was drawn back to clutch the neck-chain. But the beaming smile remained.

Karna, meanwhile, had returned his attention to the king and queen and was replying to their pleasantries: How had he learned to shoot so well? What a long way he had come, all the way from

Panchala, how good of him to make the journey. *Yes, Ma'am; thank you, Sire.* The other winners, along with the Pandavas, Lady Perta, and Drona, were standing by politely.

Drona, however, had seen the smile and half-wave and was looking at Adiratu with narrowed eyes. The weapons master waited until Karna had made his final bow. Then his stentorian voice, used to being heard over the clash of bronze in the arena, rang out:

"*Adiratu!* Is this your son?"

Every head under the canopies (except blind King Tarashtra's) swiveled toward the charioteer. Adiratu froze like a hare at bay: eyes wide on Drona, lips once again clamped between teeth, fingers clutching neck-chain. A whimper escaped his throat.

Upon receiving no reply, Drona covered the distance between the tents in a few strides, loomed over the old man—who leaned back, trembling—and flecked his face with spittle as he barked, "Adiratu, answer me! *Is that man your son?*"

The charioteer looked as if he were about to faint. Drona moved closer in … but a moment later was shoved aside by Karna, who had come up behind. Karna gripped his father's shoulders firmly but gently, steadying him; then he knelt and touched the old man's feet.

By now all except the most dignified courtiers had converged on the staff tent. There was a spectators' circle as Karna rose, turned to face Drona, and said, loud and clear:

"I am Karna of Panchala, born in Hastinapura. This is my father, Adiratu, a charioteer. My mother is Radha, a corn grinder."

Drona frowned. Karna held his stance. Adiratu stared wildly at the onlookers, who stared back, agog.

Then a screech like a hyena's made everyone jump and look round. *"Not kshatriya! Not kshatriya!"* It was young Prince Arjuna, who had pushed his way to the front of the crowd. The fair skin on his neck and chest was blotched with red; his finger, pointing at Karna, shook. He continued in the cracked voice of a boy changing to a man: "He may not compete! It is not permitted! He is not kshatriya!"

All at once the crowd was buzzing. "Not kshatriya!" "He is vaishya … no, shudra!" "No, he is vaishya, charioteers are vaishya." "Who cares, he's out either way." "How dare he! Did he think he wouldn't be caught?" "I recognized him, you know." "But what an archer! Surely they won't strip him of his prize?" "Of course they will. He is not kshatriya."

Prince Yudi, the eldest Pandava brother, was just seventeen but had the air of one older. He moved to Arjuna's side and with one hand grasped the boy's arm; the other hand he extended high in the air and held there. Compelled by the authority in that hand, the crowd stopped buzzing.

"Prince Arjuna is correct," said Yudi in a voice that was not loud, but carried. "Only kshatriya may wield weapons; only kshatriya may compete in tournaments. The son of a charioteer is not kshatriya." He looked at Karna and inclined his head slightly. "Friend, I am sorry, but you must withdraw. It is not permitted. Your prize is forfeit."

There followed a general chorus, led by the Pandavas and Lady Perta, of, "Yes, he must withdraw, his prize is forfeit"—but also a significant minority opining that it was "a shame, after he did so well." Through the hubbub Karna stood silent beside his father, who was now staring at the ground and looking about to cry.

With a snort of derision, Drona wheeled about and strode over to the weapons stand at the southeast corner of the arena. (The two blades-boys were still there, squatting in the dust and throwing their dice, unconcerned with whatever it was the grownups were doing.) Drona scooped up Karna's bow, quiver, and satchel, strode back to the canopy, and with a brisk "There are your things. Now, go"— tossed the lot on the ground at Karna's feet.

Adiratu let out another gasp and a "Drona, *please* ..." But Karna waited two more breaths, then reached down swift as a panther, grabbed the bow and one arrow, and had arrow fitted to string and aimed at Drona's chest before you could say *thunderbolt*. There were scattered screams from the crowd. Drona did not flinch but slowly raised both hands, eying the arrow's tip. It was poised an arm's length from his heart.

Who can say how things might have ended had someone not intervened?

Prince Duryodhana, who thus far had remained under the central canopy with his parents, now came stomping over to the staff tent. He was (as I have said) a muscular young man: thick-necked, with jet-black hair, black eyes, and brown skin. The beginnings of a beard fuzzed his jawline. Down his left cheek, from temple to chin, ran a pink crenellated scar, like to an old burn, which pulled the left side of his mouth into a slight but permanent sneer, disfiguring what otherwise would have been a handsome face. He wore a black dhoti and a black-dyed, plain leather vest; no jewels except for a beaten copper armband around his right bicep.

"THAT'S ENOUGH!" he roared, knocking aside a court lady and the chief carpenter as he barged through the spectators with head thrust forward. He took up a stance to one side of Karna's arrow, feet planted wide, fists on hips.

"Drona! This m-man is our guest. Yes, our, our *guest. And* a champion. A *champion!*" His seventeen-year-old voice had, unlike Arjuna's, a grown man's depth, but was marred by blurts and stammers.

"Great shooting, yes? Yes? No one could b-beat him. Not m-me, not Yudi, not even—" He turned with a crooked grin to his young cousin. "Not even the little p-prodigy with the arrows; not even our little *Arjuna.*"

Arjuna folded his arms and glared.

Karna still held his aim, but now Duryodhana spoke to him directly, almost intimately. "Sir, Sir … Karna … that is your name, yes? Karna, listen to me. I am p-prince of the Kuru, and I say you are w-welcome here. I do not care two *f-f-figs* what you are. You could be kshatriya or a shudra or a *m-mosquito*. Who cares? The point is, you have *won*. You are a w-warrior, and you, you have *won*. You shall not f-f-forfeit your prize. Lower your weapon. P-please, Karna. I am your f-friend."

Karna slowly lowered the arrow. He looked at Duryodhana and said, "I am the son of a charioteer. The prince says it is not permitted."

"NOT PERMITTED?" Duryodhana yelled it at Karna. Then he flung it over his shoulder at the Pandava brothers: "Not *p-permitted? I* am p-prince! *I* say what is *permitted!*"

"Surely, cousin," said Yudi, raising his eyebrows, "that is for the king to say."

Duryodhana paused. The lopsided grin reappeared as he replied, quite softly, "Yes, cousin. So let us see w-what my f-father says."

He held out a stubby hand to Karna and waited. For a few tense moments Karna did not react. Then he stooped, picked up his quiver and bag, replaced arrow in quiver, slung bow and all across his back, and took the proffered paw. Duryodhana went bashing back to the other tent, dragging Karna behind him and up before the king and queen. The crowd rushed to follow.

"Father! Mother! May, may I *present* ... er ... yes, Karna, Karna of P-Panchala! Karna is a w-warrior. He is the b-best with b-bow and arrow, the b-best any of us have seen. THE BEST. And yet here are my *dear* cousins, *Prince* Yudi and *P-Prince* Arjuna, saying he is *not* kshatriya and therefore *not* p-permitted to compete. Well. That may be true. But he is obviously *Arya,* so I have decided ... I m-mean to say, I ask you, f-father, if I may ... er ..." He seemed suddenly tongue-tied.

He planted his feet wider, took a breath, and went on: "I have *decided* to grant him one hundred head of cattle, twenty laborers, a p-pair of horses, and a house w-with appropriate f-farmland. ALSO! I grant him the title 'Sir Karna.' I am p-prince, and all these things are in my gift. And that, *cousins*" (with a sneer over his shoulder), "that makes him—*kshatriya!*" He turned back to his parents and bowed, a bit clumsily because his feet were so far apart.

Prince Yudi raised a forefinger. "Sire, if I may. I do not believe it is lawful for Prince Duryodhana to ..."

But King Tarashtra held up a hand. He turned to the queen and they put their heads together, their whispers making his double chin wag and her violet veil stir.

They faced front again. The king said: "My son is correct. These things are in his gift as crown ..." (the queen squeezed his elbow) "... as a *prince* of the Kuru. Kshatriya are not only born, they are also made. For this, there is precedent. Therefore, Sir Karna," (the royal eyes stared blindly ahead, but the royal head inclined slightly) "you are welcome to Hastinapura. And we congratulate you on your victory."

There was a pause. Everyone seemed unsure of what to do next.

Then one of the lady's maids said, "Oh!" One of the horse-event winners said, "Yes!" And all at once people were clapping, and more joined in as Karna, his face covered in wonder, turned to Duryodhana, seized his hand, bent to it, and kissed it. At this, the prince ducked his head and began shuffling his feet like an agitated bull; after a few attempts at "Rise, Sir Karna"—which perhaps went unheard over the swelling applause—he yanked his hand away and yelled, "RISE!" Karna straightened up, tears shining in his eyes, whereupon Duryodhana lurched forward and embraced him, slapping his back in that awkward way men have. Karna froze for an instant, but then began to return the backslaps, and suddenly both men were laughing as they thumped each other on the back, and all the spectators under the canopy (all except Drona and the Pandavas) were laughing too, and cheering, and shouting, and the joyful noise rolled on and on as if it would never stop.

≈

In the days after the tournament, the two became inseparable. Although five years the elder, Karna followed Duryodhana around like a calf its mother and treated his word—nay, his merest suggestion—as Law. The grant of one hundred head of cattle plus fief and laborers had been notional rather than actual, for the Kuru herd (which numbered more than ten thousand at the time) belonged to the clan, of course, as did all the land in the doab; and although the majority of kshatriya today keep homesteads in the countryside, back then there were just as many who lived at the palace or in town. Karna, it was clear, would remain at Hastinapura. He was given space in the soldiers' barracks on the east side of the compound and was invited, at Duryodhana's insistence, to take his evening meal with the court in the great hall. A messenger was sent to Panchala with the news that their assistant weapons master would not be returning.

The Pandava brothers treated their cousin's new ally with cold civility, nodding to him when they passed and addressing him as "Sir Karna." Arjuna, who had spent two days bowing extravagantly to Karna every time they met, on the third day received a lecture from Yudi on the manners befitting a prince and thereafter ceased his antics, although he continued to give a slight overemphasis to the "Sir." Duryodhana brought Karna with him to daily weapons practice, where Drona tolerated the champion but refused to instruct him, saying only that "the kshatriya needs no lessons from me." Adiratu, whose injections of "my son, Sir Karna" into every other sentence were beginning to annoy his fellow charioteers, could often be found watching practice from the sidelines, calling out "Oh, good shot!" and "Keep your shield up!" and "Now you've got him!" He was scrupulous about cheering all participants equally. Lady Perta, on the other hand, seemed to go out of her way to avoid Karna: if their paths around the compound ever looked like crossing she would stop, put a bejeweled hand to her forehead as if suddenly remembering an important errand, and hurry off in another direction.

It was now the morning of the seventh day after the tournament, and Duryodhana and Karna were heading for the horse barns. Karna's promised horses, unlike cattle and land, were not just notional: he was to pick out two steeds from the stables for his own. It was every kshatriya's duty then, as it is now, to train a team for battles and raids.

"The unclaimed horses are in the small b-barn, the one in the middle there; the weapons shed is over on the left," said Duryodhana as the two men walked across the training grounds. (Now that the prince was speaking one-on-one his voice was more even, with only the occasional stammer.) "The owned horses, plus the chariots, are in the two large barns over there on the right. We keep an excellent stable at Hastinapura—even b-better, I think" (the crooked grin reappeared) "than *Panchala*. You'll have your pick of forty stallions and geldings."

"What about mares?" asked Karna.

"Mares? Well, yes, we've plenty of those, too—if that's what you *Panchalans* p-prefer."

"Oh, I like mares," said Karna, jabbing an elbow into the other's ribs. "I'll ride *mares* all day." Duryodhana punched him back, and the two jostled and laughed their way along the passage between weapons shed and small barn.

But upon turning the corner, they stopped short. Ten paces away, slumped on the ground against the barn wall, naked except for a loincloth, was a man.

His face was contorted, his shoulders hunched. His left hand squeezed his right fist to his chest. Kneeling beside him was a girl of perhaps fourteen or fifteen, hair in a long untidy braid, wearing the undyed cotton shift and breeches of a lower maidservant. She was weeping, her arms around the man's neck. Blood coated his forearms and stomach, streaked his legs, and splotched the ground around him. The girl's shift was spattered with it.

Karna and Duryodhana approached cautiously. The girl was speaking through her tears; her words a combination of regular speech and hissing gibberish: "Father, please. It's all right. *Shhaassi, aassnam aghanash na vanisshh.* Father, I'm here, I'm here, *nisa, nisa,* I'll take care of you. It's all right. Everything will be all right. *Shhaassi, shhaassi.* Oh, Father …"

"WHAT'S ALL THIS?" Duryodhana shouted as they came near. The girl jumped up and went into a crouch, her arms still wrapping the man's shoulders, her head bent to the top of his, as if she expected a blow from above.

Karna gestured to his friend to stay back and squatted down in front of them.

"Now then, what's up, Uncle?" His voice was soothing, matter-of-fact: the voice of the assistant weapons master whose job it is to deal with injuries in the field. "You seem to be in a scrape. Let's have a look. No, girl, you can let go, I won't hurt him. Here, Uncle, let's see your hand. Let me see it. That's right. Open it up ... more ... there we are. Ah. I see."

They all stared at the man's right hand as he held it out. Blood was welling thickly from the place where his thumb used to be.

Karna opened his leather satchel, took out a kerchief, and pressed it firmly to the wound. "Stay still. I need to hold this here until the bleeding stops. Then we'll go wash it, put some ghee on it, and bind it up tight." He glanced up at the girl, who was now standing. She was dark-skinned like her father, with a slender frame, straight back, and large, heavy-lidded eyes.

"Where's the thumb?" he asked.

She gave a small shrug.

"Never mind," he said. "If it's totally severed you can't reattach it anyway. Was it one of the stable dogs? It'll have to be killed. Once they bite like that, they'll bite again."

"No," said the girl. "It was Drona."

Karna looked confused. Duryodhana said, "*Drona?* What do you mean, *Drona?*"

The girl regarded him unblinking. "Drona cut off my father's thumb."

"But ... but why? This m-man, I've seen him, he's a stable ... stable-hand; he has nothing to do with Drona. And anyway, who are *you?*" He jabbed a stubby forefinger at her.

The girl had the uncouth accent of an indigene, but she spoke Aryan well, with none of the giggling or whining typical of maid-servants. "I am Jaratka," she said. "My father's name is Ekalavya. We came to your country two years ago, when I was thirteen. We came from the forest south of here; Vrishni, you call it. It was many days' journey. We are Naga."

"Naga? You mean Snakes?"

Her chin lifted a bit. "No, *Naga.* Only you Arya call us *Snakes.*"

Duryodhana opened his mouth, seemed to find nothing to say, and closed it again.

Jaratka continued. "My father is very good with bow and arrows. In our tribe there is not much call for it. We use snares or short spears to catch meat. But my father, although he was ..." She hesitated for a moment. "But he wanted to be an archer. He dreamed of studying with a great teacher—a guru. My mother said it was—how do you say—ridikuluss? But after she died, my father said we would go to Hastinapura, where, he had heard, was the greatest weapons master in the world. So we came here. My father got work cleaning the stables; I, cleaning chamber pots in the women's quarters. Things were all right for us. We had food, beds. The old queen, Satyavati, she liked me, she made me one of her maidservants. But my father was not satisfied. He had ideas, and he started to go outside the town to practice."

Karna said to Ekalavya, "You had your own bow?"

Ekalavya, staring at the cloth pressed to the stump of his thumb, shook his head. He was a large, well-built man; standing, he would have been as tall as Karna.

Jaratka said, "No, he took—he *borrowed* bow and arrows from the shed. He would go in the late afternoon, after his work was done. He went north along the river to where the trees could hide him. There is a long clearing, and there he would practice, doing all the things he had seen Drona do with the princes and soldiers on the training grounds. I went with him sometimes, to help pick up the arrows. It was not wise, what he was doing, but who was to know? Nobody saw, nobody cared. I said to myself it was all right, all right as long as nobody knew, but he grew more and more skilled, and then he had another idea ..." She broke off and crouched down again beside her father, her voice angry. "I *told* you, Father, it was a *bad* idea!"

Ekalavya gave her a weak smile and reached across with his uninjured hand to pat her arm. "*Nisa, nisa,*" he whispered. "You were right, child. All the time right."

"How did Drona find out?" Karna asked. He lifted the cloth and glanced at the stump. The blood had slowed but not stopped. He replaced the cloth and kept pressing.

"Was you," said Ekalavya, looking at Karna.

"Me? What do you mean, me?"

Ekalavya's accent was thicker than his daughter's. "I see you win shooting, I hear you are made kshatriya, and I think, maybe, now iss time. I cannot be kshatriya, no, of coursse not. But if I show Drona what I can do, maybe, I think ... he will be my teacher." This brief speech seemed to exhaust him, and he leaned back against the wall, eyes closed.

Jaratka laid a hand on his shoulder. "He planned to wait for Drona in the weapons shed this morning," she said. "He asked me to come with him, because I speak Aryan better, and if there was any problem I could explain. We waited and waited in the shed.

"At last Drona arrives, and my father goes to him and kneels to touch his feet. Drona does not understand at first; he asks, Are you ill? We try to explain, but still he does not understand. So my father gets up and takes a bow and arrows and runs outside and tells Drona to come, watch, and he starts to shoot at that deodar tree there, and he shoots and shoots, one, two, three, four, five. His arrows make a perfect circle—perfect." Her finger traced a circle in the air.

Karna and Duryodhana looked at the deodar tree. It was behind one of the large barns, at least forty paces away. There were no arrows in it now.

"When he is done shooting, my father kneels again to Drona and says, 'Please, lord, you are my teacher. Command me, my teacher.' But Drona's face is so angry. I hear him say, very quiet: 'Not *another* one.' Then he kneels down, too. He says to my father, 'Very well, then, I am your teacher. Here is my first command. Put your right hand flat on the ground.'

"So my father did, his fingers spread out like a fig leaf. He was so happy; he thought Drona was going to teach him. And then Drona took a knife from his belt, grabbed my father's wrist like *this,* and ... and ..."

Jaratka dropped her head and wept.

Then she gulped, rubbed her face hard, and stood up. She reached across her father and jabbed Duryodhana's chest with her forefinger, saying, "*You.* You are the *prince.* What are you going to do about this ... this *bad thing?*" Her whole body was quivering with fury.

Karna, his expression grave and a little embarrassed, turned his attention back to Ekalavya's thumb. But Duryodhana simply stared at the girl, like a big dog unnerved and fascinated in equal parts by the depredations of a bold kitten.

❖ ❖ ❖

More beer, Sire? Please, let me refill your cup.

All this, Karna told me. But when he told me what Drona had done to the Naga man, I did not let on that I already knew some things about Drona: two things, in particular, which I'd learned from my talks with Old Queen Satyavati. I'll explain them to you.

First, Drona was born a brahmin. So what was he doing, being chief weapons master to the Kuru? It seems that as a youth, Drona had been preparing for priesthood in the usual way, living with his guru and studying the Sacred Knowledge, when one day the guru said he would no longer have him as a student. It turned out Drona had been secretly practicing with weapons, which of course no brahmin should do; moreover, when his teacher confronted him about it, he actually defied the holy man to his face and said he would not give it up. Naturally, he was sent packing.

Now here's the second thing. After he was dismissed, Drona set off for Panchala. His father had been a priest at the Panchala court years before, and little Drona used to play with little Crown Prince Drupada. Now that Drupada was king, Drona hoped to call upon that old friendship in order to get a position at the palace. But when he presented himself and told Drupada who he was, the young king was scornful.

"An old friend?" his majesty said. "What's an old friend? What I see here is a ragged student who has been insolent to his teacher, treacherous to his caste, and sent away in disgrace; in other words, nobody. As you are a brahmin, you may ask me for alms and I will give you something. But do not speak to me of *old friends.*"

Drona took the bag of food that was tossed to him—he was too hungry not to—and left the Panchala court. No one knows what he did for several years after that; Satyavati thought he might have gone as mercenary to a minor chieftain somewhere in the west. In any case, he eventually turned up here at Hastinapura, just at the time when King Tarashtra was seeking a tutor for his sons and nephews, the little Kauravas and Pandavas. Everyone assumed Drona was kshatriya. Regent Bhishma tested his skills and gave him a good report, so he was hired.

Drona became close to all the children, but especially to Arjuna, whose talent was evident at a tender age. He focused his efforts on the boy and promised he would make him the greatest archer in the world. And ten years later, he arranged the tournament.

People say it was his prize pupil's loss to a stranger that made Drona so angry. I wonder, though ...

What if the winner had not come from the court of Panchala? What if the winner had not been a caste-breaker like himself?

Might poor Ekalavya then have kept his thumb?

Well, Sire, it's late, and you must sleep. Tomorrow I will take you back further, back to the beginning, so you'll understand the origins of the rift in our family. This part of the story belongs to Satyavati. She was very old when she told it to me, and her memories of her young days came in fragments; but revealed in those fragments, as you'll see, are many truths.

Chapter 2

SATYAVATI

T*he baby was tiny, red-faced, and slick with mucus.*
Except for the rush of water, the chirr of crickets, and the sporadic hoot of an owl, there was silence in the forest. The moonlight filtering through the vine-covered banyans, deodars, babuls, and teak trees was bright enough for Satyavati, kneeling by the creek, to see the child clearly. His eyes, open and placid, regarded her as she lowered him toward the water.

"Good-bye, my son," she said. "May your rebirth be fortunate."

She leaned farther forward, taking him down past the ferns on the bank. The creek bed there was rocky, the water fast and turbulent. She straightened her arms, slowly, downward.

The baby's right heel touched the cold water and he let out a peep. Her arm muscles contracted, lifting him up. She held him there for a moment, hovering.

Then her arms straightened again … slowly, slowly … now the baby's whole foot was in the water, and this time there was no peep. Then both his feet were in, then his calves, then her hands cradling his head and bottom were submerged, then the water was roiling over his tiny thighs, splashing his tiny belly, and his face scrunched up and his hands flew out and from his just-born lungs came a wail …

Satyavati was kneeling upright on the bank, clutching her son to her breast.

After a minute she stood and wrapped him in her crumpled cotton shawl, then placed him on her shoulder and walked, bouncing on the balls of her feet, to and fro, to and fro by the water until his cries ceased and he fell asleep. She reached under her shift, feeling her inner thighs. The blood was still dripping there, but not as much as before. A porcupine waddled out of the dense woods into the clearing and over to the teak tree under which she had lain not half an hour ago; it nosed at the purplish lump of tissue that had followed the baby out of her body. She shooed the beast away and retrieved her breech-cloth from where she had left it folded on the ground. She used the shawl to strap the baby tight to her chest; with both hands now free, she drew the cloth through and around her legs and around her waist, forming loose short pants. The small bronze knife with which she had cut the baby's cord she tucked into her knotted waistband. Then she set off through the forest, following the creek.

The eastern sky had acquired a tinge of gray by the time she knocked at the gate of the ashram. The night watchman had clearly been asleep; it took much knocking before the gate squeaked open and he peered out, little eyes bleary, oil lamp in hand.

"Who is it? What do you want?"

"I have a baby."

"So? Many women do." He made as if to push the gate shut.

Her left hand shot out and blocked it. "The father lives here."

The man ejected his head a bit further, held the lamp up to her face, and peered more closely. "What's the father's name?"

"Parashara."

"Oh. Him. Well, I wouldn't doubt it."

"He came on my ferry boat. I was alone. The fog was thick that day. He forced me."

"That's what they all say." His eyes traveled up and down, taking in her round face and rosebud mouth; her curly, almost bushy, black hair; her young but already voluptuous body; and her dirt-stained, ragged clothes. The tip of his tongue probed the corner of his mouth, leaving a fleck of moisture to glisten in the lamplight. "Doesn't look like you'd mind much."

"I can't keep this baby. If you won't let me leave him here, I will report Parashara to ... to the queen."

"Oh-ho! To the *queen!* Bold words for a fish girl. That's what you are, aren't you? A fish girl. You know how I can tell?" He leaned even closer and gave several loud sniffs. "You stink of fish."

She neither retreated nor dropped her gaze, but her right hand came up to cradle the baby's head. "The queen is a River Goddess. She cares for the fisher folk. She will not like what I will tell her. Your ashram will be punished."

The man frowned and scratched his chin. His eyes moved to the bundle at her breast, then back to her set face, then back to the bundle.

He sighed, pulled the gate open, and stepped back. "All right, fish girl. Come on in."

≈

The teak tree in the clearing was two years thicker, two years taller. Satyavati's back was pressed hard against its trunk, her stomach pressed hard against the stomach of the man who was kissing her. His hands were at her temples, his fingers twined in her curly-wild hair, the soles of his dyed-leather shoes almost losing traction on the soil as he thrust his groin at hers, again, and again. The rush of creek water mingled with his moans.

"My love ... my love ... I must have you. I must *have* you."

She pressed his head to her shoulder and went on rotating her hips.

He kissed her neck, great mouthing kisses. "You will be my ... my consort ... above all other women ... I promise, only I must have you."

Her fingers slid down his naked back, briefly touched his jeweled sword-belt, moved on lower, and caressed his buttocks lightly, teasingly, through the crimson cloth that covered them. He moaned again, louder.

"Please, Satyavati ... my love ... Satya, Satya, *please* ..." His arms circled her waist and shoulders and he made as if to lower her to the ground.

She whipped her hands around, dug her nails into his chest, and shoved him away, hard. He fell back, panting, rubbing the nail-marks. She kept her hands up, ready to claw again; she too was panting, but her eyes were cold.

He fell to his knees before her and buried his face in his hands. She stayed where she was, watching him. The sun filtering through the leaves above made a tiny rainbow on his naked, bent back. The creek water rushed and bubbled as his breathing gradually slowed.

He leaned forward, grasped the tops of her bare feet, and said, "Satyavati ... I beg you. Marry me. Marry me. Be my wife. Be my queen."

She waited for a count of ten. Then, smiling, she laid a hand on his head.

"King Shantanu: I will."

≈

Early next morning Satyavati and her father, Upa, were squatting on the silty ground by the door of their hut: she roasting a catla fish on a stick over the fire, he shading his eyes as he looked east across the wide, slow river.

"No early customers today for the ferry," he said. "I guess it's just as well. The boat's leaking again. I don't know if it will take another patch."

Satyavati brought the silver-scaled fish toward her, gave the flesh a poke, and thrust it back over the fire. "Well, Papa, good news. You won't need to patch it, because I'm going to be queen, and I'll get you another boat."

Upa laughed. "Yes. Queen of the Kuru! I still can't believe it." Then he turned to her, brow suddenly furrowed. "Are you *sure* he doesn't know about the baby?"

"Yes, Papa, I keep telling you. He doesn't know. How could he?"

"No, you're right. How could he know? You drowned it, didn't you?"

Satyavati reexamined the fish. "I got rid of it."

"Yes, well, that's all fine," Upa said. "Still, child, you must be careful. You must not tempt fate. I'm sure he *will* marry you; it won't be the first time a king has married a shudra girl, and he's obviously mad for you. But now you say you're going to make him put his own son, his son by Queen Ganga, out of the succession and promise you that the line will pass through your sons instead. Don't you think he'll balk at that? What if he gets angry?"

"What if he does?"

"Don't be stupid, girl. Men are witless when it comes to women, but push them too far and they tend to recover their wits. You could lose him, and after you've played him so well—like a Ganges shark on the line. Heh. What a shame, to lose him after all that!"

"I won't lose him, Papa. You said it yourself: he's mad for me. He'll do anything."

"But why make a fuss about it now? Queen Ganga is dead, so

there'll be no more children from her. Her only son is two years old and has no protectors—other than his father, I mean. I hear he's a healthy boy, but that's nothing; a bout of flux, a fall from a horse, off he goes. And it's not as if the people know him or care about him. Why not bide your time, see what fate brings? You're only seventeen, and strong; you'll have many sons, and once you're queen, with sons, in the palace ... you'll be in a better position to arrange things, no?"

"You're wrong. The people loved Queen Ganga. They will support her son. The only reason they wouldn't is if he were sickly or deformed or deficient—which everyone knows he is not. No, they won't allow Prince Bhishma to be pushed aside for a fish girl's brat."

"Well then—if they won't allow it ...?"

"They will allow it *if* the king himself puts Bhishma out of the line. In that case, they'll have no choice. They must allow it." She took the catla off the fire and with her small bronze knife divided it onto two plates. She handed one plate to Upa, and they both began to eat.

"I don't know," said Upa, sucking fish oil from his fingers with noisy smacks. "It just seems like a big gamble."

"Maybe. But my gambles usually pay off."

He laughed again. "True enough, child. True enough. I'd never bet against you."

The river flowed on as the two ate their breakfast.

≈

The great hall of the palace was already packed with courtiers, palace staff, and townspeople, and there were scores more townspeople outside clamoring and pushing to get in. The door wardens wielded their batons, prodding backs and ribs and thighs, shouting, "Move *up!* Move *up!*" There were a few grumbles and ouches here and there, but the prodded ones mostly did not object; all eyes were on the two thrones on the dais at the far end of the hall, and everyone was trying to get nearer. In front of the dais was a clear space marked off by a rope held by two armed guards. The crowd seemed inclined to respect the rope (or the guards), but they pressed as close as possible.

On the larger and more elaborately carved of the thrones sat King Shantanu, his sword across his crimson-clad knees. Behind him stood the chief counselor, a wizened little man with a scraggy beard

like a goat's; off to his left stood a clutch of priests, solemn and dignified in their white robes. To his right in the lower and plainer throne
sat Queen Satyavati. No more dirty shift and breeches: she wore a
brilliant-pink sari edged with silver thread, silver bangles up to her
elbows, loops of silver beads on her chest, and gold and silver rings
at her fingers, ears, and nostrils. Her mouth was red with sindoor,
her wide eyes made wider with kohl. Her hair was the only thing
unchanged from her fish-girl days: a pink silk veil draped the curly-
wild mass, but did nothing to tame it. Half a dozen ladies-in-waiting
clustered around her.

Cradled in her arms, swaddled in linen and fast asleep, was a
baby.

Satyavati looked out at the crowd, red lips curved, as she dandled
the baby up and down, up and down. Shantanu was gazing at her,
his ongoing infatuation as clear as if he were shouting it aloud. He
seemed oblivious to all but his wife as the numbers in the hall swelled
until at last there was no more room for even a cat, at which point
the counselor, after several futile tries at "Your majesty," left his position, circled to the front of the throne, and made namaste. Finding
his presence still unnoticed, he leaned far to his left and lifted his
joined palms above his head as if about to execute a side-dive into
the queen's lap. The king, his attention finally caught, turned with a
benign smile and said, "Yes, Nimu. Are we ready?"

"Yes, Sire, all is ready."

The king raised a hand, palm to the audience. The garnet ring
on his finger caught the light from the window behind him; it was a
sunny winter's day, the outside air cool and pleasant, albeit unable to
touch the heat created by the throng inside the hall. The king waited
until the chatter subsided. Then he said, in a voice that did not quite
project to the back:

"People of the Kuru: Welcome!"

Light cheers from the crowd.

"This is a happy day," he continued. "One month ago, the Gods
blessed me with a son. Under the priests' supervision, I have performed the necessary sacrifices" (he nodded to the priests, whose
heads bowed in unison) "and the queen has been purified of her birth
defilement" (he nodded to Satyavati, whose eyes dipped modestly).
"Now it is my son's name-day. In accordance with the Gods' wishes,

conveyed by the priests and confirmed by the rituals, I hereby name him … *Vichitravirya*."

In the hall more cheers, a few tentative cries of "Vichitra!" "Chavitra!" and some mutters: "Vicha … what?" "What did he say?" "I couldn't hear." "Again, say it again!"

King and queen exchanged a glance; she raised her eyebrows high with a told-you-so smile. Shantanu smiled back, shrugged, turned again to the hall, funneled his mouth with his hands, and bellowed: "CHIT. We're calling him CHIT."

Much relieved laughter, nods, and cries of "Chit! Chit! Prince Chit!"

The infant in Satyavati's arms scrunched his face and broke wind. She continued to dandle him up and down, up and down.

"And there is more happy news," said Shantanu, gesturing for silence. Once he had it, however, he paused and looked again at his wife, fingers drumming on his sword. Again she returned the look— this time with no smile and only a slight raise of the brows.

The king drew in a breath, let it out, and faced the audience: "… more happy news, for today the Kuru have a new crown prince. Today I name Prince Chit my heir, before all others of my line. My friends, my clan, my people: Here is your future king!"

Some scattered cheers, but they died away. More murmurings: "What?" "What did he say?" "What future king?" Neighbor turned to neighbor, unsure what it meant.

Then a man at the back called out, "Bhishma!" and others took up the cry. Soon many of the townspeople, and even several of the palace staff, were shouting, "Bhishma! Prince Bhishma!" Some of the courtiers near the front made competing attempts at "Chit! Prince Chit!" but gave it up as the calls for "Prince Bhishma" multiplied.

Shantanu, it seemed, was prepared for this. He flicked a hand at the chief counselor, who again left his spot behind the throne, descended the two steps at stage left, and approached a small boy standing in the shadow of a pillar, chubby hands clinging to a fold of his ayah's dhoti. Counselor and ayah together pried the boy's hands loose, after which the counselor led him back up the steps of the dais (big steps for little legs) and over to the king. The scraggy-bearded man bent down and whispered something, whereupon the boy— after one panicky look over his shoulder at the crowd—dropped to his knees, leaned forward, and placed his fingers on the tops of the king's dyed-leather shoes.

The king gripped the boy by the armpits and lifted him up. He kissed his forehead, rotated him a quarter turn, and gave him a gentle push. The child, now with a more confident air, walked to the queen's throne and dropped to his knees again. But he did not bend forward to touch her feet; instead he waited with back straight, chubby hands on thighs, small feet turned pigeon-toed and pressed flat by small bottom.

Satyavati smiled down at him and (was she remembering that time by the creek in the forest?) waited for a count of ten. Then she slid to one side and patted the seat of the throne next to her. The boy stood, clambered up, and plumped down, feet sticking over the edge. With a soft "There, now," Satyavati laid the baby in his lap.

The people stood quiet before the tableau. The ladies-in-waiting leaned over the throne and cooed. King Shantanu scanned the hall, jaw set, as if daring anyone to protest.

Then a man at the back—perhaps it was the same one as before—cried, "*Bhishma!* His name means 'noble vow'! Bhishma the Vow-maker! Bhishma the Protector!"

All at once the hall was ringing with "Noble Bhishma!" "Noble vow!" "Gods preserve you, Bhishma!" "Bhishma, the Protector!"

Satyavati's smile remained firm. She kept one arm around Bhishma's shoulders, the other hand supporting Baby Chit's head. But her eyes were on the people, and her eyes were wary.

≈

"You *bought* them for me! It is not lawful!"

Prince Chit slouched on his receiving-room chair and glared at Bhishma and his mother.

"Chit, darling, why don't you just *meet* the girls," said Satyavati. "Think of all the trouble your brother went to. And they're very beautiful, the eldest one especially."

"I don't care!" He sat up, thrust his head forward, and pounded his fists on the chair arms. "I. Don't. Want. To. How many times must I say it? I don't want to marry! I want to be celibate!"

"And how many times must *I* say it," said Bhishma, arms folded on his muscular chest. "You cannot be celibate and be king."

"I don't see *why.*" Chit slouched back down and commenced kicking the base of the chair with his heel.

Satyavati clasped her hands in front of her waist—a waist somewhat thickened in the past eighteen years—looked down, and sighed. She looked up and said, "Chit, darling, we've explained this *so* many times. When your father died, you were only fourteen and too young to be king, so your brother became regent and ruled in your stead. Now you are full-grown, and believe me, if I'd had my way you'd have been crowned long ago. But the people—and the priests—must see that you will provide an heir. The line must be made certain. If you don't marry, they'll want Bhishma to go on as regent. Darling, surely you can understand."

The heel kept kicking. "*Bhishma* isn't ever getting married."

"No," said Bhishma. "I'm not ever getting married."

Satyavati threw a desperate look at her stepson.

Bhishma stepped forward, planted his hands on the arms of the chair, and leaned over. "Chit, listen to me. No—*listen to me.* I made a bargain with the king of Kashi. I gave him eight hundred cows and twenty oxen in exchange for his three daughters. Kashi is a small and poor clan, and they need those cattle. They need them badly, which means the king will not take the girls back. Do you hear? *He will not take them back.* We—no, *you*—are stuck with them. So you may as well marry them and get on with it."

He pushed away from the chair and stood back, one thumb hooked in his bronze-studded belt. "By the way, their names are Amba, Ambika, and Ambalika. Nice names, no?"

Chit had shrunk against the chair-back during Bhishma's speech. He remained there, heel no longer kicking but mouth in a sulky twist, eyeing his half-brother.

"I know you're worried about his purchasing the brides ..." said Satyavati.

"Yes, I am worried!" said Chit, his face suddenly alive with interest. "Bride-purchase is the way of the Asuras. It is not lawful. There are five lawful types of marriage." He sat up and began ticking them off on his fingers. "The way of Prajapati, when a woman is given for charity; the way of Brahma, when a woman is accepted for her dowry; the way of the Devas, when a woman is given as a fee for services; the way of the Rishis, when a woman is given for ritual purposes; and the way of the Gandharvas, when a woman chooses her husband freely. Then there are three unlawful types: when a woman is purchased—that's what the Asuras do—or abducted, as the barbarians do, or violated, as the vampires do. These girls were purchased. So your bargain was unlawful, and" (he pursed his lips) "I cannot condone it."

"Condone it or not, the thing is done," said Bhishma. He turned to Satyavati, who was standing with hands once again clasped at her waist, her gaze on her son despairing. "You'd better go get the girls, Mother. And a priest. We can at least get the betrothal ceremony over with. The wedding—we'll worry about that later."

≈

It was just a betrothal, so within the Hall of Sacraments, there was only one fire lit and a junior priest presiding. As the brides entered, escorted by Satyavati and Bhishma, Chit slouched before the fire-pit, weight on one leg and hand on hip, watching the smoke as it drifted up through the hole in the ceiling; once the ritual began, however, he stood up straighter and seemed to be paying attention.

The three young women arrayed next to him had similar facial features, which were pretty enough: wide-set eyes, high cheekbones, dainty nose and mouth. But only the eldest, Amba, had a body worth noticing: she was petite and curvy, while the two younger, Ambika and Ambalika, were off-puttingly tall and bulky. Their strapping frames contrasted with their delicate faces, and they seemed aware of the odd figures they cut, for while their older sister stood with head erect and hands loosely joined, they stood with shoulders hunched and hands clutching their elbows, as if trying to look smaller.

The ceremony was a matter of minutes. When it was over, Chit bowed to each bride in very correct fashion, then turned and led the way out of the hall with Satyavati shepherding the girls after him and Bhishma bringing up the rear. As the little procession came to the door, Amba fell back to allow her future mother-in-law to precede her. In doing so, she bumped softly against Bhishma, who stepped aside and gestured, with a half-bow, that she should go ahead. But she did not move. As the others walked out into the sunshine, Amba and Bhishma remained behind, framed in the doorway, their bare arms lightly touching.

≈

Satyavati stood at the door of the bedchamber, one ear laid against the curtain. The old king's quarters were currently unused—Bhishma wanted to keep his regent status clear, and Chit was not yet crowned—so except for the two lovers within, she was alone in the darkness. There was a window at the end of the public room off of which the bedrooms gave, and the strong moonlight through it was enough to see by. As the soft moans continued with no suggestion yet of a peak, she left the curtain, tiptoed to the window, and leaned on the sill. She stayed there, looking up at the full white moon floating just above the top of the deodar tree behind the horse barns.

After the climax, she tiptoed back and laid her ear once more to the curtain. There was silence for a while. Then:

"Mmmmm, Bhishma. You're very good."

"Thank you."

A long pause.

"My sisters are hopeless. They will make very bad queens."

"They'll match up well with Chit, then. He's going to make a very bad king."

Another long pause.

"Bhishma. Listen. Why not marry me and take the throne? You would make a good king, and I would make a good queen. I'll be with child before you know it; we'll have sons, lots and lots of sons, and together we'll make the Kuru the most powerful clan in … in the whole world. Bhishma, why not?"

"I cannot."

"*Why* not?"

"I promised my father."

"*Tcha.* Your father is dead. What matters is what the people want, and they want you. I know they do; news of the Kuru clan reaches even to poor little Kashi."

"It doesn't matter what the people want. What matters is that I made a vow."

"A vow that runs against your duty as a prince? Your duty as a man? How can that be a lawful vow?"

"A vow is a vow."

"And what if I'm with child now? Have you thought of that? Given what we've been doing the past two weeks, it's quite likely."

"You'll be married soon. The baby, if there is one, will belong to Chit."

"I could refuse to marry him. It's my right, you know. I can refuse."

"You must give grounds for your refusal."

"I'll say I was already promised."

"To whom?"

"Who cares? I'll say I already chose a kshatriya of my own clan and that he agreed. I'll say I was willing to go along with my father's plan at first, but then after the betrothal my conscience got the better of me and I told you the truth, so you sent me back."

Pause.

"If that's what you want."

"It's not what I want! I want to marry *you*."

"That's not possible, Amba."

Pause.

"Bhishma ... I love you."

There was no reply. A minute later there came sounds of rising, dressing. Satyavati crept away from the curtain and left the room.

≈

Chit was dead, of a fever. He had had a year with his two brides—the eldest girl, Amba, having been sent home in a minor scandal involving a prior betrothal—but had left nothing to show for it. The rumor around the palace was that he had been negligent in his husbandly duties.

The day after the funeral, Satyavati invited Bhishma to her rooms for the midday meal. The two sat on woven rugs, eating curried rice and roast partridge. They were alone, the dowager queen having dismissed her women once the food had been served.

"Niyoga. The law of niyoga," Satyavati was saying. She took up the flask of barley beer and refilled Bhishma's cup. "A woman whose husband is dead or otherwise incompetent may call upon another man to provide her with children. As long as that man is of the husband's family, it is as if the husband sired the children himself.

'The son is his who took the hand,' as they say. You don't need me to explain it, my dear; you know it's lawful."

"I never said it wasn't lawful. I said I would not do it." Bhishma took a swig of beer, wiped his mouth with the back of his hand, and returned his attention to the bird on the dish before him.

"Bhishma! You must do it. If you don't, the Kuru line dies. It *dies*, Bhishma."

He picked up a wing and began chewing the meat. "It's a shame all your children after Chit were miscarried or stillborn. Why don't you marry again? Try for another son. You're what—thirty-seven? It's not too late. Plenty of men would marry the queen of the Kuru."

"I'm thirty-eight. And it *is* too late. I am no longer queen of the Kuru; Ambika and Ambalika are. By Law, it is their sons who inherit."

"I'd have thought you could find a way around that."

"There aren't ways around the Law."

"You're right. There aren't."

"Bhishma ..."

He put down the wing. "No, Mother. Don't 'Bhishma' me. You talk of the Law, but nineteen years ago you used the Law to have me put out of the succession. You told my father you wouldn't marry him otherwise, and not only that, you made him make *me* swear a vow—a vow never to marry, never to sire children. I was barely four years old. All I remember is standing in front of a fire and my father telling me to kneel down and say some words. But it was a vow nonetheless, made before the Gods, and lawful. Now that vow has become inconvenient for you. Well, that's your misfortune. I will not break it."

"I see," said Satyavati. She picked off a bit of meat, put it in her mouth, chewed, swallowed. "Noble Bhishma. And if your nobility means the end of the house of Kuru?"

He took another swig of beer and shrugged. "The continuation of the house of Kuru is not my concern. You made sure of that."

When the meal was over and he had gone, Satyavati clapped her hands twice. To the maidservant who appeared she said: "Go down to the river and find my father. Tell him I want him at the palace. Tell him to come right now."

≈

49

"Well, Satya, here he is: your son."

Upa gestured toward the wild-haired figure standing next to him and proceeded to hunker down comfortably on the sandy floor before the fire-pit. The Hall of Sacraments was dark, lit only by the two torches set on the altar at one end of the spacious room (they burned there perpetually, as they do today); by the starlight shimmering faintly through the smoke holes in the roof; and by the tiny flame of the oil lamp in Satyavati's hand.

The dowager queen said, "Thank you, Papa. Did you have any trouble finding him?"

"Heh, no, of course not. You said he was at the ashram. I know where the ashram is. Though I can't imagine how you got them to take him in as a baby. Actually, no, I can imagine it—their letting you leave him there, I mean; what I *can't* imagine is why his father didn't just dump him in the forest, or drown him in the creek. Heh. Like you said you did."

"I didn't say I'd drowned him. I said I'd got rid of him."

"Yes, well, anyway, it was clever of you. But then you've always been clever. I guess you thought you might have a use for that baby someday. And now you do—eh?"

"Yes. I do."

Upa seemed to judge his contributions complete and fell to picking his teeth.

Satyavati turned to the other, who had remained still and silent during the previous exchange. She took a step or two closer, raised the lamp, and peered. Light and shadow played across the gaunt, grinning face and the shock of black hair. A demon from the forest.

"You are happy to be here," she said.

"Why not? Today I found out my mother is the queen." The voice rasped; the black eyes glowed. "I am honored to meet your majesty."

"Yes. I am your mother. But I am not the queen; at least, I am the Dowager Queen. These ladies"—she swung the lamp left, casting its dim glow on the two big women who stood there, veiled head-to-toe, huddled together—"these ladies are the queens."

"All right. They are the queens. Why am I summoned by your … grace?"

"I wish to invoke the law of niyoga. You are their dead husband's half-brother. If you impregnate them, their sons will be King Chit's sons and lawful heirs to the throne."

The glowing black eyes went to the two veiled forms.

"I see. But what if they don't want to? I've been told we ascetics can be a bit …" (the grin stretched wider, showing teeth stained red with betel nut) "terrifying."

"What they want or don't want is neither here nor there. It is their duty to produce sons."

"No doubt, no doubt. But I have no such duties. What will I get out of the bargain?"

"Much. You get to be high priest to the Kuru."

"Ah haaa … I see. That is a very generous offer, your grace."

Satyavati grabbed his wrist and drew him over to stand in front of the women. "But listen to me. You must lie with them often: every night, both of them, for at least two months. We have to be sure. And it has to be soon."

"Every night, eh?" He leaned close to the two bowed heads, sniffing their scent. "*Every* night? Even during their monthly time— their monthly bleeding?"

"No, no, don't be ridiculous. Not then."

"Oh. Too bad." He leaned back. "It might have been interesting."

"So, do we have an understanding?"

"Let me think. Yes, I think this … arrangement … will suit me very well."

"Good. I will have to inform Bhishma right away, but everyone else can wait. We'll make you high priest—I'll think of some excuse to get rid of our current one—and you can move into the palace. Then in a month or two, if you've done your job that is, I'll announce who you are, and we can share the happy news that the royal line of Kuru is secure."

"That will be happy news, indeed."

"Yes. Now, you can stay here the rest of the night—I'm sure you're used to sleeping on the floor—and in the morning, come to the great hall and we'll get you set up. If you need anything from the ashram, we can send a manservant. Papa! Are you awake? It's time to go. All right, girls, come along." Satyavati put a hand on each broad back and pushed the women before her toward the door. Upa got to his feet, yawning and scratching, and followed. The shock-haired man stayed by the fire-pit, watching them go.

When she reached the door, Satyavati turned back. "I forgot to ask. What is your name?"

The voice rasped out of the shadows: "My father named me Vyasa. But the common people call me Krishna: the Dark One."

"There are too many Krishnas these days. It gets confusing. We'll call you Vyasa."

"Vyasa it is."

"Good night, Vyasa."

"Good night ... Mother."

You might well wonder, Sire, at the questionable behavior that used to be allowed among the Arya. The law of niyoga, which encouraged barren wives to cuckold their husbands and widows to cavort with men instead of retiring decently to the forest; a queen, displaying herself in the public hall to a lot of ogling townspeople; a bride, seducing the half-brother of her betrothed; a king, refusing to perform his conjugal duties. It is all quite shocking, I agree.

I can only explain it thus: The world had become decadent since the golden age. Demons had arrived on earth, spawning and wreaking havoc, and although Brahma sent Gods to combat the demons, Gods can't be everywhere at once. Evil influences, therefore, were gaining sway. Men were becoming corrupt, falling away from the Law. As for women, they were becoming independent, proud, and ambitious—that is to say, wanton. We know the result: a terrible war that initiated this terrible age, the Kali Yuga.

But there is one thing I suppose we must be glad of. After the war, the priests, recognizing the disaster that had occurred and the dangers besetting us, introduced new rules and strictures to help men and women, especially women, back to the path of virtue. They abolished niyoga. They encouraged husbands to restrain their wives. They forbade women from going about half-covered, from wearing too many jewels, from riding (yes, kshatriya women used to ride horseback), and from mixing with men at public assemblies. And polyandry—the horrible practice whereby one wife is shared by more than one husband—the priests abolished that, too. All so the Arya might reestablish our Purity.

The olden days, however, were clearly quite different.

What happened with the royal succession? Well, once again it would have been unwise to bet against Satyavati, for her plan worked out—though once again, not without hitches. Oh, it wasn't High Priest Vyasa's fault; he was as good as his word. Every night for several months, except for one week in each month, he visited both queens' bedrooms, doing with vigor and enthusiasm (so the queens' maids reported) what their husband had been unwilling to do. And his efforts paid off: eleven months after his summoning and only days apart, three babies were born in the palace. Yes, three babies, and all boys.

First, Ambika gave birth to a son. He came out ruddy and robust, and the palace rejoiced. But almost immediately there appeared on the surface of his eyes a whitish film; his gaze grew blank, and his pupils stopped responding to light. Satyavati called in healers, promising lavish gifts if they could cure the child, but to no avail: he was blind. They named him Tarashtra.

Hopes turned to the child of Ambalika. He was weak and sickly, with a yellow cast to his skin, a poor appetite, and a tendency to fret. ("So tiresome; reminds me of Chit," Satyavati said to Bhishma.) But this boy at least had all his faculties, and he was declared the crown prince. I don't know what his given name was; from the start everyone called him Pandu, "Pale One."

High Priest Vyasa then came to the dowager queen and informed her that there was good news: he had not slacked off during those weeks when he could not lie with one of the royal ladies but had, instead, found a pretty maidservant—"an adventurous sort," he said—and spent his extra time with her. Her baby had been born a day or two after Ambalika's and was the picture of health. Satyavati said that if the high priest chose to amuse himself with shudra sluts it was his business, but the brats that came of such activities were none of hers. In response Vyasa pointed out that he, Vyasa, was her acknowledged son and the "brat" therefore her acknowledged grandson; moreover that since he, Vyasa, was standing in place of Chit, all the products of his "activities" should by Law be regarded as Chit's; moreover that the maid's boy looked a lot more promising than the two princes, one blind, the other sickly; and finally that Mother might not want to be so quick to dismiss the claims of a shudra slut, since shudra sluts (so he had heard) often found ways to rise in the world.

Satyavati dismissed the priest with a cold glare. But later she did acknowledge the maid's boy, who was named Vidura. She declared he would be chief counselor to his brother Pandu when the latter became king.

There was much more that Satyavati told me in the months after the war, when I visited her in her rooms and she lay on her settee, ancient and fat and toothless, sucking on honeycomb, having her legs massaged by her women. We'll return to her later.

But now we move on to Vidura: the boy who in all ways surpassed his half-brothers but who, unlike them, would never be king of the Kuru. I will let him tell his story in his own words.

Chapter 3

VIDURA

Vidura said:

I always loved my brother Pandu more than anyone. I knew that even though he would be king one day and I, as the son of a maidservant, would never be more than a counselor, he needed me to take care of him. I also knew that despite his addiction, he was a far better man than our brother Tarashtra. And that's not because Tarashtra was blind; it's because Tarashtra was ... well, you may judge for yourself from what I tell you about him.

Really everybody loved Pandu. Even Uncle Bhishma—that's what we boys called him, "Uncle Bhishma," although in public I had to call him "Lord Bhishma"—even Uncle Bhishma, I say, who normally had no patience for folly of any kind, would go along with Pandu's antics. At the age of three or four Pandu would jump onto his back for a "horse ride," and the stern regent would smile and oblige, galloping round the great hall or palace yard with Pandu slapping his shoulder and shouting "faster, horse, faster!" Tarashtra wouldn't have dared try that any more than I would have, but Pandu, with his guileless charm and sweet smile, got away with it.

Grandmamma (that is Satyavati, the old queen) was the only one who seemed not to care for Pandu—or indeed, for any of her three grandsons. I once overheard her saying to High Priest Vyasa that it was a shame he'd seen fit to strew his seed all over the palace, thus diluting its effects and giving her one blind prince, one yellow prince, and one useless half-breed, when all she'd asked for was one viable heir to the throne. Vyasa replied that perhaps she, Satyavati, would like to try her luck at conceiving a baby with him, as he had always wondered what an *old* woman would be like. (He was jesting, of course. I imagine he just wanted to make clear that she should not speak to a brahmin, even her own son, in such a disrespectful way.)

But everyone else loved Pandu, I most of all. As youngsters he and Tarashtra and I would play with the kshatriya and brahmin boys of the compound, and if one of them showed me disrespect—calling me "shudra scum," for instance—Pandu would rush at the offender and before he knew what was happening knock him face downward, grab his wrist, and bend his arm up high behind his back. The boy would squeal with pain and Pandu would shout with upward jerks of the arm: "What did you call my brother? What did you call him?" The boy would yell, "Nothing! Nothing!" and Pandu would let him go on yelling "Nothing!" for a while before finally relenting and allowing him to get up and apologize to me. Pandu was not strong, but he was agile. Besides, he knew none of the boys would dare raise a hand to the crown prince.

But if Pandu looked after me (unlike Tarashtra, who didn't give a fig what names I was called), I knew I also had to look after him. There was his illness, for one thing. He had that pale yellow tinge to his skin and eyes—the healers said it was from an excess of yellow bile—and he had a hard time keeping weight on, for his stomach often hurt and eating increased the pain. At mealtimes I'd challenge him to a race: the first to clean his plate was the winner, and the winner got to raid one "cow" from the other's "herd," the herds being piles of pebbles that we kept in two bowls in the playroom. Since I'd intentionally lose the races my pile was always dwindling, and every so often I would have to go outside and gather a few more pebbles to replenish it. Pandu wasn't fooled, of course, but he went along with the game and pretended to be delighted with his wins.

Worse than the stomach problems were the times when his skin would itch all over. He would scratch and scratch in a frenzy, finally saying to me with tears in his eyes, "Vidu, Vidu, I can't bear it." Then I would ask him to come with me for a swim in the river, or for a ride, or to hunt partridge—anything to distract him.

And then, amplifying his physical sufferings, there were the sufferings of his mind. Most people thought his jokes and shenanigans were signs of a happy nature; I knew, though, that underneath the façade he was afraid, constantly afraid. Of what, I didn't know and he never said. Only he would say to me, sometimes, "I wish I could sleep." And sometimes, when he thought no one was looking, he would double over and hit his head hard with both fists, repeatedly, as if to drive out a demon. I couldn't help him with any of that. I tried to be his friend, but I don't think it helped, not really. Once when he was older—I think he'd been king for half a year—he told me that his wife, Perta, wanted him to give up soma but it was the only thing that made his stomach stop hurting and his skin stop itching and his mind stop churning, and consequently he loved it and blessed it and would never give it up.

It was our father, Vyasa, who introduced Pandu to soma. (I mean, of course, our seed-father; our real father was King Chit, who died before we were born.) I think we were fifteen when he took the three of us to our first soma-pressing in the forest. There were all sorts of people there: brahmins mostly—a mix of priests, seers, and ascetics—but also soldiers, bards, even townspeople. There were some women, too. We all gathered in the wide clearing before the ashram, and the chief ascetic of the ashram invited us to be seated around the bonfire. It was a chill dark night, I recall, with only a sliver of moon.

I will not describe the ceremony to you, for nowadays the soma-pressing is forbidden to all but brahmins. But I will say that the focus was not, as the name would suggest, on the pressing of soma plants; that had happened weeks before, and the juice was standing ready in tubs along the ashram wall. Instead there were hymns, chants, and offerings into the fire, to the God Agni, very like an everyday ritual, except that woven throughout were many opportunities to drink the holy drink. And after the rite was concluded, the drinking continued all night.

Vyasa had cautioned us boys against drinking too much our first time, but once the ceremony began he became absorbed, giving himself over to the chants and gestures, and as soon as it was over he took a bowl of soma and left us, going off into the forest with another priest and several of the women. I thought perhaps they were going to engage in an even holier rite, one for initiates only; in any case, we were left on our own at the bonfire, and though I reminded my brothers what the high priest had said about overindulging, neither of them seemed inclined to listen. As the thin moon rose higher in the sky, they passed the bowl of honey-sweetened liquor back and forth, drinking again and again and trying to get me to do the same. I declined; I was feeling a little dizzy and had decided I did not care for soma.

At first they were both in high spirits, cracking jokes and falling about laughing, but after a while their moods diverged. Tarashtra grew more and more boisterous until finally he staggered to his feet and reeled away, shouting, "Who wants to play blind man's buff with a real blind man?" He was drawn in by a cluster of young men and women who were playing a game that involved passing a mango from neck to neck without using their hands. (Tarashtra, blind though he was, never had trouble finding such friends or such games.) Pandu, however, grew more and more quiet; eventually he stretched out his legs and lay back on his elbows, staring into the fire. His expression was dreamy, ecstatic ... as if he were looking on the faces of Gods. I sat up with him until he fell asleep. Then I slept, too.

≈

Pandu was crowned king on his seventeenth birthday. For a while I thought all might be well.

Uncle Bhishma had negotiated for brides for all three of us. For me he chose the illegitimate daughter of an eastern chieftain; her name was Kirti, she was kind and gentle, we were happy for the short time she lived, and that is all I will say about her. For Tarashtra he made a splendid match: the princess of Gandaram, that rich and powerful (albeit cold and savage) kingdom in the far north-west. Princess Gandhari arrived escorted by her younger brother, accompanied by a large train of attendants, and bringing with her an impressive dowry of seventy horses, seven hundred cattle, seventy chests of copper, and two elephants. One might have thought such a woman would have been the choice for Pandu, the soon-to-be king, rather than Tarashtra, the older brother whose disability had denied him the throne; Bhishma, however, had thought carefully about the qualities needed in Pandu's senior wife and, knowing he could always use junior wives to improve our alliances, had selected for Pandu a princess of Vrishni, a small, amiable land on our southwest border. Her name was Perta. Her father was a friend of Bhishma's; the two men had long discussed a union of the families. Perta was not beautiful, but she was charming, outgoing, shrewd, two years older than her prospective husband, and buxom—all of which, said the regent, made her an ideal wife for Pandu. She arrived at Hastinapura two weeks after Gandhari. Her dowry was far less rich, but her shapely figure and warm manners caused everyone to contrast her favorably with the northern princess, who was tall, flat-chested, rather too pale, and somewhat forbidding in her demeanor.

The two weddings happened quickly, followed a month later by Pandu's coronation. I was not allowed a spot on the great hall's dais, but I stood in the front row of the audience where I could keep an eye on him. I knew he'd have taken soma that morning—by that point he was drinking at least once a week, kept in supply by Vyasa—but I hoped he'd had the sense to keep it to an amount compatible with a lengthy public appearance. He had made it through the ceremony in the Hall of Sacraments with no stumbles, and now his expression and posture as he stood in front of the throne were reasonably alert. I noticed that Perta, standing before the queen's throne, was also watching him as he gave the responses to the high priest, and after he was seated and the silver circlet with the Kuru garnet placed upon his brow (the garnet being the famous jewel that was once in King Shantanu's ring), she continued throughout her part of the ceremony to send glances his way. His eyes as he looked out over the crowd had the soma glaze, but his back remained straight, his chin high, and all in all I was very proud of him.

The year that followed was a good one for the Kuru. For Pandu, I think, it was the one truly happy year he ever had. He made up his mind to grow our wealth with a series of cattle raids on neighboring clans—not Vrishni, of course, but many others. It was part of my role as chief counselor to help him strategize, and we had a marvelous time doing so, closeted with Bhishma and the army captains in the war room, scratching out diagrams on the dirt floor to show the herd locations, our moves, and the expected countermoves of our adversaries. Pandu would poke me with his stick, laughing, and say, "Remember, Vidu, how I used to raid all your cows?" And I'd come back at him with, "You always were king of the raids!" But it turned out he really did have a talent for the sport; not only was he clever with tactics and troop formations, but he could take the lay of the land, throwing aside a plan and adjusting in the moment as the situation demanded. And, the men loved him. By the end of the year he'd executed eight or nine forays, adding more than a thousand head to the Kuru herd.

All this time, he kept on drinking soma once or twice a week; as I've said, I think it was about halfway through that year that he told me he would never give it up despite Perta's objections. But Perta and I had an understanding: we both knew it was our job to keep him busy, keep him confident, and jolly him along whenever his spirits looked like sinking. Perta saw how he enjoyed bantering with me and soon devised her own way of teasing: she would pretend to be an innocent forest nymph captured by the Great God Pandu and overawed by his celestial riches, good looks, and prowess:

"Oh, Pandu," she would purr, laying a hand on his forearm as they sat together at supper in the great hall, "I can't imagine what a God like you could want from such a lowly creature as I. These rags of mine ..." (she looked down with exaggerated modesty) "I'm ashamed to wear them in your radiant presence. I must, I simply *must* take them off. See, I'm taking them off right now! Or shall we retire to your chamber, Your Divine Gloriousness, and I'll shed them there?" Then Pandu would laugh, and kiss her, and they'd get up and rush out of the hall, she leading him by the hand.

It was quite early on that I fell in love with Perta. This occurrence did not worry me: she was Pandu's wife, and I loved him more. I think in a way my love for her was an aspect of my love for him, born of our mutual, unspoken agreement to be his guardians. It was as if she and I stood side by side watching over him, as parents watch over a child in the cradle. But I did admire her vivacity—of which I myself had little—as well as her intelligence, which she deployed on her husband's behalf. And yes, I admit it: I admired her lovely figure. I used to dream, now and then, of taking her to bed and caressing those breasts.

≈

As for our brother Tarashtra: he knew he would never be king, and since he had no interest in kingly pursuits—neither statecraft, nor strategy, nor the management of land or livestock—his situation suited him well. I did wonder, for a while, if he might be drawn to the Sacred Knowledge. He spent a great deal of time with Vyasa, the two of them going often to the forest together for soma-pressings and, Tarashtra said, "other rituals." It was not unprecedented among the better kshatriya families for a son with a disability or deformity to enter the priesthood, even though his caste would seem to exclude him, and I thought perhaps Tarashtra would follow that path, for he and the high priest certainly got on well. But when I asked him once at supper whether that was his intent, he scoffed.

"What, spend my days memorizing ten thousand hymns and chants? Tippy-toeing around the Hall of Sacraments, flapping my arms this way and that, slicing bird necks and sloshing ghee into the fire? And being scolded by a lot of old white-robes if I pronounce a word wrong. No, thank you. That all sounds more your line, Vidu— sorry, *Counselor Vidura*."

He drained his cup of beer, belched, and rose from the table. (We, the Kuru nobility, had recently taken to eating at low wooden boards; they say the practice had originated at the court of Panchala and spread from there.) The small boy assigned to be his guide hurried up to take his arm. I watched them make their way across the hall to the priests' section, where Vyasa sat. Tarashtra waved the boy away and squatted down behind the high priest with a hand on his back, whispering in his ear. A lascivious smile spread across Vyasa's face. He lifted his cup of lassi (even back then, brahmins were not permitted alcohol) and made the proper oblation, pouring a few drops of the sweet milk onto the floor; he turned to his neighbors left and right and bowed, again very properly. Then he got up, raking his hands through his shock of black hair, and threw an arm around Tarashtra's shoulders. The two men went out together into the warm evening.

Tarashtra's wife, it was known, did not approve of how he spent his time. Like Queen Perta, Princess Gandhari was two or three years older than her husband and had a steadier head; unlike Perta, she seemed disinclined to use feminine charms to coax her husband away from his questionable activities. As I've noted, she was too tall and slender for beauty (though she had a stately grace to her), so she may have realized that flirtation was not her best tool. Instead, she worked on Tarashtra's pride. He didn't have a lot, but all men have some, and Gandhari was good at perceiving that soft voice that must have risen occasionally to his mind—the one that said *he* was the first-born son, so why wasn't *he* king?—and amplifying it.

I remember one suppertime conversation between them. That evening, Tarashtra, Gandhari, and I made a party of three at the royal table in the great hall, the rest of the family having taken the meal in their rooms. The two of them sat on one side of the board, I across from them. They ignored me, as was typical; generally speaking,

Pandu and Perta were the only ones of my relatives who paid me any mind.

Gandhari took a small bite of her lamb-with-mint and said, "My lord, are you going out with the high priest tonight?"

"I expect so. Why?" said Tarashtra.

"I was just curious. King Pandu is holding a meeting in the war room to plan the raid on that western clan, I forget their name, Nam … Naim something."

"Naimisha. What of it?"

"Nothing, nothing. I just thought you might have been invited."

"I was invited! I don't care to go. Why would I involve myself in such idiocy? Tearing around the countryside stealing cows. I can't ride, and even if I could, it wouldn't interest me."

"No, dear, of course not. I only wondered."

"Well, you can stop wondering. I have better things to do."

"Yes. It's just that Pandu … no, never mind."

"What? What about Pandu?"

"No, no, I really shouldn't say. It is not my place to speak of these things."

"*What about Pandu?*"

"Well, since you insist … it's just that yesterday Queen Perta confided in me. She said she's very worried about the king. He's drinking more and more soma. It's affecting his mind, she said. Sometimes he'll stop in the middle of a sentence and when people ask him what's wrong, it's as if he doesn't hear them; he just sits and stares. And then when he's gone two or three days without any, his hands start to shake and he can't focus at all. Perta is really very worried. Quite frankly, so am I. What's going to happen if he loses his wits entirely? Who'll run the country then?"

"Huh. Bhishma will run the country. As usual."

"But Bhishma cannot be king. The Kuru need a king, Tarashtra."

Tarashtra sat frowning, tapping the butt of his knife on his plate. Then he rounded on his wife, his unseeing eyes directed at the red bindi on her forehead, and hissed: "It is not your concern!" He struggled up from the table, his feet catching a little on the hems of his dhoti, his pudgy stomach wobbling. "Dog!" he shouted. The small boy hurried forward and took his arm. He stomped away.

Gandhari and I were now alone. She continued to sit and finish her meal: legs crossed, back straight, hair coiled smoothly under her head veil. Eventually she finished eating, wiped her knife daintily with her handkerchief, and tucked the knife into her waistband. Then she raised her eyes to mine. In them, I saw a challenge.

≈

Bhishma knew he had compromised on wealth and prestige by choosing Perta, but he'd thought she'd be good for Pandu and, more important, good to produce sons. When her first pregnancy ended in a miscarriage, he accelerated the search for a second queen.

One of Pandu's cattle raids had been on Madrasa, a land just north of us. The king of Madrasa was renowned not only for his riches but also for the beauty of his eldest daughter. After the raid, Bhishma noted the quality of the animals taken and decided that the riches, at least, were no mere rumor. He entered forthwith into negotiations for the daughter's hand. There was no reason to fear that the king had taken offense at his cattle being raided; on the contrary, it had been a demonstration of the prowess of the Kuru and, hence, our desirability as an ally.

The talks took a few months, after which the fifteen-year-old Princess Madri arrived in Hastinapura accompanied by an enormous wedding party that strained the town's ability to accommodate them all. Her dowry exceeded even Gandhari's, including as it did nine hundred head of cattle, fifty horses, five elephants, many chests of silver and ivory, dozens of bolts of Madrasa cotton cloth, and a large collection of weaponry. The uncle who escorted her carried a jovial message from the king: With these gifts, not to mention his daughter, he hoped to encourage King Pandu to leave his cows alone from now on.

Madri's beauty, it turned out, was as real as her father's wealth. When she entered the Hall of Sacraments for the marriage ceremony—dressed in an emerald green sari embroidered all over, not just at the hem, with gold thread and dripping with silver, gold, and actual emeralds—there were gasps from the assembly. In those days brides did not come fully veiled to their wedding (no doubt the new way is better), so her gorgeous face and form could be seen by all. She was tiny, perfect, like a jeweled figurine of Rati, Goddess of Love. That is what I thought, at any rate, as I watched her walk with Pandu seven times around the sacred fire.

At first, Pandu seemed a little intimidated by her; his manner toward her was very formal. Madri, for her part, was careful to defer in all things to Perta, the senior wife. And Perta's confidence remained high. Even though she had lost her baby and at nearly twenty-one was a little past her prime, she was sure of Pandu's ongoing love and dependence. At supper the two continued to flirt, hold hands, and laugh together while Madri sat quietly by with beautiful eyes lowered, beautiful hair rippling in dark waves down her back, beautiful skin glowing in the torchlight like oiled deodarwood. I could not keep my eyes off Madri; nevertheless, I suspected it was still Perta who shared the king's bed most nights.

For all her influence, however, Perta had not been able to keep Pandu from his greatest and most abiding love. Her open disapproval of his habit had, in fact, caused him to adopt a new approach: rather than having Vyasa deliver jars of the juice to his rooms and indulging there, he had begun a daily program of "hunting" in the forest. At first nobody questioned it; he had always liked hunting, was good at it, and of course it's an appropriate pastime for a king. He would set off early in the morning with a large group of men and ladies of the court (I among them), and together we would pursue the stag, boar, hare, or whatever was in season. But after an hour or two Pandu would contrive to lose the party and ride off alone, heading—as it later transpired—to the ashram, where he would be invited in by the ascetics to "rest." And there he would spend the remainder of the day, and often the best part of the night, drinking soma.

Once I finally realized what he was up to, I resolved not to allow him to go off alone again. The next day I stuck to him like a kudzu vine to a tree, and when he and I arrived at the ashram, I pretended to be pleased at the idea of a break and refreshments. We tied up our horses and went in. Pandu, clearly made ill at ease by my presence, called for lassi. We sat for a few minutes with him staring about the room, yawning and fidgeting, the lassi untouched. Then he stood up and said that it was too hot for hunting, so we might as well go home.

Looking back, I can see that all I did was drive him to more subterfuge. If I hadn't been so conscientious … but Perta said I mustn't blame myself. There was no one to blame. Not even Madri was to blame.

When we got back to the palace, Pandu was in a foul temper. He shouted at the stable boy for not coming quickly enough to take the horses, kicked a brown dog that slinked past his feet in the yard, and stormed off to his rooms. I followed, worried what he might do in this state. As we came through the doorway of the king's quarters he was yelling for water and a towel, but—it being the hottest part of the day in high summer, and all the courtiers and servants, knowing the king was away, having found a cool place to nap—there was no one there.

Or rather, it appeared at first there was no one there. For out from behind a pillar stepped—Madri.

She looked frightened to see us and quickly knelt to the ground with palms pressed together at her forehead. She was wearing a plain pale green dhoti, chest-band, and veil with no jewels, not at all the standard costume for a queen.

"What ... Madri? What are you doing here? Where is everybody?" Pandu's tone was harsh, his expression irritated.

"M-my lord. I am sorry. I ... forgive me. Queen Perta ..." Her voice was trembling, almost inaudible.

"What's that? Speak up, for Gods' sake."

"My lord, Queen Perta told me to leave ... to leave the queens' quarters. She said I was not to return today."

"Perta said that? Why? What did you do?"

"I ... I don't know, my lord. Her majesty said she was ... she was ..."

"Yes, yes, she was what? Speak *up*."

"She said ... she said she was s-sick of my s-simpering face." Two tears spilled out of her beautiful eyes and rolled down her beautiful cheeks. "I am sorry, my lord. I have offended her. It is my fault."

Pandu gave a deep sigh and ran a hand over his scalp. "Oh, I see." He rubbed the back of his neck, sighed again, and chuckled. "I'm afraid Perta doesn't like you very much."

"No, my lord. I apologize most deeply."

"She told you to get out, and you didn't know where to go, so you came here. Is that it?"

"Yes, my lord. She ... she would not allow my women to come with me."

"Yes. Well, never mind. She'll get over it. Don't worry, I'll speak to her about it." He went to the girl and took both her hands, quite gently. "Come now; get up, no need to be kneeling in the dirt like that." He helped her to her feet. He leaned down and dusted off the knees of her dhoti. Then he walked her over to the big chair by the window and sat, drawing her onto his lap. He took a corner of her veil and used it to blot away her tears. She was half his size and looked like a child being comforted after taking a bad tumble in the play-yard.

"Now, then. Since Perta has tossed you out and you can't do whatever it is women usually do all day, we'll have to find something else to amuse you with. What would you like to do? Hey?" He jiggled his knees up and down. "We'll do anything you want."

Madri's eyes were still lowered, but she was smiling a little now. "Oh, my lord, you are very good. I would like to do whatever *you* like to do."

Pandu chuckled again. "Well, what *I* like to do is go hunting. But most people around here don't want me going hunting. My brother the counselor, for instance ..." He lifted his chin to indicate me, standing in the doorway. "*He* doesn't want me hunting. He doesn't think it's good for me. Do you, Vidu?"

Madri looked at me. I saw passing in turn across her face, first, confusion; next, comprehension; and finally—was it hope?—I'm not sure. But after a moment she turned back to her husband, placed her arms about his neck, and said:

"*I* will go hunting with you, Pandu."

≈

Within a month, it was clear that the king had entered a downward spiral from which he would not escape. He was now going every day to the ashram, accompanied by Madri and seven or eight courtiers, hand-picked by him for their willingness to join his revels. No—not revels, for he was anything but merry. Let us say, his excursions. I went with the party once, telling him I wanted to give soma another try; he eyed me suspiciously, then shrugged and said, "Why not? But I'm warning you, Vidu, if you're thinking to stop us, you're wasting your time."

I stayed all day and part of the evening with them. It was like a scene from hell.

Upon arriving at the ashram we went into a big room seemingly used for multiple purposes: slaughter of birds and small animals for sacrifice or consumption, cooking of meals, extra sleeping space for the ashram's visitors, toilet facilities for when residents found the night air too cold or just didn't have the energy to go outside. It was windowless, dank, and filthy. The residents clearly knew the drill: without being asked, two servants carried in a tub of juice, placed it in the middle of the floor, and distributed bowls. Our group gathered round, filled their vessels, and settled down in various spots to drink. I tried to join Pandu and Madri, who sat together in a corner, but he waved me off; Madri nestled against his shoulder, and for the many hours I stayed there, the two of them barely moved except to return to the tub to get more soma. Several of the courtiers sat at first in a group, talking and laughing, but after a while they drifted off to their own corners, there to slump, glassy-eyed and nodding, unmindful of the bits of excrement, human and animal, that dotted the floor around them.

After that experience I accepted, finally, that there was nothing I could do. Every few weeks there would be a stretch of days, perhaps two or three, when Pandu would remain at the palace and try to do a king's work; then he would call his priests and advisors into the great hall or war room and make a pretense of discussing state affairs. I joined those sessions, as was my duty, but said little. I could see him dying, and it broke my heart.

Perta and Gandhari, being women, had a different reaction. Upon realizing that the childless king was not long for this world and the succession therefore in doubt, they were both seized with a single purpose: to give birth to sons.

Soon after Pandu took up with Madri and departed (so to speak) for the forest, Perta let it be known that she was pregnant again. Soon after that, Gandhari made the same announcement. Gandhari, like Perta, had had a miscarriage the year before, but this time luck was with both ladies; they made it through their first six months without incident, the babies quickened inside them, and the race was on for who would be delivered first. Perta edged Gandhari by twelve hours: her son Yudishtira was born in the morning, Gandhari's son Duryodhana on the evening of the same day.

One might have thought the two would now rest easy. They did not. Perhaps their grandmother- and mothers-in-law had warned them, based on bitter experience, of the dangers of pinning hopes on just one boy child; in any case, it was only a month or two until both were pregnant again. For Gandhari it wouldn't have been too difficult; Tarashtra had no lack of enthusiasm for women and no trouble begetting offspring, as was made clear by the several boys running around the town and the servants' quarters that he proudly acknowledged as his. (Several girls, as well, but to them he paid scant attention.) Gandhari was not to his taste—"my bony wife," he called her—but no doubt she could attract him if she put her mind to it, and besides, he'd been delighted with the birth of little Duryodhana. Perta, on the other hand, had a bigger challenge: Pandu was now rarely at home and weakening fast, with no real interest in anything but soma. I suspect, though I have no way to know, that she fell back on her old game of forest-nymph-captured-by-God, which Pandu had always loved. Had she waited until one of his good days and surprised him at bedtime with a full-blown drama, he might well have responded favorably. (I suppose I should also mention that since both ladies naturally had the services of wet nurses, they were not distracted by the need to care for an infant.)

However they managed it, their bellies swelled again, and in good time two more sons arrived. First, Gandhari had Dushasana, a strong boy like his older brother; a week later, Perta had Bimasena. The latter took after his grandmother and great-aunt in size: he was the largest baby anyone had ever seen. It was fortunate that Perta's hips were broad and accommodating, for a thinner woman might have been torn apart pushing out such a giant.

And then there was Madri. She also grew heavy with child. I cannot believe she had had any thoughts of the succession or of her potential position as mother of an heir; the only thing she had ever cared about, I am convinced, is gaining and keeping some small measure of Pandu's love. You might wonder that her womb was able to sustain a pregnancy after all that soma, but she had never indulged to the extent the king had; she was merely his faithful forest companion, eager to do whatever he liked to do. The thought of them rolling on the floor of that squalid room in the ashram, in full view of their fellow addicts, fills me with horror. Perhaps she, taking a cue from Perta, encouraged Pandu in his God fantasies.

She had a hard labor and died in the end, lying on her bed in the queens' quarters with Pandu holding her hand and Perta stroking her forehead. The final irony was that she surpassed her sisters-in-law in the baby wars, for she gave birth to twin boys: Nakula and Sahadeva, both of whom survived and who immediately became known as Naku and Saku. Naku inherited some of his mother's beauty. But never again did I see her equal.

≈

One week after Pandu died—he, too, died in his bed, not in the forest, for which I thanked the Gods—Bhishma called a family meeting.

Gathered in the public room of the king's quarters were: Old Queen Satyavati, now sixty, fat, lavishly bejeweled, insistent on taking the one chair; Perta, seated on a stool against a wall, head uncharacteristically bent, eyes red from weeping; Tarashtra and Gandhari, standing close together by the window, his expression unreadable, her left hand under his right elbow; Prince Shakuna, leaning on the wall near his sister and brother-in-law (I have not yet spoken of Shakuna; he was the younger brother who had escorted Gandhari to her wedding and afterward remained with us at Bhishma's invitation); High Priest Vyasa, cross-legged on a rug in the middle of the floor, grinning and chewing his betel nut; and—a surprise to us all— the dowager queens Ambika and Ambalika, out of their rooms for the first time in the four years since Pandu's coronation, two veiled figures hunkered massively on two hassocks in a corner. I myself had carried a stool to the doorway and seated myself where I could see everyone.

Bhishma was standing by the old queen, one hand on the chairback, his other thumb hooked in his bronze-studded belt. His hair had touches of gray now, but he was still as powerfully built as ever. He looked down at Satyavati and said with the ghost of a smile: "Well, Mother. Here we are again."

Satyavati, toying with a string of beads, frowned and said nothing.

Bhishma addressed the group: "My thanks to you all for coming. The situation is this. The king is dead. His eldest son, Yudishtira, by rights is the heir, but Yudi is a toddler and obviously cannot take the throne. So, I find myself regent—again." (Tarashtra made a scoffing sound; Gandhari laid her right hand gently on his right bicep.) "However," Bhishma continued, "I have no desire to rule for the next fifteen years. I am past middle-age, and it is time to think about my retirement. Besides, we have here another son of the royal line"—he gestured to Tarashtra—"who is capable to serve."

Tarashtra's head snapped toward Bhishma. His mouth dropped open. Gandhari's right hand pressed a little harder.

Bhishma continued: "Moreover, the Kuru need a king, not a regent. Therefore, I propose the following: Prince Tarashtra will take the throne, with the understanding that once Prince Yudi reaches his majority—and assuming there emerge no defects in the boy's body, mind, or character that would make him unsuitable to rule—Tarashtra will step down, and Yudi will be crowned."

Everyone, suddenly, was looking at Tarashtra. He did not know that we were looking at him, of course, and perhaps didn't realize that we all saw his left hand reach across his flabby chest and grip Gandhari's right hand, which was still pressing his right arm.

"I cannot think there would be objections to this plan," said Bhishma; "nevertheless, I do not have authority over these matters of succession. Indeed, it is not clear who does have authority, nor what the Law prescribes. I have consulted the priests" (he nodded at Vyasa, who in response merely widened his grin and chewed harder) "but they are at odds on the question. So it seems to me we must simply agree—as a family."

For the next half hour we discussed it. Perta was against the idea; she did not understand, she said, why Bhishma could not rule on her son's behalf until he came of age. "After all," she said, mustering up a brilliant smile, "you do it so well, Lord Bhishma." She obviously did not like the thought of Gandhari's husband on the throne and Gandhari's son nearer the throne, even if it was only temporary. But the high priest spoke out in favor of Tarashtra, quoting at length from the Sacred Knowledge about the origins of the monarchy and underlining the absence of any specifications that a king must have eyesight. Gandhari said she had always believed strength of *mind* to be the critical quality in a king; she looked pointedly at Perta as she said this. Prince Shakuna, of course, backed his sister and brother-in-law. And then Ambalika shocked everyone by rising from her hassock in the corner and saying, in a tone that was soft but definite, "My son is dead. My sister's son must take his place." She sat down again, and as far as I know, neither she nor her sister ever said another word to anyone in that room.

When Bhishma asked for my opinion, I hesitated. I knew

Tarashtra would make a wretched king, but I also knew that my longtime love for Pandu and my grief at his death (not to mention my affection for his widow) would cause me to be biased against our brother. Like Perta, I wished that Bhishma could continue as regent; I understood, however, his desire to begin putting worldly cares aside as he glimpsed, on the far horizon but visible nonetheless, the God Yama approaching with his deathly noose. I also thought about what would happen should Bhishma stay regent but die before Yudi came of age, leaving us in the exact same quandary but this time with no Bhishma to help us navigate it. I reflected on all this. Then I stood, looked an apology at Perta that I hoped she could see, and said to the group, "It is right that my brother Tarashtra should hold the throne for the son of Pandu."

Finally Bhishma turned to Satyavati—who had not spoken thus far—and said, "Well, Mother?"

The old queen sat silent, fingering her string of beads, as a minute passed. At length she sighed, heaved herself to her feet, and waddled over to the couple by the window. She stood looking at them for a moment. Then she bowed her head; not to Tarashtra, but to Gandhari.

She left the room, and we all followed. The next day Tarashtra was crowned king—Gandhari, queen.

And there you have the first part of Counselor Vidura's story. As I noted, he seemed pleased at my interest in him and relieved to have someone to talk to after all those years, even if it was only a young girl. You'll be surprised at some of the things he told me later.

What is it, Sire? Why the puzzled look? Ha! I know what it is. I can see the question forming on your lips ...

What about Arjuna?

That's what you're wondering, isn't it? You have counted up the babies on your fingers. On your left hand, the sons of Tarashtra: Duryodhana and Dushasana. On your right, the sons of Pandu: Yudi, Bimasena, and the twins Naku and Saku. But where is Arjuna?

I'll tell you where Arjuna was: he was about to be implanted in Perta's womb—it must have happened soon after the family meeting, perhaps that same night—by Vidura.

Vidura, as I hope I've made clear, was a modest man, reluctant to discuss or even to imagine unsavory activities. He was especially respectful of priests; he never said a word against Vyasa, for instance, despite everything that twisted old brahmin did to enable Pandu's addiction and Tarashtra's perversions. He also disliked talking about women. His own wife had died in childbirth some ten months after they were married; the child, a girl, also died. I believe he loved his wife, but he would never speak of her or the baby. As for his infatuation with Perta, he always portrayed it as a kind of corollary to his love for his brother. Although he admitted to "admiring her lovely figure" and even said, once, that he dreamed of her breasts, he never told me directly of his passion for her or how they came together. But I'm sure all Perta would have had to do is to show up in his room that night, looking for comfort.

Two months after Pandu died, Perta announced with joy that she was pregnant. The child was assumed to be Pandu's, of course; there was no reason to think otherwise, even when the baby arrived two weeks later than might have been expected based on the last possible date that Pandu could have contributed to the project. "This one took his time," said Perta, smiling down at little Arjuna in her arms, the family gathered round her bed. Gandhari had wanted Tarashtra to be godfather, as he was to Pandu's other sons, but Perta insisted that it be Vidura, "for Vidura was always Pandu's most faithful friend." She handed Arjuna to the counselor and he stood there, holding his brother's fifth and last child in his arms and feeling a love such as he'd never felt before suffusing his body like ... "like the glow of soma," he told me. But then he corrected himself and said it was not like that at all, it was simply that he felt great affection for the child and the mother, and he made a silent vow to Pandu's soul, waiting in Yama's kingdom to be reborn, that he would look after them both.

So now you know about Arjuna.

There is one other thing, a small thing, which I should perhaps explain before continuing. I mentioned that at the tournament organized by Drona fifteen years later, Queen Gandhari was wearing a violet silk veil that covered her whole face. She did not wear this veil in the first few years of her marriage to Tarashtra; at their coronation, however, she put it on, declaring that it was not fitting for a king to have a queen whose abilities in any way exceeded his. She vowed never to remove the veil from that day forward, and with this vow of hers she earned the people's love and respect.

They called her Sati: "the Good Wife." And as you shall see, her thoughts were ever on her husband and sons, as a good wife's thoughts should be.

Chapter 4

GANDHARI

T*hings are looking up for me. I may still be a hostage, but at least now I'm the brother of the queen,"* Shakuna said with a smile. He was lying full-length on Gandhari's bed, hands clasped behind his head.

Gandhari removed her veil, laid it neatly on top of the clothes chest, and turned with a look of annoyance. "Get off of there, Kuku. I'm exhausted. I want to lie down."

Shakuna sat up and moved to the foot of the bed. He leaned back against the wall with one leg extended, the other ankle resting on his knee, and scratched the sole of his foot.

"That was a good idea you had about the veil. I watched the people when you came out on the dais after Tarashtra. They were whispering in an awestruck sort of way. They were calling you 'Sati' by the end; I heard them."

Gandhari slipped off her shoes, got onto the bed, and stretched out, propping her feet on her brother's thigh. "Yes, well, they've always preferred Perta to me. I needed something."

"I think it worked. Anyway, you're queen now and she isn't. What are we going to call her, now that she's not queen anymore?"

"I don't know. I'm sure she won't want to be called 'Dowager Queen.' She'll think it makes her sound old. And we've got the two dowager queens already—not that they ever leave their rooms. I suppose she'll just be 'Lady Perta.'"

"They left their rooms yesterday. For Bhishma's meeting, I mean."

"Yes. That was unexpected." Gandhari closed her eyes. "I'm *so* tired. That ceremony was endless. Rub my feet, will you?"

Shakuna pushed the hem of the purple sari out of the way and commenced rubbing.

"Dhari ..."

"Mmm?"

"What's going to happen to me, now that you're queen? Will Bhishma decide it's enough, and let me go home?"

"You mean enough to ensure that our father doesn't attack the Kuru?"

"Yes."

Gandhari opened her eyes and looked at her brother. Although nineteen, a grown man, Shakuna was slight of frame and boyish of face; luckily for him he was also a formidable swordfighter, light-ning-fast and wily, and not bad as an archer, either. In the first few months after Gandhari and Tarashtra's wedding, when he had been "invited" by Bhishma to remain at Hastinapura, he had been just fourteen and even smaller, causing many members of the palace staff to place bets against him in training skirmishes. They soon learned not to do that. Another thing they learned not to do was to play dice with him—not for serious stakes, anyway—for the Gods seemed to guide his hand at every throw. "Born lucky!" Shakuna would say as he collected yet another cloak, knife, or jewel from a challenger.

"I doubt Bhishma will think the threat has been reduced," said Gandhari, "just because Tarashtra is king and I'm queen. He might think there's *more* of a threat, actually, because word will reach Gandaram that the Kuru now have a blind ruler, and that will make us look weaker than before."

"I suppose you're right. And then there was Madrasa in between us and Gandaram, acting as a buffer, but with Madri dead, it's just as likely that her father will join with our father to attack Kuru. He won't have any reason not to."

"Exactly. And Bhishma knows all this, so he'll probably decide he needs you as extra insurance now more than ever." She bumped his leg with her heel. "Keep rubbing."

"I *am*. But Dhari, here's the thing ..."

"What?"

"Even if Bhishma did say I could go home, I wouldn't want to."

"I know—because you couldn't bear to leave your dear, darling sister!" She punctuated each of the last three words with a kick.

Shakuna laughed. "You know what would be the best thing about leaving? Not having to rub your smelly feet every day!"

More kicks were delivered.

"Ow! Stop it! No, I'm serious, Dhari, listen. If I stay here, I can help you work it so that Tarashtra stays king and you stay queen. I know Bhishma thinks we all agreed Prince Yudi will take over when he comes of age, but I don't see why we should go along with that. Tarashtra was the eldest son, not Pandu; it was always his right to be king, and your eldest son has the right to be king after him. That's the Law. Obviously."

Gandhari smiled, one eyebrow raised. "And you're thinking if you stay here, *you* can obviously be chief advisor to a blind, incompetent king, whereas if you go home, you're just the third son of a highly competent king who hasn't much use for you except to marry you off to some tiresome girl for the sake of her dowry and expect you to make babies with her."

Shakuna smiled back. "Yes. Obviously."

"And then when Tarashtra dies, and my son becomes king ... or wait ... *will* my son become king? Or does my dear brother have another plan? What could my dear, darling brother be thinking right now?" This time she dug the nail of her big toe into his thigh.

"*Ow! Stop it!* I'm not thinking anything like that! Of course Duryodhana will be king, and I'll support him. It's just that I have a better chance of being somebody here than I do back home. Tarashtra can't stand Counselor Vidura, he calls him Counselor Stick-up-His-Arse, but he likes me well enough. I'll get closer to him and I'll—no, *we'll* be his advisors, you and me. We'll be the power behind the throne."

"Hmm. Don't forget about Bhishma. All that talk about retiring—I don't believe it for a minute. He's not going anywhere. And he's always been the power behind the throne."

"Well, he's always had the people's backing. But you, Madam Sati, with your virtuous veil, maybe you'll be the one with the people's backing now."

Gandhari looked over at the clothes chest and sighed. "Yes, maybe I will."

She sat up, put an arm around her brother's shoulders, and gave them a little squeeze. "All right, Kuku, I really need to dress for the feast. Time for you to go."

"But it all makes sense to you—what I said?"

She nodded. "It all makes sense to me. Go on, now. See you at supper."

He hoisted himself off the bed and left the room. Gandhari went over to the chest, picked up the large square of thin violet silk, draped it over her head, and secured it with its matching band. Then she clapped her hands to summon her women.

≈

Years passed. Crown Prince Yudi was now seven; his cousin Duryodhana the same. Bima and the twins, Naku and Saku, were six; Dushasana the same. And Arjuna was five.

On a bright morning in the eleventh month, the boys were all on the training grounds having an archery lesson. Standing on the south side of the arena were the king, the queen, Prince Shakuna, Lady Perta, Counselor Vidura, and Lord Bhishma, along with a small entourage of retainers, ladies-in-waiting, man- and maidservants. It was an informal party. Earlier that day Bhishma had suggested that they might like to see the progress the boys were making under the new weapons master, Drona, who had been hired a few months ago and seemed to be working out well; Bhishma cautioned, however, that there must not be any fuss to distract from the practice. The cool of winter had lingered, obviating any need for canopies or fans, so they would simply walk out to the grounds and watch casually.

The hawk-faced weapons master had set up a target of two stakes a forearm's length apart, the goal being to shoot between them. The boys had arrows with blunt tips and quarter-size bows. Drona was a stickler for both safety and etiquette: after each student made his shot, he was to bow to the instructor, bow to his fellow students, retrieve his arrow, and return to the back of the line. Only then was the next boy permitted to step to the mark and take aim. While in line, they were to stand still and straight, bow in one hand, single arrow in the other, awaiting their turn. And as they took aim, they were to say the following words: "I salute you, mine enemy; may your rebirth be fortunate!" Any boy forgetting these rules earned a sharp rebuke and a cuff on the ear.

On the sidelines, Perta was whispering to Gandhari: "Now, my dear, it is Yudi's turn. Here he comes to the mark. I know a mother shouldn't say it, but he has *such* a noble bearing. Only seven years old, and already you couldn't mistake anyone else for the crown prince. Look, now he's taking aim ... now he's saying the words ...

oh, never mind, how silly of me, of course you can hear him saying the words. There goes the arrow ... and it's through! *Well done, Yudi!*"

At her loud cry, Drona threw an irritated glance at the observers. Bhishma said, "Lady Perta, please."

"Sorry, Lord Bhishma, sorry. It's just so exciting, I can hardly contain myself. Look at the boys, all so grown up. Honestly, Gandhari, I don't know how you can bear not to see them. If I were you, I know I couldn't resist lifting that veil and taking a peek. You're awfully strong-minded." She giggled, then leaned close to the queen and said, much more softly, "But then, you and I both know that silk isn't *entirely* opaque—don't we?"

Gandhari so far had neither moved nor spoken. Now, however, she turned her head to the right and down a little, so that the fall of cloth, eyeless, seemed to stare at Perta. The ever-present veil, secured by a violet silk band about her brow, gave many people the uneasy sense that behind it there might be the face of a celestial, or a demon, or—perhaps—no face at all. Perta's mouth fell open and her eyes widened; she looked for a moment like a rabbit hypnotized by a snake. She closed her mouth, cleared her throat, and turned back to the exercises.

Yudi had made his bows, retrieved his arrow, and returned to the lineup, all with perfect decorum, earning a nod and a slight smile from Drona. Bima was next; though a year younger than Yudi, he was already a head taller and a foot wider than his brother and was allowed to use a half-size bow. His voice on "I salute you, mine enemy" was like the howl of a wolf cub, causing Perta to clap her hands to her ears and remark with a laugh, "Goodness, that Bima! He'll deafen us all!" His arrow went wide of the posts but flew twice as far as Yudi's had. He, too, completed the rest of his round correctly and received a nod from Drona.

Then it was Duryodhana's turn. As he walked to the mark his head was down and forward, his feet scuffing on the hard-packed dirt. Drona made no comment but went over and, laying hands on the boy in a brisk series of moves starting at the bottom and moving upward, arranged feet, legs, hips, torso, shoulders, and arms in the proper posture, with bow flexed and arrow on the string. Lastly he grabbed the boy's scalp hair and levered his chin up a notch. Then he stepped back and waited.

Duryodhana began in a voice nearly as loud as Bima's: "I salute you, mine enemy. May your ... m-m-may your ..." He stopped.

Over on the sidelines, Gandhari stood up a little straighter.

"M-m-may your ... re-b-b-b ... b-b-b ... b ..."

The weapons master turned to regard the line of boys. Not one of them moved. He turned back to Duryodhana and continued to wait.

"M-may your re-b-b ... b-b-BIRTH ... b-b-b ... b-b-b ..."

Tarashtra let out a "*Pshh!*" and threw up his hands. Shakuna put a fist to his mouth and bit a knuckle. Perta said quietly, "Oh, my." Bhishma, arms crossed on his chest, frowned and shook his head. Vidura watched, silent and still.

"B-b-b-BE ... f-f-f ... f-f-f-f-f ... f-f-f ..."

Little Arjuna, in the lineup, used the tip of his arrow to scratch his nose. Drona snapped his fingers with a glare; Arjuna jumped and lowered the arrow.

"F-f-f ... f-f-f ... f-f ... f... FORTUNATE!"

Everyone on the sidelines let out a breath. Duryodhana pulled the bowstring a little farther back, cocked the arrow up at an angle, and let it fly; it went straight through the posts but fell short of Yudi's distance. He bowed to Drona, bowed to the other boys, went and retrieved the arrow, and returned to the line. Drona made no sign of either approval or disapproval.

Naku, Saku, and Dushasana each took their turn, with varying degrees of success. Arjuna performed remarkably well for a five-year-old. Then Drona seemed to decide that the lesson had gone on long enough—or perhaps sensed that the audience, that is to say his employers, were growing bored. He instructed his students to place their weapons on the stand and proceeded to shepherd them over to the grownups.

The five Pandavas rushed to their mother, who dispensed hugs and kisses all round. "My big boys! You all did *so* well. Yudi, you look ready to ride a chariot into battle tomorrow. Oof, Bima, don't crush me! Naku, Saku, you were *splendid*. Arjuna, my precious." Arjuna, after giving his mother's still-slender waist a vigorous squeeze, ran to Vidura shouting, "Uncle Vidu, pick me up, pick me up!" Vidura did so, smiling and ruffling the boy's hair.

Meanwhile, Duryodhana and Dushasana were being embraced by the king and queen, with affection though in a cooler fashion.

Duryodhana pressed his head into his father's fleshy belly; Tarashtra patted his son's back, his white-filmed eyes directed out over the grounds, and said, "All right then, Duryo. All right, then." The two boys seemed unfazed by their mother's veiled countenance as she bent down to kiss their foreheads through the silk. Shakuna began to shadow-box with Dushasana, who shrieked happily as his uncle danced about throwing punches that never landed.

Drona stood back, waiting until the ruckus had subsided a bit, then stepped forward and bowed to the company. He addressed the king and queen with, "Your majesties. I am honored to serve you." He bowed to the other men: "Lord Bhishma. Prince Shakuna. Counselor Vidura." Then he turned to Perta, made namaste with his palms, and said, "Lady Perta, your sons are exceptionally talented. I am fortunate to be their teacher."

Perta beamed and made namaste in return. "Thank you, Chief Weapons Master. It is they who are fortunate, having a guru such as you to teach them."

Drona bowed again, acknowledging her compliment. Then he turned to the king, who was standing with his arms around the shoulders of his two sons, and said, "Your majesty, with your permission; it is time the princes put away their weapons."

"Yes, yes, of course," said Tarashtra. He raised his voice: "Off you go, all of you! Do as Drona says. Put the bows and arrows away."

The seven boys, obedient, let go of hands and waists and stopped their roughhousing. As they began to leave, Duryodhana, going as usual with head down and forward, bumped into Bimasena. Bima responded with a light shove—which, coming as it did from the burly boy, caused the other to stumble and nearly fall—and said, "W-w-w-watch out, D-D-D-Duryo!"

Duryodhana's face twisted into a mask of hatred. He flung himself at Bima—who after the quip and the shove had kept walking away—leaped onto his back, hooked a forearm around his windpipe, and squeezed. Bima reared back, gasping and clawing at the forearm, but Duryodhana hung on tight. It was only a few seconds before Drona, Bhishma, and Vidura converged on the pair and yanked Duryodhana away; Bima, however, had clearly been rather badly hurt. His knees buckled and he fell to the ground, coughing, crying, holding his throat.

Perta rushed to her son. "Bima! Oh, Bima!" She sank down and wrapped her arms around him. On her knees, she was no taller than he.

Duryodhana, face still contorted with fury, was being restrained by Bhishma; the king and queen were standing back, Shakuna between them, his hands gripping both their elbows. The members of the entourage were hovering about, whispering to one another in half-horrified, half-excited tones. In a few minutes Bima's coughing lessened, whereupon Perta looked over her shoulder and said, "Vidura, please." He came, and they helped the boy to his feet.

Vidura said, "He's all right. Let's get him back to his room and he can lie down."

Perta nodded and made to go. Then she stopped and said, "Wait."

She turned and walked back to the trio of king, queen, and prince, her face blazing with a fury to match her nephew's. She planted herself in front of the queen, leaned in to a palm's breadth from the veil, and hissed: "You tell your little monster to *leave my boys alone.*"

She rejoined Vidura, and the two of them led Bima away.

≈

"He *cannot* go on stuttering like that! It's humiliating!"

Tarashtra was standing in the middle of the bedchamber being undressed by his manservants. Gandhari was sitting on the king's bed, veil in place.

"Really, dear, I don't know what you expect me to do. It's a phase. He'll grow out of it."

"When? When will he grow out of it?"

"Eventually."

"Eventually! You've been saying that for years. He's seven!"

"Yes. Only seven."

"Not *only* seven. *Seven!*" Tarashtra stuck out his arms so his vest could be removed.

"The Pandavas make it much worse," said Gandhari. "Especially Bima. I've told and told Perta to make him stop teasing Duryo, but she won't do a thing about it. 'Bima's just high-spirited,' she says. High-spirited! That boy is a menace."

"You do realize he's supposed to have his First Purification next month. How is he going to get through the ceremony? A solid hour of him going b-b-b and f-f-f, with Vyasa grinning like a freak and Perta saying 'Oh my' and Bhishma standing around with his arms folded on his beefy chest. I'll go mad. Mad, I tell you."

"I'm sure it will be all right, dear. I'll get Vidura to coach him in advance. He's always better when he has a chance to practice first."

"Vidura, coach him? More likely sabotage him. Stop that fumbling, you idiot!" Tarashtra dealt three or four hard slaps to the hands and face of the servant who was kneeling before him trying to untie his dhoti; the youth fell back, wincing and pressing his eye. The king went on: "Vidura has one thought in his head, and that's supporting those Pandava brats. Well, to be fair, two thoughts: he thinks about screwing their mother, too." He snickered.

"Dear. Don't be vulgar." Gandhari waved a hand at the servants. "You can all go. I'll do the rest." She waited until they had left the room before removing the veil. She draped it over the bedpost, went to Tarashtra, and bent down to deal with the dhoti.

≈

The queen asked Counselor Vidura if he would mind very much helping Prince Duryodhana prepare for his First Purification. With his usual courtesy, Vidura agreed. Over the next few weeks he had the boy come to his rooms daily to rehearse the words and procedures, and as the time approached he asked Yudi, Bima, and Dushasana to join them, for they would be Duryodhana's stirrup-men and play a large role in the ceremony. (Back then boys of the same age served, not older relatives as is the custom now.) Bima had been a stirrup-man at Yudi's First Purification a month ago, so they were familiar with the rite; Vidura, however, thought Duryodhana would grow more comfortable if the boys practiced all together.

On the afternoon before the big day, Vidura had arranged for a dress rehearsal in the Hall of Sacraments. He kept the group to the essential few: just himself, Duryodhana and his three young attendants, Vyasa (presiding as high priest), Shakuna (who would present the candidate at the altar), and the king. The coterie headed over to the hall shortly after the midday meal.

Meanwhile Gandhari and her women were in the queen's

quarters, spinning flax. The hot weather would arrive soon, and with it the need for linen.

"… and if only you could see him, Madam, I know you would agree with me. He's not the handsomest man I've ever seen, but he's one of the most attractive!" The lady's fingers moved faster as she plucked another flax fiber from the heckling comb and twisted it onto the long strand wound around her spindle.

"He's certainly attractive for a weapons master," said another lady. "They're usually so scarred and battered. I don't like that look in a man. Drona has all his fingers, and no scars to speak of. Nice, smooth skin … all over."

A third lady said, "It sounds like you've made quite a study of him. Was it his *whole* body you examined, Padma?" She waved her spindle lewdly. "Do tell!"

"Tell, tell!" said all the women, giggling and waving their spindles at Padma. But Gandhari, behind her veil, gave only the lightest of laughs before saying in her low cool voice, "Ladies, really. That's enough. The Chief Weapons Master is married, as are most of you."

There followed groans and cries of, "We *know*." "It's too *bad*." "Oh, Madam, don't rub it *in*." Fingers plucked and spindles twirled, propelled by more giggles.

Suddenly there came the sound of bare feet pounding down the corridor. Heads turned to the door. Six-year-old Dushasana burst into the room and ran to his mother.

"Mummy, Mummy, come! Come quick!"

Gandhari put a hand on the boy's back. "Dusha, what is it? Why aren't you at the dress rehearsal?"

"It's Duryo, it's Duryo! Mummy, Mummy, *come*." He tugged at her hand, leaning nearly horizontal toward the door.

Gandhari pulled him back around in front of her and held him by the shoulders. "Dusha. Slow down. What are you saying? What's wrong with Duryo? Slowly, please."

The boy clenched his fists, his arms rigid and trembling. He took a deep breath. He let out the breath. He said, slowly:

"Duryo fell into the *fire*. He's hurt *bad*. You have to *come*."

Gandhari stood, tore off her veil, and ran from the room.

Dushasana followed on her heels. The violet square of silk fluttered in the air behind them; the women, transfixed, watched it float to the floor. As it touched down, they rose as one and went after their mistress.

≈

Gandhari entered the Hall of Sacraments. Over by the main fire pit, Shakuna and Vidura were kneeling on either side of a supine Duryodhana, pinning his shoulders to the ground. The high priest was also crouched there; he had a jar of ghee in the crook of an arm and in the other hand a cloth with which he was trying to dab Duryodhana's face, but the boy was not allowing it: he was flailing about, screaming "NO, NO, NO!" The whole left side of his face was a lurid mess of red, pink, and white.

Gandhari ran to them and stood looking down. Then she looked up and around the hall. She ran to the altar, grabbed a large bowl off its stone top, ran to a tub of water in a corner, filled the bowl, and strode back to the group. She shouted to the priest, "Move!"—and dumped the water on Duryodhana's face.

She ran back to the tub, refilled the bowl, returned, and dumped the water. Again. And again. On the fifth trip, she returned with the bowl but did not empty it; instead, she squatted down, said to her brother and the counselor, "Let go of him. Get back," and put the full bowl next to her on the floor. She unwound the shoulder drape of her sari and dunked it in the water. When it was sopping wet she lifted it out and began wringing the water onto the burn; the boy put his arms up to fend her off, but she placed a hand on his chest and said, "That's enough. Lie still," whereupon he turned his right cheek to the floor, closed his eyes, and lay still, whimpering. Gandhari continued to dunk the sari and wring the water, over and over again.

"Oh, what *shall* we do?" "Is he *dying?*" "Oh, *poor* Prince Duryo!" The queen's women had by this point arrived and were gathered around, weeping and chattering. (They would have shown up much sooner had Padma alone not kept her head and, realizing that to have nine or ten ladies-in-waiting dashing through the palace and across the compound would only attract unwanted attention, insisted they all walk slowly and decorously to the hall.) Vidura had risen and collected Yudi, Bima, and Dushasana, taking them off to one side; the three boys were huddled against him, their faces pale and strained. Prince Shakuna, after observing his sister's actions without comment, had gone to the altar to fetch another bowl, filled it at the tub, and returned; he set down that bowl, took away the old one, and was now exchanging and refilling the bowls as needed. High Priest Vyasa had retreated to the far side of the fire-pit; he was pacing to and fro, tipping and re-tipping his jar of ghee so as to spill drops of golden liquid into the flames, all the while muttering words that were not audible over the women's wails.

Ten minutes passed. Gandhari kept wringing the water and Shakuna kept swapping the bowls. At last she stopped, letting the wet swath of purple drapery drop onto the floor between her feet. She turned to her brother and said, "I need a clean cloth."

Shakuna called out to the women, "A clean cloth! Who has a kerchief, anything?" There was a patting of waistbands and a delving into chest-bands; someone produced a square of cotton, which was passed to Gandhari. She folded it into a rectangle, wet it, wrung it out, and laid it on her son's face. She took his hand and brought it up to the cloth, saying, "Hold that there. Good boy. Now, can you sit up?" She reached behind his back to help him. Still whimpering, but less than before, Duryodhana sat up holding the compress to the burn.

Gandhari touched the other side of his face, gently probing. She lifted each eyelid and looked at each eyeball. She ran her fingers over his scalp, his neck, his shoulders, his back, inspecting them all. Then, seemingly satisfied that there was no additional damage, she looked again at her brother and asked, "What happened?"

Shakuna said, "He fell into the fire-pit. Not right into the flames. But his face hit the hot stones."

"How did he fall?"

Shakuna looked down and to one side. "He ... just fell."

Gandhari gripped her brother's cheeks in a one-handed vise and turned his face to hers. "Kuku. Tell me. Was he *pushed?*"

Shakuna met her eyes and shrugged.

Gandhari stood up slowly. The sari top dangled in a long wet clump down the front of her skirt, leaving her upper body covered only by her chest-band. Her hair had come undone and hung disheveled down her back. A couple of the women hurried forward to help her, but she brushed them off and approached Vidura, who was still standing apart with his arms around Yudi, Bima, and Dushasana, pressing them to his brown robe.

Confronting the foursome, Gandhari pointed a finger at Bima; then she crooked the finger to beckon him. Her face was a blank; her half-naked torso was shining with damp; she was like a cobra rising up, tall and slender and graceful, fixing its prey with cold eyes. Bima took a faltering step forward. Big as he was, he was only six and clearly terrified.

Gandhari said, softly: "You pushed my son into the fire?"

Bima's mouth gaped a little. He did not answer.

Gandhari said it again, louder: "*You pushed my son into the fire?*"

Bima's face crumpled, and he began to cry.

Gandhari lunged forward, grabbed him by the shoulders, and shook him hard. "YOU PUSHED HIM! YOU PUSHED HIM! YOU PUSHED MY SON INTO THE FIRE!" Bima flopped to and fro like a scrap of cowhide being worried by a puppy.

Counselor Vidura reached over the boy's head and slapped the queen's face.

She gasped, let go, and fell back, one hand pressed to her cheek. Bima collapsed to the ground and sat there, sobbing.

"Your majesty; forgive me." The counselor bowed to the queen. "Prince Bimasena did not push Prince Duryodhana."

Gandhari did not seem appeased. "Then who? Was it Yudi?" She glared at the eldest Pandava. He flinched, but met her angry eyes with dignity impressive for a child.

"No, Madam," said the counselor. "It was his father."

Gandhari looked confused.

"His *father?*"

"Yes, Madam."

"You mean … *Tarashtra?*"

"Yes, Madam. The king." Vidura's expression was impassive.

"But … where is the king? I remember now, yes, he was to be here, at the rehearsal. Did he leave? Did he go to get help?" She glanced around the hall.

"His majesty is there." Vidura gestured, palm upward. Everyone turned to look. There by the doorway, in the shadows, stood the king.

The queen's women, with cries of "Oh!" and "Your majesty!" dropped into court curtseys: left leg crossed behind right, palms flat on right knee, head down. No one else moved.

Tarashtra had his small-boy-guide-dog with him. (It was still a small boy, the king not liking the idea of a grown man leading him about the palace.) With a brusque "Go," he now emerged from the shadows and started across the space. His gait beneath his crimson robe was dignified, but his hands—his hands were shaking, just a little.

As he came up to Gandhari, she merely stared at him. Her failure to curtsey to her husband in this public setting was remarkable, but of course went unnoticed by him.

"Tarashtra," she said. "What happened?"

The king puffed up his chest and cleared his throat. "Good afternoon, my dear. Yes ... most unfortunate." He shook his head, sighed. "Poor Duryo. He fell. I trust he's all right now?"

"He is badly burned. On the face."

"We must get the healers in immediately. They'll fix him up."

"Tarashtra ..."

The king held up a pudgy hand and began speaking quickly. "I must tell you, my dear, though I'm sorry to say it, the rehearsal did not go well. Not well, not well at *all*. That coaching you had Vidura give him: worse than useless. The poor boy could barely say a word. Terrible. It was terrible. Where is Vidura?"

Vidura said, "I am here, your majesty."

Tarashtra wagged a finger at the counselor. "Now listen to me, Vidu. I know you prefer the Pandavas. I don't say there's anything wrong with that. You always liked Pandu, he was their father, and I understand your feelings. But I won't have you trying to undermine my son. It's not fair, and I won't have it. Do you hear me, Vidu?"

"Yes, Sire. I hear you."

The king turned back to his wife and went on. "So, as I say, poor Duryo, it was not going well *at all*. And I lost my temper, just a bit. He was stuck on b-b-b-b-b and I told you, Gandhari, I told you it drives me mad—I *warned* you, you know I did—so I admit it, I gave him a smack, a very small smack, on the back of the head. I won't apologize for it. No, I won't apologize; sometimes children need a smack. Just like women, sometimes. They need a little smack, help them pull themselves together. Yes. And after my ... the little smack, well, I guess he tripped and fell. Burned himself, it seems. But not too badly."

He tipped his head up and called out to the air, "Not too badly— eh, Duryo?"

His cry echoed off the mud plaster walls: *D-D-Duryo … ryo …o … o …*

Gandhari looked at her son, still sitting on the ground with his uncle beside him, the wet cloth pressed to his face.

The king extended a trembling hand to his wife. "Gandhari … not too badly?"

Gandhari looked back at her husband. She reached out and took the hand.

≈

"Winner in archery: *Karna of Panchala.*"

Applause greeted Karna as he walked across the training grounds. Under the royal canopy, the king leaned and whispered to his wife, "Who is this one again? Do we know him?"

The queen turned her face to her husband's ear and whispered back, her veil stirring: "No, dear. He's not one of ours. He's from Panchala."

"Ah. But Duryo won the sword-fighting, didn't he?"

"Yes, Duryo won the sword-fighting."

"Good, good. I can't tell you how glad I am he beat that little prat Arjuna."

"Yes, dear. But remember, we must be gracious to all the winners."

"Gracious? I'm always gracious! You know I'm always gracious."

"Yes, I know you are."

The king and queen ceased whispering and sat upright again on their stools.

Out in the arena, Drona said: "Lady Perta will present the garlands." On the king's left there was a minor bustle as Perta rose from her seat and beckoned to the maidservant with the tray of marigolds to follow her.

The queen leaned toward her husband. "Dear."

"What?"

"When we greet the winners, remember not to refer to Duryo as the crown prince."

The king sighed, bringing a hand up to rub his brow. "I know, I know. It's a habit I've fallen into lately. I'll try to remember."

"Thank you. We have to be careful, especially now that he and Yudi are seventeen."

Out in the arena, the winner of the jousting received his garland from Perta.

The king leaned again. "Vidura made a point of it in council the other day. He said—in that prissy way of his—he said, 'Your majesty, I must note that Crown Prince Yudi is now of age. It is time we begin thinking of the transition.' I didn't answer him at first. Made him wait. Then I said, very calmly, 'Counselor Vidura, all in good time. Prince Yudi is not yet married. I believe, according to the Law, a king must have a wife.' He had no answer for that! Damn him, anyway, that pompous, tight-assed ..."

The queen placed a hand on his upper arm. "You're right, dear, of course you're right. But the thing is, Lord Bhishma is already seeking a wife for Yudi. Before we know it, he *will* be married. And then what?"

"I don't know. I don't know. I mean—sometimes I think—I mean it's not as if I *enjoy* being king. Nothing but endless council meetings and judging the townspeople's stupid disputes, not to mention the hours and hours I have to spend in the Hall of Sacraments with the damned priests. Gods, the boredom. I hate it. I hate all of it. Maybe I *should* step down."

The nails dug into the chubby loose flesh. "Ow!" hissed the king, yanking his arm away and rubbing it. "That hurt!"

The queen did not apologize. Instead she pulled him in close again and put her veiled mouth right up to his ear. "Tarashtra. You *cannot* step down. If you step down, Duryodhana will never be king."

"Yes, yes, I know, I *know*. He must be king. I *want* him to be king. I just—sometimes I wish ..." he went on rubbing his arm, his fleshy lips pushed out in a pout.

"What do you wish?"

"Nothing. It doesn't matter anyway, because I don't see how we can stop Yudi from getting married and being crowned. Bhishma will see to it. You know he will."

"Yes," said the queen with a sigh. "We can always trust Bhishma to see to it."

They drew apart and sat erect again. Out in the arena, Perta was having an oddly long conversation with the archery champion from Panchala.

The queen leaned over once more. "Dear ..."

"*What?*"

"Don't worry about Yudi. We'll figure something out."

"Who's *we?* You and Shakuna? What are you two cooking up?"

A pause. "It's probably best you don't get involved."

"Hmm. Yes. That probably is best. Well, I'll leave it to you, then." He yawned. "Gods, is this thing ever going to be over?"

The crowd of townspeople was dispersing, heading for the roasting pits.

"It's over," said Gandhari. "Here comes Perta with the winners. Now, remember what I said about 'crown prince.'"

"I'll remember," said Tarashtra. They both rose, her hand lightly under his elbow.

I asked Gandhari about her mad dash to the Hall of Sacraments on the day her son was burned. She said it had not attracted as much notice as you'd think. That everyone was used to her with the veil— indeed, had not seen her face for five years—afforded her a kind of disguise: without it, she was assumed to be a lady-in-waiting sent on an urgent mission by the queen. And afterward she had one of her women go back and fetch the veil and a dry sari, then had the men and boys leave the hall first and she and her ladies a little thereafter, in twos and threes.

Duryodhana's First Purification was postponed. The story was put about that at the rehearsal he had very unfortunately tripped and fallen onto the hot stones of the fire pit, but that thanks to the quick thinking of his father and uncle the damage was not too bad. He wore a bandage for a month and was well tended by the healers while the priests performed extra sacrifices to Agni to speed his recovery. When the bandage was removed there was an ugly scar running from temple to jaw and pulling his mouth to the left, but his father said a scar was the mark of a real soldier, which made the boy beam with pride. He liked to show off the scar to the other boys of the compound: "Go ahead, touch it!" he would say, and they would touch it with looks of awe.

After the injury, moreover, his stutter diminished. It did not go away entirely, but it improved, and at his First Purification—when it finally came about—he did well.

The next ten years in Hastinapura were uneventful. Thanks in large part to Lord Bhishma's steady hand (and I suppose we must give King Tarashtra some credit), it was a time of peace and prosperity. There were the usual cattle raids among clans; even a full-on battle or two over territory, led by Bhishma. But for the most part, the Kuru tended their herd and crops, swapped brides with their neighbors, and minded their business. As for the Pandava and Kaurava boys, though little love was lost between them, they did not quarrel too much. Drona, for one, would not have tolerated it, so they rubbed along.

But when Karna showed up at the tournament, beat Arjuna, and was made kshatriya, tensions increased. The Pandavas sensed danger: the balance of power had shifted, subtly, in their awkward cousin's favor.

Chapter 5

KARNA

The queen, expressing a desire for more exercise, had instituted a morning stroll around the compound with her brother and two sons. Duryodhana's friend, Sir Karna—"such an adept young man, however did we do without him"—was also invited. The queen's ladies were not.

On today's walk in the winter sunshine, the five had paused for a rest near the roasting pits north of the horse barns. A clump of head-high elephant grass screened them from view of the palace. A rug was spread for the queen; the men squatted in a semicircle around her, Karna a little back from the others.

"And the marriage negotiations are complete? You're sure?" Gandhari plucked a long grass stalk and ran it between finger and thumb.

"Yes. Bhishma announced it in council this morning," said Shakuna. "It's the youngest daughter of the King of Madrasa, if you can believe it. Madri's little sister."

"Really? Goodness! His dead stepmother's sister—how did Yudi take the news?"

"Graciously, of course," said Duryodhana, grimacing. "He stood up and b-bowed to B-Bhishma and made a speech thanking him for his—what was it, Dusha?"

"His assiduous efforts," said Dushasana. He had grown up to be a short and muscular young man, similar in looks to his older brother, but with a shaggy mane of hair.

"Yes, his *assiduous efforts*. He said he was m-most pleased with Bhishma's assiduous efforts that had led to such a *suitable b-bride*. Gods! Yudi!" He turned his head and spat.

Shakuna scratched his close-cropped beard. "He really is

sickening. I always want to slap him when he makes those pompous little speeches. Say, Karna—what if you just took care of this whole thing for us with a stray arrow on the training grounds?" He mimed pulling and releasing a bowstring. "Twang! Oops! No more Yudi. Problem solved."

Karna turned to Duryodhana with a look of alarm.

Shakuna rolled his eyes. "I'm joking, Karna. It's a joke."

Karna mustered a weak smile.

"Enough jokes," said Gandhari. "If the negotiations are complete, we don't have much time. We need a plan. Shakuna, you said you had one; let's hear it."

The prince grew serious. "Right, yes. Here it is. I figure the main thing we need is for the people to turn against Yudi; better still, against the Pandavas in general. If the people turn against *them*, we can persuade them to turn to *us*. If the Pandavas are out, the Kauravas are in. So the question is: How do we make that happen?"

"That's no good," said Dushasana. "The people loved King Pandu. The soldiers especially loved him. They'll back his sons no matter what."

"No, no. Not no matter *what*. Support is never no matter *what*. Give people a good reason to shift allegiance, and their allegiance will shift."

"What do you have in mind, Uncle?" asked Duryodhana.

Shakuna paused, looking from face to face as if to prepare them for something big.

"Rape," he said. "I have rape in mind."

"What on earth are you talking about?" Gandhari said, snapping the grass stalk in two and tossing the pieces aside. "Stop being dramatic and get to the point."

Shakuna rolled his eyes again. "You're so impatient, Dhari. Look: everyone sees the Pandavas, and Yudi especially, as noble and virtuous. Supreme gentlemen, paragons of Law. They even say Yudi is an incarnation of the God Yama—who used to be just the God of Death, you know, but now the priests say he's the God of Law, too. Why should Death and Law be the same thing, I wonder? It's an interesting question ..."

"*Tsk!*" said Gandhari, and her sharp-toed shoe drew back as if to deal a kick.

Shakuna glanced at the shoe and continued: "... yes, anyway, the thing is: suppose it turns out the Pandavas *aren't* noble? What if instead they're vile kidnappers, despoilers of virtuous women? If the evidence is unassailable, well, there's the character defect that'll disqualify Yudi, or any of the five, from taking the throne. Even Bhishma will have to admit it's impossible. Tarashtra must remain king, and Duryo will be crown prince."

Dushasana's brow furrowed. Gandhari, behind her veil, was silent. Karna looked uncertainly at Duryodhana.

Duryodhana said with quiet ferocity, "The Pandavas—*rapists*. Yes, that w-would do it. But how … oh! I know. You'll get a girl, a girl to lie about it."

Shakuna nodded, smiling broadly. "You've pegged it, Nephew. We'll arrange a bachelor party for Yudi and the boys. As their uncle, I'm the right person to host it, and naturally I'll supply the entertainment. The bridegroom must get a little premarital experience, after all. And his brothers, too: Bima and the twins are seventeen, Arjuna is nearly sixteen, high time they were in the saddle" (he glanced at his sister) "so to speak. So we'll find a girl, a very respectable girl. I already have one in mind. And we'll pay her to be the entertainment. But really what we'll pay her for is to be a credible victim. She'll escape the party and run back to town with her tale: kidnapped, beaten, gang-raped, nearly killed. By whom? By the Pandavas!"

A light breeze riffled through the elephant grass. Away by the compound's north wall, a covey of partridges emerged from a stand of thorn bushes. They came hopping and fluttering over to the cooking pits and began to forage around the rims.

"Who's the girl?" asked Dushasana.

"Someone I know. That is, I know her mother—a lovely woman …" (he stroked his lower lip) "recently widowed, with six little daughters, no sons; most unlucky for her. What must she have done in a former life to earn such bad karma? At any rate, they have no real means of support, no close relatives, and even though the father was a respectable tradesman, naturally the girls have no marriage prospects now."

"Are they vaishya?"

"Yes, cloth weavers. The mother can't afford materials anymore and takes in washing. The older girls help. The youngest are mere babies. The neighbors have been generous; still, they'll be beggars within a month if someone doesn't rescue them."

"And you'll offer to rescue them," said Gandhari.

"Yes. We'll give mamma a position as court weaver; the older girls can be upper maidservants and live in the compound. A happy idea, isn't it? Everyone wins."

"Which of the girls is the one?"

"The eldest; Ani is her name. She's fourteen and beautiful. Fragile-looking, but tough as teak underneath. Clever. And desperate to help her mother and sisters. She's just right for the part."

Duryodhana broke in: "She's a v-virgin?"

"Yes, of course. I told you, they're a respectable family."

"Then it's a b-big risk for her. What if—what if the mother won't allow it?"

Shakuna raised an eyebrow. "She'll allow it. If she's uncooperative, I can spread tales of our relationship all over town. In which case, people won't even give her their laundry."

Duryodhana rubbed his scar and did not reply.

"Well? What do you think?" Shakuna looked around the group.

"It makes sense to me," said Dushasana, "as long as the girl's reliable."

"I'll vouch for her. Gandhari? What say you?"

The queen was looking at the partridges (though, of course, she could not see them). She turned back to her brother and said, "Yes. It's a good plan. We're not likely to contrive a better one. But Kuku—it will be your show. Don't make a mistake."

"Don't worry, I won't. Duryo? You seem doubtful. Remember, this is all for you."

Duryodhana thrust his head down. His hands were clasped between his knees; he squeezed them rhythmically as he spoke.

"You ... you'll m-make sure that girl, w-what's her name, Ani? You'll make, make sure she doesn't *really* get hurt?"

"Of course she won't really get hurt. I'll coach her well. And she'll be paid well."

"P-paid well. Yes. And the Pandavas ..." He raised his head. "The Pandavas will be *f-finished.* Won't they, Uncle?"

"Oh, yes. They'll be finished."

"All right, then. Let's do it." He squeezed his hands hard, as if crushing a bug.

"I guess that settles it," Shakuna said. "Although, wait: we haven't heard from Karna. Sir Karna?" His smile grew ironic. "What are your thoughts on our plan?"

Karna looked at Duryodhana.

"Say what you think," said Duryodhana.

Karna looked at the ground, tugging on one of his golden earrings. "I … I do not wish to offend Prince Shakuna …"

"Offend me? How could *you* offend me? Spit it out, Karna, there's a good fellow."

Karna let go the earring and looked up. "Forgive me, my lord, but the plan does not seem … honorable."

A crease appeared between Shakuna's brows. But an instant later it was gone, and he laughed and said, "Honorable? I never claimed it was honorable. The question is: Will it work? Will it ensure that your friend becomes crown prince? Surely, Karna, you want to support Duryodhana. Think of all he's done for you."

Karna flinched. He looked down again and said softly, "Of course. Yes. I will support Duryodhana."

"Good," said Shakuna. "Then we're in agreement. I'll put things in motion."

The men rose. The queen held out a hand, and her elder son helped her to her feet. Karna gathered up the rug. The five resumed their morning walk around the compound.

Gandhari, leading the way on Duryodhana's arm, looked back over her shoulder and said to her brother, "We'll have to think of a good place for this bachelor party."

Shakuna said, "Way ahead of you, my dear. I know the perfect spot."

"Oh? Where?"

"The Lacquer House."

≈

"That's it? It doesn't look like much," said Karna.

To get to the Lacquer House, one went north along the main road or river road and then west along a forest path; an hour's ride, a three hours' walk. The wood-frame wattle-and-daub structure sat wide, long, and low in a clearing in the trees, the ground around it strewn with pine needles and dead leaves. Wooden steps in front led up to a veranda.

"It's not much from the outside," said Duryodhana, reining in his horse next to Karna's. "But wait till you see the inside. King Shantanu had it built for Queen Satyavati as a w-wedding present. It was their love nest."

"Looks more like a barracks," said Karna. "Why *lacquer* house?"

"You'll see."

They dismounted, tied their horses to the hitching post, and walked up the steps, the rickety boards creaking beneath their feet.

Passing through the narrow doorway, they entered a room some thirty paces long and fifteen paces wide. The floor was made of wood planks. Along the right-hand wall was a series of four archways that appeared to lead into smaller side chambers. In the middle of the space was a ring of wooden posts around a circular platform which, judging by the moth-eaten blankets and pillows strewn across its surface, had once served as a bedstead. There were no windows, yet the room was suffused with rosy light, and on the floor were several large squares of brighter light crisscrossed by dark lines. If one looked up, one saw why: there were three skylights, each made of dozens of pink glass tiles held in a lattice of wood, through which the afternoon sun shone. In the two back corners were capacious chair swings, suspended from the ceiling by bronze chains. One of the swings held a heap of dirty sheepskins; on the other, the chains on one side had snapped, causing it to drop askew. The whole place smelled of dust and mildew.

"Looks like there's some f-fixing up needed before the party," said Duryodhana.

Karna did not reply. He was staring at the walls.

He was staring because every inch of them was covered with glossy red lacquer, and etched into the lacquer, traced in black ink, were scenes of such extraordinary ... well, I will try to describe them. (Remember, Sire, I am an old woman and these things long ago lost their power to shock me. Also, I have vowed to tell you the truth.)

Across the red walls, men and women had intercourse in an amazing variety of positions. Men and women pleasured each other orally, digitally, and with flowers, feathers, fruits and vegetables. Down in a corner, three men converged on one woman, penetrating her mouth, vagina, and anus; up near the ceiling, five women converged on one man and were penetrated by his penis, two thumbs, and two big toes. On the left wall a group of men engaged in a dance, each with a woman perched on the tip of his enormous erection, her legs wrapping his back as he pranced in a circle with his fellows; next to the dancers there was a trio of women flogging a trio of men, the men on hands and knees with mouths stretched wide. On the right, the spaces between and above the archways were devoted to beasts: tigers, horses, dogs, jackals, deer, birds, monkeys, rabbits, snakes, and exotic combinations thereof cavorted with one another and with human partners. The main door was framed by an intricate border of vulvas and phalluses. Wherever one looked, the black lines seemed to lift off the scarlet background and vibrate with ecstatic force: an orgy all-inclusive, all-pervasive, and never-ending.

"Um," said Karna.

"Quite something, eh?" said Duryodhana, bending to scrape a clod of dirt off his boot.

Karna walked to the animal wall and peered at two monkeys engaged in mutual oral gratification. With his forefinger, he traced the red-and-black spiral of a monkey's tail.

"It's incredible. Did King Shantanu bring all his women here?"

"No, that's the odd thing; only Satyavati. He m-made it just for her."

"Really? It must have taken years. For the craftsmen, I mean."

"Four years. He had them do one wall each year, and then he'd b-bring her in the springtime. Of course there was furniture and everything then."

Karna walked to the back wall and gazed up at an image of the Goddess Kali treading on the supine form of her husband, Shiva. She was naked, her stomach distended as if pregnant. Her right hand gripped a sword; from her left hand dangled by the hair a man's sev-ered head. Her tongue protruded long and red, and around her neck floated a garland of skulls. Shiva lay below her, his shaft pointing straight up, his face tense with delight.

"I suppose she was very beautiful," Karna remarked.

"Who? Oh, Satyavati. Yes, so they say. Hard to believe now. She's so f-fat."

"I don't know. I can still see it."

Karna rejoined Duryodhana by the exit. As they turned to go, he gave the walls one last perusal and said, "Good place for a bachelor party."

"It is. And now you see why it's called the Lacquer House."

On the way back, they decided to stop and see Ekalavya.

After the incident with the hacked-off thumb, Duryodhana had arranged for the Naga man and his daughter to have a dwelling in town along with a small pension. Karna had suggested that, given his talents, the Naga might be given a job as a palace blades-man— fletching arrows, honing swords, and so forth—but the prince had immediately quashed that idea.

"And be under Drona's eye every day? I don't think so! You want him to lose his whole hand? And the kshatriya won't want a f-filthy Snake touching their weapons."

"True. I hadn't thought of that," said Karna.

"Anyway, how much can a man do with a missing thumb? No. The girl was right. They're my responsib ... *sibility*. I need to look after them."

So Ekalavya and Jaratka moved into a tidy little hut in town. They had a goat for milk, a few chickens, and supplies of grain and lentils to eat and exchange in the market. Besides doing odd jobs for neighbors, Ekalavya gathered wood and whittled arrow shafts, which he sent to a palace contact (who saw no need to reveal the source, the quality being high and the cost low) in exchange for more foodstuffs. Jaratka chose to remain as maidservant in the old queen's quarters; indeed, Satyavati had taken a shine to the slender girl with heavy-lidded eyes and would not have spared her. She went in early each morning and attended for most of the day, coming home to prepare a cooked meal for her father in the late afternoon.

Late afternoon, Duryodhana had found, was the most convenient time for his and Karna's regular visits.

Entering the town of Hastinapura, the two men reined in from a canter and began to ride slowly through the grid of narrow streets. Townsfolk moved aside for them, the women throwing appreciative glances at Karna on his roan gelding and somewhat less-appreciative glances at Duryodhana on his black. On either side above, smoke curled from roof-holes. The smell of stew-meat, rice, and lentils wafted from doorways, and the riders raised their heads to sniff; as they came up the lane toward the Nagas' house, however, they covered their noses. Only shudra lived in this section of town, so the sewer ditch down the middle of the lane lay open—unlike those in the vaishya sections, which had clay covers—and although in winter the stench wasn't overpowering, still it was unpleasant. Stopping at the door, they dismounted and tossed their reins to an urchin who ran up, eager to earn a copper bead for his services.

Ekalavya, as was his wont, was sitting at the back of the one-room hut next to the hearth, a big pile of sticks to his left and a small pile of arrow shafts to his right. As Karna leaned in with a "Namaste, Uncle!" the tall, dark-skinned man put down his knife, jumped up, and came toward the visitors with a smile of welcome. He bowed low with palms pressed together.

"Ah, my lords! Lord Duryo, Lord Karna. Come in, come in. Iss such happiness, such honor to see you."

"Not *Lord* Karna," said Karna with a laugh. "Remember? Just *Sir* Karna."

"*Sir* Karna, *Sir* Karna." Ekalavya laughed too, his weathered face showing traces of the good looks that must once have been his. "And *Prince* Duryo. You must forgive! I am still not speaking him well. And to us, you are both great lords, yes? Iss not so, Jaratka?"

The girl at the hearth had made a proper court curtsey when the two men entered, but right away had turned back to the fireplace and continued stirring the contents of the copper pot hanging on the bar. She had grown in recent months and was now nearly as tall as Duryodhana, her upright carriage and long braid of hair giving the impression of even more height. Keeping her back to them, she replied: "Yes, Father. They are great lords."

The room was furnished with two sleeping mats with blankets, a few sheepskins, and a set of shelves that held pans, dishware, and eating utensils along with woodworking tools and an oil lamp. Unlike in Karna's parents' home, the cups and plates were ochre in color and crudely made. A waist-high water jar stood in one corner, a broom, spade, and bucket in another. Propped in a niche on the back wall was a clay plaque carved in bas-relief: it showed a snake with a crown of flames, poised as if to strike. A bracket next to the niche held an unlit torch.

There was no table, but Ekalavya arranged sheepskins in the middle of the floor and begged Karna and Duryodhana to be seated.

"Let's have a look, Uncle," said Karna, leaning forward and

taking the man's right hand to examine it. "Excellent … excellent. It's really healed up well. No pain to speak of now?"

"No, no pain," said Ekalavya, tapping at the stump. "See? Just itch, sometimes."

"Yes, that's normal. Nothing to worry about." Karna released the hand and sat back with a look of satisfaction. "And how is work? You're keeping busy?"

"Oh, yess. I help many people, cleaning, fixing. I clean the sewer ditch when it stop up. And I am whittling fass-ter. Now I make many arrows every day. Do I not, Jaratka?"

"Yes, Father. Many arrows."

Karna and Ekalavya continued to chat about this and that.

Duryodhana had not said a word since arriving. He was sitting cross-legged on the sheepskin, rubbing his scar and looking at Jaratka. As she turned from the hearth and reached for a serving bowl on the top shelf, the armhole of her shift gaped, revealing the side of her breast. Duryodhana froze, fingers pressed to scar, mouth slightly open. Lifting down the bowl, the girl turned to face them, whereupon the prince flushed red, ducked his head, and folded his arms tightly on his chest.

"Father, the meal is almost ready."

"Thank you, child, thank you. It smells very good. My lords, will you not stay? Pleasse. Iss not what you are … what you are used, I know, but, such honor if you would stay. We have plenty. Plenty to share."

Nobody spoke. Karna glanced at Duryodhana, who kept on staring at the floor.

"Father, you know they can't stay." Jaratka's expression was severe. "We have talked about this many times."

Ekalavya looked unhappy. "No … I mean, yess, you have said. I know. The Arya lords cannot eat with Naga."

"Not just the lords, Father. No one. *No one* can eat with us." Her fingers gripped the bowl. "To eat with us means they are defiled. Dirty. I'm not going to explain it again."

Ekalavya looked even more unhappy and said nothing.

Karna took a deep breath, slapped his palms on his knees, and said in a hearty voice, "Well, we've taken up enough of your time. It's good to see you looking well, Uncle—and you, Miss." He nodded at Jaratka. "Come on, Duryo." He stood and made to leave.

Duryodhana did not move.

Karna took another step toward the door. "Prince Duryodhana. Are you coming?"

Duryodhana finally looked up—but at Jaratka, not Karna. He said in a pleading tone: "W-w-w … why shouldn't we stay? We can stay. We *will* stay."

"Yess!" said Ekalavya, his tone gracious and glad. "Pleasse, you stay."

"NO!" The word snapped from Jaratka's mouth like a whip-crack. Her two hands holding the bowl were shaking. "Are you mad? If it is found that you, the crown prince, ate with Naga—with filthy Snakes—the people would turn on you. You … you would be *dead!*"

Duryodhana lurched to his feet, stumbled, and regained his balance. "I am *not* the crown p-p-p-prince!" he cried. "I will *never* be king! So let them turn on me, let me b-b-b-be dead! What does it m-m-matter?" His hands, clenched at his sides, were shaking like hers. "I just want … I want … oh, you *know* what I want!"

The two glared at each other, their faces close enough to feel each other's breath. For a moment it seemed they might fall together—to attack or embrace.

Then Jaratka took a step back and lowered her gaze.

"We also would be dead. The townspeople would drive us out as—how do you say?—as *polluters*. And the Naga would not take us back. My father and I would be homeless." She met his eyes again, and now it was her turn to plead. "You do not want that, do you?"

After a few more seconds of glaring, the prince looked away and sighed.

"No, I do not want that."

"No. So you must go. Please. Go now."

She put the bowl on the floor and made a proper court curtsey. Ekalavya, seeing her do so, got to his feet and bowed; his eyes were wet, but his bearing was dignified.

Karna was already outside, handing a copper bead to the urchin. Duryodhana came out of the house. The two men remounted and rode off down the street.

≈

Several weeks later, the five morning walkers gathered again behind the clump of elephant grass near the roasting pits. This time they remained standing, Karna a step back from the others.

The queen said, "Let's have the report."

"Everything's coming together nicely," said Shakuna. "I was concerned at first, because when I told Yudi I wanted to give him his bachelor party he looked confused—I don't think he knew what I meant—but fortunately his mother was present, and she was thrilled. She said of *course* there must be a party, that it was tradition, and all the boys must be included, and I said naturally they'd all be included, and then Yudi said I was most kind and that he'd be pleased to attend any—let's see, how did he put it—yes, any *customary celebrations*."

Dushasana made a gagging noise.

Shakuna continued: "He was even more pleased when I told him there'd be plenty of dice games; you know how he likes to gamble. So he went away happy. Then Perta pulled me aside and said it was so difficult, the boys having lost their father and no one to look after them when it came to men's affairs. She asked if I was going to handle everything. I said yes and she was not to worry because I would make sure nothing was overlooked. *Nothing*—I said it pointedly. Then she asked where I planned to hold the party, and I said, at the Lacquer House. Her eyes got big and she said, 'Ooh, the Lacquer House! What a good idea! Do you suppose I might drop by, just for a short time?' And I said hmm, well, such events are by tradition strictly male and she wouldn't want to cause her sons to feel constrained in any way, now, would she? She blushed and said no, no, it was just that she'd always longed to see the Lacquer House, and I said I *quite* understood and perhaps, after the wedding, I might arrange a special tour there just for her and her ladies. She perked up then and said I was too thoughtful and she appreciated what I was doing for her sons. So, there you go. We're all set." He beamed round at the group.

"What about the girl," said Gandhari. "Ani, was that her name? Did she agree?"

"She did. I spoke with her and her mother together. As soon as they heard my proposal, they didn't hesitate. Like I said, she's a smart girl."

"And she knows what she has to do? To play the victim, I mean?"

"Yes. I'll be coaching her over the next few days. She'll be well prepared."

"When's the party?" Dushasana asked.

"Seven days from now. Invitations go out tomorrow. There'll be a full moon on the night." He glanced up at the sky and rubbed his palms together. Then, with a sly smile at Karna: "We'll see *you* there, Sir Karna; you won't want to miss the fun."

Karna inclined his head. "Thank you, my lord, but I think I will be busy that evening."

"Busy. Is that so? Well, you must suit yourself." Shakuna turned to the queen. "Let's go, Dhari. Oh, listen—make sure the king doesn't come. We don't want him mixed up in it."

"Don't worry," Gandhari said. "He knows to stay clear." She took her brother's arm, and the two of them led the way across the compound.

≈

Midnight, and the full moon shone through the window of Duryodhana's receiving room, lighting up the game board for the men squatting on the floor.

Only a few retainers were in attendance on the prince that evening. Shakuna had issued, via messenger boys, close on a hundred invitations—"a big crowd and lots of confusion, that's what we want"—and most of the men of the compound, kshatriya, brahmin, and vaishya, had set off for the Lacquer House some three hours ago in a boisterous pack. Thanks to a beer barrel supplied by Shakuna to the barracks that afternoon, many had made an early start on the festivities. Duryodhana, however, had not gone. "We don't want *you* getting blamed for what happens," said his uncle. "Best that you not be feeling well." So the prince had claimed an aching head, and Karna, along with a couple of old soldiers, had stayed behind with him.

A gray-haired kshatriya rolled the dice and cackled with glee. He moved his last ivory-elephant piece to the finish line and said, "Game to me!"

"Pavel wins again," Duryodhana said with a yawn. He wagged three fingers at a serving boy. The boy went to a chest on a table, removed three copper beads, and took them to Pavel, who with a look of satisfaction proceeded to string them on the cord he wore around his neck.

Duryodhana got up from his squat. "Come on, Karna. I'm dead

b-bored. Let's go for a ride, shoot some hare. There's plenty of light for it."

"Is your head better, my lord?" asked Karna, also getting up. "I'm glad."

"My head? Oh—yes, much b-better. No, no," (he waved a hand at the others) "you needn't come. Karna, you come."

"Yes, my lord."

The two retrieved cloaks and bows from an anteroom. They exited the palace by a back door, crossed to the barns, stocked their quivers from the weapons shed, collected their horses, and were soon riding out the south gate with the wardens bowing low. It was late winter now, and though they pulled their cloaks across their chests, the air was nippy rather than freezing.

"Nice night," said Duryodhana. "Nice and calm."

"It might have been better to stay in," Karna remarked. "There must not be any question of your being involved in the ... you know."

"Ha. The gang rape? Yes, I guess it's a risk. But I couldn't stand those old geezers another m-minute. Anyway, I'm sure Shakuna has everything under control."

They were no more than thirty paces beyond the gate when they saw a figure running toward them up the road that led to town. The strong moonlight showed it to be a man wearing the undyed breeches and tunic of the lowest caste.

"Who's that?" said Duryodhana, reining in his horse and squinting at the runner. "It looks like ... no, wait. Yes—it is! I think it's Ekalavya!"

"What in the world?" said Karna.

They rode forward to meet him. As the Naga approached, he recognized them and began to wave and shout: "Lord Duryo! Lord Karna! Help, help!"

Karna called out, "Uncle, is that you? What's the matter?"

The tall man came up to them and grabbed onto Karna's stirrup, panting hard. His eyes stared; his mouth opened and shut, opened and shut, like a fish out of water.

Karna bent down and touched his hand. "Ekalavya! What has happened?"

Ekalavya made an effort to gather himself. He spoke, gasping between the words:

"The men ... the men. They come. They come in the house.

They ... they say Lady Per ... Perta? Lady Perta, she wantss a Snake, a Snake girl. They point at Jaratka, they ... they tell her to come with them. I say no, NO! I get in front of her and try to stop them, I try, I try ... but they have swords." He stooped and pressed his forehead to Karna's foot. "Pleasse, pleasse, you must help her. I beg you. I beg my lords."

Duryodhana urged his horse around Karna's and came up behind the Naga. He leaned down and seized the man's shoulder, wrenching him round.

"Ekalavya. Look at me. Do you mean to say that men from the palace—soldiers—came and took Jaratka? Just now?"

"Yess! Just now! Two men! She say no, she will not go, but they, they laugh and say ..." He closed his eyes as if trying with all his might to recall. "They say: *Lady Perta wants a Snake girl for the party.* Then they grab her, she screams and I scream, but no one helps us. They take her, I do not know where. So I run, I run to find you. Lord Duryo, I beg, I beg ..."

Duryodhana straightened up and looked at Karna. His face was tight with horror.

"They took her for the party. A Snake girl. It's tradition."

Karna swung his leg over the roan's back and jumped down. "Uncle," he said, "we know where she is. We will go to her. Here, you must ride behind me. I'll help you up."

Ekalavya hesitated only for a second. Then he turned to the horse, clutched the saddle, put his foot in Karna's laced hands, and struggled up. Karna remounted in front, swinging his leg forward over the roan's neck. Ekalavya wrapped his arms round Karna's waist as they wheeled about to follow Duryodhana, who had already kicked his horse to a trot, shouting, "We'll go by the river!" They cantered down the short slope, turned left, and in a moment were galloping north, the full moon on the water keeping pace alongside them.

≈

The moonlight barely penetrated the pines and deodars around the forest path that led to the Lacquer House, and they had to slow to a trot, though they were aided by the lanterns stuck in the ground at intervals (another of Shakuna's arrangements). When they came to the edge of the trees and were about to emerge into the clearing,

Duryodhana dug his heels into his horse's flanks, but Karna leaned over, seized the reins, and said, "Wait."

"What are you doing?" said Duryodhana angrily. "Let me go!"

"We don't know if she's in there."

"Of course she's in there! W-where else w-would they take her?"

"No, I mean we don't know if she's there *yet*. Likely she's not. They would have used a chariot, and that means taking the main road, not the river road. It's smoother, but longer."

"We don't know that."

"Yes, we do. No, Duryo, listen. If they'd been on the river road, we would have overtaken them. They had a ten-minute start on us at most."

Duryodhana turned to Ekalavya. "As soon as they took Jaratka, you ran to us?"

"Yess, yess." He nodded hard, still clasping Karna's waist. "The men come, they take her, and I run to find you. I know you are the only ones can help."

The prince readdressed Karna. "You're right; they're still on the way. So we'll go in and wait. We'll say we changed our minds, decided to come to the p-party after all." He thrust his chin at Ekalavya. "He'll have to stay here. When they show up with her ..."

They looked across the clearing. From the house came a buzz of revelry and snatches of music. Torchlight made a narrow saffron rectangle of the doorway; a rosy glow emanated from the skylights into the darkness above. Men spilled out and around the building, standing or squatting in small groups, hoisting clay tankards of beer that they refilled from barrels on the veranda. Over to the right, a line of horses stood at makeshift hitching posts driven into the soil. Grooms and horse-boys, chatting, dicing, or snoozing, leaned or lay on the beds of the wagons, carts, and chariots drawn up nearby.

Presently a young brahmin stumbled out the door and down the steps, staggered over to a pine sapling, hitched up his robe, and urinated; when he was finished, he staggered back and tried to mount to the porch, but tripped, fell backward, and lay there motionless, his robe still hiked around his waist. The group of men seated on the steps threw him uncurious glances and returned to their drinks.

"I guess we'll just have to p-play it by ear," said Duryodhana.

"Come on, Uncle, let's get you down," said Karna, dismounting and helping Ekalavya to do the same. The Naga did not seem to like the idea of staying back, but he obeyed Duryodhana's curt instruction to "wait here; don't let anyone see you." He retreated into the shadows and watched the pair as they led their horses across the clearing.

They tied the roan and the black to the one free hitching post, left their bows and quivers hanging from the saddles, and proceeded to the house. Navigating around the passed-out brahmin, they walked up the steps and pushed their way through a group of men massed at the entryway. In that group was Drona, the chief weapons master; he made way for them with a look of mild surprise, but did not greet them.

The main room was packed and loud. Though the crowd was mostly male, there were also perhaps a dozen women whose bronze hoop earrings marked them as prostitutes. The guests milled about, hovered near beer barrels and food tables, or lounged on floor cushions. In the back corner where the broken swing had formerly hung was a low dais where two flutists and two drummers played a rollicking tune. In the other back corner, a dice game was underway. The round platform in the center made a stage for three dancing girls; they were bare-breasted, and below wore only short skirts with fringe that shimmered as they undulated. A gaggle of men ringed the stage, hooting and cheering. One of them was Karna's father, Adiratu.

The room was lit mainly by the moon-glow coming through the skylights, but there were also torches in stands and oil lamps on tables casting pools of light around the space and onto the red-lacquered walls. Most of the guests were taking no notice of the etchings—with a couple of exceptions. Over by the left wall, some men and girls were trying to recreate the scene with the women perched on the dancers' erections; since the men were very drunk, however, the most they could do was hoist the girls up on their loins, prance around for a few beats, and collapse to the ground with roars of laughter. Halfway down the right wall, High Priest Vyasa, his arm around a lanky whore, was gesturing at a depiction of a woman and horse copulating. He took hold of the whore and began moving her long limbs this way and that, fitting his groin to hers and adopting various positions, all the while keeping his eyes on the horse-and-woman etching. He seemed to be trying to work out how such a feat might be possible.

The four archways along that wall now had curtains hung

across. Guarding the rearmost curtain were two frowning kshatriya, burly arms folded on their burly chests. They bore no weapons— Shakuna having decreed that, for this occasion, everything except eating-knives be left at home—but looked capable of beating any would-be intruder to a pulp.

"That room at the back," whispered Duryodhana. "The Pandavas are in there."

Standing at the first archway was the host himself, Shakuna, resplendent in a blue-green dhoti and a plum-colored cloak sewn at the shoulders with peacock feathers. He was pulling back the curtain shouting, "Come on, Counselor! Don't take all night, people are waiting." He stood there, popping his head in and out of the side chamber, saying, "Come along, come along," until at length there emerged Counselor Vidura, his pale face beaded with sweat, retying his brown dhoti with deliberate care. Shakuna clapped him on the shoulder. "What was that, three times? She certainly liked you, my man! Well done!" Vidura looked embarrassed and walked off with head down, still arranging his waistband.

Shakuna turned to the crowd, cupped his mouth, and called above the music and chatter: "Rahul! It's your turn! Hey, you there— go find Sir Rahul and tell him …"

Suddenly he caught sight of Duryodhana and Karna in the entryway. His mouth dropped open; his brow furrowed; he seemed at a loss. But the next instant he recovered himself and came toward them, smiling with arms outstretched.

"Why, if it isn't Prince Duryo and the splendid Sir Karna! What a surprise! I thought you two weren't coming!"

He leaned in to embrace Duryodhana and whispered, "What are you doing here?"

Duryodhana gripped him by the shoulders, pushed him back, and cried: "Good evening, Uncle Shakuna! What a p-p-party this is!"

Karna bowed. "Yes, you've outdone yourself, Prince. Allow me to congratulate you."

Shakuna gave Karna a curt nod and readdressed his nephew with a look of concern. "Duryo? I thought you weren't feeling well."

"Oh, I'm m-m-much better. Much better. I decided I just couldn't m-miss it."

"I'm so glad. But this crowd, the smoke … it's not good for your head. Come, let's step outside, get some fresh air." Shakuna spun them around, placed his palms on their backs, and ushered them out the door. "Make way, there! Prince Duryodhana needs air."

He herded them onto the veranda and over to a beer barrel, where he filled two tankards for them and said loudly, "Let's get you away from this crowd where you can breathe." He led them down the steps, across the clearing, past the horses and carts, and into the shadow of a big deodar at the edge of the trees.

"What is going on?" he said, taking their tankards from them and placing them on the ground amidst the tree roots. "You were supposed to stay home, both of you."

"We have a p-p-p-p ..." Duryodhana took a deep breath. "A *problem.*"

"What problem? Everything's going fine, fine." Shakuna rubbed his hands. "Yudi and his brothers are in the back room with three high-caste whores. Ani's there, too, hiding under the bed. When the boys have finished and rejoined the party, the whores will mess her up a bit—black her eye, rip her clothes, nothing too drastic. Near dawn, things are winding down, she'll make her exit. There are windows in the side rooms; all she has to do is climb out, and I'll make sure there's no one to see. I've got a boy waiting to take her back to town, and after that, she knows what to do. She won't come to any harm. You have to trust me."

"*No!* I'm not talking ab-b-b-b ... a-b-b-out *her!*"

"You're not? What, then?"

"It's ... it's ... *listen*, it's ..." Duryodhana's mouth stretched in a helpless grimace.

Karna said, "My lord. Lady Perta had her men go into town and take the Naga girl, Jaratka. It seems she wanted a Snake for the party—a present for her sons. The girl's father came to us for help. The men will be arriving with her any minute now."

Shakuna looked at Karna as if waiting for him to go on. "And?" he said.

"And ... well ..." Karna looked at Duryodhana.

"*And they're going to rape her!*" said Duryodhana.

Shakuna scratched his beard. "I'm not sure what you're getting at. That Snake—the one who had his thumb cut off by Drona—you're talking about his daughter?"

"Yes!" said Duryodhana. He seemed relieved that his uncle was finally grasping the point. "Ekalavya. His daughter is Jaratka."

"And she's coming to the party?"

"Not *coming* to the party. *Abducted*. W-w-w-we have to *do* something!"

Shakuna paused. His eyes narrowed.

"All right, Duryo. If I understand you—which I'm still not sure I do—you are upset because your Aunt Perta arranged to have a Snake girl sent to the party. Now, I confess I'm disappointed in Perta, since I specifically told her I would take care of everything; on the other hand, I can't fault her for wanting to do something nice, something traditional, for her sons. I guess you know this girl's father, and I guess you feel beholden to him since that incident with Drona. And I agree, Drona behaved badly; it's to your credit that you've been helping the man. But let's be clear ..."

A rumble of chariot wheels resounded deep in the forest. All three looked over to the gap in the trees where the path emerged. A spasm of anguish crossed Duryodhana's face.

Shakuna resumed: "Let's be clear: They're Snakes. Outcastes. Not Arya; not Pure. I doubt this man will even care if his daughter is deflowered. Why should he? Either way, you'll go on helping him, won't you?"

"*Of course he'll care!* AND *SHE* WILL CARE, AND *I* WILL CARE!"

Heads on the veranda turned in their direction.

"For Gods' sake, lower your voice," Shakuna hissed. "Now, Nephew, you listen to me. I don't know what's got into your head about this girl, but you need to remember something: This whole plan is for *you*. It's about getting rid of the Pandavas and making *you* crown prince. If it succeeds, you'll be king. If it fails, we're all done for—you, me, your mother, your father, your brother, and your faithful dog Karna, here."

The rumble of wheels was getting louder.

"The plan is working. I will make sure it works. But hear me, Duryodhana ..." He leaned in close to his nephew's face. "*Don't fuck it up for some stupid Snake girl.*"

With a swish of his feathered cloak, he marched off back to the house, pausing to jest with the men on the steps before proceeding up and through the doorway. As he disappeared within, a two-horse chariot burst from the trees and circled the clearing, wheels jouncing and skidding on the dry, stony soil. In the vehicle stood two kshatriya: one held the reins while the other stood behind, hands on the shoulders of a slender figure. They halted on the opposite side of the clearing and disembarked. The second kshatriya waited, gripping the slender figure's arm, while the driver tied up the horses to a branch. Then all three headed for the house.

Duryodhana said to Karna: "Come on. Bring your b-beer. Follow my lead." They picked up their tankards and moved out of the shadows.

Striding quickly, both parties nearly collided at the steps. Some of Duryodhana's beer spilled on his black leather vest, and he cried out, "Damn it, w-watch where you're going!"

The driver, recognizing the prince, fell back. "Prince Duryodhana! I beg your pardon, my lord." He bowed low. The other man, also bowing, pulled Jaratka roughly aside.

Karna, glaring at the two, used his cloak to dab at his master's vest.

"Leave it, Karna, leave it," said Duryodhana, brushing him off. "Never mind, lads! No harm done. Glad you could m-make the party. Ishana, isn't it? And you are …?"

"Mohanu, sir," said the second kshatriya, bowing again.

Jaratka stood as if she were made of stone. Her eyes were wide, terrified.

"Mohanu, yes, of course. And what have we here?" Duryodhana jerked his thumb and grinned. "B-brought your girlfriend, did you?"

The men seemed set at ease by his genial manner. "It's a Snake girl, my lord," said Mohanu, pulling her forward with an air of pride. "Sent by Lady Perta for the Pandavas."

"A Snake girl! Did you hear that, Karna? Now the p-party's really getting started!" He clapped his hand on Karna's shoulder. Karna attempted a jolly leer.

"Say, lads …" The prince adopted a confidential tone and motioned for the two men to come closer. "I don't suppose I could sample the goods first? I happen to know the Pandavas are occup-p-p … *occupied* at the moment, with some v-very talented ladies; be a shame to interrupt them right now. What do you say? You could just slip her into one of the side rooms for me."

The men looked doubtful. "Well, my lord," said Ishana, "I don't rightly know. Lady Perta said specifically it was for her sons. As a gift. I wouldn't … I mean …"

"Of course, of course. It was just a thought. Wouldn't want to get you b-boys in trouble, now, would we?"

"No, my lord. I'm sorry, my lord."

"No, no, it's my fault. I shouldn't have asked. Well—let's deliver the gift, shall we?"

He took Jaratka's right arm and began to escort her up the steps, Mohanu on her left side, the others following. As they squeezed through the crowd by the doorway, he put his head next to hers and whispered, "Trust me."

He led them along the right-hand wall through the milling, dancing, lounging, cavorting guests—Vyasa seemed to have given up on the horse mechanics and was now putting the whore through her paces in a rather ordinary position atop a heap of cushions on the floor between the second and third archways—to the backmost curtain, where stood the two burly guardsmen. "Delivery for the P-Pandava boys!" he cried. "One Snake girl, gift from Lady Perta."

The guardsmen scowled down at him.

Upon receiving no response, the prince scowled back. "Hello? I'll say it more slowly. Here is a *gift* from Lady *Perta* for her *sons*, the *Pandavas*. Step aside and let us enter."

The bigger guard swept his eyes over the five of them. "I'll take her in, sir," he said.

"Fine," said Duryodhana. "Get on with it." He released Jaratka's arm ... but then, as if with a sudden thought, pulled her round to face him and shoved her back against the wall. "Wait a minute. She's a bit dirty. Karna—got a rag?"

Karna quickly dug in his leather satchel and pulled out a cloth.

"Good. Clean off her face." Karna came forward, wet the cloth with his tongue, and began to wipe Jaratka's cheeks and forehead. While he was doing so, Duryodhana leaned in close again and whispered: "Let them take you in. I'm going outside and around to the w-window. Be ready to jump when I call."

Jaratka had been staring past them into the crowd, her face a frozen blank; now her eyes shifted to meet Duryodhana's, and her chin dipped in an almost imperceptible nod.

"All right, she'll do." Duryodhana presented her again at the archway. "Remember, compliments of Lady Perta." The big guardsman seized her arm and took her inside.

"Come on," said Duryodhana to Karna, and they headed back

down the long room. But as they passed the stage with the dancing girls, Karna's father spied them, waved, and called out: "My shun! Shir Karna! Hello, my shun!" He reeled toward them. "Karna! Sho good, sho good to shee you ad … *hic* … adda pardy!"

Karna made a hasty namaste, said, "Hello, Father," and tried to move on, but Adiratu flung his arms about his neck, saying, "My shun! Sho proud! Sho very, very, very *proud*."

Karna said, "Father, excuse me, I must go," and tried to disentangle himself. Adiratu hung on, repeating, "Sho *proud*," and Karna, struggling to get free, lurched backward into a table bearing a tray of sweetmeats and an oil lamp.

The table tipped. The lamp fell sideways onto the heap of cushions where, a minute ago, Vyasa and the lanky whore had lain. The oil spilled over a cushion that was pressed against the wall. The lamp's wick touched the oil-soaked fabric. A small tongue of flame leaped up, licking at the red lacquer.

Adiratu had also stumbled backward and in doing so had knocked into a fat elderly brahmin lumbering toward the food table. The brahmin shouted, "You clod!" and gave Adiratu a box on the ear, causing Karna to jump forward, grab the brahmin's wrist, and wrench it behind his back with a snarl. A small scuffle ensued, drawing a few other guests over to watch. Duryodhana was tugging at Karna's elbow, saying, "Leave it! Come *on*." Adiratu was weaving to and fro, shouting, "You show 'im, Karna! No butt-faced brahmin is gonna inshult *my* shun!" The observers began chanting, "Fight, fight, fight!" as more people gathered round, hooting and clapping, eager for a brawl.

A sheet of fire rose up the wall between the archways.

The *whoosh* was not audible over the party noise, but the sudden blaze of light caught everyone's attention. There were cries of "Whoa!" "What the …?" "Gods!" as the flames traveled left and right over the top of the arches, down the other sides, and up and over again, spreading outward faster than the eye could follow. As the watchers stood open-mouthed, the entire wall caught fire. An instant later all four curtains did, too.

As thick black smoke began to billow, a few people screamed. Someone yelled, "Out! Everyone out!" There was a general rush for the exit. Duryodhana still had Karna by the elbow; he pushed his friend in the other direction, shouting, "That way! Go back!" The two men forced their way upstream, buffeted by the stampeding crowd. It took them a minute to beat their way to the rear archway, which was now blocked by a curtain of flame.

The Pandavas' guards were no longer there—perhaps they had fled—but someone was there: Vidura, the chief counselor. He was struggling with a stone water jar, trying in vain to drag it from its corner. "It's no use! Here!" Karna cried. He grabbed a bronze torch-stand, yanked out the torch, doused the torch in the water jar, and began using the base of the stand to jab at the curtain, pulling down flaming bits of cloth to clear the doorway. Vidura and Duryodhana stamped on the charred scraps as they fell to the floor. By now the fire had engulfed all four walls, the black-and-red etchings dancing like hell fiends in the orange and yellow light. The smoke and fumes were making it harder to see, but once the curtain was mostly down, the three men were able to dash through the opening.

The side chamber was seven paces wide by ten deep. A bed on the left wall, piled high with pillows and sheepskins, was the only furniture and took up a good third of the space. Here there was no lacquer; instead, draperies of red silk covered the walls. Opposite the doorway was a window, set chest-high, which at the moment was flanked by the big guardsman and Bimasena; they were help-ing Arjuna to climb out. Standing to one side with cloaks wrapped around their noses and mouths were the other Pandavas; once Arjuna had jumped, Bima and the guard began to help them out in turn. The high-caste whores were kneeling huddled together on the bed, half-naked and shrieking. Jaratka was nowhere to be seen.

Duryodhana made a quick tour of the chamber, pulling aside the silk drapes, coughing into the crook of his arm as smoke and heat poured in from the main room, now an inferno. Saku was lifted onto the windowsill; as he jumped, Duryodhana rushed over and leaned out after him, scanning the ground below. Bima and the guard made to lift him up, too, but he shook them off and ran back to Karna and Vidura, who were dragging the women off the bed.

"She's out there, I saw her! She must have been the first out!" he said to Karna.

"Good!" Karna cried. "Help us with these three, then we'll go." Each of them took hold of a whore and half-carried her, still shriek-ing, to the window. Bima and the guardsman helped bundle the women out. Counselor Vidura was next. Then Duryodhana.

Bima seized Karna's bicep. "Up you go," he said.

But Karna stopped, hands braced on the window frame, and said, "Wait." He turned back to the chamber, squinting through the thickening fumes. He said, "Go. You both go. I'll follow."

Bima said, "Karna, don't be stupid! Come on!"

Karna said, "No. Go. I'm right behind you."

"It's your funeral," said Bima. He climbed to the window and jumped. The guardsman followed.

Karna, coughing hard, went to the bed, dropped onto his stomach, and looked beneath it.

Under the bed was a girl, also lying prone, her face turned toward Karna. Her eyes were squeezed shut, her veil covering her nose and mouth.

"Ani," said Karna. She opened her eyes.

Karna reached under the bed, grabbed her hand, and dragged her out. He picked her up, carried her to the window, set her on the sill, and said, "Jump!" She jumped. He climbed up, stuck his legs out, and jumped after her.

As his feet hit the ground, the skylights exploded. Great blooms of fire rose from the roof of the Lacquer House. All around the clearing, people ducked and covered their heads as shards of pink glass cascaded down like rain.

Straightening up, Karna saw dozens of people running helter-skelter or kneeling on the earth, coughing and gagging. Some were already at the line of hitching posts, yelling at horse-boys and fumbling with bridles as panicky steeds reared and whinnied. Others were stumbling, dazed, toward the path that led back through the forest. One man's cloak was on fire; he ran, howling, until another man tackled him and rolled him over and over in the dirt, beating at the flames with his hands. From the burning house came terrible screams.

There was all the confusion Shakuna could have wished for, and no one paid Karna any mind as he grabbed Ani's hand again and pulled her over to his master, who was standing with the Snake girl at the edge of the trees.

"Here's our rape victim," Karna said.

Duryodhana and Jaratka had their arms wrapped tightly around each other, her dark head pressed to his shoulder, his scarred cheek wet with tears. They did not reply.

❖ ❖ ❖

I know, Sire. Horrifying. The bards call it the worst house fire in a hundred years.

The casualties? Well, of the one hundred and twenty people who had been at the party—guests, harlots, musicians, dancers, manservants—about half were either outside or in a side chamber and able to jump out a window. Of the sixty in the main room, half escaped in time. The other thirty faced a pile-up at the doorway and were trapped by the fire and smoke. Lacquer being so flammable, an enormous blaze was the work of minutes.

Shakuna made it out. So did High Priest Vyasa and his lanky whore. Drona, as I've said, was already outside, as was Dushasana. The reasonably sober guests had better luck than the stumbling-drunk ones; the young better luck than the old; brahmins and kshatriya better luck than vaishya. So hot had been the fire and so total the destruction that, when the outcaste charnel-men came to clean up the site, the blackened bodies were unrecognizable. But some were identified by their jewelry: the slim bronze neck-chain of Adiratu was returned to his son, Sir Karna, of whom he had been so proud.

In the midst of the chaos, Duryodhana and Karna had simply mounted their horses, pulled Jaratka and Ani up behind them, and ridden off down the forest path. Neither of the men remembered Ekalavya or thought to look for him, and of course Jaratka did not know her father was there. Later, his ash-covered body was found on the ground near the veranda steps, a pink glass roof tile nearby. He must have run toward the house when he saw the flames. When the skylights burst, one of the few unshattered tiles struck him on the head.

But the four young people were unaware of this as they cantered along the river to Hastinapura. The majority of the survivors took the main road, and those who took the river road were mostly walkers whom they easily outpaced. When they arrived back at the palace, Karna offered to take Ani home; she insisted, however, on following through on her agreement. "We made a bargain with Prince Shakuna," she said. "If I do not keep it, my family will starve." Black from smoke, scraped and bruised from being dragged across the floor, and bleeding from the shower of glass, she already looked as if she'd been well abused, and after Jaratka helped her make some strategic rips in her clothes they all agreed she made a credible victim of gang rape. As the moon sank below the horizon she staggered into town, wailing for all she was worth.

Her appearance made a sensation. Her mother played it up, pounding on neighbors' doors, shrieking, "Oh! My daughter! Rape! My poor, sweet girl! Raped by those monsters! Help her! Help my daughter!" In a matter of minutes half the town was awake and in the streets, buzzing with the news. Several householders from the shudra section added weight to the story by stating that, indeed, a chariot had rolled by shortly before midnight, they had heard it, in fact they had happened to be awake at the time and had seen it, it was a chariot with two evil-faced kshatriya ... no, *two* chariots with *four* kshatriya ... no, a whole *train* of chariots and kshatriya. What? Did you hear that? The cowards! Sending all those men to abduct a poor, defenseless girl. A respectable girl, we all knew her father, a fine man he was, and her mother, that poor widow, what a good woman she is, doing her best for her family, they're only just scraping by, and now this happens—terrible! Those Pandava princes think they can get away with raping a poor, defenseless, fatherless girl, do they? We'll see about that! The Law doesn't constrain just us; it's for the palace folk, too. We'll go to the king. And the queen. Yes, the queen—Sati, the Good Wife—she'll see justice done. Justice, justice for Ani!

By dawn there was an angry mob outside the compound gate, yelling to be let in.

Meanwhile, king and queen had been awakened and were in the great hall being briefed on the fire by Shakuna and Duryodhana. Ladies and maidservants stood about, twittering their shock. Bhishma was on the dais, too, listening to the report with a grim face. Lady Perta showed up and became hysterical; only after Shakuna assured her that he had seen all five of her boys safe, that Vidura was with them, and that they would surely arrive at any moment did she calm down and allow her women to lead her to a stool in a corner, wrap her in shawls, and bring her a hot drink. Gandhari wondered aloud how the fire had started, but no one could give her an answer. Tarashtra asked if there was danger of the whole forest burning, dry as it was, but Shakuna said he thought not, given there was the river to the east of the house and creeks to the north and south, which would form a barrier. (And as it turned out, thanks to the lack of breeze that night, the fire did not spread beyond the house.)

The old queen, Satyavati, came to the hall having heard the news. She was flanked and supported by two of her ladies, her weight now almost too much for her to carry alone. Behind them came a couple of manservants bearing a settee, which they placed to one side of the dais. She collapsed onto it, wheezing, and allowed her women to arrange the pillows so she could recline and watch in comfort. When they told her the Lacquer House was no more, she closed her eyes but showed no other reaction.

A little later the Pandavas finally did arrive, disheveled but obviously unharmed. Their mother rushed to them and threw her arms around each in turn—with an extra-hard embrace for Arjuna and another for Counselor Vidura—crying that never, never again would she let them out of her sight. Everyone heard about Bimasena and how he had bravely led the escape for his brothers. Everyone wondered again how the fire could have started.

All this to-do, however, was as nothing compared to the furor that overtook the hall when the king, upon hearing there was a crowd outside the gate shouting about rape and justice, gave the order that they should be admitted.

Three days later a tribunal was held, with King Tarashtra presiding and Prince Shakuna as chief prosecutor. The girl Ani was the principal witness, and a very convincing one. The details she gave of the rape—each brother taking his turn, she said, while the others held her down and laughed—were gruesome; her gratitude toward her saviors, Prince Duryodhana and Sir Karna, was touching. Her mother and some townspeople testified in support of her story. The big guardsman, testifying for the defense, said that he had brought in a Snake girl, a gift from Lady Perta, but had seen no other girl in the room; under cross-examination, however, he confessed that he had seen other women in the room and had assumed they were whores, but could not swear they were *all* whores. Vidura also spoke on behalf of the Pandavas but had to admit that he had been occupied "for at least an hour, wasn't it," said Shakuna, "in one of the side chambers, so you haven't any idea what the Pandavas were doing then, have you?"

By Law, none of the accused was permitted to speak.

King Tarashtra's face was grave, almost sad, as he rendered his judgment. "I wish I could pass off this unfortunate incident as a boyish prank, or a case of young men's over-exuberance on the eve of a wedding. Perhaps no one would blame me if I showed leniency to five beloved nephews," (he shook his head and sighed heavily) "but I would blame myself. The Law is the Law, for princes as for commoners, and it is a king's duty—his particular duty—to display no bias when it comes to higher castes versus lower, or palace folk versus townsfolk. We are all Kuru, are we not? Moreover, the rape of a virgin is nothing less than an atrocity. Therefore ..." He rose from his throne, and Gandhari rose, too.

"Therefore: I decree that the Pandavas be banished from Hastinapura for a period of two years. Furthermore, I decree that any decisions as to the succession be postponed until their return; this includes the question of Prince Yudi's marriage. And finally, I decree that during their banishment, my eldest son, Duryodhana, be styled Crown Prince of the Kuru."

Two weeks later the Pandavas departed, heading, on Lord Bhishma's advice, to the court of Vrishni where their uncle Vasudeva was king. Perta professed to be elated at the prospect of seeing her royal brother again. They gathered in the palace yard on a fine spring morning, the first day of the new year: a small train consisting of the Pandavas on their horses, a dozen armed kshatriya, some twenty man- and maidservants, and a pack elephant with its mahout.

There was also a covered cart carrying Perta and her ladies. Just before the call to move out, Perta left the cart and approached the king and queen, who were standing in the main doorway to bid fare-well. She took Gandhari's hand, leaned in close, and said:

"You heinous bitch. I'll repay you for this—you and your monster son."

The veiled countenance turned and stared, but this time Perta showed no fear. She merely smiled, dropped a curtsey, walked back to the cart, and climbed in. Soon the procession was wending its way out the gate.

PART TWO

THE BRIDEGROOM CHOICE

Chapter 6

KRISHNA

2 0 — 1 9   Y E A R S   B E F O R E   T H E   W A R

Krishna said:
   I was overjoyed when my cousins the Pandavas showed up at the court of Vrishni. *Krishna Vasudeva,* I said to myself as I sat beside my father watching them make their bows and present their host gifts—*Krishna Vasudeva, at last you're going to have some nice friends.*

I observed each of the new arrivals with intense interest. First my Aunt Perta, who I'd always heard was a great beauty. She certainly had an excellent figure, accentuated by a richly embroidered scarlet sari, but I was disappointed with her face: too sharp for my taste. My father descended from the dais to greet her with the honor due his sister and a former queen of the Kuru. He had had a third throne placed on his left, matching mine on his right; he took her hand to lead her to it, begging that from now on she look upon the Vrishni as her own clan and people. Her words in reply were charming, as was her smile, and her movements were elegant as she ascended the steps and seated herself upon the throne. I reminded myself that grace and refinement are, after all, what count.

Prince Yudishtira was next. He hadn't been given a throne, but my father did stand and bow to him, showing respect for his status as crown-prince-in-exile. He, too, was richly dressed; I had never seen a dye of such deep crimson, and his cloak was adorned with gold thread. (I was glad I had put on my best cloak to receive them; no embroidery, but it was a decent blue with a fur lining.) Even more impressive, though, was his poise. He delivered a speech thanking my father for his hospitality, expounding upon the long friendship between Kuru and Vrishni, conveying Lord Bhishma's special compliments—my grandfather and the famous regent had been close, apparently—and expressing many other worthy sentiments. He was so eloquent, so genteel. And his diction was smooth and clear, with no trace of a country accent: not a single broad *a*, nasal *e*, or buzzing *v*. Having endured for the past two years the hideous drawl of all the supposedly high-caste people around here, I found his voice incredibly refreshing. He ended by insisting, with a self-deprecating smile, that we all call him "Yudi." Charming!

Prince Bimasena, now; when he lumbered forward with his thighs like tree-trunks, his chest like a beer barrel, his head almost scraping the ceiling, I hardly knew what to think. Was he a lout? The embarrassment of the family? But when he began to speak, I knew I had misjudged him. Though he was a bit loud, his accent was good and his manner, though forthright, in no way loutish. And his sense of humor was evident from the start: he made a quip about how we were not to worry if there was no bed large enough to accommodate him, for he was quite happy sleeping in one of the barns and would do his best not to terrify the horses. We all laughed. My father assured him that the palace carpenters (we have just one palace carpenter, but never mind) were already hard at work building a "Bima-sized bed," and we all laughed again.

Naku and Saku, the twins, were presented together. Naku—oh, my! His stunning beauty more than made up for his mother's lack. Although, I recalled, Lady Perta isn't his real mother. That famous princess of Madrasa, the one who was said to resemble the Goddess of Love, she was his mother. So that made sense. I noted his delicate yet manly features, his skin like oiled deodarwood, and especially his gorgeous wavy hair that fell to the small of his back. I contemplated, briefly, growing my hair out like that; but then I thought, being so tall, I might look a bit freakish with long hair and dropped the idea. Naku smiled and chatted in a most pleasant fashion, expressing his delight with everything and everyone he had seen thus far in Vrishni. As for Saku—his real name is Sahadeva, but they're Naku and Saku—he was clearly the quiet one. He allowed his gregarious twin to make most of the remarks, but what he did say was exceedingly articulate and demonstrated that he had already taken the trouble to learn much about our country and clan.

Then Arjuna stepped forward. And it was all over for me.

He was neither as poised as Yudi nor as witty as Bima nor as informed as Saku. He was certainly not as handsome as Naku. But he had a quality about him; I'm not sure how to describe it. It was as if ... as if he were more alive than the others, indeed, more alive than anyone I'd ever met. His pale skin and dark hair glowed as if reflecting torchlight, though it was daytime and the torches in the hall unlit. His white dhoti and silver-threaded vest sparkled like snow on the mountains. When he looked at me, I felt as one sometimes does before a thunderstorm: there's that tingling in the air, that sense that invisible celestials are flying by singing in high, lovely tones, and it makes the back of one's neck shiver. Years later, the story went about that he was a partial incarnation of the God Indra (and I of the God Vishnu! which I did find amusing). Not being a priest, I of course can't say whether the story is true. What I can say is this: When I first set eyes on Arjuna, I might have been struck by lightning.

≈

Vrishni is an unbelievably backward place. I know because when I was ten, my Uncle Kansa, king of the faraway land of Mundra, sent a messenger to my father asking if he'd be willing to send his younger son (me) to be fostered there. My uncle had had terrible luck with children: his four wives had produced nothing but girls, and now that he was getting on in years, he was afraid he'd be left without a son to succeed him. When my father summoned me to tell me the news, I think he assumed I'd be afraid or at least reluctant to go. But I needed no urging.

Up until then I'd spent most of my time in the cowherds' village with my older brother Balarama, both of us sleeping and taking our meals in the house of Balarama's mother, a vaishya woman. My father thought it a healthier life for us than living in the palace: "Plenty of fresh air and exercise," he said, "plus you'll learn animal husbandry from the ground up." Balarama and I had a fine time with the village boys: climbing trees, stick-fighting, holding races on the silt flats by the river, and generally doing everything except herd cows. Yes, a fine time—but I never enjoyed it as Balarama did. Though tall, I was not especially athletic, and often I would slip off to join the girls and sit with them under the fig trees while they braided one another's hair, played jacks, and gossiped. Or I'd be in the house with my stepmother, helping her make her delicious honey cakes fried in butter. I always felt boys were a bit loud and stupid. And the lessons Balarama and I took on the palace training grounds, from a weapons master who spat phlegm and picked his nose, did not lead me to form a better opinion of grown men.

So when my father called me to him and said my Uncle Kansa wanted to foster me at his court and possibly make me his heir, I was intrigued. "Mundra is hundreds of kosa to the southwest," my father said. "It is on the sea."

On the sea! I'd heard of the sea and immediately formed a picture in my mind of what it must be like. When I arrived in Mundra after a three-week journey, I demanded of my escort that they take me straight away, before even greeting my uncle, to view the sea. It was not at all what I'd expected; it was much better. I was enchanted!

And the town itself, and the people—they, too, were beyond anything I could have imagined. To begin with, everything was so clean! In Vrishni we just relieved ourselves in any convenient outdoor spot or into chamber pots whose contents the servants would dump into the yard each morning. In Mundra they had what they called "privies," which were special pits with tunnels underneath that were flushed regularly with earth and water, sweeping the sewage directly out to the harbor. The buildings of the town were made of the usual materials—mud-brick with mud plaster—but they were large, with many windows, and all but the houses of shudra had floors made of wide, smooth stones fitted together: "flagstones" they were called. Many people, not just palace folk, had stools, beds, shutters, rugs, even chairs. And instead of plain roof-holes for the hearth fires, there were, running up the outsides of the houses, hollow pillars of brick with tin cylinders on top: "chimneys" and "chimney pots."

Mundran customs were equally sophisticated. For instance, instead of trading goods in the marketplace—one goat for five sacks of rice, say—they had something called "money." Money was seashells: little black-and-brown spotted ones with a slit on the bottom. In the marketplace or anywhere else, one could trade money for anything one wanted; or, one could take something one had, whether it was cloth or grain or jewelry or chickens, trade it for money, then take *that* money and trade it for something altogether different. People could even exchange their work for money. Senior staffers at the palace were paid in seashells rather than foodstuffs. Really an ingenious system, and one I wish all the Arya would adopt.

I spent six years at Mundra and wanted to stay forever. Everyone, including my Uncle Kansa, was exceptionally kind to me. In later years, there arose a ridiculous story about how it had been foretold I would cause his death and that therefore he'd wanted to kill me and had only invited me for that purpose. Well, let me tell you: for the six years I was under his protection not only did he make no attempt on my life, he also treated me in every way like his own son, and he continued to do so even after one of his wives managed, finally, to produce a boy. I suspect the evil tale was put about by his enemies as a way to turn the population against him—much like the tale put about by the Pandavas' enemies that they'd raped that girl. When it's a question of gaining power, some people will lie like demons.

Alas, when I was sixteen there came a messenger saying that my brother Balarama had died and I needed to come back to Vrishni. I made the return journey with a heavy heart. After the beauty and refinement of Mundra, the drabness of home seemed so unbearable that for a time I considered departing this life. But then I said to myself: *Krishna Vasudeva, chin up; you never know what tomorrow may bring.*

And after two excruciating years, my patience was rewarded. The Pandavas arrived, and things began to look a lot brighter.

≈

I could tell my cousins didn't think much of our palace—which in truth is scarcely worthy of the name, given it sits right next to the town, practically *in* town if I'm honest, with no separating wall and not much other than its size to distinguish it from an ordinary house—nor did they think much of the kshatriya and brahmins of the vicinity, male or female, with their rough manners and low tastes. But the Pandavas were too well-bred to show their disdain. They professed eagerness for the game in our "unspoiled forest" (luckily our local Snake tribe gives us no trouble), and the six of us soon fell into a routine of hunting in the early morning, assisting my father with his councils and audiences at midday, and either more hunting or some training exercises—archery, sword- and spear-fighting, wrestling, or charioteering—in the afternoon. After supper we would engage in discussions of politics, strategy, and Law (about which Yudi and Saku were especially knowledgeable), or else have a bard brought in to entertain us with songs and stories. A few of our Vrishni bards aren't too terrible.

I loved all my new companions, but Arjuna—Arjuna was my joy. Right from the start I became his hunting and training partner. Yudi, as the eldest, might have expected me to pair up with him, but he, with his unerring sense of what was fitting, was more concerned that his talented younger brother have a worthy teacher and guide, and since our chief weapons master (as I've said) was repulsive, it made sense for me to take Arjuna under my wing. When he arrived he was sixteen, I eighteen. His all-around natural ability was beyond question and his skill with bow and arrow already superb; his sword technique, however, lacked polish, and he had not yet had much practice shooting from horseback or chariot, so I determined to bring him along in those areas. In addition to sparring every day on the grounds, we spent hours hunting together in the forest. He was most impressive with birds: he could shoot them down in mid-flight with amazing accuracy. East of town there was a large, flat field where the grass was short, and there we did most of our chariot practice, me at the reins and him standing behind shooting at the targets we'd set up along an oval track.

Oh, what I felt during those chariot rides … The horses would be pounding down the field, manes and tails flying, mouths straining at the bit as I drew them round the turn, and the wheels rattling and the floor of the chariot jouncing so it was all I could do to keep my balance. Yet none of this was the cause of my breathless excitement. It was Arjuna behind me: standing aslant, his calf braced against mine, his elbow brushing my shoulder blade as he drew the bow taut, waiting, waiting … then letting the arrow fly with an explosive "Aah!" The sweet smell of him in my nostrils made me dizzy. He would place his hand on the small of my back as we rounded the next turn, just for a moment, and the heat of that hand went right through my back and into my loins and it was all I could do not to yank the horses to a halt, turn round, and crush his body to mine in an agony of need.

I went on for a year and a half like that, spending much of each day with him but saying nothing about my feelings. Finally, on a late afternoon in the fifth month, driving back from the field where we'd been able to stand only an hour's practice in the torrid pre-monsoon heat, I decided I had to speak.

We drove up to the barn, disembarked, and set about unhitching the team, rubbing them down, and seeing them stabled with water and hay. (The few stable-men we have are clods and not to be trusted with my war horses.) While we were inside we heard drops of water hitting the roof. "Relief at last!" I said, and Arjuna grinned as he wiped his sweaty chest and tossed the towel to a stable-boy. Next we needed to make sure the chariot had been put away properly and to store our weapons, so by the time we came out to the barnyard the rain was well and truly underway, though as yet there was no abatement to the heat.

Arjuna was about to set off across the yard, which was already a maze of puddles, but I pulled him back to the doorway. "Wait a bit," I said. "If you get soaked after all that exercise, you'll catch cold."

He laughed and gave me a friendly punch in the arm. "What an old nursemaid you are! Always fussing about my health."

"Old nursemaid! That's what you call me? Your host, your guru? Crown prince of the Vrishni?" said I, feigning offense.

"Like an old mother hen, clucking away!" He crossed his arms and leaned sideways on the doorframe, still laughing up at me. But then he looked out at the falling rain, and his face grew serious.

"No, you're right, Krishna. I shouldn't tease you like that. You are my host. And my guru. You've taught me more than anyone— more than Yudi or Bima, more even than Drona. And I'm truly grateful; not just for your instruction, but for your friendship. Why, if it hadn't been for you, I don't know how I would have managed … well, I mean, being banished to such a place … such a, um, distant country …" He hesitated, clearly not wanting to insult me again. I found his confusion adorable.

I reached out, laid my hand on his shoulder, and left it there. He did not move. The rain pelted down, splashing in the puddles, cascading from the clay spouts on the roofs of the buildings around the yard, spraying droplets of mud onto our shoes and ankles. The smell of hot dust soaking up water was intoxicating. His torso, neck, and face were glistening with damp. I lifted my hand from his shoulder and held it suspended in the air; then I reached, slowly, to touch his cheek …

With a piercing shriek, my sister Subhadra burst out the back door of the palace and into the barnyard.

I whipped my hand away as Arjuna straightened up. We watched as Subhadra began to jump and dance in the puddles, around and around, squealing. She was, if you can believe it, wearing nothing but a loincloth and chest-band, and the chest-band was rather too narrow to contain her breasts, which I was surprised to see had grown—she was thirteen and a half, so this must have been recent— to womanly size. I glanced at Arjuna; he was staring wide-eyed, mouth agape, as if he'd never before seen such a sight (and I imagine he hadn't). I was just about to dash out into the downpour, grab my sister, and drag her back to her quarters where I would give her the scolding and possibly the beating of her life, when she spied us and came bouncing over.

"Krishnaaaa! Arjunaaaa!" She threw her hands in the air and tilted her face to the sky. "It's *raining*! Isn't it *wonderful*? Rain rain *rain!*"

She pushed past us into the barn and stood laughing in the entryway, shaking the water from her hair. The loincloth and chest-band were made of pale-yellow cotton and, soaked, had turned transparent. She may as well have been naked. Her total lack of shame stunned me; I didn't know where to look or what to do.

"Subhadra! For Gods' sake, cover yourself," I said, fixing my eyes on her forehead. "Arjuna, go get her a towel."

"Arjuna will *not* get me a towel! *Arjuna* is going to come dance in the rain with me!"

I grabbed her arm and gave it a shake. "*Prince* Arjuna. Stop this nonsense, you're much too old for it. Where are your ladies?"

"Ha! That's funny." Her voice was shrill with contempt. "My *ladies*. I don't have *ladies*. I have *one* lady, and she isn't even a lady. She's a servant. Ye Gods, Krishna, you are so full of *poo*." Her hands were on her hips, her breasts thrust out and jiggling as she spoke.

With a *Tcha!* of exasperation I strode off to find a towel, a horse blanket, anything to cover her up. A clutch of stable-men were squatting near the barn's rear door, playing dice; one of them had a shabby cloak round his shoulders and I shouted at him to give it to me. He did, and I rushed back to the front, shaking out the cloak as I went, preparing to throw it around my naked sister.

But the entryway was empty. And looking outside I saw, to my everlasting dismay—Arjuna and Subhadra, dancing in the rain.

≈

My mother, who was the sister of Uncle Kansa, had died giving birth to Subhadra. Parturition was an ordeal for my delicate mamma; six stillbirths had preceded my brother Balarama's arrival, and she did not pull through her ninth lying-in. I had loved her and was sad to lose her. My father, left with a motherless girl-child, hadn't the least idea what to do with it. He gave the squalling infant a pat, handed it to a maidservant, and put the whole thing out of his mind.

Subhadra was a non-factor in my boyhood. When I left for the seacoast she was four, and I barely knew she existed; when I returned, she was ten and still (I thought) just a skinny brat. Over the next few years I saw little of her—typically she took her meals in her rooms, though on feast days she would join my father and me at our table in hall—and from what little I did see, I concluded that she had been brought up, or should I say dragged up, with shocking neglect. She had no manners, no grace, no modesty. Her hair was never combed, her clothes often dirty. Her face, though pretty enough, radiated stupidity. (Not that girls need to be intelligent, but one does appreciate something going on behind the eyes.) Then there were her constant shrieks and giggles, which gave me a headache and, what was worse, usually seemed prompted by some petty cruelty or misfortune: a servant dropping a dish, the clubfooted daughter of the cook being teased by the kitchen boys, a sack of puppies being taken out to drown, her old maidservant stamping on a spider and displaying the mess on the sole of her shoe. Her enjoyment of such things was most distasteful.

After the Pandavas arrived, my father seemed to harbor some hopes of my Aunt Perta taking her in hand: the daughter she never had, motherly instincts, that sort of thing. He had Subhadra join us at supper in their second week. Perta took one look, made a moue of disgust, and never gave the girl another glance.

All in all, you can imagine how I felt when she hooked her claws into Arjuna. Oh, it was planned, you may be sure of that, and the plan well executed. Arjuna, aged seventeen and a half, had had little experience of women; his first and only adventure, he'd told me, had been two years before at Yudi's bachelor party with a trio of whores who, though skilled, were a bit long in the tooth and went about their business with a jaded air. Subhadra's performance in the rain that afternoon would have struck him as fresh, exuberant—not to mention sexy. Afterward she took him to her room to "dry off" and, I suspect, straight to her bed. How she knew what to do with him there I don't know, but I wouldn't put it past her to have practiced in advance with a town boy or two. As I say, she had next to no supervision. And absolutely no shame.

Much as she might have liked to, she did not come between me and Arjuna. He and I continued as friends; indeed, for him there had been no change. For me, though, things were never the same. Although I still loved him, loved him dreadfully, I knew from the moment I saw the two of them frolicking in the downpour that he would never love me.

Ah, well; it had been a vain hope all along. And I suppose I should count myself lucky, for unlike many thwarted lovers, I could still be with my darling every day. I could still teach him and talk with him, ride with him and hunt with him, all without restriction—except, of course, for the one restriction that mattered.

I vowed I would go on doing all I could to help and protect him, him and his brothers. I would be their most stalwart friend, their most trusted advisor. During my time in Mundra I had learned much about statecraft, God-craft, and the military arts; now I could put that knowledge to use in service to the Pandavas. Their exile was drawing to an end: in six months they would return to Hastinapura, and despite the scraps of news that had trickled in from Kuru, via our own scouts or the occasional merchant or bard, it was anyone's guess what kind of welcome they would receive upon their arrival back home. From what we could tell, the blind king and veiled queen were still firmly on the throne, and their son, the scar-faced, stuttering Duryodhana, was still being styled "crown prince." The signs were ominous. So, I decided I would go with them when they went back and help them however I could, whether that meant speaking on their behalf, participating in negotiations, or simply offering moral support.

As it turned out, however, the Pandavas and Kauravas were to meet before the period of exile was over—and not in Hastinapura.

≈

"A bridegroom choice? Are you sure?" asked Saku.

The five brothers and I were seated with my father around the table in his receiving room, which also served as his council chamber. Our high priest, who doubled as chief counselor, was there as well.

"I mean," Saku went on, "it's a fairly archaic custom. The way of the Gandharvas, they used to call it. Not a form of marriage one sees much these days."

"Very true, your highness," said the priest. I averted my eyes as he spat a red glob of betel juice onto the floor. "And a form that, in my humble opinion, should never again be seen. Shocking, is what it is. A maiden, permitted to sit in the arena and watch men competing at archery and swords—even wrestling!—and then, instead of her parents in their wisdom making the choice of a husband for her, *she* makes the choice. Lewd, is what it is. Not only does it encourage lustfulness, but it gives young women, indeed all women, the idea their preferences matter. What comes of that? I will tell you what: disobedience, debauchery, and the destruction of society. Disgraceful, is what it is. Thankfully, here in our country we have put a stop to such barbaric practices. People say the Vrishni are rustics, but in matters of real consequence, in matters touching on the Law, we are more civilized than many of our neighbors. Yes, yes ..." (another red dollop splatted in the dirt) "*much* more civilized."

"Thank you, High Priest," my father said, "for your sagacious words." He put his fingertips to his graying temples and rubbed, briefly. Then he turned to Saku and said, "The messenger was explicit: the Princess Draupadi's bridegroom choice will be held on the first day of the twelfth month—that's two and a half months from today—at the Panchala court, with invitations extended to young men of royal blood from the clans of the Arya."

"We must all go and compete!" cried Naku, sweeping back his long hair and smiling his lovely smile. "Isn't the princess of Panchala supposed to be very beautiful?"

"Yes, very beautiful," I said, smiling back. His enthusiasm, as ever, was contagious. "But hold your horses, Naku. We need to think. There's opportunity here—if we're strategic about it."

"Yes," said Yudi, "we must be careful. We should not all enter the tournament."

"Why not?" asked Naku, looking crestfallen.

"Because," said I, "it will look as though the Pandavas are desperate. We don't want to remind the Panchala king of your somewhat precarious position. With all due respect to his holiness," (I threw the priest a chilly glance) "even in a bridegroom choice, the girl's parents have influence. They can veto her selection if they think it inappropriate. The process is not as free-wheeling as all that."

The priest looked sour and mouthed his betel nut.

I went on: "But it would not look ill, I believe, if two of you were to compete. The question is: Which two?"

"What about you, Krishna?" Arjuna interjected. "It's not just us who should have a chance. You're a young man of royal blood. Will you not participate?"

He was looking particularly well today, and I let my eyes rest on his face—the high cheekbones, the arching brows—for perhaps a moment too long before replying.

"Oh ... I may enter, or I may not. We'll have to see. The main thing right now is to figure out how to work this situation to *your* best advantage. If the Pandavas return from exile having made alliance with Panchala, that changes the whole situation. The balance of power would shift decidedly in your favor."

"It would indeed," said my father, "although the tricky thing with a bridegroom choice is predicting the whims of the girl."

"How do you mean, Sir?" asked Yudi.

"I mean you never know whom she'll choose. It might be the man who wins the most events, but then again, it might not be. I remember one such occasion, many years ago ..." His gaze went to the window. "Great champions came from far, dozens of them, many from wealthy clans. The tournament was held in a majestic arena on the verge of the sea. Each evening when the sun sank down, the sky was like fire on the water. And the competition! You never saw such shooting, jousting, wrestling. The princess might have chosen from those who took the top prizes, or from those who brought the richest gifts. But in the end she chose a prince who had acquitted himself well, but not outstandingly well; a prince from a small and backward land ..." He trailed off, his eyes soft with memory.

He brought his attention back to the table. "Ahem. Yes. My point is, you never know who will strike the girl's fancy. All you can do is put your best foot forward."

"Well then," said I, "I think it makes sense for Yudi and Arjuna to enter. Yudi, you're the eldest. By right you should be married already, but your enemies stripped you of that right; as you know, the king of Madrasa refused to wait for your return and gave his youngest daughter to another. So you should have this opportunity."

Yudi inclined his head, his expression dignified. Bimasena gave his older brother's back a pat with his giant paw.

"And Arjuna …" I twisted around to look at my love. He had gotten up from the table and gone to the mirror that stood in a corner. This mirror, as tall and wide as a man, was one of my father's prized possessions; made of an alloy of two-thirds copper, one-third tin, and with a surface smooth as silk, it produced an image of surpassing clarity. Arjuna was standing before it, pulling an invisible bowstring and aiming an invisible arrow, intent on his reflection. *Silly peacock,* I thought, fondly; but his form, I must say, was perfect.

"And Arjuna," I said again, a little louder, "you are likely to win the most events, or at least to do extremely well. As my father notes, that does not guarantee the princess will choose you. But it gives you a fine chance."

Arjuna turned away from the mirror and regarded us, his head high. "Thank you, Krishna," he said. He bowed to my father. "And you, Sir. I will strive to be worthy of your confidence."

"Very well, that's settled," I said. "I'll send the messenger back with our reply."

We all got up—the priest taking time to eject one last gob of spit—and filed out of the room. Most of us took a right turn to go in the direction of the great hall and thence about our business; Arjuna, however, took a left turn toward the women's quarters. As he walked away, I heard a high-pitched giggle down the corridor.

Krishna Vasudeva, I said to myself, *you're a clever man.*

Krishna confessed to me his hope that Arjuna would catch the eye of the Panchala princess, be chosen as her husband, and as a result forget all about Subhadra. As you know, Sire, it did not work out that way. Although Subhadra was never to be his senior wife, Arjuna married her before he returned home and stuck by her through everything that happened in the years to come. He seemed to find her amusing. Certainly her passion for him never waned, as was evident when she took part in his burning-jackal show (you'll recall she held the torch).

King Vasudeva raised no objections to the match; indeed, when Arjuna came to ask for his daughter's hand, he barely waited for the question to be out of the young man's mouth before leaping to embrace him. Vasudeva may have been a neglectful father, but he was no fool: he knew his situation, knew his daughter, and knew a gift from the Gods when he saw it. The wonder is that in the five months Subhadra had been carrying on with Arjuna before he left for the bridegroom choice, she had not become pregnant. Perhaps her maidservant-ayah helped her manage the situation.

Krishna always blamed his sister for weakening Arjuna's character. He never understood that Arjuna was already weak—like a beautifully shaped and painted bowl that in the kiln has acquired an internal crack, a crack that will someday cause it to fall apart. To be fair, such a crack remains invisible until the moment of shattering. So how could Krishna have perceived it? He knew Arjuna was vain, but vanity isn't much of a fault in one so talented. I have been dismissive of Arjuna's feats, but the truth is, he was a warrior who in his prime outshone nearly all others of his day; perhaps only Karna was ever his equal. So if he was a bit pleased with himself, well, many would argue he had a right to be.

His real flaw, however, was buried far deeper and was at stark odds with his public image. When it emerged, Krishna (I think) simply couldn't believe it had been there all along. He needed someone to blame for it—someone whose acid-like stupidity and cruelty he could imagine had eaten away at the strong spirit of his beloved, making that spirit crumble when the crucial test arrived.

Poor Subhadra. I've often wondered what it was like for her, the motherless, friendless girl-child, ignored by her father and big brother, left to be cared for by a cackling old woman whose idea of fun was stepping on insects. When the Pandavas arrived, she must have seen a glimmer of hope. Who can blame her for that? And I admit it makes me laugh, just a little, when I think of her donning that skimpy loincloth and chest-band each afternoon as the monsoons approached, waiting and watching for Krishna and Arjuna to return from chariot practice, praying to Indra to send the rain, send the rain, send the rain *now*. She hadn't much to work with. But what she had, she used well.

And now, Nephew, we must see what was going on back at Hastinapura during the Pandavas' banishment. Once again, it is the night of the Lacquer House fire. We are in the rooms of Old Queen Satyavati.

Chapter 7

SATYAVATI

Well, Mother," said Bhishma, raising his cup, "whether it's this week or next week, it's somewhere around this time, and seventy-seven is an impressive age. So: Happy birthday. Gods grant you many more years of this life." He tipped a few drops of beer onto the floor, extending his arm away from the leather stool on which he sat. Then he raised the cup to his lips.

The old queen, reclining on her settee, gestured to the yawning maidservant to refill her cup and reciprocated her stepson's gesture. The beer drops glistened in the moonlight before melting into the hard-packed dirt.

"Thank you, my dear. Seventy-seven! Seems I'm going on forever. You know what the townsfolk are saying about me, it's too funny … Sisi! Here, put the cup on the table and hand me that plate of rice balls; goodness, must I knock you on the head every time I need something? There, child, you can go back to bed, I won't need you anymore tonight; go on, I know it's late, off you go … Now, Bhishma, you'll appreciate this: They're saying I was born of a fish and am a partial incarnation of the Goddess Kali." She glanced up at the ceiling. "Heh. Kali! I've always loved her, her and her garland of skulls, so it does tickle me."

"With the Gods, you never know," said Bhishma. He left the stool and got down on the rug, stretching out his legs in their indigo dhoti and easing the bronze-studded belt around a waist that, though still muscled, had in recent years acquired a slight paunch. "Perhaps it's true."

"Heh. Perhaps it is. She's Goddess of the Night—among a lot of other things—and it's certainly true that I can't sleep at night anymore. I hardly ever put my head down until near dawn. It's kind of you to keep me company now and then."

"Not at all. I'm the same. Ever since I entered my sixties, sleep eludes me."

"Just a pair of old insomniacs." She shifted her torso, wincing. "*Oof.* I shouldn't have let that girl go to bed. Everything's slipping down."

"Allow me." He rose, went to the settee, rearranged and plumped the pillows. "How's that?"

"Much better. Thank you."

He resumed his seat on the rug.

"Now tell me," said Satyavati, her cheek full of rice ball, "why aren't you at Yudi's party? Oh, I know all about it. Don't tell me you disapprove of such affairs."

"Hmm. Actually, I wasn't invited."

"What? How odd. How could you not be invited?"

He took another swallow of beer and shrugged. "When the topic came up in council, Shakuna said—I think these were his exact words—'Lord Bhishma, I will not insult you by presuming that one of your advanced years and august dignity would find any amusement in a bachelor party.' I couldn't very well say, 'Oh yes, I would!' So I bowed and let it go."

"Huh. He obviously doesn't want you there. I wonder why."

She stared into space, fingering one of the many strings of beads on her voluminous chest. Then her brow creased, and she looked again at her stepson. "You know, I'm not too happy about this marriage you've arranged for Yudi. Another princess of Madrasa. It's a rich clan, extremely rich, and they're just to our north. The king acts friendly—I remember all those jokes he made when Pandu raided his cattle, years ago—but the fact is, rich kings like to get richer, and having his daughter seated on a throne in Kuru is liable to make him weigh his chances of turning an alliance into a takeover."

"Rich princesses bring rich dowries," said Bhishma.

"I know. Like Gandhari. But that only proves my point. You were worried about the king of Gandaram getting notions—yes, you were, don't deny it—which is why you took Shakuna hostage."

"I *invited* Prince Shakuna to remain with us after his sister's wedding."

"Like I said, took him hostage." She popped the last rice ball into her mouth. "Don't get me wrong; you were wise to do it. Problem is, it didn't entirely work, because now we've got a Gandaram queen *and* a Gandaram prince ruling the Kuru. And if Yudi does end up on the throne—which I'm quite sure Gandhari and her brother will go to any lengths to stop—but even if he does, we'll be in the same quandary, with another foreign queen. Only worse, because Madrasa sits right on our border."

"So what are you saying? That Kuru princes should marry only Kuru girls?"

"Yes. That's exactly what I'm saying. It's much safer."

"Bringing no dowries? No alliances?"

"What need have we for dowries? Our herd is enormous. The doab yields grain in plenty. We have three copper mines, two tin mines, forests of timber. Our kshatriya are well-trained and well-equipped, our horses well-bred. Our vaishya are skilled and productive. If we want more cattle we can raid some; if we want ivory or spices or silver we can trade for them. And raiding and trading, I'm sure you'll agree, are nobler pursuits than waiting for some outland missy to come prancing in with her boxes of jewels and strings of elephants."

Bhishma sighed. "All you say is true. We're well situated here. We don't need the dowries. But ..." He shook his head. "I'm afraid we do need the alliances. A clan without allies ends up isolated; the countries around it start trading with others, they start eyeing the clan's cattle, and eventually they start to wonder why that clan should exist at all. No. We need allies. And brides are the way to make them."

Satyavati pursed her lips and fiddled with her beads. "Maybe, maybe," she said. "But I still say homegrown girls are best. Look, what does the wife of a king really need to do? What's her one and only job?"

"Sons," said Bhishma.

"That's right. Sons. If she doesn't produce sons, strong sons, all the jewels and elephants and alliances mean nothing. So I say pick one of our own, as long as she's good-looking, intelligent, and fertile. Kshatriya, vaishya, shudra—it makes no difference."

"And if she turns out not to be fertile?"

"Then put her aside and find another girl and slap her in the king's bed as quickly as possible."

"I see." A wry smile. "Just as my father, King Shantanu, did with you?"

Her eyes flashed. "*I* was fertile enough! I had two perfectly good sons. It was those stupid girls, Ambika, Ambalika, they're the ones to blame. First they made no effort with Chit, then I had to bring in Vyasa and *force* them to do their duty—no thanks to *you*, by the way—then they produced those wretched babies, Pandu and Tarashtra ... Useless cows! They made me sick. I'm glad they're dead, I don't care if it's evil to say it."

She was seized with a fit of choking coughs. Bhishma got up, rubbed her back, poured her another cup of beer.

"Thank ... thank you. *Oh.* Gods. Thank you, Bhishma. I'm all right now."

She lay back, fanning herself with the empty plate.

Bhishma reseated himself on the stool. "Poor old Ambika and Ambalika. Their sister, Amba—she warned me they would make very bad queens."

"How right she was! Amba. I remember her well. Pretty girl. Now *she* would have made a very good queen." Satyavati chuckled, her temper seemingly restored. "It's really too bad you didn't take her up on her offer. She practically hurled herself at you."

"Mother. Be serious. If Amba and I had announced we were getting married and taking the throne away from Chit, what would you have done? I shudder to think."

"Ha! You're right. I would have made an unholy fuss."

"We would have seen the wrath of Kali, then!"

"I would have had your skull for my garland!"

The old queen and the venerable regent shook with laughter.

The full moon, beginning its descent, was now visible in the room's west window. The air outside was cool and still. Satyavati used a corner of her shawl to dab at her kohl-rimmed eyes in their pads of flesh. "Ah! It is funny to think of us, back in those days. Although ..." Her voice grew softer, entreating. "You're not all regrets, are you, my dear? Never king, no, but you *are* the most famous man of our age. The whole world knows Lord Bhishma of the Kuru."

He looked to the window, shading his eyes against the strong moonbeams. "The whole world? Well, a lot of the world, anyway." He looked back at the queen. "What does fame matter, when I have no sons?"

She was silent, her expression unhappy.

"On the other hand," (his wry smile returned) "I do have a granddaughter. And based on what I see of her, she looks like growing up to be more of a son than most."

"Yes, Shikhandi! I hear she's a little warrior."

The smile grew doting. "Little hoyden, more like. She and Drona's son, Ashwattama, are best friends, and they run wild. The boy has taught her to swim, wrestle, even a bit of swordplay ... she's not bad for a girl, not bad at all. Drona doesn't approve of her, but" (the smile grew to a grin) "he can't tell his son not to play with Lord Bhishma's granddaughter."

"The chief weapons master is a man of strict ideas," said Satyavati.

"He is indeed. Shikhandi is nine now. Ashwattama's ten. In a year or two we'll have to separate them; she'll have to be assigned some ladies and keep to the women's quarters, learn to behave properly ..." He sighed. "I know it must be. Still, I can't help feeling sad about it. She'll hate being penned up."

"You give her riding lessons, don't you?"

"I do, yes. We go out nearly every morning. Well, kshatriya women need to ride; I know some of the priests would like to put a stop to that, but I believe in the old ways. I figure I may as well teach her properly. And she's got a good seat. Just yesterday, listen to this, a toad hopped across the path, and her pony reared way up—there's many a boy would have fallen, even a few men—but she stuck fast. I was very pleased with her. Naturally, I didn't say anything; we just kept going through the forest. But I was very pleased."

"You're fond of her. It seems Amba was right to send her to you; was it a year ago? You were annoyed at the time."

"I was. Her arrival was ... unexpected. And that message Amba sent: 'Here's your granddaughter, her mother and father are dead, I will soon be dead too, I hope you can find room for her.' I found it disrespectful. But then Amba was never much for proprieties."

"You didn't think of refusing? Of sending her back to Kashi?"

"No. I wouldn't have done that."

He drained the last of his beer and leaned to set the cup on the table. As he sat up, running a hand through gray-and-white streaked hair, he looked a trifle sheepish.

"You know what she calls me?"

"No, what?"

"Papa-Beesh."

≈

Satyavati was snoring, the rice-balls plate fallen to the floor beside her. Bhishma stood at the window, looking at the moon sinking behind the trees on the rise west of the compound. He sniffed; there was a slight smell of smoke in the air. A homesteader burning leaves, perhaps.

He went to the settee, pulled a light blanket over the old queen's bulk, picked up the plate, put it on the table. Then he made for the door—

—and found his way blocked by two young men and a girl, all three sooty, scratched, and breathing hard.

"Uncle Bhishma! What ..." cried Duryodhana, stepping back and shoving Jaratka behind him. His scar was glaring pink through the black streaks on his face.

"Duryo? And Karna! What is this?" said Bhishma, also stepping back.

"We, um, we, we need to see the old queen. Something b-b-b ... something *not good* has happened."

"I don't understand. What has happened? Who's this girl?"

From the settee: "Duryodhana! Is that you? Get in here. What's going on?"

The three entered the room. Satyavati, struggling to prop herself up, waved a be-ringed hand to beckon them.

"Come, come. What on earth—Gods, you're all black! Is that Karna? What have you two been up to?"

They approached. Duryodhana and Karna bowed. Jaratka kneeled, palms together at her forehead.

"Good lord. *Jaratka?* Is that you?"

"Yes, my lady." The girl lowered her arms but stayed kneeling with hands clasped.

The queen went into another coughing fit. "*Oh.* Gods. *Hem.* What have you been doing? You all stink of smoke. No, wait ..." She heaved herself to a sitting position and planted her feet on the floor, knees wide, one hand on her fleshy hip. With a flick of the other hand, she indicated Karna. "You. Explain."

"Your grace," Karna said, placing his hands at his sides and directing his eyes at a spot above her head. "We were at the Lacquer House, at the party—I mean, Prince Duryodhana and I. There was a fire. The house burned. We escaped, but some did not. It looked like the house would burn to the ground."

Bhishma broke in, his tone sharp. "How many were inside?"

"My lord, I don't know ... perhaps eighty, ninety."

"The Pandavas?"

"They were inside, but they escaped with us. We all got out the window of one of the side rooms. They'll be on their way back now. The chief counselor was with them."

The regent's face showed relief. "I must wake the king and queen. Come to the hall, both of you, as soon as you can. They'll want to know the details." He strode out of the room.

Satyavati looked down at Jaratka. Besides being dirtied all over with soot, the girl had a large cut on her forehead, from which blood, now dried, had run down onto her cheek. Her left arm was covered with tiny scratches.

"Karna? Why is my maidservant in this state?"

Karna said, "Ma'am. It seems Lady Perta sent some men to the Snake, I mean the Naga girl's home, to bring her to the party."

"To *abduct* her," Duryodhana said.

"Yes, to abduct her. She was to be Lady Perta's gift to the Pandavas. Duryo, I mean Prince Duryodhana, he, I mean we, went there to help her."

Satyavati's eyes went from one, to the other, to the other.

"We were there when the soldiers arrived with her," Karna continued. "We tried to get her away, but we couldn't—not then. When the fire began she was inside with the Pandavas. We broke into their room, thinking to rescue her, but she had already jumped out the window."

Duryodhana opened his mouth again, but Satyavati held up a hand. She leaned toward the kneeling girl. "Jaratka: Is this true?"

Jaratka lifted her head. "Yes, my lady. It's true."

Satyavati took hold of the girl's chin and turned her face this way and that. With gentle, fat fingers, she touched the dried blood on the cheek. She shook her head and said, "*Tsk.*"

"Great-grandmother, p-p-please," said Duryodhana. "She needs a safe p-place to stay tonight. I thought, since she is in your service, you m-m-might ..."

"Yes, yes, of course she must stay here. That cut looks a bit nasty. But we'll get her cleaned up, no fear, leave her to me. You'd better go to the hall now." She clapped her hands together three times and, turning toward an inner doorway, called:

"Sisi! Vinata! Wake up in there! I need you!"

She readdressed her great-grandson. "Oh … and doesn't she live with her father? You should send word to him. I'm sure he's worried sick."

The two men stared at her, then at each other.

"Her father!" said Karna.

"Ekalavya!" said Duryodhana.

"Eh? What about him?" said Satyavati.

"He, he was *there,*" Duryodhana said. "He ran from town to tell us, and we took him w-with us to the f-forest."

"But we didn't bring him back," Karna said, laying a hand atop his brown mop of hair. "We told him to wait for us. We forgot all about him."

Jaratka clambered to her feet, her face incredulous. "My father was *there?* We must go back! We must find him!" She grabbed Duryodhana's hand and made to pull him toward the door.

"Jaratka!" said the old queen. "Stop it. Don't be silly. You can't go galloping back to the Lacquer House now; what good would that do? Your father is quite capable of walking home on his own. I'm sure he's fine. You'll see him later."

Turning again to the inner doorway, she clapped her hands five times and shouted:

"Sisi! Vinata! Come *on!*"

The girl Sisi and a plump lady-in-waiting appeared, rubbing the sleep from their eyes. "*There* you are," said Satyavati. "Must I always scream myself hoarse? Yes, all right, never mind. Look, here is Jaratka. She has been in a fire. Take her to my chamber, get her cleaned up, and get her something warm to drink. Wash this cut and bandage it up. Wash it well, do you hear? Then put her to bed. Go on, my dear. No—I said go on. Your father will be fine."

Jaratka looked over her shoulder at Duryodhana as she was led away.

"Now," said the queen, "off you two go. The king will want the report."

144

Duryodhana and Karna bowed and turned to leave. At the door, the prince looked back.

"Grannie ... thank you."

"Yes, yes. Off you go."

Once they had departed she sat still, wheezing softly, for several minutes. Then she looked up at the ceiling. There, barely visible in the gray dawn light that was just beginning to suffuse the room, was a panel of red lacquer.

It was etched in black with a figure of the Goddess Kali. Her right hand held the sword, her left the severed head. Her belly protruded. Her garland of skulls floated upward as she danced upon Shiva, lying supine with his penis erect, his face tense with delight.

The old queen, smiling, twirled a white lock of curly-wild hair.

Then she dropped her gaze, clapped her hands, and called, "Sisi!" When the girl appeared, she said:

"Go get two of my men. I need my settee carried to the great hall."

≈

It was the first day of the new year, and the Pandavas, banished, had departed for Vrishni that morning. The old queen had not gone to see them off (though she had attended the tribunal two weeks before). Now she was having her midday meal in her rooms, reclining as usual, with Jaratka massaging her legs and Duryodhana seated on the leather stool across the low table from her. The Naga girl was in the costume of an upper maidservant: dhoti, long-sleeved tunic, and cotton veil, all in forest green.

"So, my boy," Satyavati was saying, "you managed to get rid of them, eh?" She handed Jaratka her empty plate. "Another slice of beef pie, there's a good girl. And peas—smoosh them for me. That's right. My teeth are not what they were." She took the plate and applied herself to the pie. "For two years only; still, gives you time to figure out something else. Nicely done."

"Great-grandmother, I don't know w-what you mean," said Duryodhana. There was a hint of a crooked grin before he folded his arms and looked sideways at Jaratka.

"Heh. You know exactly what I mean. Although I'm sure it was your mother and uncle, not you, who fixed it up. Gang rape! Yes, it's just the kind of thing Shakuna would think of. He's clever, that one." She paused to chew a large mouthful.

"Not that those sons of Pandu didn't deserve what they got," she continued. "They may not have raped anyone—oh, of course they didn't, that little piece Ani put on a good show, but it didn't fool me—but their mother, now, with what she did to Jaratka—to *my* maidservant, mind you. Well, that never came up at the trial, no need to bring it up, but *we* know what Perta did, and I say it's not right. *And* Jaratka's poor father; we must lay that at Perta's feet, too."

She shook her head and ate some peas.

"Queens are supposed to protect girls, especially shudra girls. I know Perta isn't queen anymore, but she used to be. And I know you aren't shudra, my dear, you're Naga, but really," (she waved her napkin at a fly) "what difference does it make? The priests, they're always going on about caste, but I say, for a girl, caste doesn't matter. Women and girls—we're our own caste. We have to make our own way, whoever we are."

She handed the plate back. "Oof! I'm full. A few pieces of honeycomb, I think. Better give me another napkin, too. Thank you. Do a little more on my left calf, dear." Jaratka set to work, pressing in deep with her thumbs. "*Ahh. Ooo. That's good.*"

There was quiet for a while as the girl massaged the old queen's calf, the old queen sucked on honeycomb and grunted with pleasure, and the prince looked at the girl. Now and then she returned his look, meeting his eyes with a small smile.

"So the next thing we have to think about," said Satyavati, wiping her sticky fingers, "is how to get you two married."

They both started.

"*What?*" said Duryodhana. "That's ... I, I, I mean to say, that's imp-p-p-p ... *impossible*. Isn't it?"

"Nonsense. You're the crown prince now, aren't you? You can marry whom you like. And you'd better be married soon, to someone or other, if you want to get on that throne."

"B-b-but my father ... and Bhishma ..."

"Your father won't care. He hates being king. He can't wait to step down and get back to his, shall we say, preferred activities. And if you've got a wife, it gives him the perfect excuse. As for Bhishma, he won't like it, but he has no authority to stand in your way. No, your mother is the one you have to worry about. Not that she has authority, either, not by Law, but she'll seek a means to stop you, and she'll seek hard."

"Oh. I see. B-but …" He looked at Jaratka. Her eyes met his; her lips parted; her shoulders gave a tiny shiver.

Still looking at Jaratka, he said, "You'll help us, then, Grannie?"

"Heh. Yes, I'll help you. Believe me, I know girls, and this girl …" She reached out a plump, sticky hand. Jaratka took it in her dark, slender one.

"This girl will make a very good queen."

≈

One month later. Fans were not yet needed indoors, but Satyavati had had the straw blinds hung over the windows to shield the room from the strengthening afternoon sun.

" … and the crucial thing is to get your son on the throne," she was saying to her granddaughter-in-law. "That is all that matters, my dear. You know it is."

Gandhari drew the edge of her veil outward, brought the cup of lassi underneath, and sipped.

"Oh, indeed. I know that's what matters."

"Then you know that what also matters is getting your son married as quickly as possible. Once he's married, Tarashtra can step down with dignity. To be sure, Duryo will need to go on calling himself 'crown prince' until the Pandavas return, but if he's king in all but name—and if his wife is with child, even *has* a child—they'll have a difficult time unseating him."

"Maybe. But the people might not like it. Nor the soldiers. There's many who still back the sons of Pandu."

"*Pff.* The townspeople won't care. You're forgetting how much they love *you.* Your regular visits to—what was her name again—Ani? Yes, to Ani's house with your little baskets of food, and making her one of your maids, and her mother court weaver—I have to hand it to you, my dear; if they weren't swooning for Sati before, they are now. You've played your part well."

The draped head bent in acknowledgment.

"As for the kshatriya, you and Tarashtra have done such a good job of bribing them this past month—all that extra beer and beef, the chariot races—most of them are now firmly with the Kauravas, too. In any case, it's only a few old codgers who even remember the days of Pandu and his cattle raids. No. Duryo won't meet with any resistance to speak of."

Gandhari took another dainty sip of lassi.

"But the main thing," said Satyavati, driving a forefinger into her enormous, pink-silk-swathed thigh, "is to get him married. And whom does he want to marry? Jaratka."

"A maidservant. A Naga girl."

"Right. A Naga girl! Famously eager in the bedchamber, famously fertile. And *this* Naga girl is attractive, well-spoken, plucky, and clever to boot. What could be better?"

"Lord Bhishma won't stand for it. He'll want Duryodhana to make a useful alliance."

"Huh! Lord Bhishma is not the king. I know it's his favorite pastime, running around making deals for brides, but he has no say in this."

A pause.

Gandhari said, "Do you really think my son loves this girl?"

"Oh, yes. He's besotted with her. He won't look at anyone else."

"Hmm."

Another pause.

"Well, then. I must see what I can do." Gandhari put the cup on the table and rose. "Thank you so much for your counsel, Grandmamma. Now I'm afraid I must go."

"I'm so glad you see it my way, my dear. We must have more of these little talks. I'm always pleased when you young folk come to visit me; such a comfort to an old lady."

"Of course. The pleasure is all mine."

The queen dropped a neat curtsey and left the room.

≈

Two weeks on. Satyavati had her women—Vinata, Sisi, Jaratka, two other ladies-in-waiting, and one other maidservant—gathered around her settee, sitting on stools or on the floor, all of them embroidering men's vests or cloaks. The old queen preferred embroidery to spinning, and male attire to female. Her plump fingers had no trouble with the needle, and her eyes, even in the fading light of early evening, were still good for the close work.

148

"Almost done!" she said, holding up a black linen vest with red flames stitched around the hem and sleeve-holes. "Jaratka, what do you think? Too flashy for Duryodhana?"

Jaratka looked up from the cloak she was working on. "It's beautiful, my lady. But ..." She smiled and shrugged. "I am not sure he'll wear it."

"Heh. He must wear it! It's my express wish as his great-grandmother that he wear it on his wedding day. Eh, my dear? We'll see that he wears it!"

"Yes, Ma'am," said Jaratka, bending her head again but continuing to smile. The three ladies-in-waiting exchanged glances, lips pinched. The old queen paid them no mind.

The women worked on until the light was nearly gone. Then Satyavati laid aside the vest, flexed her hands, and said, "That will do, girls. Time to tidy up for supper."

There was a flurry of getting up, putting away, lighting lamps, and coming and going between inner rooms and outer. In the midst of the bustle, there came the sound of tramping feet down the corridor. Two manservants wearing the king's crimson appeared in the doorway, stood to attention, and bowed.

"What's this? Is there a message from the king?" said Satyavati, her expression curious as she handed off the flame-embroidered vest. "Don't crumple it, Sisi! Hold it flat. It's not a bundle of hay."

The shorter of the two manservants stepped forward. "My lady. The king has asked us to fetch the Snake girl, Ja ..." He looked over his shoulder at his fellow, who whispered, "*Jaratka.*"

"... the Snake girl, Jaratka. The king requires her."

Jaratka had just emerged from the inner room, carrying a comb and a copper hand-mirror. Upon seeing the men and hearing her name, she froze.

Satyavati frowned. "What do you mean, the king requires her? She's busy at the moment. What does he need her for? If he wants something mended, surely it can wait."

The two men exchanged a glance.

"Ma'am. I don't know, Ma'am. The king just said he—requires her."

Satyavati's mouth dropped open. Her eyes widened. Her hand clutched the edge of the settee.

Nobody moved or spoke for a count of five.

Then, with a quick breath and a smoothing of her sari: "Fine. I'll send her along shortly. Tell the king she'll be there in half an hour. You may go."

"My lady, um, I apologize, but the king said immediately."

"And *I* say my maidservant is busy just now and will be there shortly. Now *get out* before I have you both whipped!"

The men snapped to attention, bowed, and left.

Jaratka dropped the comb and mirror, ran to the settee, and fell to her knees, her arms around Satyavati's shoulders, her forehead pressed to Satyavati's breast. She did not make a sound, but she was quaking.

The old queen brought her hand up to cradle the girl's head. "Sshhh … sshhh. It's all right, child. Sshhh. I promise you, everything's going to be all right. You'll see."

The waiting women were clustered in the inner doorway, some looking mystified, others satisfied. Satyavati snapped, "Go away, all of you. Leave us." They beat a retreat.

She unloosed the Naga girl's arms and gently pushed her upright. The dark face with the heavy-lidded eyes was a study in despair.

"Now, my dear. That's enough falling apart. We don't have much time; we need to discuss things, and you must listen. Can you listen? Take a breath." Jaratka took a deep breath and let it out.

"Good girl. You've always had courage, and that courage is going to serve you well now. Come, sit by me." She heaved herself to one side and patted the seat next to her. Jaratka got up and sat down, her slender hands encased in Satyavati's fleshy ones.

"Here's what you must understand: Tarashtra likes variety. He will tire of you within a few weeks, a couple of months at most. So all you have to do is grit your teeth and go along with it for that short time, and then he'll be done with you and it will all be over and forgotten, and you can go on with your life. Do you see?"

"Yes, my lady. But …" The girl closed her eyes.

"Yes? But?"

"Prince Duryodhana …" A tear welled from each eye and slid down.

"Duryodhana does not need to know. Look at me, Jaratka. *He does not need to know.* And I will make sure—trust me on this—that *nobody* tells him."

"But what if … if …"

"You get pregnant? Yes. That is the one thing we really do have to worry about. You must not get with child. So, I'm going to be very blunt now and tell you a few things; they won't be a guarantee, but they will help. First, you must ..."

There followed ten minutes of explicit instruction.

"... can you remember all that? Good. Now, go wash your face and comb your hair. No need to change clothes, but I'll give you one of my veils; it will help you feel you've got a bit of armor, at least. Take the pale-green one with the silver. It's never suited me, but it will suit you. You know where it is, don't you? Go and get it."

Five minutes later, Jaratka returned. The tear-streaks had been washed away. The new veil was wrapped around her head and neck, its ends flowing down her back. The pale-green silk with its pattern of silver leaves looked well with the forest-green tunic and trousers.

"There, now. You look beautiful. Come here and I'll tell you one last thing."

Jaratka came forward. Satyavati took her hand and said:

"No matter what that repulsive fool does, you just remember: You're a hundred times better than he could ever hope to be."

She held the girl's hand for a little longer, looking hard into her eyes as if trying to transfer strength from her old mind into the young one.

At last she called out, "Vinata!" and when the woman appeared in the doorway, said, "Go with Jaratka to the king's quarters. Then come straight back. I'm going to want to have a talk with all you ladies."

After the two had gone, she lay back and stared at the lacquer panel on the ceiling. She bared her teeth. She clenched her fists. She whispered:

"Damn that Gandhari! Damn her to hell!"

≈

As the end of the second month approached, the heat grew. A maid-servant with a straw fan was now stationed behind the settee in the afternoons.

"Gandhari, my dear, it's good of you to visit me again so soon. More halva?"

"The pleasure is always mine, Grandmamma. And it's delicious. But no, thank you."

"Ah. You're so careful with your figure." Satyavati patted her own enormous stomach. "I admire your discipline. I suppose Tarashtra likes you so thin? He likes skinny women?"

"He ... I ... I could not say. The king is so occupied these days."

"Of course, of course. I was only teasing. You have given him two fine sons, eh? He ought to leave you alone, at this point. So crude, isn't it, when husbands go on pestering their wives, after those wives have more than done their duty."

"The king treats me very well."

"Oh, I know, Tarashtra is blameless in that regard. He has never demanded that you keep him amused. He amuses himself, does he not? He was always good that way. He and Vyasa ... my, the things they'd get up to! I used to be quite shocked, hearing about their adventures. But then, how much better it is to have a husband of that sort than one who's always underfoot. Eh? Don't you agree, my dear?"

"I suppose. Yes."

Satyavati popped a square of halva in her mouth and munched.

"Just for example, it's come to my ears recently—you know how servants talk, you simply can't shut them up—it's come to my ears that the king is spending all his extra time these days with one of the palace maids. I don't know which one, but they say she's exceedingly young and pretty. Do you know which it is?"

"Really, I couldn't say."

"No, of course not, why should it matter to you? I only wondered because I've heard a few whispers that it's an outcaste girl. You know I'm not prejudiced about such things—I've made my own position very clear, regarding Jaratka—but I know how *you* feel about it." She licked the sweet crumbs from her fingers with loud smacks.

"On the other hand, I daresay it's just a silly rumor. Probably spread by the girl herself. Girls, especially low-caste girls, do love to make dramas. Oh, they surely do. Why, that was the first thought I had when that town girl—what was her name? *Tsk.* I can *never* remember her name. Sisi, what was that town girl's name, the one who said the Pandavas raped her?"

"Ani, my lady."

"Ani! That's it. When she testified at the tribunal, the first thing I thought was, 'She's making it all up.' I have an intuition about these things, and I just knew she was lying. Well, then the king judged as he judged, the Pandavas were sent away, and I had to admit I was wrong. Still, I've had some chats with her mother since then—I've had her in to discuss materials for my summer clothes—and it's funny, because I've asked her about what happened that night, and some of the things she says don't ... well, they don't quite add up. Wouldn't it be funny if the whole thing *was* a lie? About the rape, I mean. If Ani recanted, the Pandavas would have to be called back and the whole case reopened. Imagine!"

More smacking of lips on fingers. "Are you sure you won't have another halva?"

"No, thank you."

"Ah, well. Then I'll just have to eat the rest, won't I? Heh. Goodness, listen to me rattling on about old news. You must find me awfully tiresome."

"Not at all, Grandmamma. What you say is very interesting."

"I'm so glad you think so. Sisi! Come round here and hand me the other plate. Yes, *today*. Honestly, Sisi, sometimes ..."

She accepted the plate and picked up another nut-crusted square.

"But of course it's all mere speculation—I mean about the king's carrying on with the outcaste girl, and about Ani's lying. Just idle chatter. No harm done, as long as we keep it to ourselves, an amusement for us ladies. What we don't want—what none of us wants—is for this idle chatter to reach the men. Tarashtra, Shakuna, Duryodhana: they have important things to worry about. We won't bother *them* with our trivial tales."

She fixed Gandhari with her puffy, kohl-rimmed eyes.

"Will we?"

A pause.

"No," came the low, cool voice from behind the violet silk. "No, I see no reason to bother the men with such tales."

"No reason at all. Oh, my dear, I do enjoy our talks. I feel you really understand me."

"Yes, Grandmamma. I feel exactly the same way about you."

≈

As predicted, the king tired of Jaratka in a matter of weeks, ceasing to send for her before the year's fourth month was out. Satyavati's women did not talk; nor did Gandhari say anything to her son. Others, to be sure, may have whispered in kitchens or back corridors about the king's latest plaything, but there was no cause for servants' gossip to come to Duryodhana's ears, and in any case, he was away for much of that time overseeing the expansion work on one of the copper mines out west near the Yamuna. When the rains arrived, Jaratka was back full-time in the old queen's quarters, with Duryodhana once again a regular visitor.

Throughout the monsoons he came faithfully each afternoon, sitting on the leather stool across from his great-grandmother, entertaining her with stories of his doings as the water dripped or poured outside. Sometimes Karna came, too. The old queen would tease him:

"Now, Sir Karna, we must find a bride for you, as well. I'm sure you have no trouble attracting the ladies; still, you must be careful. Nothing is worse for a man than the wrong wife. But don't worry, I'm here to help. Now, let's think. What about Lady Padma, in the queen's quarters? She's awfully lively. Pretty eyes, pretty hair ... big hips, too, good for childbearing. Oh, dear—now I've embarrassed you. Look, Duryo, your friend is blushing. But it only makes him more handsome, does it not? Handsome as Indra, he is! Jaratka, my dear, I don't know ... you may have picked the wrong man!"

Jaratka had always been quiet, and had of late grown quieter. Nevertheless, she gave her mistress a demure smile before bending again to her embroidery. Her long, dark braid hung down over the green-and-silver silk veil, which was wound several times about her neck and shoulders. The prince sat gazing at her. Anyone could see he was drunk with love.

In this pleasant way, the rainy season passed. But as the sixth month wore on, Jaratka's skin acquired an ashen tinge; she nodded over her sewing in the afternoons; in the midst of her duties she would stop and lean on the wall or windowsill. Satyavati observed these things but did not comment. Then there came a morning when Jaratka rose from her sleeping mat in the old queen's bedchamber, stumbled to the chamber pot in the corner, and retched.

"I ... I apologize, my lady." She sat up, pressing her hands to her temples. Then she doubled over and retched again. "Oh ... oh. I am *so* sorry, my lady. I don't know what is wrong with me. Please excuse me. I will clean this up right away."

"You'll do nothing of the sort," said Satyavati, heaving herself to a semi-reclining position. She had felt tired at a reasonable hour the night before and had decided to go to bed rather than sleep on the settee, keeping the Naga girl with her and banishing the rest of the women to the outer room. "One of the sweepers can take care of it later. Get a towel and wipe your face. Then come over here and sit."

Jaratka obeyed.

"When did you last have your monthly time?"

"My ... oh, you mean my blood time?"

"Yes."

"Oh ... um ... I don't know. It was when the king ... when I was ..." She hung her head and spoke softly. "I mean, I know it was then, because I told him it was my blood time and he insisted that I please him by ... in another way. I said I would go, so as not to defile him, but he said he didn't care about that."

"I see. And you haven't had it since then?"

"No, my lady."

Satyavati pinched the bridge of her nose.

"My dear. Why didn't you tell me?"

"You mean ... why didn't I tell you I hadn't had my blood time?"

"Yes."

"I ... well, it often does not come for a few months. Sometimes three, or even four months. It has been that way ever since it started. Do you think ..." Suddenly her eyes grew wide. Her hands went to her stomach. "Oh, no. No. My lady, you don't think ... I did everything you told me to do! Everything! I promise!"

Satyavati patted the girl's knee. "I believe you, child. I believe you. But as I said, those methods aren't perfect. And now it's too late to do anything about it. If I'm counting right, you're almost three months along." She tapped her own thigh with her fist. "It's my own fault. I noticed you were getting tired, but I thought, no, it's just the rains ..."

"Then I am dead," said Jaratka.

"What? Nonsense, you're not dead. You're just going to have a baby. Happens to the best of us. Let's see ..." She stared into space, drumming her fingers on the blanket. "Maybe I could send you somewhere. But where? If only the queen were on our side, but, ha!

She's not. No, there's nowhere to send you, so the only thing to do is stay and brazen it out."

She tapped a forefinger on a fat cheek. "We mustn't lose our heads. You're hardly the first maid to receive the king's attentions, and assuming it's a boy, he won't be unhappy; quite the opposite, in fact. *If* it's a boy, you'll be able to parlay it into something ... jewels, certainly, but also a promotion to court lady. Official consort, even. Oh, he won't bother you again, don't worry about that, but you may as well get the title ..."

"But, my lady!"

"What, what?" She patted the girl's knee again. "Really, child, your situation is not unusual. And I'll make sure you get the best of care."

"*Duryodhana.*" The word was a wail of misery.

"Ah." The old queen looked down at the blanket. "Yes. I had forgotten about him."

The two women sat silent, heads bent. Through the window came the morning coos of pigeons.

"Well," said Satyavati at length. "As I said: we'll just have to brazen it out."

≈

"P-p-p-p ... p-p-p ... *pregnant?*"

Duryodhana pressed his hand to his scar and stared at Jaratka open-mouthed.

The Naga girl was kneeling between settee and table, palms on her thighs, eyes down. The green-and-silver veil wrapped her head and neck, its ends falling almost to the ground. Outside it was twilight; the room's oil lamps and torches were lit; the table was laid with an array of supper dishes. The waiting women had all been sent away for the evening.

Satyavati was sitting upright, feet on the floor, one arm around Jaratka's shoulders. "Yes, Duryodhana. Pregnant. And before you go flying off the bowstring, you need to know something else. Duryo?" She snapped her fingers at him. "Are you listening? You need to know that this is the king's doing. He sent for her. She had no choice. So if you're looking for someone to blame, you can blame your father.

Although if it comes to that, blame your mother; she's the one who put him up to it."

Duryodhana said nothing. The scar beneath the pressing hand was turning dark pink.

"I expect the baby will be here in the spring, sometime after the new year," Satyavati continued. "Until then, it's probably best you stay away. We don't want any gossip about you two; we want it kept very clear that this child is the king's. Now the good news is, if it's a boy, Jaratka's status will rise significantly. She'll be made a lady, a kshatriya. That will make it a lot easier for the two of you to be married; nobody can object to your marrying a girl of your own caste. So ..."

"M-m-m-m ... *married?*"

"Yes, married. That's what you've been wanting, isn't it? Well, this is going to make it easier for you. It's really to your benefit, my dear." She smiled and nodded.

Duryodhana's eyes started from his head. "You ... you ..." His fingers squeezed at the scarred flesh, now turned a lurid red. "*You ... you ...*"

He stood up, leaned down, and with his right forearm swept all the dishes off the table.

"YOU FILTHY SLUT! YOU FUCKING WHORE!"

He lunged forward, planted one hand on the table, and with the other hand seized his great-grandmother by the throat.

"YOU SOLD HER! YOU FILTHY, FAT OLD WHORE! I'LL KILL YOU!"

Satyavati's eyes rolled back in their sockets. Her hands waved helplessly in the air.

Jaratka leaped up and grabbed Duryodhana's wrist, tugging at it. She pried at his fingers, shouting, "*Stop it!* Let go of her!" but he hung on. After a few seconds she put her mouth below the copper armband and bit, hard. He yelled and fell back. The old queen slumped forward, gasping and red-faced, spittle frothing on her lips.

Jaratka threw her arms out like a shield. When the prince gave no sign of renewing his attack, she turned and bent to her mistress: "My lady, are you all right? Oh, my lady. Oh, my dear." She pressed her face to the white curls. "Wait, wait, let me get you some water." She retrieved a cup from the floor, ran to the water jar in the corner, filled the cup, and returned. "Here, my lady. Try to drink." She wiped the swollen lips, lifted the cup to them. Satyavati spluttered and coughed but managed to swallow a little. Jaratka helped her lie back on the settee. She arranged the cushions. She went and got a cloth, dampened it at the water jar, and sat down next to the old lady, gently mopping her face and neck.

Duryodhana stood watching them, rubbing the bloody bite mark on his right arm, breathing hard but saying nothing. Outside, it was now full dark.

Still tending to her mistress, Jaratka threw him a sideways glance and said, "Get out."

"W-w-w ... what?"

"I said, get out."

"B-b-but ... No. Jaratka, p-please, I ..."

She rose from the settee, picked her way through the mess of crockery on the floor, and stood before him. The veil had fallen back about her shoulders. She was nearly as tall as he, and their eyes were on the same level.

"These are Queen Satyavati's rooms. You will leave. I will not see you again."

He reached and took her by the shoulders, shaking her slightly. "*No.* My love, my love, p-p-p ... *please.* Why didn't you *tell* me? I w-would have protected you! I w-would have *killed* my father b-before letting him touch you!"

The heavy-lidded eyes shone cold with contempt.

"You are worse than your father. I would rather he touch me than you."

Duryodhana's face warped in monstrous pain. He turned and ran from the room.

≈

On the fifteenth day of the first month, roughly one year after the Pandavas' departure, in the old queen's quarters, Jaratka gave birth to a baby boy. The labor was relatively easy; the infant, however, had no left arm. The king was present at the birth—he had always loved the evidence of his virility—but upon hearing the appalled whispers of the midwives and demanding they tell him what was wrong, he stomped out of the room in disgust. "Kill it!" he shouted over his shoulder at Satyavati as his small-boy-guide-dog led him away.

Satyavati did not kill it. Instead she kept the child in her rooms, letting mother and baby sleep in her bedchamber and relieving Jaratka of most of her duties. The boy was nicknamed Vaishamya— "Lopside" in the common tongue—and except for his deformity, he was perfectly healthy. He smiled, rolled over, sat up, and gripped his rattle right on time. Having only one arm, he did not crawl very well, but he scooted about on his bottom most efficiently.

When Vaishamya was six months old, on a bright autumn morning after that year's monsoons had come to an end, Satyavati sent a maidservant to find the high priest and beg him to attend her. The white-robed brahmin arrived forthwith, grinning and chewing his betel nut. He bowed to the old queen, ensconced on her settee.

"Mother. What a joy to receive your invitation. It's been ages."

"Hello, Vyasa. Please, sit down. Everything well with you these days?"

He seated himself cross-legged on the rug. "Couldn't be better. Couldn't be better. Of course, the new crop of priests, the ones that came in this year—seriously, the worst I've ever seen. They barely know the catechism. It's a trial to me, a sore trial. Still, mustn't complain." He reached for a small bowl of nuts on the table. "May I? I don't want to dirty your floor."

"Of course."

"Thank you." He emptied the nuts onto another dish, sat back, and expectorated into the bowl.

"Do help yourself to lassi."

"Ah, lovely." He poured a cup from the ewer and sat back again. "Well, now that we're all caught up; there must be something you need, so let's hear it."

"Hmm. Yes, actually there is. It's something important, and I believe only you can help."

"Now, where have I heard that before?"

"Oh, for Gods' sake, Vyasa. You've done extremely well out of our bargain. Forty years ago I made you high priest to the Kuru, and I'm sure you haven't regretted a single day."

The gaunt face glowed with mirth. "Mother, dear, you mistake me. As I've always said, I'm endlessly grateful to you for pulling me out of that ashram and giving me such a nice job. Such nice perks, too. Kings for children; smashing parties. It's all been simply ..." (he spat another red glob into the bowl) "... divine."

Satyavati rolled her eyes. "Yes, well, I'm glad. Anyway, here's my request. I have this baby, and ..."

"*Another* baby? Indra save us—at your age? It must be true what they say about you being a Goddess!"

"Vyasa, so help me ..."

"Sorry, Mother, sorry. I apologize. Please, continue."

She sighed loudly and took a sip of lassi before resuming. "My *maidservant* has a baby. A son, by the king. He's called Vaishamya, because he only has one arm. When he was born, the king told me to kill him ..."

"*Tsk.*" The priest shook his head. "I'm afraid my boy Tarashtra doesn't have much empathy for cripples. Odd, when you think about his own disability and the way we've all supported him nonetheless."

"Indeed," said Satyavati. "But in any event, I did not follow Tarashtra's instructions. I kept the child, and his mother, here in my rooms. He's six months old now: a fine, robust boy. Good-looking, except for the arm. Alert. Sleeps and eats well. He's ready to start solid food and cow's milk."

"He sounds wonderful. And how do I come into this cozy family story?"

"I want you to take him. Adopt him. After all, he is your seed-grandson."

"Ah. I see."

The two sets of black eyes regarded each other unblinking.

"Well? What do you say?" she asked.

"I don't know. As I did forty years ago, I have to wonder: What's in it for me?"

Satyavati's fingers went to her throat and lightly scratched the pink welts that had never quite gone away. "Vyasa, I am an old woman. Long ago, I was queen; I have not been queen for many, many years. I have nothing to offer that you would think valuable."

"But?" He said it with a smirk and a raise of the eyebrows.

"But," she said, "here is something to consider: If it is true about my being an incarnation of the Goddess Kali—mind you, I'm not saying it *is* true, but *if* it is true—I would think you'd want to avoid displeasing me."

The smirk faded. The gaunt face looked uncertain, then ... afraid.

He lowered his head and spat once more into the nut bowl. When he looked up, the grin was back in place.

"Well, Mother, I daresay I can oblige. I mean, these young priests," (he shook his head) "not a one with potential. Now, if I have my own boy, I can train him up properly and he can succeed me after I'm gone."

"My dear. What an excellent idea." The old queen, smiling, fingered her strings of beads.

"Yes," said the priest, putting the bowl on the floor and running a hand through his shock of gray-and-white hair. "In fact, the more I think about it, the more I think this ... arrangement ... will suit me very well."

Now, Sire, I'm sure you realize that Duryodhana and Jaratka did eventually reconcile. That I, their daughter, am sitting here before you is proof that they did. They were apart for a long time, though: more than a year and a half would pass before they would see each other again. The old queen made no further attempts to hide the fact of Vaishamya's birth, so Duryodhana no doubt heard about it; he did not comment on it, however, to Karna or to anyone else, nor did he try to visit his great-grandmother afterward. He occupied himself with assisting his father in council and hall, traveling on forestry and mining projects, and daily hunting and weapons training. It seems he never said a word to his father about what had happened.

The king did not confer kshatriya rank on Jaratka. The baby, though a boy, was deformed, which meant she had failed, so her status remained vague: a Snake, but a Snake who had enjoyed the king's attentions; an outcaste, but an outcaste who lived in the old queen's rooms, wore the old queen's veil, and touched the old queen's food. On the other hand, once it became clear that she and the crown prince had had a falling out, her fellow waiting-women grew much friendlier. They all helped look after little Vaishamya, keeping the secret of his continued existence with sisterly solidarity and declaring "our poor Jaratka" sadly ill-used.

The secret became an open one, of course, after the baby was adopted by Vyasa and moved to the high priest's quarters. Indeed, Vyasa made a point of talking about "my new son" in the king's presence. "A most engaging child; *so* unfortunate he lacks an arm," he would say, loudly enough for everyone around the council table to hear. "But then, it is well known that the Gods smile on cripples. Disabilities needn't stop a man from advancing in life. Isn't that so, my boy? Sorry … *your majesty.*"

Tarashtra, it seemed, had decided to let the matter go. "Adopt whatever brats you like, High Priest," he'd say with a yawn. "Adopt a hundred of 'em. All the same to me."

Meanwhile, the question of the crown prince's marriage became paramount. Not only was Duryodhana nearing twenty now, but the Kauravas knew their advantage depended on his being married and on the throne before the Pandavas returned from exile. Many discussions were held in council, with proposals of this or that princess from this or that clan; the prince himself, however, refused to take any interest in the matter, saying only, "Uncle Bhishma knows best." And Bhishma, oddly enough, failed to tackle the issue with his accustomed energy. He hemmed and hawed and said that perhaps there had been too many foreign influences on the Kuru of late (Shakuna looked sharply at him then); perhaps a homegrown girl, in this case, would be a better choice. Then, when this or that lady of Hastinapura was suggested, he gazed out the window and said he wondered whether it weren't best for a young man to choose his own bride, for after all, he was the one who had to live with her. This bizarre statement met with puzzled looks all round.

All this was told to me by Chief Counselor Vidura, who, of course, was in those council meetings. He said that the news of Princess Draupadi's bridegroom choice, when it arrived in the middle of the ninth month, had a galvanizing effect. The possibility of an alliance with Panchala—a clan that, though once of middling reputation, had been steadily gaining wealth and power ever since the succession of King Drupada eighteen years ago—was too appealing for even the new, lackadaisical Bhishma to ignore. Soon the group was deep in plans for the prince's retinue, what gifts to bring, when to depart. There was also speculation about which other lords from which clans would be there.

"The Pandavas," said Shakuna. "The Pandavas will be there."

Whereupon Duryodhana sat up, leaned forward, and said:

"Then by all means, let me go and compete."

Chapter 8

VIDURA

V*idura said:*
    I did not want to go on the trip to Panchala. But King Tarashtra asked me to go, invoking the honor of the Kuru, so I felt it was my duty.

"Look here, Vidu," he said, after the other council members' footsteps had receded down the corridor. He had requested I stay behind when the meeting broke up. "I want you to go with Duryo to this bridegroom choice. I want you to help him. He's not been himself ever since that girl, I forget her name, that Snake girl, in the old queen's rooms—ever since she rejected him. Oh, don't think I don't know about that; everyone thinks I'm unaware of what goes on around this place, everyone thinks my wife and Shakuna run it all and I just dodder along doing whatever they say, but I didn't fall off the ox cart yesterday. I know a thing or two, especially about girls. And I know my son was mad for that girl. Surprising, eh? That a prince should fall in love with a Snake. But there you are; there's no accounting for the arrows of the Blind God. Heh! I always liked the thought of the God of Love being blind like me." He chuckled to himself while scratching his groin.

"Duryo was upset about my having fun with her. Now, why he didn't just send for her after I was done—or even before I was done, because I wouldn't have minded, I'm never stingy about such things—why he didn't just take his own initiative in the matter, I cannot comprehend. All that mooning about: it never pays with women. Gives 'em the idea they've got the whip hand. And that's clearly the idea the Snake girl got, because she turned him away. Oh, yes: she told him to leave her alone, the little cunt. Mind you," (he snickered) "she had enjoyed my favors. Perhaps I spoiled her for anyone else. Ha-ha! Ha-ha!" The scratching hand moved upward to his bulbous belly, which shook as he laughed.

"No, no ... I'm just joking, Vidu, just joking. It's well known that Snake girls will go with anyone; they're always ready for a romp. But again, that just makes it all the more baffling why my son didn't simply summon her, screw her, and get her out of his system." He sighed and shook his head. The scratching hand ascended to his flabby jowls.

I continued to wait, silent.

Finally he placed his hands on the table and patted it with a down-to-business air. "So, to my point: Duryo is going to need help. Even at his best the boy has always been a bit unstable—comes from his mother's side—and right now, he's not at his best. I fear that at this tournament, he might not only do poorly, he might do something to embarrass himself. And if he embarrasses himself, he embarrasses the Kuru. We can't have that, can we?"

"No, Sir," I said. I was in full agreement with him there. "We cannot have that."

The upshot was that as winter neared its end, I found myself riding southeast on the road to Panchala with Prince Duryodhana; Sir Karna; Chief Weapons Master Drona; and Drona's eleven-year-old son, Ashwattama. With us were some fifteen kshatriya and three times as many cooks, charioteers, grooms, manservants, launderers, sweepers, and bearers. There were wagons for the food, fodder, and tents; pack elephants for weapons, stools, sleeping mats, extra clothing, cookware, and sundry equipment; plus a couple of chariots (the king had thought one was enough, but I insisted upon two) in case they were needed for the competition. We brought six warhorses and two priests. A few whores attached themselves to the train.

We five would not have chosen each other as traveling companions, but then, choice had had little to do with it. Karna was there at Duryodhana's insistence. Drona, like me, was there on king's orders: his job was to coach our candidate and keep in him top form for the events. Ashwattama was there because his father thought it would be an educational experience for him. And as I've said, I was there to make sure my nephew did not fall apart in front of the entire civilized world, thereby wrecking the repute of the Kuru clan.

Our destination was Kampilya, the principal town of Panchala and seat of the Panchala court. As we were going in easy stages, the fifty-kosa journey down the Ganges would take approximately ten days. The road follows the river but does not stick to it; it wanders away by as much as half a kosa, veers back to the riverbank and away again, running mostly through forest except where the trees have been cleared for a town or village. Past Kampilya, I knew from bards' tales and merchants' reports, the road runs on southeast another hundred kosa to where the Yamuna merges with the Ganges. Years later, after the war, I would have the opportunity to travel myself to that great meeting point and stand on the rocks of the promontory. What a sight it is: the Yamuna, roaring and raging, hurls herself into the arms of Mother Ganges, and that most sacred of all rivers scoops up her daughter with barely a "Hush!" and proceeds onward, calm as dusk and wide as half the sky.

But at that time I was concerned only with my assignment, which was to get Prince Duryodhana to the tournament, help him win, and get him back home with his prize, the Princess Draupadi. I say it was my assignment; I do not say it was my desire.

≈

The first three days of the journey passed uneventfully. Drona, Ashwattama, and I rode at the front of the cortege, the two priests alongside us, while Duryodhana and Karna rode a little back with the other kshatriya, and the rest of the train straggled along behind. It being late winter and the weather dry and cool, the ground was firm and the going easy. Each day we made camp by midafternoon, after which Drona would conduct a training session with the prince and some of the soldiers; during that time, Karna generally went hunting, and I would observe some of the exercises and later go for a walk in the forest or along the riverbank.

Drona, it was clear, still wanted nothing to do with Karna. His relationship with Duryodhana, however, seemed cordial enough. Standing beside Drona on the edge of a makeshift training ground, watching the prince spar with a partner, I would hear him murmur, "Nice parry" or "That needs work." At length he'd approach his student and have a brief discussion, demonstrating this or that technique while Duryodhana watched and listened, then repeated the maneuver, usually to an approving nod and grunt from the hawk-faced instructor. I am no judge of martial arts, but Duryodhana did appear to me to have grown as a warrior in the past year. His speed and strength with the sword, especially, was remarkable.

On the fourth day we overtook a group of six or seven brahmins traveling on foot. They had come from Vrishni, they told us, and like us were headed for the bridegroom choice—though naturally, they were not going to compete.

"There will be tremendous alms and feasting, courtesy of King Drupada," said their leader, a cheerful, white-bearded old priest whose name was Dhaumya; I had dismounted and was walking beside him as we neared our camping spot for the afternoon. "And we hope to meet many others of our caste from far and wide. It will be a joy to share speech with them. In Vrishni, remote as it is, we are always in some danger of losing our exactitude in the rituals: a word mispronounced here, a line transposed there, a gesture muddied. Sometimes" (he leaned in and his voice sank to a whisper) "I worry that we've dropped *whole sections* of hymns. So it is crucial to get together on occasion with our brothers from other clans and compare notes."

"It is indeed," I replied. "Even in Hastinapura, which I think I may without undue pride call a center of learning, I often notice some egregious mistakes. Once, if you can believe it, our own high priest left off the entire final verse of the Indra Invocation."

He gasped in disbelief.

"I assure you, it's true," I said. "And it goes to show how important are these opportunities to meet and keep one another on our toes."

"Well said, well said. And you, Sir," he continued in a respectful tone, "if I may ask: Are you brahmin?"

I hesitated. I was thinking about my kshatriya father, my brahmin seed-father, and my shudra mother.

"No ... no," I said. "My father was King Chit of the Kuru. But my mother was not his wife. I am chief counselor to my brother, King Tarashtra."

"Ah," he said, nodding and stroking his beard. "Kshatriya, then. Yet you seem to know much about the sacraments. Perhaps you were attracted to the priesthood at one time?"

"I confess I find the Sacred Knowledge compelling, very compelling. But my path was set early in life. It was decreed by my grandmother, Queen Satyavati, that I would be counselor to my brother the king. So that is what I have been, and am, and will always be."

"Satyavati!" His eyes grew wide. "Of course, the old queen of the Kuru. They say she is an incarnation of the Goddess Kali, born of a Ganges fish. Tell me, is it true?"

I shrugged. "I cannot say. She has certainly lived a long time. But she has never taken much notice of me, or of my brother. She likes Bhishma, our former regent."

His eyes grew wider still. "Lord Bhishma! He, too, is renowned. Ah ... it must be wonderful to belong to such a clan. Such resources as you have. Such history."

"You must come visit us in Hastinapura someday," I said, liking this old priest. "You and your colleagues must come. We would be ..." (I thought about saying "honored" but decided that would be too much) "pleased to have you."

"Thank you, Counselor Vidura! You are too kind," he said.

We walked on in silence for a bit. Up ahead through the trees I could see the clearing where our camp was already being pitched.

"Tell me," said I, "What do you hear of the Pandavas? I mean the five princely brothers of the Kuru, who were exiled to your land. Do you know anything of them? Are they attending the tournament?"

"Oh, indeed, the Pandavas," said he, nodding. "Sons of our lady Perta. I do not belong to the Vrishni court, so I cannot speak with assurance. But I *hear* they are all five attending, and that the eldest and the youngest will compete."

"Yudi and Arjuna," said I. "Yes, that makes sense."

We entered the clearing.

"I see you know these princes well. And you must also know—is it their cousin?—the prince who leads your party." He cocked his head at me with a mischievous grin. "Now, if I were to place a wager on one of them at the bridegroom choice, how would you advise me?"

"Hmm," I said. He had put me at ease, so I found myself dropping my guard. "It's difficult to say. Prince Yudi is a safe bet to win many events; Prince Duryodhana, as well. But if you want to know whom the princess is likely to pick as a husband ..." I winked at him. "There is no contest. Bet on Arjuna."

≈

With Duryodhana's permission, I invited the Vrishni brahmins to join our party. They rode in one of the wagons or walked as we continued along the way. Our own two priests at first turned up their noses at the country bumpkins, but Dhaumya with his genial, deferential manner soon won them over, and within a couple of days all the holy men were walking together at the back of the caravan, debating, reciting, and laughing as they went. I would leave my horse to a groom and fall in with them for an hour or two; their conversation was most enjoyable.

On the evening of the sixth day, Dhaumya came to my tent and told me the priestly cohort was planning a Sunrise Oblation for the following morning.

"I do hope you will come, Counselor Vidura," he said. "I will be officiating myself. I'm a little nervous, to tell you the truth; it is a beautiful but demanding ceremony, extremely intricate, and I would welcome a friendly face in the seats."

I told him I would attend with pleasure. The Sunrise Oblation is one of the most ancient of rituals, yet in these latter days it is performed rarely, having been replaced by the twice-daily Agni Oblations, the first of which theoretically happens at dawn but actually happens whenever the royal family is up and ready. In olden times, upper and lower castes would rise with the sun; today, the superior orders tend to drag themselves out of bed when the morning is half gone, so there isn't much call for an early service. In my life there had been only two or three Sunrise Oblations performed in Hastinapura, and High Priest Vyasa, who generally got up around noon, had certainly not presided at them. So I was eager to see one done.

I told Dhaumya I would persuade the prince and chief weapons master to come, too. He appeared excited at the luster we three would add (in his view) to the proceedings, and thanked me profusely.

Duryodhana, when I put the request to him, was willing enough. "What about it, Karna?" he asked. "Think I can get up that early?" He was lounging on his camp bed juggling a couple of eating knives in one hand. Up went one knife and up went the other before the first was caught, the sharp blades tumbling over and over in rapid succession. The hour was late, the tent's interior dimly lit. He never fumbled.

Karna was cross-legged on a sleeping mat, honing the tip of a spear. "Sure, let's go," he said. He flicked a sidelong glance at me and added, "... my lord."

"Very well, Uncle Vidu. We'll b-be there." The knives flew up and down, up and down.

I went out and through the darkness to Drona's tent. He and his son—a wiry boy with short-cropped hair and a beaked nose like his father's—were sitting outside by their campfire. As I approached, they rose to greet me.

"Chief Counselor," Drona said, making namaste. He frowned at Ashwattama and snapped his fingers toward the ground. The boy quickly knelt, leaning to touch my feet.

I stepped back, abashed. "Oh, Drona, he doesn't have to do that here."

"Yes, he does," said Drona. "All right, Ashwa. That will do." Ashwattama rose and stood at attention, eyes down.

"How may I help you, Counselor?" Drona asked.

"I wanted to let you know, the brahmins, the ones from Vrishni who've been traveling with us—they're performing a Sunrise Oblation tomorrow. I am going, as is Prince Duryodhana. I was hoping you'd join us. You *and* your son." I smiled at Ashwattama.

"A Sunrise ... really?" Drona appeared taken aback.

"I know, it's hardly ever seen these days," I said. "It's an interesting opportunity, especially for the boy. To witness such an ancient ritual, I mean."

He glanced at Ashwattama. "Oh, indeed, indeed." His eyes shifted back to me, then to the fire, and he rubbed his mouth with his palm. I did not know why he seemed nervous. I thought perhaps he did not wish to go but was too polite to tell me frankly.

"Of course," I said, "if you are busy ..."

"No, no," he said, holding up his hand in denial. "Your invitation is most kind. I would like to come. Ashwattama, too. As you say, it's a fine opportunity for the boy."

"Excellent," I said. "They've selected a site on the riverbank. We're just a quarter of a kosa west of the river here, so it's a short walk. We'll begin a half hour before dawn."

"I'll have my bearer call me. Thank you again, Counselor."

"Chief Weapons Master."

As I made to leave, he looked pointedly at his son, who bowed low.

≈

After all that, I arrived late to the ceremony. My bearer woke me well in advance, but I fell asleep again, and when he called me a second time it was less than half an hour to sunrise. I dressed in a panic and ran the whole way to the river, stumbling over tree roots in the dark. Bursting, breathless, out of the woods and down the strand, I saw the oblation was already underway. The land on the far side of the Ganges was flat and treeless; the horizon was streaked with violet, pink, and gold, the streaks mirrored in the dark water. The priests stood around the fire in a semicircle facing west with their backs to the river—the sacred fire was small, no bigger than a campfire, but built up with sandalwood, which gave off a sweet scent—while the participants, perhaps forty in all, sat on the pebbly sand in rows facing east. Some had brought blankets or towels to sit on.

I was just going to slip in at the back, when to my further mortification Duryodhana twisted round, waved, and shouted, "Uncle Vidura! Up here!" So I had no choice but to make my way up the side, walk along the front row with everyone staring, and sit down in the space he made for me on his left. Drona was on my left, with Ashwattama next to him. I think Karna was sitting in the row behind with some of the other soldiers. As I scuttled to my seat, Priest Dhaumya, presiding behind the fire, halted the chant and made namaste with a welcoming smile, then with a nod indicated to his fellow celebrants that they could continue. I clasped my hands in my lap and tried not to breathe too loudly. The essential requirement for any sacrament is that it be performed precisely, with not a word flubbed or a pause too long. I was keenly aware I had ruined the whole thing.

But nobody else seemed particularly perturbed, so after a few minutes of sweaty immobility I relaxed a bit and began to mark the proceedings.

The Sunrise Oblation is unique among rituals in that it focuses not on a God who manifests himself in natural phenomena—such as Agni (fire), or Indra (thunder and rain), or Vayu (wind)—but rather on the God of Wisdom, Brihaspati, and the Goddess of Speech, Vacha. One might even call it a meta-ritual, for it pays homage to the Sacred Knowledge itself and the means by which the Sacred Knowledge is expressed and transmitted. So far I did not recognize any of the hymns (as I've said, the ceremony is rarely performed), but I enjoyed seeing how the priests took up the verses in turn, handing off smoothly from one to the other, never in the same order but with no hesitations. Either they had rehearsed a long time, I thought, or else in their movements there was a code indicating who was to chime in next. There were no offerings of blood or ghee into the fire, only the chant and the gestures.

All the time the eastern sky was growing brighter and brighter, until at last a bolt of white light shot from the horizon, across the water and straight into our eyes. At that moment, the priests pivoted to face the sun and began to sing a hymn I did recognize; one, in fact, that I knew well. It is a hymn to the origins of speech, and it begins thus:

> Brihaspati! When men sent out the first utterances of Speech, all that was excellent and spotless was revealed through love.
>
> When the wise in spirit created language, cleansing it like flour through a sieve, friends saw and recognized the marks of friendship; their speech bears the blessed sign.

Why did I know this hymn? My mother used to sing it to me as a lullaby.

My mother, as I have told you, was a maidservant impregnated by Vyasa during his early days in the palace of Hastinapura; she was the "shudra slut" who had occupied the high priest's nights when he was unable to lie with one of the two bulky queens from Kashi. What I have not told you is that Vyasa liked my mother and continued to spend time with her even after he had fulfilled his bargain with my grandmother, spawning my two brothers and me. He described her not only as "adventurous," but also as one of the most intelligent women he had ever known, with a keen interest in topics that usually mean nothing to shudra, let alone female shudra: topics such as history, Law, and the Gods. (Shudra are expected to acknowledge the Gods, of course, but as they do not undergo Purification, they must leave it to the higher castes to participate in the sacraments and intercede on their behalf.)

She had a prodigious memory, Vyasa said, and a thirst for learning. She begged him to teach her hymns from the Agni Oblation, that being the sacrament she had heard the most about, and when he demurred—realizing it might be awkward to have a maid roaming about the palace chanting verses to the Fire God—she asked him if there were other hymns he might teach her, hymns nobody would recognize. He thought of the Sunrise Oblation. Perhaps it amused him to think of his shudra friend knowing songs from an arcane ritual, one with which even many brahmins are unfamiliar. So he taught her a few, this one among them. She, in turn, would sing it to me when she put me to bed.

> With sacrifice the path of Speech they followed, and found her harboring within the Rishis. They dealt her forth in many places; seven singers make her tones resound.
>
> One man with sight has never seen Speech; one man with hearing has never heard her. But to another she shows her beauty as a loving wife, well-dressed, reveals herself to her husband.

The priests, facing the rising sun with arms lifted high, continued to intone. I was overcome with emotion, remembering my mother leaning over me as I lay drowsy on my mat, her face veiled by evening shadows, her voice sweet and low as she sang and I stroked her cheek.

Suddenly I heard a voice right next to me, chanting the words. Jolted from my reverie, I turned in shock, half expecting to see my mother's ghost. She was not there. But what I saw was nearly as strange.

It was Chief Weapons Master Drona, singing so quietly that none but I, and Ashwattama on his other side, could have heard him:

> One man they call a laggard, dull in friendship; they never urge him on to deeds of valor. He wanders in profitless illusion; the voice he hears yields neither fruit nor flower.
>
> No part in Speech has he who has abandoned his own dear friend. Even if he hears her, in vain he listens; he knows nothing of the path of righteous action.

How can I describe the look on Drona's face? He looked happy, painfully happy, as a man might look who returns home after decades of travel in foreign lands and realizes all those years were wasted, for here was his heart all along. Yet when he sang the line about "he who has abandoned his own dear friend," his mien became all sadness. And with these next verses his voice cracked, and I wondered if he might actually be about to cry:

> Unequal in quickness of spirit are friends endowed alike
> with eyes and ears. Some are like shallow water tanks; others
> are like ponds fit to bathe in.

> When brahmins sacrifice together as friends, they leave one
> far behind for lack of attainment; and some who count as
> brahmins wander off.

> Those who neither step back nor move forward, who are not
> true brahmins or pressers of the soma; having used Speech
> in a bad way, they spin out their thread in ignorance.

I faced the river again, embarrassed to have witnessed ... what? I did not know, not then. Much later my grandmother told me about Drona's past: how he had been born a brahmin; had studied the Sacred Knowledge with other brahmin boys but rebelled against his caste, practicing with weapons and as a consequence being dismissed by his guru; and had subsequently traveled to Panchala in hopes of a welcome from his old friend Drupada, but was scorned by the newly crowned king and turned away to wander the world—casteless, friendless, alone.

I did not know any of this then. I sat in the front row, watching the chanting priests and the rising sun but hearing only Drona's voice, fraught with pain, as he sang:

> All his friends rejoice in the friend who comes in triumph,
> having won fame and victory in the contest. He is their
> blame-averter and food-provider. He is fit for deeds of valor;
> he is worthy to win the prize.

≈

The Sunrise Oblation had taken place on the seventh morning of the journey. As we drew nearer to our destination, the forest began to thin and the road to widen, with more villages along the way where we stopped to replenish our provisions. We came across bands of travelers who were also going to the tournament. They were not entourages like ours; only packs of commoners eager for the show, the feasting, the gambling, and the drinking. But I was getting the sense this would be a mighty gathering.

On the ninth afternoon we made camp in a large, dusty field half a kosa from the river, along with many other parties large and small. Drona marked off an arena with stakes and ropes and proceeded with the training session. I could sense his irritation when an excited crowd clustered around the perimeter, hooting and cheering as Duryodhana, Karna, and the other soldiers engaged in wrestling matches and, a little later, sword- and spear-fights. The people were clearly in the festival spirit. When it came time for archery, Drona tried to clear them from the target side, striding over and shouting, "Move! Do you want an arrow in the face?" But the rabble merely shied back, the men guffawing and the women giggling, only to reassemble at the rope as soon as he walked away.

Seeing it was useless, Drona rolled his eyes and signaled to the men to go ahead with the practice, but after someone's arrow flew wide of the target and grazed the shoulder of a boy in the crowd, causing his parents to go into fits—his mother screaming "My son! My son is maimed for life!" and his father stomping about bellowing curses and swearing vengeance on all kshatriya—the chief weapons master called a halt to the session and told everyone to go to their tents and get some rest. He then asked "Sir Karna," in a tone more courteous than I had ever heard him use, if he would "please go and see to the boy's injury." (Karna did. It turned out to be the merest of scratches.)

I approached Drona as he was walking around the makeshift arena, rolling up the rope, and asked him if he'd like to join me on a walk down to the river and back. He stopped, looked at me with tired eyes, and said, "That would be nice." He called to Ashwattama, who ran over and took the rope coil from him. The two of us headed off across the field.

"There's a path," said Drona as we approached the tree line. We took it and walked along in the sun-dappled shade. Up in the branches, parrots squawked. I heard a woodpecker rat-tatting.

"What do you think of Prince Duryo's chances?" I asked.

"I like them," Drona replied. He had picked up a long stick off the ground and was using it to push aside vines and light brush, clearing the way for both of us. "He's come along this past year."

"It has seemed so to me, too. He does you credit as his guru," I said.

"He has great strength and agility. And he takes direction."

We walked along. It was chilly under the trees. I pulled my cloak around me.

"You are cold, Counselor? Shall we go back?" Drona had no cloak, only a vest, but he was not a man to notice the weather.

"No, no," I said. "I'm fine."

I loosened my cloak and tried to look hardy.

"But I hear the Pandavas are coming in from Vrishni," I said. "If Prince Arjuna competes, surely he'll beat the whole field. You always said he was the best you'd ever seen."

"He has the most natural talent, certainly. Whether he has honed that talent these past two years or let it go to waste—that I don't know."

"Oh, surely he wouldn't let it go to waste. He was always dedicated. He practiced hard for you."

"Yes. He was dedicated. But when a boy is sent away—separated from his teacher, from his friends—it's hard to know what will come of it." He flipped a brown earth snake off the path with the end of his stick. "Exile is a hard punishment."

"You think the Pandavas' punishment was unjust, then?"

"I did not say that."

We walked along. I kept my eyes on the ground, watching for snakes.

"*I* think it was unjust," I said. "I think there was no rape. I think the queen and Shakuna set them up."

"I wouldn't doubt it," Drona said. "It's the kind of thing Shakuna would think of."

I looked sharply at him. "Then? If it was all a lie, designed to get rid of the Pandavas and put Duryodhana on the throne? If their banishment was unlawful?"

He stopped and faced me. "What are you saying, Counselor?"

"I'm saying that if the Pandavas were unlawfully exiled, it is our duty to help them. It is your duty to help your students. It is my duty to help my nephews. We can't let Duryodhana win. He mustn't become king."

"Duryodhana is also my student. And your nephew."

"But his claim to the throne is false!" I pulled my cloak tight around me, shivering not with cold now, but with anger. "It's not right! You love Arjuna. *And* his brothers. How can you stand by if you believe they have been so monstrously treated? If you believe the Law has been violated?"

He looked at me for some time before replying.

"Counselor, you seem to know much about the Law. I admit I do not. I only know my job, which is to train the sons of the house of Kuru in weaponry and deportment. That is what King Tarashtra and Lord Bhishma hired me to do, thirteen years ago."

He jabbed the stick into the soil several times.

"Did I like teaching the Pandavas? Yes. I thought them extremely talented. Did I *love* them? No. That is not a word I would use to describe how a teacher regards his students. And it is not right for a teacher to have favorites. So if I did show favoritism for Pandavas over Kauravas, that was wrong of me, and I am ashamed to have done it."

"But," I said, "if you think they were wrongly accused, wrongly exiled …"

"The king's decrees are not for me to judge," he said, turning and continuing along the path a few paces. Then he stopped again and looked back. His face was contorted with anguish.

"Do you really think I would be so mad as to go against the wishes of my employers? The people who took me in, who gave me a position—who have asked me no questions and kept me with them all this time? What sort of a man would I be if I repaid their loyalty with disloyalty? What sort of a man turns against his friends?"

I wondered for the second time in as many days if he were about to cry.

"I am sorry, Drona," I said, reaching out to touch his arm; he flinched back. "I did not mean to offend you. Of course, you owe loyalty to your employers. That is only right."

He turned and walked on. I followed.

Soon we emerged from the trees. The river lay before us, the late-afternoon sun sparkling on its surface. Scores of sandpipers ran to and fro at the edge of the water, their feet leaving no marks on the wet silt. We walked halfway down the strand and stood side by side.

"What are you going to do?" Drona asked.

I watched one bird darting back and forth, back and forth, as if undecided about its course in life.

"I don't know," I said. But then, against my better judgment, I burst out with: "No! I do know. I am going to make sure the Pandavas get what is owed them. Especially Arjuna."

He gave me a piercing look. "Even if you have to break the Law to make sure of it?"

I know I should not have revealed my intention to him, but at that moment I didn't care. Although at that time I did not know his story, perhaps something in me sensed he might understand— understand the need to break the Law for the sake of love.

I nodded, looking down at my feet. "Even if."

Your majesty, I think we'd better stop there. It's late. And tomorrow you're rendering judgments in hall, are you not? You need your rest. Especially with the way the rains are going.

My goodness, the rain … in my fifty-six years I don't think I've ever seen such monsoons. All day, all night, it just keeps coming down. The river frightens me with its height. I hope it doesn't breach its banks and flood the compound.

If it does, what will you do with the Snakes in the horse barns? I can't bear the thought of leaving them to drown. There are children among them, you know; it's not good for children to have wet feet … Well. I won't think about that now.

Ha! If it gets too bad, we'll just have to ask Arjuna to intercede for us with Indra. After all, he's on speaking terms with the Thunder God. "Indra lives in me," he says. It must be a tight squeeze for poor Indra!

All right, Nephew, no need to look disapproving. I'm just an old lady, having my bit of fun. Heh. Oh, dear. Sometimes we have to laugh at the Gods, don't we? They torment us with fire and flood and disease, wage war on us endlessly, and yet we go on living and dying and living some more. Truly, the Gods are no match for us.

What's that? You want to know what happened at the bride-groom choice?

Very well; I guess we can go on a little further. I'll tell you the next part, and then you really must go to bed.

Nagira! Bring me my shawl. No, I *don't* know where it is. Really, dear, you might look in the clothes chest.

Just put it around my shoulders. That's right. Goodness, this damp; it seeps into the bones.

Now then, Sire. About Princess Draupadi ...

Chapter 9

DRAUPADI

18 YEARS BEFORE THE WAR

L ook, Tadyu! Just look at this one!"
Draupadi held up a sky-blue sari with silver threads
running down it like drops of rain. She threw its top over
her shoulder, held out the full skirt, and twirled. "And look what
else! There's a necklace to go with it ..." She cast her eyes around
the dressing room with its abundant furniture, rugs, and curtains.
"Harini, what happened to the necklace?"

"I put it away with the others, my lady. Wait, here it is." The
woman rummaged in a teak jewelry chest and removed a sparkling
heap that shook out into a dozen connected strands of beaten silver. She brought it to her mistress and draped it around her neck.
Draupadi struck a pose with wrists overhead and back to back, fingers spread like lotus petals. All her ladies and maidservants—seventeen of them, for it had amused her father, King Drupada, to gift
her a new waiting-woman each year on her birthday—laughed and
clapped.

"See, Tadyu?" said Draupadi. "Isn't it beautiful? And earrings to
match. No, never mind, Harini, he can just imagine them. Tadyu,
what do you think? I was planning to wear this dress on the second
day of the tournament, but it's so pretty, and it's my favorite color, so
maybe on the last day, instead of the gold-embroidered one ... oh, I
just don't know."

Her twin brother, leaning on the windowsill, put his fist to his
mouth and seemed to give the matter earnest thought. Eventually
he said:

"I would wear the gold one on the *first* day, because on the
first day, you want to make an entrance. On the second day, father
will bring some of the important guests to meet you; you'll want to

look nice, but not forbidding, so you should wear something plain, maybe even dhoti-and-veil; casual, like you're at home, not too many jewels. Then the last day ends with the banquet, and you'll be seated with the winners. That's when you should wear that light blue thing. It looks good on you. You want to look really good that night." He folded his arms with a firm nod. "That's what you should do."

Draupadi went to the mirror that covered a good part of one wall. She chewed her lip as she regarded herself. "Yes ... yes, I think you're right. The gold on day one, casual on day two, maybe my lilac, and this one for the banquet. With the necklace. Oh, Tadyu!" She spun to face him and did a little dance of joy. "They're all going to be competing for *me!* Isn't it exciting?"

"Unbelievably exciting. Can't wait." He shook his head. "Girls have all the luck."

"Pssh. You're just jealous because I'm the center of attention for once."

"Let me point out that I'm never going to have a *bride* choice. Father and the council will choose my wife for me. *I'll* never get to sit in an arena and watch a bunch of girls prance around begging me to pick them." He arched his back, put a hand behind his head, and spoke in falsetto: "Ooo, Prince Tadyu, choose meee!" He slouched down on the sill again. "If only."

"Too bad, so sad!" Draupadi made a face and turned again to the mirror.

Tadyu left his perch and stood beside her, looking into the polished copper. His straight black hair was shorter than hers, but otherwise they were a matched pair: pale skin, wide-set gray eyes, narrow nose, full lips, and slender build. Reflected behind them were the shadowy forms of the waiting women going about their work or gossiping in the corners of the large chamber.

"Only thing is, Padi," said Tadyu to his sister's image, "you'd better be careful. Careful who you choose, I mean."

"Why be careful? They're all princes. They can't enter if not."

"Just because a man is a prince doesn't mean he'll make a good husband."

Her puzzled eyes met his in the mirror. "I'll have three whole days to look them over. All those events, plus the banquet. I'm going to pick the *best* prince. You think I don't know what I want?"

"I'm sure you do know. But Father isn't going to let you pick just anyone. Prince Nothing-clan will be out, no matter how much you like him."

She pouted. "I know *that*. I wouldn't want Prince Nothing-clan, anyway; I'm not some fourteen-year-old ninny. I told you, I want the best."

"I'm just saying. Girls always like the handsome men, or the rich men. But what you really want is someone who'll be nice to you."

Her pout gave way to a complacent smile as she stroked the necklace's multiple loops. "Men are always nice to me."

"*Now* they are. Doesn't mean your husband will be. He won't have to be. That's why you must choose carefully—now, while you've got the upper hand."

Draupadi did not appear to be listening anymore. She was holding out the skirt of the sky-blue sari and shaking it so the silver threads shimmered in the mirror like falling rain.

"Tadyu ..."

"What?"

"You have to ... will you sit with me for the whole thing? Help me decide?"

"Hmm. I'll try. But Father will probably want me to go around with him, greet the nobles, distribute alms to the brahmins and all that. It's a big deal for him, you know, this tournament. He wants everyone to see who we are. How rich we've become."

Draupadi looked down. "I know. I know it's not about me. Not really." She gave the skirt another small shake.

"Well, it isn't as if he could do it without you. You're the reason everyone's coming."

"Yes." Her chin came up and the complacent smile returned. "Yes. I guess I am."

≈

A roar went up from the crowd as Draupadi appeared on the west rim of the enormous bowl. The rising sun lit the gold embroidery covering her sari, making her shine like the morning star. Her veil, jewels, tiara, and fringed parasol—the latter held above her head by a lady-in-waiting—also flashed gold. She paused there on the top step, palms raised in namaste to the cheering throng; then, lifting her skirts out of the dust, she began her descent to the royal platform.

The clamor grew. Every eye was fixed on her as she walked slowly down, down the long flight of stairs, her female entourage—all in saffron yellow—following several paces behind.

The arena had been dug and quarried six tiers deep. The surface of the oval field (one hundred fifty strides long, seventy-five wide) was rolled and scraped to perfect smoothness. The bend of each tier was reinforced with logs of timber, and the flat part where people sat was covered with a thick layer of gravel, depriving the rains of their power of erosion. Drainage was provided by a deep ditch circling the field with a system of tin pipes leading out and away. One could only imagine the man- and elephant-hours that had been required.

King Drupada had wanted the structure set on the outskirts of Kampilya, both to show off the town and for ease of access; the master builder, however, had explained that digging down so far, so near the river, would mean striking the water table and creating a permanent lake. The king had glowered and summoned more builders for their opinion, but when they all said the same, he had agreed to move the site to higher ground half a kosa away, recovering most of his good humor when the master builder promised that a grand avenue, lined with fig and lemon trees and wide enough for four chariots to travel abreast, should run from palace to arena. The work had begun in the tenth year of the king's reign and completed seven years later; that is to say, last year.

The seating was arranged by caste. On the first tier, closest to the field, sat the brahmins; on the second and third, kshatriya; on the fourth and fifth, vaishya; and shudra were permitted to stand around the top, at ground level, and jostle for a view. Given that the carts of the food and drink vendors were also located up top—not to mention the men's and women's latrine pits, which were placed discreetly behind brick walls at one side of the meadow—an argument could be made that the shudra had the best of it. In any case, every tier was filled, which meant some eight thousand spectators, all of whom had packed in early to ensure a seat.

On the field in a line stood the thirty-six contestants, representing, it was said, some twenty-four clans. No distinct impression could be had of them at this point, except that they were a diverse group: all heights, girths, complexions, and postures. They were dressed the same—plain gray dhoti, bare chest, with a thin leather cord around each neck—and for these opening ceremonies, they carried no weapons. Standing in front of them was the tournament master, an imposing figure in a gray cloak, gripping his tall staff of office.

Having arrived at the third tier, Princess Draupadi turned right onto the royal platform, which was situated atop a massive stone jetty extending out to the brink of the field. Its back part was canopied, with stools set in rows; the front was open, affording the spectators a good view of the royals from anywhere in the stadium. Several dozen courtiers were already there; like the rest of the audience, they stood and applauded as Draupadi walked. Prince Tadyu was also there; he did not applaud, but remained at attention as his sister made her way to the front of the rostrum. She stopped and curtsied to him, and he bowed back, equal to equal. Then she took up a position behind her chair—which was elegantly carved but low-backed, so as not to block anyone's sightline—and turned to face the top of the stairs down which she had just come.

The people roared again as King Drupada appeared on the verge. He wore a plain black dhoti and a plain black cloak, as if to make clear that it was his daughter, not he, who was the focus of this occasion; on his chest, however, were many gold chains, and on his brow a gold circlet with an egg-sized black jewel. A gold-hilted sword hung in a black scabbard at his thigh. Vaishya and shudra knelt, brahmins and kshatriya bowed, and everyone held their proper pose, silent, as he descended the stairs to the platform. He walked with ease, arms swinging, dispensing smiles and waves: the proud yet genial host. The eight men of his personal bodyguard marched behind in two columns, spears at the vertical.

Arriving upon the platform he went to his daughter, raised her from her curtsey, kissed her forehead, and led her forward to the balustrade, where he lifted her hand in his, presenting her to the throng. The loudest shout so far rolled like thunder around the huge stadium.

After a suitable interval, Drupada turned and, with a gracious incline of the head, seated Draupadi on her chair. Then he re-faced the arena, held up his hands for silence, and commenced upon this short speech:

"Clans of the Arya! Lords and ladies, priests and seers, friends and guests—I bid you welcome to Panchala. We are glad you have come. Your presence does us honor.

"This is the bridegroom choice of my daughter, the Princess Draupadi. Today and for the next three days, she will observe and assess the competitors for her hand. Never has there been such a contest, with such splendid examples of young manhood, of unalloyed Purity, as we shall see here displayed. I do not know how my daughter will choose," (he shook his head, smiling, at Draupadi; she pressed her palms to her cheeks as if in dread of the weighty decision) "but choose she must. For this form of marriage is the way of the Gandharvas: an ancient and virtuous form, approved by our ancestors, sanctified by the Gods. And I have sworn to honor her choice. Moreover, I have disallowed all gifts, for my daughter is not for purchase. He who would win her must do so on his own merits, by means of skill, courtesy, and valor. Never has there been a prize of such worth; may he who is worthy of the prize succeed!

"Over the course of the tournament, there will be distribution of alms to the brahmins" (polite applause from the first tier); "gifts of grain and cloth for each kshatriya and vaishya family" (applause from the second through fifth tiers); "many animals have been slaughtered for your dinners" (general applause); "and beginning at sundown—free beer for everyone!" At this last statement, lusty cheers rose from the whole arena.

King Drupada waved in acknowledgment, then gestured once more for quiet.

"I know our competitors are eager to show their talents. Indeed, I am sure they cannot wait to join the fray. So, without further ado …" He lifted both arms, palms to the sky. "Let the games begin!"

More cheers and applause as the king seated himself on his stool, which for this occasion was a plain campstool just like the rest, placed to the right of and a little behind his daughter's chair of honor. Tadyu took a matching seat on the other side. The courtiers sat down, too, and throughout the arena there was a great bustle of people arranging blankets and rugs, rummaging in picnic baskets, complaining about the sharp gravel, and hailing the vendors of sweets and roti who had begun to range over the arena's twelve staircases, lugging their containers and holding up their fingers to show the number of copper beads they would take in exchange for their wares. A number of people were streaming up the stairs heading for the food and drink carts, whose owners would accept a variety of goods in barter in case one hadn't brought any copper. Everywhere there was that sense of excitement blended with disgruntlement that characterizes all large public events.

At one end of the field, a tunnel led beneath the tiers to a cavernous room where the contestants stored their weapons, ate, and rested. At the king's signal to begin, all thirty-six men had marched into the tunnel and disappeared from view; they had not, however, retreated to the ready room, for when the tournament master began to announce the names, each man reappeared immediately and ran to take his place on the field for the first event: wrestling.

The tournament master had a booming voice that carried to the top seats:

"Prince Daiveya of Madrasa!"

"Prince Avinashu of Kashi!"

"Prince Yudi of Kuru!"

"Prince Arjuna of Kuru!"

"Prince Baiju of Naimisha!"

"Prince Rishana of Mundra!"

"Prince Duryodhana of Kuru!" ...

Each contestant's name and emergence from the mouth of the tunnel met with a noisy ovation from his fellow clansmen scattered around the arena. Once all were paired up in their appointed spots, a dozen referees ran out and took up positions.

At the tournament master's "On your mark," each man faced his partner. At his "Get set," they crouched down. At his "Go!" they lunged forward, and the bouts began.

≈

The midday sun was unseasonably hot, and Draupadi had summoned the waiting-woman with the parasol to give her and her brother some shade. Tadyu had pulled his stool up close to her chair. On the field, the spear-throwing event was underway.

"No, not that one," the princess was saying. "*That* one—the strong-looking one, with the short black hair and beard. The one who's up next. He placed first in the wrestling."

"Oh, him. He's one of the Kuru," said Tadyu.

"That's what I thought."

"His name is Yudi. No, wait: that's another Kuru. Duro ...

Duryoda? Duryodhana? Yes, Duryodhana. He's the crown prince, I'm pretty sure."

"Duryodhana." Draupadi turned to the three ladies seated in a cluster on her right. All four put their heads together, whispering and giggling. Below, Duryodhana was just stepping forward to make his second throw; when he launched the javelin and it flew a great distance, landing right in the center of the farthest circle marked on the ground, the ladies squealed and clapped. Draupadi clapped, but did not squeal.

She leaned back into the parasol's shade. "I like him. Duryodhana."

"He's been doing well," said Tadyu. "The Kuru are a good clan. Old wealth. Powerful. Father certainly wouldn't mind if you chose him."

"Oh, I don't know *yet*. We've a long way to go. I'm just saying I like him."

"And I'm just saying you could do a lot worse. Although ..." Tadyu knit his brow and scratched behind his ear. "I just remembered: there's some question about the succession. With the Kuru, I mean."

"What question?"

"I don't know, exactly. Some dispute between two sides of the family—about who's the real heir. That chap Duryodhana is the crown prince, but the other Kuru, that Prince Yudi—he also has a claim to the throne, apparently. He and his brothers. But they were banished for a while because of some crime they committed. I think."

"Where did you hear all this?"

"In council, last week, when Father was going over the list of contestants. I wasn't really paying attention. My point is there's some conflict there, so choosing a Kuru could be risky."

Draupadi rolled her eyes. "Successions and heirs and banishments. How am I supposed to know about all that? Nobody tells me such things. Anyway, it's the same in every clan: you men are always fighting over who's to be king, and once you've got it figured out, you start fighting over who's to be the *next* king. It won't be any different no matter which prince I choose. No matter what happens to him, I'll have the same job."

"What job is that?"

"To keep my husband happy and produce sons."

Tadyu gave his sister a thoughtful look. "Hmm. Can't argue with you there."

They turned their eyes again to the action on the field.

"Now here comes that third Kuru," Tadyu said; "he's quite young, they say. Our age. His name begins with Ar ... Ar-something."

"Arjuna?" said Draupadi.

"That's it! Arjuna. How did you know?"

"Father sent the tournament master yesterday to recite the list to me and my ladies. It seems I pay better attention than you. All right, here he goes, watch." She laid her hand on the balustrade and leaned far forward. "Oh, well thrown! Bravo!"

Arjuna, hearing her call, looked up at the royal platform, smiled, and inclined his head. He shook his dark hair out of his eyes and kept on smiling at her as he went to collect his spear.

Draupadi's cheeks flushed pink. She sat back on her chair, fingers pressed to her lips. Then she leaned left again and said to her brother:

"I like *him,* too."

≈

The first morning had included wrestling, jousting (with blunt-tipped staves), and spear-throwing. There was a break at midday, during which most people climbed the stairs to ground level and sought out food, water, or latrines. The beer barrels would not be rolled out until evening, but long lines formed at the roasting pits in which turned on spits the sizzling carcasses of steers, goats, and sheep—more evidence of King Drupada's wealth and generosity. Upper-caste families had set up their tents in the meadow and could retreat there for a nap; shudra and less-prosperous vaishya could walk five hundred paces to the verge of the forest and lie down under a tree until the gong sounded for the afternoon events: horse and chariot racing.

First up were heats on horseback: four riders at a time, ten times around the oval, with disqualification for going out of bounds or blocking another horse too obviously. Saddle blankets in bright patterns marked the riders' clans. Up on the royal platform, the princess and her ladies were in a tizzy of excitement, placing bets and cheering for their favorites.

"Mine's winning! Mine's winning!"

"Look, Kashi on the outside! Here he comes! Goooooo, Kashiiiiiii!"

"Madrasa! Come *on*, Madrasa! Yes ... yes ... *yes!*"

"Oh, no ... *no!* Did you see that? He cheated, no fair!"

"Madrasa wins! I win, I win, ha-ha! Pay up, Harini!"

Lady Harini turned her back to the field, plopped down on the balustrade, and pouted. "He galloped right in front of my Kashi prince. Why didn't the referee call it? It's not *fair*."

The other lady smirked and held out a hand, flexing her wrist with affectation. "One copper bangle, please. *As* agreed!"

"Go on, Harini, pay up," said Draupadi, laughing. "Win some, lose some!"

Harini, still pouting, worked a bangle down off her forearm and handed it over.

The eight heats yielded eight semifinalists, who ran two more heats to determine who would go head-to-head in a match race. The two finalists hailed from distant lands: a prince of Gandaram (the son of Shakuna's eldest brother, as it happens) and the prince from Mundra. The Gandaram prince won, to Draupadi's delight; she had bet heavily on him, knowing that her father sent traders to that far northwestern country to acquire horses from what were said to be the finest herds in the world.

Chariot races came next, which brought the crowd to a new pitch of stomping, whistling, and yelling as steeds and drivers thundered round and round the field, tipping and even crashing on the turns. Not all the contestants had brought a chariot, let alone two; there were only twenty entrants to the event, and several of them had to bow out when they broke an axle or did some other irreparable damage to their vehicle. But Duryodhana and Arjuna both made it to the semifinals, along with the princes from Madrasa and Naimisha. Arjuna and the Naimisha prince then matched up in the day's last race.

The king, who had spent most of the day out among his guests, had returned to the rostrum for the chariot races. When Prince Baiju won, he gave a derisive snort and remarked to his daughter, "Naimisha! Luck was with him. We certainly can't credit those horses."

As the sun dropped to the western lip of the great bowl, the contestants lined up once more at the center of the field. Knotted on the leather cords around their necks were bits of colored ribbon indicating the points they'd won and in which events. The referees examined the ribbons and used sticks to mark each man's tally in the dust at his feet; then the tournament master stalked down the line, right to left, noting the tallies; and back again, left to right, tapping some men on the shoulder and passing others by. The ten men who had received a tap stepped forward. Duryodhana and Arjuna were among them; Yudi was not. (It later transpired that Yudi had been running on no sleep, having joined an all-night dice game the evening before.)

Up on the platform, Tadyu approached the balustrade. His father had assigned him the task of closing each day. As he raised his arms, the setting sun at his back made two spindly black shadows that extended down over the field and up the tiers on the other side: the arms of a God or demon, reaching across the bowl of the universe.

"My *friends!*" It came out a squawk. He coughed and tried again.

"My friends." (That was better.) "This concludes the first day of the bridegroom choice of my sister, the Princess Draupadi. All the contestants have performed nobly. Please join me in applauding them."

The audience complied.

"But only these …" (his forefinger moved, counting quickly) "only these *ten* will advance to the next round. Let us congratulate our semifinalists."

Another, louder ovation.

"And now, it is time … we thank you … I mean, we are *honored* …" His voice cracked again, and his arms began to droop. Behind him, the king frowned.

A raucous shout from below: "*Where's the beer?*"

Tadyu laughed. He brought his arms up high again and shook his fists in the air.

"Beer up top! Come and get it!"

A deafening huzzah; a rush for the staircases. Tadyu collapsed onto his stool and mopped his brow with the hem of his cloak.

Draupadi leaned over and placed a hand on her brother's shoulder. "Well done," she whispered.

≈

The first event of the second day was steer-roping. As it was getting underway, King Drupada, his chief counselor, and his son stood behind the princess's chair and conferred.

"That is correct, your majesty," said the chief counselor. His voice was clipped, precise. "Two of the semifinalists are of the Kuru clan, but one of those two—Prince Arjuna—belongs to the set of brothers who were banished from Kuru these past two years. They're known as the Pandavas. Arjuna's sponsors include his brothers, naturally, but (and herein lies the question) they also include the crown prince of Vrishni, which is the clan that's been hosting the Pandavas in their exile."

The king stroked his full black beard. "So, is he to be considered Kuru or Vrishni?"

"Exactly, Sire. You've seen the problem. The two sides of the family are not on good terms. If we honor one side, we risk offending the other."

"I couldn't care less about offending Vrishni," said the king. "A worthless clan; no cattle to speak of. On the other hand, if these men are all Kuru, we should tread carefully."

"Quite so," said the counselor. "But here is one more thing, Sire: should Prince Arjuna make it to the chariot archery—as you know, that's the final event tomorrow—the person registered as his charioteer is none other than the crown prince of Vrishni."

"What?!" said the king. "How odd! Are you sure?"

"Yes, Sire. Like you, I was astonished when I heard, so I asked the tournament master, and he assured me it's true. Prince … Krishna, I believe his name is, will be the driver for Prince Arjuna, should he make it to the finals."

"Huh," said the king, shaking his head with a frown. "I guess it's too late to tell them it's not allowed. But I don't like it. A kshatriya, doing a vaishya's job. No, I don't like it."

"Perhaps Arjuna won't achieve the finals, Father," said Tadyu. "Then we won't have to worry about it."

"That's not the point," said the king, waving his hand irritably. "Word of this will get out, even if he isn't in the finals. People will assume I condone this sort of caste-mixing. Which I don't. If he's a crown prince, why didn't this Krishna enter as a contestant, for Gods' sake? What can he be thinking?"

The counselor gave a discreet cough. "If I may, Sire …"

"Yes, yes, what?"

"I would suggest that you *not* invite the Kuru-Vrishni cohort to meet her highness. Invite only the regular Kuru faction. And invite *all* of the latter—whomever they've sent, noble or otherwise. That will send a clear message as to where your favor and disfavor lie."

The king stroked his beard some more. "Yes, that makes sense. So we'll invite Mundra, Gandaram, Madrasa, and Kuru—the *regular* Kuru—and that's it. In that order. Tadyu, you can start bringing them up when the roping event is over. Be sure to space them out a bit. Allow each group to stay for half an hour or so."

"Yes, Father."

"Good. Well, I'm off to mingle. Counselor, come, we need to discuss the next round of alms for the brahmins. The fruit baskets are looking meager; we need to throw some flowers on top, or feathers, something …"

Throughout this entire exchange, Draupadi's eyes had been on the steers and rider-ropers charging around the field below. But instead of chatting with her women, she was sitting quietly with head tilted to one side. She appeared to be thinking.

≈

The sun was nearing its zenith, the swordfights had concluded, and the target-archery event was well underway when Tadyu climbed the stairs to the royal platform for the fourth time that morning. Behind him came the delegation from Kuru, followed in turn by an honor guard of two of the king's men.

One of Draupadi's ladies, an older woman with a creased but merry face, whispered in her mistress's ear. The princess, who was slumped in her chair waving a straw fan at her bare midriff, blew air from puffed cheeks. "Lord, Mimi. Is this the last lot? Please say it is."

"I think so, Princess. Goodness, it's hot today! You're all in a muck. Here, let me give you a wipe. Sit up, now."

Mimi poured some water from a jug onto a kerchief and quickly mopped Draupadi's neck, arms, and chest, being careful not to wet the lilac silk chest-band or dhoti. The princess sat still as a doll during the procedure.

"You'd think it was the third month, not the twelfth," said Mimi, smoothing the long black hair under the lilac veil with a wrinkled hand. "There, Ma'am, you'll do. Here they come. Smile, now. Ooh ... that one is awfully handsome!" She stepped back, tittering.

Draupadi rose and turned to greet the men approaching along the platform.

Tadyu had grown more adept with each introduction. He ushered the guests forward with a lordly air. The guards retreated and the trio lined up in front of the princess; they were empty-handed, the king having been quite clear about his no-gifts policy.

"Sister," said Tadyu, "may I present our distinguished visitors from the Kuru clan, sponsors of Crown Prince Duryodhana. This is Counselor ... uh, *Chief* Counselor Vidura, uncle to the crown prince."

Vidura bowed deeply. Draupadi made namaste, raising her hands high to her forehead and lowering her thick-lashed eyes.

"Chief Weapons Master Drona, the crown prince's guru."

Drona bowed deeply. Draupadi made namaste again.

"And here is Sir Kar ... um ... Sir *Karna*, the crown prince's friend."

Karna did not bow. He stood with arms at his sides and mouth slightly open, staring at the princess. He looked as if he'd just been struck on the head with a mace.

Draupadi, who had raised her hands again to return the expected salutation, lowered them and waited. Her brows went up a little, but she did not seem perturbed. Drona, next to Karna, shot him a frown. Vidura seemed to be watching the field, where another archer was stepping to the line to take his turn at the target. For several moments, no one moved or spoke.

Tadyu, his cheeks reddening, cleared his throat and said, "I apologize, Sir. I must have ... I think I got your name wrong. Is it not Sir Karna?"

Drona jabbed an elbow into Karna's ribs and hissed, "*Bow*," whereupon Karna seemed to recall himself. He blinked hard, stiffened his back, and bent low to the princess. Draupadi raised her hands and dipped her chin.

As Karna straightened up, she gestured toward the balustrade and said, "Please, sirs, join my brother and me." She did not wait, but went to her chair and sat down. Vidura and Drona hung back until Tadyu had seated himself on his sister's left; they then drew up stools on his other side. Karna, however, hastened to the princess's

right and lowered himself onto the stool there. He began by looking
out at the arena, but his eyes slid sideways, then his head revolved
a little, then a little more, and before a minute had passed he was
staring straight at Draupadi again. His two hands gripped the strap
of his leather satchel. His mouth remained open.

Draupadi turned to him with a gracious smile. "I hear Kuru is
a beautiful country, Sir Karna. Is your principal town right on the
river?"

Karna shut his mouth and swallowed. "Yes," he said.

"Yes, it's beautiful, or yes, it's on the river?" Her eyes were teasing.

"Um ... both."

"I see. What's the name of the town?"

"Hastinapura."

"What a nice name. Is it very far from here? How long is the
journey?"

Karna did not reply. He swallowed again.

"Sir Karna?"

"Oh ... sorry. What did you say?"

"I asked, how long is the journey from Hastinapura?"

"Oh. Um ... it depends."

"Depends on what?"

"On ... different things."

Her smile grew a little fixed. "Well, how long is the journey
generally?"

"I don't know. Five days. Or ten. It depends."

No longer smiling, Draupadi turned to regard the field. On her
other side, Tadyu was talking with the Kuru counselor and chief
weapons master. She took a breath, restored her pleasant expression,
and turned back to Karna, whose gaze had not left her face.

"What do you think of our arena, Sir? Do you have one like it?"

"No," said Karna.

"Well, what do you think of it? Isn't it grand?"

He shot a glance at the stadium. "It's all right."

Her lips pressed together in a thin line. "I'm so glad you approve."
She turned away again and leaned forward to watch as the next man
approached the mark to shoot. It was Prince Arjuna, and his arrow
hit the bullseye, raising a cheer from the crowd. Karna appeared not
to notice. He continued to stare at the princess as she applauded
gaily. His hands continued to grip the satchel strap.

"Who do you want to win?" He blurted the question.

Draupadi stopped mid-clap with a look of surprise. "Oh, I …
I don't know …" She sat up straight, put her hands in her lap, and
adopted a formal tone. "All the contestants are marvelous. I don't
know how I shall ever choose."

"Yes, but you'll have to choose," he said. "So who will it be?"

She crossed her arms and gave a hiss of exasperation. "Well if you
must know, I like that Prince Arjuna, the one who just went. Oh …"
She brightened a bit. "I just remembered. He's a Kuru, isn't he? Do
you know him? What's he like?"

Karna looked down at his feet. "I could not say."

Her eyes narrowed. "What exactly is it that you do in
Hastinapura?"

"I'm a soldier," he said softly. "Just an ordinary soldier."

"You're more than an ordinary soldier if you're part of the Kuru
delegation. My father doesn't invite just anybody to the royal platform, you know."

He shrugged, his eyes still downcast. "I am Prince Duryodhana's
friend."

"Oh, then you know *him* well, at least," she said, her eagerness
returning. "What's *he* like? Do tell me!"

He looked up, frowning. "Why do you care about him? You said
you liked Arjuna."

Her expression grew crosser than ever. "I do! And I like
Duryodhana, too. He's done very well so far. Perhaps I'll pick *him* as
my bridegroom."

Suddenly, Karna looked afraid—terribly afraid.

"No. No." He shook his head. "You would not like Duryodhana."

"What *do* you mean? You just said you were his friend!"

"I am, but …" His hands clenched and unclenched on the
satchel strap. "No. Don't choose him. You would not like him."

Draupadi sat up straight again and drew her veil across her
bosom. "Well, now I'm intrigued. I hope Prince Duryodhana wins a
lot more and gets to the final. I hope I meet him at the banquet. Him
and Prince Arjuna. They both seem absolutely perfect." With a toss
of her head, she turned away and leaned over to speak with the men
seated on her brother's left.

Karna stared at the back of her head. His face was a study in
miserable longing.

It is doubtful that any of the three hundred banquet guests had ever seen a room so brightly lit. Suspended from the ceiling of the great hall of the Kampilya palace were some three dozen wooden wheels, like wagon wheels laid on their side, with an oil lamp attached to the end of each delicately carved spoke. The effect was of myriad stars twinkling overhead. As they dined, many of the ladies kept their heads down with veils pulled forward against the brilliance; the men shaded their eyes with their hands as they squinted upward, exclaiming about the design of the fixtures and speculating about the cost.

There were exclamations, as well, about the royal table at one end of the hall. It was circular—which wasn't unusual—but its top was a full arm's length above the ground, and each guest there was seated, incredibly, on a chair.

"Look at them up there! Like parakeets around a birdbath," remarked one of the princes who had failed to reach the semifinals. He was sitting in the usual way at the next table, which was of normal height. His quip raised laughter from his companions. King Drupada's downward twitch of the lips was the only sign that he had heard the jest.

Fourteen parakeets perched on high. Princess Draupadi, in her sky-blue sari with the silver-thread raindrops, was seated across from her father facing out to the hall; on her right was Prince Duryodhana, the winner of the tournament, in his black dhoti and black leather vest; on her left, Prince Arjuna, the runner-up, in his white and ivory. Next to Duryodhana was Chief Weapons Master Drona; then Sir Karna, who ate and drank with eyes fixed on the princess; then Counselor Vidura; then old priest Dhaumya, who had been invited at Vidura's request; and finally, on the king's left, Prince Tadyu. Next to Arjuna sat his four brothers—Yudi, Bimasena, Naku, and Saku—and, on the king's right, Prince Krishna of the Vrishni. Resting on an ebony plinth in front of the princess was a large double-handled cup, wrought of silver and carved with swirling vines flecked with leaves of onyx.

The tournament, everyone agreed, had been a huge success. The third day had begun with a crowd-pleaser, a horse-sport of the king's own invention in which all thirty-six of the original contestants divided into two teams and galloped about the field swinging long wooden mallets in an attempt to hit a ball through goalposts at either end. Points were awarded to those who hit goals and those who prevented goals, though it was unclear what to do when (as happened more than once) someone hit the ball through his own team's goalposts or decided to wield his mallet like a jousting stick in order to knock his rivals to the ground. The constant confusion of the referees and the king's bellows of correction from the royal platform did nothing to dampen the audience's enthusiasm for the boisterous new game. The arena was abuzz: "We must arrange for this to be played back home in Madrasa!" "In Kashi!" "In Mundra!"

The atmosphere had grown more serious with the announcement of the final event. Four men would compete in the chariot archery: the two Kuru princes, the prince of Gandaram, and the prince of Naimisha. The contest was preceded by a parade around the field, each man standing and waving to the cheering throng, his driver at the reins, his horses decked out with jeweled bridles and egret plumes. Up on the royal platform, the princess's ladies were in a frenzy of speculation. The princess herself sat quietly watching, her father leaning now and then to murmur in her ear. Occasionally, she murmured something back.

Arjuna won the event handily. The Gandaram prince came second, Duryodhana third, and the prince of Naimisha fourth. But Duryodhana had come into the third day with the most ribbons on his neck-cord, so when the four men lined up for the final count by the referees, he and Arjuna had the same tally scratched in the dust at their feet. Even so, it was the princess's privilege to select the winner and runner-up; after all, it was her bridegroom choice.

She descended the stairs—flanked by the king's full bodyguard and followed by two ladies-in-waiting, each of whom carried a rose garland, one red, one pink—and crossed the field to the finalists. The stadium held its breath as she went down the line, speaking a few words of congratulation to each contestant. You could have heard the swish of a tiger's tail as she lifted the pink garland and stood looking from man to man, as if in indecision. When she looped the pink roses over Arjuna's head, indicating second place, a great shout of approval went up (for many had had bets on Arjuna). Then silence fell again as she collected the red roses; and when she draped them on Duryodhana, the roar for the winner would have drowned out the roar of the ocean churned by the First Gods in their quest for the elixir of immortality.

Now, in the banquet hall, course three of ten was just arriving. It was hilsa fish, deboned and cooked in a turmeric-and-mustard sauce, one fish per diner. The serving-men ran panting with their trays, struggling to get three hundred individual plates out at more or less the same time. The beer-maids with their ewers were also hard pressed, rushing to and fro in response to tankards waved aloft and shouts of "Fill up, here! Fill up!"

At the royal table, Arjuna was speaking to the princess; at least, he had begun his remarks with "Your highness," but was now addressing the whole group.

"… and when I saw the targets that had been devised for us, I could not have been more delighted. Any archer can hit a stationary target, but a *moving* target, now, that's another story. Not many archers are adept with *moving* targets, but my guru Drona" (he nodded across the table, smiling, and Drona nodded back, grave-faced) "always insisted that I put in hours—hours, Drona, do you remember?—shooting at birds and other live game. And then Prince Krishna and I did the same, in Vrishni. Wonderful hunting in Vrishni!" Putting a finger to his brow, he threw an insouciant salute in Krishna's direction. Krishna lifted his cup in smiling response.

"So," Arjuna went on, "when the tournament master demonstrated the device for us, how it fires wooden discs up into the sky, and I realized it was just like shooting grouse that the beaters send up, only from a chariot—well, I immediately grasped the situation and felt perfectly confident. The other finalists, now, they didn't seem at all confident. My cousin Duryodhana, he turned quite pale. Didn't you, Duryo? Ha! I thought you were going to faint!" He grinned round, inviting everyone to share the joke. His brothers chuckled.

Duryodhana seemed unflustered by the jabs. Leaning back at ease in his chair, he took a swig of beer and addressed King Drupada: "Indeed, Sir, it was a quite a challenge you set us. How did you come to create such a device?"

The king, looking pleased, launched into an explanation of his invention. Arjuna had taken a breath as if to continue his soliloquy on moving targets, but fell silent and toyed with his fish as the king talked on with animated gestures.

Duryodhana turned to the princess and said in a loud whisper,

"Your highness, I fear my cousin needs some help with his f-fish." He leaned forward, staring past her at Arjuna, who was probing gingerly at his plate with his knife. "*Ssst,* Arjuna! The fish has had its b-bones removed. You can just eat it. Use your spoon."

His whisper carried round the table. A few people turned to look.

Arjuna used his spoon to shovel a big piece of hilsa into his mouth and chewed, glaring at his cousin, who stared back blandly. The princess covered her mouth to suppress a giggle.

The king finished his disquisition. He directed a question to Priest Dhaumya, and the conversation around the table broke up into twos and threes.

"Your cousin seems displeased with you, Sir," said Draupadi, her eyes twinkling. "Do you two always spar like that?"

"Oh, we tease each other," said Duryodhana. "It's all in good f-fun. I have the greatest respect for all my cousins, of course."

"Is it true they were in exile for the past couple of years?"

He nodded, sighing. "Quite true. Yes, my father had to b-banish them. They went off to Vrishni. Everyone in Hastinapura has m-missed them terribly. Well," (he raised an eyebrow) "perhaps not *everyone.*"

"Dare I ask why they were banished?"

The crooked grin pulled askew. "You can dare."

She leaned closer, eyes wide. He put his lips next to her ear and whispered:

"Doesn't mean I'll tell you."

She reared back, laughing, and dealt a light slap to his arm. "You beast! Now you *have* to tell me."

"Ow!" He massaged the arm in mock pain. "Not if you're going to use v-violence."

"Oh, please! As if a mighty warrior like you could be hurt by a woman!"

He laughed. Then he looked down at the table. The fish dishes had been removed, and the fourth course (a vegetable curry) was being served in small bowls. He leaned aside to allow the serving man to place the bowl before him, at the same time rubbing his other arm. There was a small red mark there, just below the copper band.

After a short pause, he said: "It's the w-women who do the m-most hurt."

She looked at him curiously. "What do you mean by that?"

"Oh …" He raised his head, smiling again. "I don't m-mean anything. Look, I'd rather hear about you and Panchala. What about that arena your father built? What a p-place!"

"Isn't it? It's only been open for a year, but we've already held all sorts of games and races there …" She talked on, and Duryodhana listened, putting in a question now and then.

Around the table, the conversations continued.

As the fifth course (leg of mutton glazed with mint sauce, one per table) was being set down, King Drupada was speaking in a frosty tone to his neighbor on the right:

"… and is it the custom in Vrishni for princes to drive chariots?"

"Well, King Drupada," replied Krishna, "since I am the only prince in Vrishni, and I drive a chariot—on occasion, that is—I suppose I would have to say yes. Mutton? Here, let me hold the plate for you while you carve."

Krishna swept aside his blue fur-lined cloak and handed the dish to the king with an air of condescension. The king opened his mouth to retort but, confronted with the mutton, shut it again. He picked up his knife, gripped the leg bone, and sawed at the meat with vigor.

The sixth course (ribs of beef, well charred) arrived at the tables.

Arjuna, his voice a little slurred, was bantering with his brothers. "Course I woulda done better in the spear-throwing, only Naku had to go and break my bes' spear on the way here. I couldn't do a … do a *thing* with my second-bes'."

"Hah! As if it would have made any difference," said Naku. His face was a bit pink, making him even handsomer than usual. "You've always thrown like a girl, 'juna."

"A girl! Thass rich coming from you, Prince Long-hair. If you were any prettier, you'd … you'd *be* a girl."

"Ooh! I'm so hurt. Ha, I'll be a girl any day. Better than an elephant, like Bima!" Naku extended his arm out from his nose and waved it over Bima's plate with a trumpeting noise.

Bima hoisted his tankard out of the way of the swinging arm. "Watch it, brother! Insult me all you like, but spill my beer and you'll see what a raging elephant can do."

Naku, Saku, and Arjuna instantly began pounding on the table, chanting, "El-e-funt! El-e-funt!" Bima, laughing, made to rise and knocked his chair over in the attempt. Yudi, putting a hand on his brother's bulky shoulder, said something in his ear. Bima picked up the chair and reseated himself, looking chastised. Krishna leaned over to offer more praise of Arjuna's performance in the final event. Talk of chariots, horses, and archery ensued.

The seventh course (partridges in mango sauce) was served.

Yudi leaned toward his youngest brother and said quietly, "Arjuna."

"What?"

"You need to be speaking with the princess."

"Huh? I have been shpeak ... speaking to her."

"No, you've been speaking to the table. You need to speak with *her*. Make yourself pleasant. Make sure she chooses you."

"Of course she's gonna choose me." He snickered. "She's not gonna choose ol' Scar-face."

"I wouldn't be so sure. They seem to be getting along. She's been laughing all evening."

Arjuna threw his cousin a quick, contemptuous glance.

"Thass cause she finds his stuttering funny."

"No. She likes him. It's obvious."

Arjuna rolled his eyes. "Oh, all right, all *right*. I'll talk to her. Look, here I go."

He turned to Draupadi and loudly asked her to guess the number of partridges he had once shot in a single day. She seemed startled, but gave him her attention with a polite smile and proceeded to listen to his tale of hunting prowess.

The eighth course (an elaborate pudding with layers of rice, cream, nuts, and fruit mixed with honey) was set down in a great bowl on each table.

Chief Weapons Master Drona, on Duryodhana's right, had been taciturn all evening. He kept patting his hip, as if feeling for a sword. (As in the stadium, weapons were disallowed at the banquet.) King Drupada, although he had spoken to every other guest at the royal table, had so far not said anything to Drona; now he took a breath as if bracing himself for an unpleasant task, directed his gaze left, and said:

"Well, Drona. It has been a long time." He drummed his knife lightly on the table. "Ah ... my apologies. I suppose I should say *Sir* Drona."

Drona, unsmiling, said: "Chief Weapons Master Drona." He made the king a tiny bow. "Your majesty."

"What? Oh. Yes. Chief Weapons Master. That's what you do in Hastinapura, eh?"

"Yes, your majesty."

"Ah. Well ... it certainly has been a long time." The king addressed his son. "Drona and I used to play together as boys, Tadyu. Can you imagine? Here, in Panchala. We were just eight or nine years old. The things we got up to. I was the crown prince, and he was ... yes, well. It was a long time ago. Ha! The things we got up to. Didn't we, Drona?" He shook his head, chuckling, and drummed the knife some more. "Old friends. Old friends."

Drona, stone-faced, said nothing.

The king glanced around the hall as if seeking an exit. "Well ... Chief Weapons Master ... it's good to see you. Perhaps we'll have a chance to talk again soon. I hope so. Yes."

Drona gave another tiny bow. "Your majesty."

The king turned to his right. "Prince Bimasena! Why did you not enter the tournament? Surely you would have swept all before you ..."

The ninth course (several cheeses, sheep and cow's milk, served with roti) came out from the kitchens.

On the ceiling fixtures, a few of the oil lamps had gone out. Duryodhana, who had re-engaged the princess's attention, pointed upward and made a comment. She laughed. As he spoke on, she caught her father's eye across the table and smiled. The king smiled back at her, stroking his black beard and nodding gently.

Arjuna rehashed the tournament with his brothers and Krishna. Tadyu and Dhaumya chatted about the unseasonably warm weather. Karna watched the princess laughing with his friend. Drona stared straight ahead and ate a hunk of cheese.

Counselor Vidura, his cheese course untouched, was flicking his eyes from king to princess, princess to king, and back again.

The tenth and final course arrived: trays of beautiful little cakes, cut in fanciful shapes, drizzled with pomegranate juice and sprinkled on the top with actual sugar. Oohs and aahs wafted around the hall.

Draupadi made one more smiling comment to Duryodhana and looked again across the table at her father, her brows raised in a question. The king leaned back in his chair and gave her a nod of unmistakable approval. She smoothed her silver necklace and adjusted her sky-blue veil. Then she leaned forward, reaching for the silver-and-onyx cup …

"King Drupada!"

All heads turned toward Counselor Vidura. He was sitting up straight, eyes bright, cheeks flushed. Draupadi froze with her hands halfway to the cup.

"Uh … yes, Counselor?" said the king. "Is something wrong?"

"Oh, no, Sir, no indeed," said Vidura, his voice strangely loud. "Nothing at all wrong. It's just that I wanted to tell you an amusing story about Crown Prince Duryodhana. You'll appreciate it, I know. It's really very amusing." He glanced round the table, baring his teeth in a grin that was almost a grimace. "You will all think so."

The diners, including Duryodhana, looked back at him with expressions of mild surprise.

"Uh … very well," said the king. "Please. Tell us the story."

"Yes," said Vidura. He picked up a piece of roti and began to crumble it as he spoke. "You see, two years ago, our prince fell in love. Madly in love. Which isn't unusual for a young man, of course, but the thing is, the girl he fell in love with, she was a … she was …"

The breadcrumbs scattered from his fingers as he rubbed them together, harder and faster. The grin became a rictus.

"She was a *Snake*."

All eyes flew to Duryodhana. His face was a blank.

"That's right!" said Vidura. "A Snake. Now, listen …" All eyes flew back to him. "You might think it was just a boy's first adventure, getting a bit of experience—nothing wrong in that. But no, no, I assure you, our prince was in *love* with this Snake girl. She was a maidservant in our old queen's quarters, which in itself is highly improper, I know, but then old people do get these fancies. They will have their way. Our dear old queen even let this girl handle her food, if you can believe it."

King Drupada was leaning forward now, his attention riveted on the counselor.

"At any rate," Vidura continued, his voice growing still louder, "Prince Duryodhana simply worshiped this Snake girl. He wanted to marry her. He actually *asked* her to marry him. Now here is the really funny thing; you'll never guess what. You'll never, never guess."

He scooped up another bit of roti, squeezing it in his fist. His voice rose nearly to a scream as he beat the table:

"*She. Turned. Him. Down.*"

He held up his hands, waving them and letting fall the squashed roti. "Yes—a Snake girl—turned down our crown prince! The gall of her! Oh, but he was terribly upset. For a while we all thought he might do away with himself. His parents were *very* worried."

People at nearby tables were now staring.

"And you'll hardly believe this, Sire, but I happen to know ..." He leaned far forward, chest on his plate, head thrust toward the king, eyes bulging. His voice became a violent hiss:

"*He is still in love with her.* Still in love with that outcaste girl. You mark my words, Sire: once he's king, he'll be taking her as his second wife. Or I should say—his *real* wife."

He sat back up, breadcrumbs sticking to his shirtfront. He brushed at them, grinning round the table again. "Ha-ha! Such a funny story, isn't it? Princess Draupadi—don't *you* find it funny?"

Draupadi was sitting far back in her chair, rigid as a statue.

"Oh, I know it sounds ridiculous, but Drona, Karna," (he turned to his left) "you two were there. You can bear me out, can't you?"

Drona's arms were folded, his face impassive; he shook his head at Vidura ever so slightly. Karna was looking at the princess with distressed eyes; he appeared not to have heard the question.

Suddenly, Yudi spoke. "I can bear you out."

The king turned to him. "So this is true?"

"Yes, your majesty," said Yudi, "all quite true. I know, because our mother sent that very same Snake girl to my bachelor party, two years ago. She was a gift to my brothers and me. And Duryodhana came to the party—he and his friend Karna—in order to rescue the girl. He did not want her ... defiled." He turned to his cousin. "Isn't that right, Duryo?"

Duryodhana's face was still a blank. His left hand rubbed the spot below his copper armband as he turned slowly toward Yudi.

"Yes. That's right."

Around the royal table, there was silence. Throughout the hall, the munching of cakes, swilling of beer, and tipsy chatter continued.

The princess looked at her brother; he gave her a rueful smile and a small shrug.

She looked at her father, smoothed her necklace, and nodded, once.

The king got up, came around the table, and pulled out her chair for her. She stood. He raised his hand and waited until the noise in the hall had ceased.

He said: "My daughter has made her bridegroom choice!"

Draupadi reached forward, using both hands to lift the silver cup. She held it before her as the two champions rose and faced each other.

She turned left—and gave the cup to Arjuna.

I know, I know—the mild-mannered Vidura! I don't blame you, Nephew, for being incredulous. But he confirmed, when I asked him years later, that he had indeed said those things at the banquet. He told me it had taken all his courage, but he thought of his brother Pandu and his silent promise to protect his son, and that thought drove me on.

I admit I still feel a little angry with Vidura. Had Draupadi married my father instead of Arjuna, none of the terrible events, including the Great War, would have followed. Although, karma being what it is, who can say? We can no more change the consequences of our ancestors' actions than our descendants will be able to change the course we are laying down for them with our own actions today. Fate is fate.

After the bridegroom choice there were still two weeks until the end of the Pandavas' exile, so they went from Panchala back to Vrishni, accompanied by Krishna and taking Arjuna's new wife, and her dowry, with them. The dowry was not nearly as lavish as they had expected; King Drupada, when he presented them with the single wagonload of goods and the dozen or so horses (not even terribly good horses), made a comment to the effect that the tournament had wrung him dry and that, in any case, an alliance with Panchala was the real dowry. Yudi looked displeased but nevertheless made a speech expressing his gratification at the long friendship between the two clans being at last made formal.

They started for Vrishni immediately after the marriage ceremony, so Draupadi's wedding night occurred on the road. She and

Arjuna were provided with a tent of their own, naturally, but it was odd (she later told me): Arjuna invited all his brothers to dinner that night, and the five of them sat late eating, drinking, and talking, ignoring her completely. Eventually she crept outside and went to the tent where her ladies—the two her father had allowed her to take with her—were sleeping. She went in, lay down between them, and wondered what she had done.

Some hours after midnight, she heard Arjuna calling her name. She got up and rushed back to the big tent. He was standing just outside it, weaving a little; his face in the light of the campfire was annoyed. He grabbed her by the wrist and pulled her within. Yudi, Naku, and Saku had gone, but Bima was still there, stretched out leaning against a tent post, addressing himself to a plate of meat bones in his lap. Arjuna stepped over his brother's legs and stumbled to a mat in the corner where he dropped to his knees, at the same time beckoning to Draupadi with a flailing hand. When she approached, he seized her, pushed her down in front of him onto all fours, and yanked her dhoti down about her thighs. He fumbled with his own pants, then grabbed her hips and entered her with a great heaving thrust. He humped away for a minute, shuddered in release, and fell forward onto her, crushing her body to the mat. He lay there for a while. Finally he rolled off and lay supine with one arm flung over his eyes. His heavy, regular breaths soon told her he was asleep.

For the rest of the journey, the Pandavas continued to drink and talk late into each evening, sometimes joined by Krishna—although he would always make his exit early, claiming a need for his "beauty rest." Draupadi would leave the tent around midnight, unnoticed, to go sleep with her women. Arjuna did not call for her again.

Upon arriving at the Vrishni palace, they were met by Lady Perta, who flew into the yard and dispensed wild hugs to "my boys, my precious boys—you're back, you're back!" She even had a hug for "Krishna, sweet nephew; thank you for looking after them!"

Draupadi had climbed down from the women's cart and was standing beside it, hands clasped at her waist, eyes lowered. Perta caught sight of her.

"Oh! And this must be your bride. We all heard from the messenger that Arjuna had won—my clever darling, I knew you would, it was no surprise to *me*—" (she gave Arjuna another squeeze) "and here she is!"

She went to the princess and embraced her. "My dear, *welcome* to our family. Let me look at you." She put her fingers under Draupadi's chin and pushed her head up. "Oh, but Arjuna! Boys! She's simply beautiful! I never saw such a lovely creature. Isn't she beautiful, Krishna? Boys, what are you thinking, leaving her standing alone like this? Come now, all of you. Help her inside. Make her feel welcome. Come, come."

The five Pandavas, obedient to their mother, clustered round as Perta gripped the back of Draupadi's neck and propelled her toward the door. "Now, dear, don't worry about a thing. I know it's hard, leaving your home. But it's all right. From now on, you belong to *all* of us."

Surrounded by her new relatives, Draupadi disappeared into the palace.

PART THREE

THE DICING

Chapter 10

KRISHNA

Krishna said:

I couldn't believe my eyes.

When we—the Pandavas and I and our small cortege—rode into the Hastinapura palace yard on the first day of the new year, I saw: nobody. Not the king, not the queen, not Prince Duryodhana; not an uncle, not a brother, not a junior priest; not so much as a stable boy was there to welcome us. An old maidservant was shuffling past as we came through the compound gate (the wardens had not denied us entry, at least); upon seeing us, she started like a scared rabbit and hastened her steps. Other than her and a couple of mangy dogs making a meal of a dead bird over by the water trough, the yard was utterly empty.

We had sent men ahead to announce our arrival, so I knew we were expected. Counselor Vidura, in fact, had ridden out the day before to meet us on the road and had given every indication of joy (or what passes for joy in a man so reserved) at his nephews' return from exile. On the last leg of the journey he had stuck close by the women's wagon carrying my Aunt Perta and the two brides, Draupadi and Subhadra. Now, as I turned my horse and rode back down the line to see if he had any idea what was going on, I saw consternation on his face. I waited to say anything until I had drawn up beside him and could speak softly.

"Counselor, what is this? Why is there no one here to greet us?"

"Prince Krishna, I ..." His fingers plucked at the collar of his brown cloak. "I don't know what has happened. Please, will you wait here just for a moment while I go see ..."

He alighted, handed the reins to a groom, and went at a jog across the yard and through the main doorway.

I rode back to where the five Pandavas sat their horses in a line. I pulled up next to Yudi on his chestnut gelding.

"We can take this as a sign of things to come," I said.

Yudi nodded, thin-lipped. "I had not expected a celebration. But this blatant discourtesy … I fear you are right. They plan to mistreat us again."

No palace yard is ever that quiet at mid-morning. It was clear this was no mere oversight: people had been told to keep away.

"They are afraid of you," I said.

"Why afraid? I don't understand. We do not seek to harm them."

"You seek the throne."

He turned to me with knitted brow. "It is not a matter of my seeking it. I am the former king's eldest son. Tarashtra is merely a regent. The throne is mine by Law."

"And all Law-abiding people would agree with you. But I'm sure the Kauravas don't see it that way."

He faced front again. "They cannot set themselves against the Law."

"Can't they? I think they will try. This non-welcome is only the first taste of what they're planning."

He did not reply. On his other side, Bimasena on his massive dapple-gray steed was beginning to emit rumbling sounds from deep in his chest, similar to wolf growls.

"Take comfort," I said to Yudi, "in knowing they have good reason to be afraid. You have made a formidable ally who will back you in your claim."

He smiled. "Two formidable allies."

"You mean Vrishni?" I said. "Of course; us, too. But Vrishni is nothing beside Panchala. If it comes to a fight, Panchala will be the ally that counts. Just as the Panchala princess is the wife that counts. My sister is …" I winced as a piercing squeal reverberated from the women's wagon behind us. "My sister Subhadra is very *lively,* but she is not to be compared to Draupadi. I hope Arjuna realizes that."

"He assuredly does," said Yudi. "But you are forgetting something, Krishna."

"What's that?" I asked.

"Yourself. Our best ally in the fight—if there is a fight—will be you."

I confess I was gratified to hear him say it.

≈

The council room would not fit our number, so we convened in the great hall. The early-evening sun was strong through the west windows. King Tarashtra had seated himself on the dais while the man-servants were placing wood-and-leather stools in a circle on the floor, but I suggested in my most diplomatic tone that it might be difficult to hear the king's words with him so far away; we would all hate for his majesty to be left out of the conversation, so would he not deign to join us? At that he pursed his lips, grunted in assent, levered his crimson-robed corpulence off the throne, and had his guide-boy lead him down the steps. I begged him to take the open stool on my left, and he did so, plopping down with a sigh followed by a shout for someone to bring him a beer. With many bows and smiles, the rest of us took our seats.

I had mostly figured out who was who among the Kauravas. I'd already met Prince Duryodhana and Counselor Vidura, of course, at the bridegroom-choice banquet; likewise Drona, the chief weapons master with the hawk-like face. Vyasa, the high priest, was easy to pick out in his white robes. The slight fellow with the short beard and plum-colored cloak, sitting across the circle from me chatting with the priest but regarding me out of the corner of his eye, I guessed must be Prince Shakuna, the king's brother-in-law.

Prince Dushasana was the stocky young man with the mop of black hair, seated next to his brother; I knew this because he had been the one who, two mornings ago, had finally come out to greet us in the palace yard. His manner had been casual, almost insolent: "Dear me, have you been waiting? My royal parents beg you to excuse them: they are busy with affairs of state. My brother, the crown prince, is out hunting." Now he sat with legs sprawled and arms folded, staring at the Pandavas with a smirk. I saw that Bimasena was staring back, his arms (which were twice the size of Dushasana's) also folded, his lip curled in a sneer.

Seven of them, six of us—but there was still one stool vacant, directly across from the king. I wondered if the servants had mis-counted. Then the hall's external door was darkened by a figure which, upon entering, proved to be a muscular man with gray-white hair wearing a dhoti of indigo, a belt studded with bronze, and a stern look on his weather-beaten face. *Lord Bhishma,* I thought. He went to the empty seat, bowed to the king, bowed to Duryodhana. To my surprise he then turned and bowed to Yudi, who was on my right. After that he sat down, hooking a thumb in his belt and resting the other hand, age-spotted but strong-looking, on his knee.

"Everyone is here, Sire," said the counselor. Tarashtra nodded, handed his tankard to the boy, cleared his throat of phlegm, and spoke.

"My dear nephews." He directed a benign smile at the five of them. "Let me be the first to welcome you back to Hastinapura. You have been in exile two long years, and in your exile you have, I am sure, reflected on your crimes—or should I simply say, your *transgressions* —and have made the appropriate penitential oblations. It gave me no pleasure, no, none at all, to send my flesh and blood away from me. If your pain has been great, mine has been greater. Yes, indeed; much greater. I have missed you terribly."

He adopted a mournful expression, at the same time sticking out a hand for his beer. He took a swig, said, "Terribly ... terribly," set the vessel on his knee, and continued.

"But all that is now in the past. I am overjoyed to welcome you home. For Hastin ..." (he belched) "Hastinapura *is* your home, and you must regard it as such. You must make yourselves free of the premises. Suitable quarters will be provided; horses, clothing, and so on. Drona will be delighted to have you back in his training sessions, won't you, Drona? And you must join us at supper, at the royal table. No, no—I insist. You are family, after all."

He lifted the tankard again, draining it. After a second, louder belch, he handed it back to the boy and addressed Vidura. "Well, Counselor. Is there any other business today? Oh ..." He put a hand to his brow and turned his blind eyes on me.

"Prince Krishna. How rude of me! You are also welcome; stay as long as you like. Though I'm sure the bucolic charms of Vrishni are calling, eh? We must not keep you. You will miss your sister, Subhadra, but she'll be safe with us, I assure you; oh yes, quite safe. I will make sure she is not abused. All that sort of thing is in the past for these Pandava boys. Mistreatment of women, I mean." He wagged a finger at them. "Isn't that right, boys? From now on, you'll be models of propriety."

Turning back to Vidura, he said, "Nothing else, then, Counselor?

Good. We're adjourned." He patted his plump thighs and made as if to rise.

"Wait!" said Naku. "What about Yudi's claim?"

His outburst was followed by Saku's more measured tones: "Yes, Sire. We need to discuss our brother's claim."

"Claim? Claim? What claim?" Tarashtra remained poised on the edge of his seat, his expression annoyed and (I thought) a touch anxious.

"Sir," said Yudi, "they mean my claim to the kingship of Kuru."

Tarashtra tipped his head up toward the ceiling. "Ah. I see. And what is the basis for this ... *claim?*"

"You know very well what it's based on!" Arjuna cried. "He is the crown prince! He's been the rightful king ever since our father died!"

"Your father?" Tarashtra said mildly. "Do you mean *his* father, or *your* father, Arjuna? I confess I get a little confused, sometimes, about you boys' parentage."

I did not know what he was implying. Everyone knew the Pandavas had two different mothers, but they were all the sons of Pandu, surely.

"I mean *our father,*" said Arjuna, his pitch rising, "our father, Pandu, who was the lawful king. Yudi is his eldest son. You were only allowed to take the throne because Bhishma didn't want to be regent anymore, so he made a deal that you could rule until Yudi came of age. Well, now Yudi is of age. He should be king."

Tarashtra's fleshy lips stretched into a broad smile. "You're absolutely correct, Arjuna," he said. "Abso*lute*ly correct."

I had been about to speak, but this apparent capitulation caught me off guard.

"Yudi *should* be king," Tarashtra went on, "and *would* be king, except for one very important point about the—how did you put it?—the *deal.* A very important point of which you, dear nephew, seem to be unaware. Of course you weren't even born then, so how could you know anything about the *deal,* as you call it."

He turned to his left. "But *you* were there, Counselor Vidura, and you'll certainly remember." He cast his eyes up to the ceiling again. "And Shakuna will remember. And Bhishma. Yes ... I distinctly recall what Bhishma said. He said, and I quote: 'Tarashtra will take the throne, with the understanding that once Prince Yudi reaches his majority—*and assuming there emerge no defects in body, mind, or character that would make him unsuitable to rule*—Tarashtra will step down, and Yudi will be crowned.'"

He pressed his palms together, fingers pointed straight ahead. "No defects in body, mind, or character. Was that not one of your stipulations, Lord Bhishma?"

"It was," said Bhishma.

The palms swept up and outward. "And can we not all agree that the forcible rape of an innocent Arya girl indicates a rather *serious* defect in character?"

Bimasena leaped to his feet. "IT'S A LIE! WE DIDN'T RAPE ANYONE!"

Duryodhana, Dushasana, and Shakuna sprang up, too; none was carrying a sword, but Shakuna drew his knife from his belt. Naku, Saku, and Arjuna also rose with their hands on hilts. Across the circle the men glared at one another.

Better do something, I thought. But before I could do anything …

"Sit down, all of you," said Bhishma.

He had not moved; he had barely raised his voice. After a brief hesitation, they all sat down.

Aha, I thought. *We see where the real power resides.*

"The king is correct," said Bhishma. "The defect in character indicated by rape is a bar to the succession. And …" He held up a hand as Bima looked about to protest again. "And, while some may question the Pandavas' guilt, to raise such questions now is futile. There was a public trial in which they were lawfully convicted. If Prince Yudi were to take the throne now, the people would question his fitness to rule, and rightly so."

"The people!" That was Arjuna. "Who cares what the *people* think?"

Bhishma turned to him with a slight frown. "The people care about the Law, Arjuna. We have taught them to do so. If we ignore the Law, we teach the people to ignore it. And if the people ignore the Law, it is the end of the Kuru; the end of us all."

Arjuna stared back at the regent; the hatred in his eyes startled me a little.

Yudi said, "What do you propose, then, Bhishma? Are we simply to stay here, disgraced, living off our uncle? What is our status to be?"

"Yes," said Naku. "What's our status?"

Everyone looked again at Bhishma, who for the first time seemed unsure. He tapped his fingers on his knee and said, "I don't know. But we must agree on something. The well-being of the clan depends on it."

Shakuna leaned forward. "Sire, there is nothing more to discuss. If Prince Yudi can't be king, he and his brothers must simply stay here, with your permission and at your pleasure. If you ask me, they should be on their knees thanking you for your generosity—you and Crown Prince Duryodhana, both."

The younger Pandavas glowered. Bima muttered, "Not acceptable."

Krishna Vasudeva, I said to myself, *now is the time.*

I stood up. "Your majesty," I said, "might I be permitted to speak?"

"What? Who is that? Krishna?"

"Yes, Majesty. If I may ..."

Tarashtra waved his refilled tankard at me. "Yes, yes, go ahead."

"Thank you, Sire." Arranging my blue cloak to best advantage, I stepped to the middle of the circle and stood tall yet at ease, facing the king.

"The House of Kuru is confronted," I said, "with a dilemma. Prince Yudi has a claim to the throne based upon his birth. But there is reason to deny that claim, based upon his conviction of a serious crime. Lord Bhishma" (I pivoted and made him a small bow) "says that to call into question the Pandavas' trial and conviction would serve only to sow lawlessness among the people. I agree with him."

Arjuna looked stricken. "But Krishna!" he said.

I held up both hands. "Please, Arjuna, hear me out. Lawlessness among the people, we say; but what if there were no people?"

"What?" said Tarashtra, spluttering into his mug. "No people? What are you saying, Krishna? Kill all the people? Ha! Not that I have any liking for the people. Wretched trash, most of 'em. Still, I can't just do away with them. No, no—I can't do that."

"Not at all, Sire," I said. "I am speaking of giving the Pandavas a new land. A land where there are no people."

Silence. Puzzled faces. I was pleased with my effect so far.

"The Kuru own all the doab," I went on, "all the land between the Ganges and the Yamuna. But nearly the entire population lives here in the east, on the Ganges. Out west, the land is sparsely populated. After five kosa you won't find a single homesteader."

"There are p-plenty of indigenes out west," said Duryodhana. It was the first time he had spoken. "I've b-been out there. I've seen them."

"Oh, to be sure, Prince Duryodhana, to be sure," I said. "But we are not speaking of indigenes. My point is, there are no *people* in the west; no Arya. And that means his majesty might give the Pandavas a domain there, by the Yamuna, in which they can make a fresh start. No people, except the ones they might eventually attract. No soldiers, except the few they might persuade to go with them. No cattle, other than what they might raid or barter for. And no women; except, of course, for their revered mother, and Arjuna's two lovely brides."

I smiled at Arjuna. He was looking skeptical.

"A kingdom without people?" said Yudi. He was clearly skeptical, too.

"Yes, your highness." I stepped close to him, put my back to Tarashtra, and spoke sotto voce. "The important thing is to get the land and the title. The people can come later."

As I turned again to the group, I saw Vidura leaning to whisper something in the king's ear. Duryodhana and Dushasana also had their heads together.

Shakuna spoke up: "So you're saying his majesty should divide the kingdom. That he should give up territory and allow a new king to sit smack on his western border. How, pray, is that in the best interest of the Kuru?"

I shrugged. "All his majesty will be giving up in the way of territory is a small stretch of wilderness. As for another king on his border: that king will be his own nephew, from whom he has nothing to fear."

"Nothing to fear?" said Shakuna. "I doubt that. I doubt that very much." He sat back, slapping his knife blade on his palm. "But then, I am not Kuru; it is not for me to say. Lord Bhishma: What do you think of this plan?"

Bhishma, I noticed, was looking at me with something like respect. "I think," he said, "it is a plan worth considering."

I made him another small bow.

After that the discussion continued for some time, with varying degrees of heat. The Kauravas did not like the idea of Yudi being granted a king's title and ownership of land, however wild; the

Pandavas, in turn, did not like the idea of being (as Arjuna put it) "exiled once again to the middle of nowhere." But High Priest Vyasa, when asked whether there was anything in the Sacred Knowledge forbidding such an arrangement, said he couldn't think of a thing. And Counselor Vidura, though I half expected him to insist upon the Pandavas' rights (for it had been clear to me, ever since his interesting little performance at the banquet, whose side he was on), seemed disinclined to put himself forward—for which I was grateful, having as I did the goal in sight and not wanting it put in jeopardy by any foolish grandstanding.

To Tarashtra, I kept emphasizing how far away the Pandavas would be: two or three days' journey. They would not be popping in. "And I know how painful you will find their absence, Sire," I said. "But I know, too, that you are the most unselfish of rulers. You never allow concern for your own suffering to influence your decisions."

That sealed it. Tarashtra, after a few more whispers with the counselor and much throat-clearing, proclaimed that this plan—despite the considerable pain it would cause him—was for the best. His decision, he said, was to grant his nephews a parcel of land along the east bank of the Yamuna extending two kosa east and five kosa north and south. "Give it what name you will," he said.

"And I am to rule that land? As king?" asked Yudi.

"Of course, Nephew," said Tarashtra. "Rule away. And you may have a few cows to take with you. *And* an elephant. No, no, I insist; you are family, after all." He chuckled. Then he stood up. Everyone else stood up, too. "Nature calls," he said, kneading his lower belly. "I'll leave you to work out the details." He departed, led by his small guide-boy.

We all remained standing in the darkening hall. No one said anything for a while.

Finally, Saku broke the silence: "The whole east bank of the Yamuna is thick forest. The Khandava Forest, it's called. We'll have to clear it if we want to build there."

"And how are we supposed to do that," said his twin, "without a slew of woodcutters?"

"Yes," said Arjuna. "We have no men. No axes. How are we going to clear a forest?"

His sweet face still showed a sense of betrayal. I wanted to reach out and smooth that look of hurt from his brow.

"How will we clear the forest, Krishna?" he repeated.

"We'll burn it," I said.

≈

I admit that when I saw the first tribeswoman come dashing out of the trees, her long hair ablaze, the baby in her arms screaming, I felt a twinge of dismay. But Yudi quickly used a couple of arrows to put them out of their misery, and after that, we all did the same, the Pandavas and I, deploying our longbows with speed and efficiency against the Naga men, women, and children as they fled the burning Khandava. We did the same service for the larger animals: many deer, many boars, a couple of panthers, even a tiger. I took down the tiger myself; it was an impressive sight as it came tearing out of the smoke and flame, jaws gaping, tongue slavering, waves of heat rippling off its black-and-saffron flanks. I skewered it through the eye; it reared up with a great snarl and flailing of paws, then fell dead. The smaller creatures—hares, rabbits, jackals, birds, and so on—most of those we had to let be, although Arjuna took shots at some as they ran or flew past. As usual, he rarely missed. (Looking back on it, I wonder whether this was when he first got the idea for his burning-jackal show.)

This was our fourth expedition to the Pandavas' new land. Our previous trips, the purpose of which had been to scout and plan, had taken up the spring. Now the hot, dry summer had set in: ideal fire weather. King Tarashtra was less than pleased by our continued presence in Hastinapura; he had apparently expected us to pack up and leave right after we had made our agreement, but I asked that we be permitted to stay on for a few months, pointing out that it would not look well if he sent his nephews off to the wilderness with no chance to prepare and they perished out there. He thought that over for a minute. Then he said he did not know why I was telling *him* these things, for *he* would be only too delighted if his nephews stayed at home forever; after all, it was not *his* idea that they should desert their family and set up on their own. I asked if we might stay until the middle of the fourth month. He tapped a finger on his lower lip. "End of the third," he said. "Done," I said. So that became our deadline.

Vidura accompanied us on each trip west. His sadness at the

Pandavas' impending departure was (unlike his brother's) clearly genuine, but he was also determined to be useful. He helped me and Saku calculate the extent of the forest, the pattern in which it would likely burn, and the distance we would need to stand away. He also came up with the idea of clearing a strip of grassland about thirty paces from the tree line—a *fire-break*, he called it. "Agni cannot travel if he has nothing to feed on," he said. So, on our second visit we brought plows, spades, and rakes with us and set to creating a space that the fire would not cross.

It was while we were doing this work that Vidura noticed our watchers. He came up to me as I was raking a newly plowed section of the break, cocked his head toward the tree line, and said quietly, "Prince Krishna. Look there."

I looked but saw nothing. "Where?" I said.

"*There*," he said. "Under that babul. They're in the shadows."

I looked again. This time I saw five dark faces—two shoulder-high, one chest-high, two waist-high—and realized it was a family of indigenes. I thought I could make out a male, a female, an elderly female, and two young ones.

"I see them." I started to rake again. "Naga, most likely. Nothing to worry about."

"I did not realize there were people in there," he said.

"Yes, well, most forests have a Snake tribe or two," I said, continuing to scrape and pull at the loose dirt and grass.

"How are we going to move them out?"

"Move them out?" I leaned on my rake, puffing; this fire-break was hard work. "What do you mean, move them out?"

"Before we set the fire."

His expression was earnest. I realized suddenly that he was concerned not about our safety, but about the Naga's.

"There's no point trying to get them to leave, if that's what you're suggesting," I said. "If we go in there, they'll kill us."

"We could call a few of them out and explain the situation."

"How? It's not as if they speak Aryan!" I was getting a little impatient with him. "Counselor, there are thousands of creatures in that forest. Not just Naga; beasts of all kinds. I know it's unpleasant to think of them dying, but I'm afraid that is what has to happen if the Pandavas are to have a home—if they are to have any chance at all. I

219

intend to build them a new domain, but I need somewhere to build it. It can't be up in the trees."

"What if you built the new residence here, in the grasslands?"

"Two kosa from the river? With a forest between? How will they get water?"

"There are creeks to the north and south ..."

Now I really was becoming annoyed. "A creek will not water a herd of cattle. Nor a town."

"Yes ... I see." He nodded, but his eyes were still worried.

We both looked again to the shadows under the trees. The watchers had disappeared.

Arjuna came trotting toward us on his horse, a wooden plow dragging askew on the grass behind. "Uncle Vidu!" he called merrily. "You're a genius! Who else would have thought of such a way to beat the Fire God?"

Vidura smiled up at him, as did I.

"I'm off to plow farther up," he said. We both gazed after him as he cantered away with his dark hair flying and white dhoti rippling.

After that, Vidura said nothing more about the Naga. And indeed, the fire-break worked exactly as he had predicted: the flames advanced to the edge, but they did not cross it, and we on the far side were protected from the inferno.

≈

The forest took two days to burn. When the flames had finally subsided and the ground cooled somewhat, we rode through the charred and smoking landscape, assessing the work that remained to be done. Many large trees would still need to be felled, although the smaller trees and underbrush had all burned nicely to the ground. Ponds and brooks that had boiled away would need to be cleared of the piles of dead fish, frogs, and turtles clogging them. In search of the best building site, we rode all the way down to the river; there were many corpses there—of creatures that had chosen a watery rather than a fiery death—drifting slowly downstream. Out in the middle there was a lone, live panther with just its head and forepaws out of the water, clinging to a blackened branch. It hissed at us, its yellow eyes gleaming.

There were corpses half-buried in the ash of the forest floor, too, and many more out in the eastern grassland where we had shot them down. We could not touch them, of course, but this did not worry me overmuch, for I already had a plan to recruit several dozen indigenes from the country around Hastinapura: outcastes whom no one would object to our collecting and taking with us, and who could, initially, perform much of the labor, including dealing with the dead, that would be needed in order to build the Pandavas' new home. These indigenes would also be our farmhands. It was not too late to plant a few crops; barley, spelt, and peas grow quickly, as do squash and cucumbers, and what with the cows we could wangle from Tarashtra, plus the fifty or so I could get from my father in Vrishni, we would not starve.

An army was another story. We had our own few men, of course, and I thought we could persuade some kshatriya of Hastinapura to come with us: some of the older ones who remembered King Pandu, perhaps. Also some of the poorer ones who lived out of town, had missed out on the Kauravas' bribes, and would welcome a chance to improve their lot. Vrishni, again, could spare us a handful. But any real army, supplied with real arms, would likely need to come from Panchala. The princess Draupadi was our trump card there; I was worried, however, by her father's stinginess with her dowry. Would he support us willingly? Or would I need to force his hand—and if so, how would I do it?

These thoughts occupied my mind as we rode back from the Khandava. I was at the rear of the party, with the Pandavas and the counselor in front of me. My five friends were joking and laughing, their spirits buoyed both by our recent adventure and by the pros-pect of adventures to come. Vidura was riding apart, eyes on the ground. I kicked my horse up next to his.

"Counselor, are you well?"

He looked at me with a wan face. "Oh ... yes, Prince. I am well. A little fatigued. All that char and ash ... it affected my breath."

"My eyes are still watering. But please, no more 'Prince.' You must call me Krishna."

He nodded. "Very well—Krishna. And you must call me Vidura."

I smiled in acknowledgment. We rode on for a while in silence, veering left and putting a little distance between ourselves and the others. Their laughter floated toward us on the smoke-smelling breeze.

As we passed the scorched corpse of a deer—it must have escaped our arrows and run a long way before collapsing—Vidura said abruptly: "You revel in it."

"I'm sorry?" I said. "I revel …?"

"No," he said, "I mean you and the Pandavas. You kshatriya."

"We revel in what?"

"In death."

I was taken aback. "Well … death is our business. Fighting, hunting, war. It's what we are trained for. I wouldn't say we *revel* in it. Why would you think that?"

He did not answer, but glanced back at the dead deer.

"And what," I went on, "do you mean by *you kshatriya?* You yourself are kshatriya, are you not?"

"It's not at all clear what I am," he said in a bitter tone.

"Your father was king of the Kuru, wasn't he? That seems clear enough."

"And my seed-father is brahmin, and my mother was shudra. So what does that make me?"

I could tell he was upset and suspected he wanted to unburden himself of something. I arranged my face in a look of sympathetic interest and said, "Go on."

"I just don't know," he said, his hands clenching on the reins.

"Don't know what?"

Suddenly it was as if floodgates had opened. "I don't know if I did the right thing! Krishna, I swore I would help Arjuna, help the Pandavas, even if I had to go against the Law to do it. An injustice was perpetrated on them. I was sure of that. I wanted to correct it. So I told that tale at the banquet, because I knew it would make the princess reject Duryodhana and choose Arjuna, but now I just don't know if I was *right*."

"Was the tale false?" I asked. "I can't think it was, since Duryodhana and the Snake girl are married now." (This had happened right before our return from Vrishni.)

"The tale was true. That's not the point. The point is I am chief counselor to King Tarashtra, my brother, who charged me with protecting his son, with protecting the interests of the Kuru. That was my duty, my clear duty, and I did not adhere to it." His left hand came up and pressed his temple, as if trying to press away a deep pain. "Drona warned me. He warned me about what happens when people try to … but I didn't listen."

I considered asking more about Drona, but decided that might take us down a rat hole from which we'd never emerge.

"As I see it," I said firmly, "you have no reason to fault yourself. You told the truth. How could telling the truth be wrong?"

He looked at the ground and shook his head, his fingers still pressing.

"Also," I said, "think about this: if Duryodhana had managed to make alliance with Panchala, thereby putting himself in a stronger position, he might have killed his cousins as soon as they returned from exile. He and his brother likely would have murdered them outright. By telling your tale at the banquet, you probably saved their lives."

At this, Vidura looked even more upset—shocked, even. He sat up straight in the saddle, looked me in the eye, and said:

"No, Krishna, you're wrong. Duryodhana would not kill his cousins. He can be impulsive, yes, and he longs for power. But he is no murderer."

I raised my brows at him and said nothing.

"On the other hand," (his head drooped again) "what do I know of killing? Killing, as you say, is a kshatriya's business. It is not my business. And I certainly do not revel in it."

"What *do* you revel in, Vidura?"

"In the Law. Or at least, I used to. Now … I'm not even sure I know what Law is."

We rode on toward Hastinapura.

Yudi (as you shall see, Sire) was right about Krishna. He turned out to be the Pandavas' best ally; their secret weapon, if you will. Out in the wilderness—the "land without people"—what would their chances have been, had Krishna not been there to help them?

On the last day of the third month, Krishna and the Pandavas set off west with ten cows, twenty-five men and manservants, forty indigenes, and one elderly elephant. Draupadi, Subhadra, and Perta remained in Hastinapura—"until my boys have built their splendid new palace," said Perta, "for we girls simply can't live outdoors! But we'll come just as soon as we have a place to lay our heads, which I know will be in the blink of an eye." The three women gathered in the palace yard to see the men off. Perta sniffled. Subhadra wailed. Draupadi did not make a sound.

Arriving on the burned banks of the Yamuna, the settlers were met by King Vasudeva with fifty men, fifty cows, a cartload of weapons and tools, and—to everyone's surprise—a priest. The priest was Dhaumya, the white-bearded brahmin from Vrishni who had joined the Kaurava party on the way to the tournament and presided over the Sunrise Oblation. He had volunteered to go, expressing his excitement at "getting in at the start of a marvelous new venture, where the Gods' assistance will be paramount."

Vasudeva stayed for only a moment. He enfolded his son in a tight embrace, saying, "I wish it could be more," nodded to the Pandavas, and was up on his horse trotting away south, followed by his one bodyguard, before anyone could thank him.

Ash still floated in the air, coating the black trunks of trees and speckling the bloated bodies washed up on the river-bank. The sixty cows stood dumbly or ambled down to the water to drink. A few of the men and outcastes went to drink, too; others stayed standing where they were, looking around with dubious faces. The elephant nosed half-heartedly at a defoliated branch. The sky above was a yellowish gray, and there was a stink of rotting flesh.

"What lovely country!" Priest Dhaumya said. "What will you call your new domain?"

Krishna flicked a flake of ash from his forearm. "We haven't decided," he said. "All I can say is, the monsoons had better come early this year, or we may as well call it Yamaloka."

"Ah," said Dhaumya, beaming. "Then you must ensure the Rain God's favor. Call it— *Indraprasta.*"

Chapter 11

GANDHARI

17 YEARS BEFORE THE WAR

T he queen, hearing of her elder son's return from the bride-groom choice, dispatched a maidservant to request his immediate presence in her rooms. She then sent her women away and seated herself on a stool by the window to wait. The late-winter morning sunshine was unseasonably warm; she removed her shawl and let it fall to the floor.

When Duryodhana arrived, she rose, went to him, and embraced him. The violet silk brushed his scarred cheek.

"My son. My dear son. You're back."

He bent to touch her feet, then rose and embraced her. "Hello, Mother. Yes. I'm b-back."

She did not hold him long, but pulled away and stood with both his hands in hers. "What news from Panchala?"

"I took first place in the tournament," he said. (She drew in a breath.) "But … in the end, the p-princess did not choose me."

She let out the breath and let go his hands. He walked to the window and leaned on the sill, looking out at the training grounds. There, a few dozen kshatriya were gathered around Chief Weapons Master Drona: some kneeling to touch his feet, others clapping him on the shoulder, all giving him a hearty welcome home.

"Whom did the princess choose?" she asked.

"Arjuna."

Her shoulders slumped, but only for a moment. She went and stood beside him.

"We must think about what's next. Have you told your father?"

"No. They said he isn't up yet."

"Oh, of course; it's not yet noon. Good. You must let me tell him. He'll be angry, especially when he hears Arjuna won."

"I know. He'll b-blame me."

"Actually, I think he'll blame Vidura." She turned around and sat on the sill. "But in any case, his anger will blow over quickly; it always does. The bigger question is how we're going to counteract the advantage the Pandavas now have. The only sure way is to get you a wife, a wife who'll give you a son. There's no time to lose."

Duryodhana made no sign of assent or dissent, but his left hand rubbed the mark below his copper armband.

≈

Gandhari placed her empty dish on the low table before the old queen's settee.

"That was delicious, Grandmamma. And I'm so grateful for your help; thank you."

"Oh, my dear, no need to thank me," said Satyavati, brushing crumbs from the great swell of her pink-swathed bosom. "As I've always said: we understand each other, you and I."

Gandhari nodded and continued: "Now, you're sure the Snake girl—I mean, Lady Jaratka, as she will soon be—are you sure she won't reject him again? Not that I would blame her. I'm aware of what my son did to you; how he abused you. I gave him quite a talking-to about that, and he was contrite; nevertheless, it was unforgivable, and I worry that the Sn ... that *Lady Jaratka* will not forgive him. I know how she loves you."

"Tush," said Satyavati. "She loves him more. And I gave *her* a talking-to, as well."

"I'll take your word for it. But you, Grandmamma—you are still on our side? On the side of the Kauravas?"

The old queen pursed her lips, deepening the deep creases there. "Kauravas, Pandavas ... I don't know about all that. I'm on *your* side, my dear. I'm on Duryodhana's side. More than anything, I'm on the side of the House of Kuru."

Gandhari nodded. She reached for her cup of lassi, brought it underneath her veil, and took a sip. She replaced the cup and said, "That gives me comfort. Yet I'm still not sure the king will agree to this marriage. Even if I make her kshatriya ..."

"Which is your prerogative, as queen," Satyavati interjected.

"Yes, but even so, there's still the matter of the baby, Vaishamya.

The high priest may have adopted him, but everyone knows his parentage. I do worry that …"

"You worry entirely too much, Gandhari." The old lady heaved herself upright and placed one bare foot on the floor. "Answer me this: Who rules the world?"

"What an odd question. The Gods, I suppose."

"No, I mean the everyday world; the world around us. This palace, this clan."

"The king, of course. The king and his council."

"Wrong! The king *thinks* he rules. It's the same in every kingdom, chiefdom, farmstead, and household, down to the lowest fisherman's shack. The men *think* they're in charge. But the men are deluded, Gandhari; deluded by their muscles, their weapons, their authority, their bluster—and most of all, by their tallywhackers."

"Their tally … oh, Grandmamma! You're too much."

"Ha! I may be. But I'll tell you who really rules the world." She wagged her hand back and forth between the two of them. "*Us.*"

"You and I rule the world?"

"Don't pretend to be obtuse, child. You know I mean *women.* Queen or maidservant, kshatriya or shudra, Arya or Snake, it makes no difference: we women rule the world."

"We women," said Gandhari. "Hmm. You may be right."

"Of course I'm right! *If*, that is, we have the wits and the will for it," said Satyavati, brushing more crumbs from her capacious pink lap. "So, speaking of wits, here's another question: What will you say to Tarashtra so he'll let this marriage take place?"

Gandhari was silent for a while. Then she said, "I'll tell him this is the fastest way to get Duryo a wife. I'll remind him that any inter-clan negotiation for a bride will take months, and that we don't have months. I'll remind him Arjuna is returning from exile with not just one bride but two, and one or the other will be pregnant before we know it."

"Very good," said the old queen.

"Also …"

"Yes?"

"Also, I'll make sure he has a distraction. Something to keep his mind occupied."

"His *mind?* Oh, my dear… and I thought you were making such progress."

"Sorry, Grandmamma. Not his mind. I meant to say ... his *tallywhacker.*"

The two queens laughed and laughed.

≈

Two days later, Gandhari summoned Duryodhana to her rooms again. This time, she had seated herself on her carved wood chair with the purple cushion. On her right sat Satyavati, her bulk over-flowing an extra-wide stool. On her left stood Jaratka, wearing a forest-green silk dhoti, matching chest-band and veil, red slippers, and silver jewelry.

Upon entering, Duryodhana stopped short. His eyes went from one woman, to the other, to the other.

"Duryodhana," said the queen. "Please, come in."

"M-mother." He advanced a few steps and bowed to her, then bowed to his great-grandmother. His face was wary.

"Come here, my son." She held out a hand to him. He approached and took it.

"You know the situation, Duryo. Your cousins will be home next week, having made alliance with both Panchala and Vrishni. It has become imperative that you be married, and married quickly. I have spoken with your father, and he agrees."

"Yes, Mother. I know." He was still glancing from side to side. "And ... who am I to m-marry? Are negotiations already underway? I suppose Bhishma is taking care of it."

Satyavati said, "Bhishma isn't involved in this one."

Duryodhana dropped his mother's hand and stepped back. "I don't ... I don't understand ..." His toe scuffed at the hard-dirt floor.

"Duryo," said Gandhari, "we all agree it will be best for you to marry Lady Jaratka."

His mouth fell open. "Lady ... *Lady* Jaratka?"

"Yes, Duryo," said Satyavati. "Your mother has made her kshatriya. And your father has agreed. So we're not going to have any more nonsense. I told you long ago it was my dearest wish to see you two married. I even embroidered you a wedding vest—red flames on it, some of my best work—and I intend to see you in it before I die. I am a very old lady," (she coughed pathetically) "and I absolutely *forbid* you to disappoint me. Do you hear me, Duryo?"

He stared at her as if he simply could not take it in.

"Duryodhana!" said his mother. "Your great-grandmother asked you a question. What do you say?"

He gave a small gasp, ducked his head and said, "Yes, Grannie."

"Good," said his mother. "And now, what have you to say to Lady Jaratka?"

Duryodhana turned slowly to his right. Throughout the previous exchange Jaratka had stood still with hands clasped, head down; now, she lifted her chin and stared straight into his eyes. He stared back, unblinking. As on that afternoon two years ago in Ekalavya's hut, an observer might have imagined they were on the verge of a mutual attack.

Then, suddenly, Jaratka smiled: a smile such as no one in Hastinapura had ever seen on her face: a smile of such gaiety, beauty, and assurance that no man seeing it could have resisted its invitation. Duryodhana took two steps forward and seized her by the waist. She flung her arms about his neck. He picked her up and swung her around and around, both of them laughing with pure joy.

≈

They were married on the day before the Pandavas' return from exile. Jaratka, although she had been supplied with a rich trousseau including wedding finery, insisted on wearing the old green-and-silver veil that had belonged to her mistress. Duryodhana wore the flame-embroidered vest. Satyavati was at the front of the audience, multiple pillows propping her upright on her settee, which she had ordered be carried to the Hall of Sacraments for the occasion. At the conclusion of the ceremony, after first greeting the king and queen, the newly-weds went to her, knelt before her, and touched her feet.

"Stop that nonsense!" she sputtered. She raised them up, joining their two hands and squeezing tightly. "Now you be good to each other," she said, her old eyes misting a little, "and don't fight too much. Go along now, go along. I want my supper."

≈

The Pandavas arrived home. A couple of days later, while the men were having their meeting in the great hall, Gandhari invited Perta and the three new brides—Jaratka, Draupadi, and Subhadra—to join her on a charitable trip to town.

The palace yard was warm in the early-evening sunshine. "I make these visits once a month," the queen said to the ladies as they waited for their horses to be brought around and the cart with the food baskets to be drawn up. "It's good for the townspeople to see that the royal family cares about them. And I would have us all be seen to care, not just me."

"Gandhari, what a charming idea," said Perta, fussing with the waistband of her scarlet dhoti. "Goodness ... I haven't worn riding trousers in an age. I hope they don't slip off! Isn't this a charming idea, girls? After all, my Yudi will soon be married and taking the throne. Then there will be a new queen, and all us ladies, of *whatever* background" (she smiled sweetly at Jaratka, who did not smile back) "must rally round her and ensure she has the people's support. Not to mention, Gandhari, the time you'll have on your hands then; your charity work will be something to keep you busy."

"Yes," said Gandhari, "if Yudi takes the throne."

"I don't know what you mean by *if*," said Perta, knotting the waist tie with a yank. "He is the rightful king, surely."

"We women can't know what the men will decide," said Gandhari. She placed a foot in the stirrup and rose to sit her black mare. "It's not for us to think about such things."

"Oh, no, indeed," said Perta, getting up on her white mare, "I never think about such things. I was only saying what a charming idea this is."

The sun was nearing the horizon as they headed out the gate, two armed guards following at the back of the party, maidservants walking with the cart or, in the case of the queen, leading the black mare by the bridle. Jaratka sat straight in the saddle but appeared ill at ease. Subhadra flopped about, kicking at her horse's flanks and shrieking whenever it tried to trot. Draupadi rode with the firm seat of a true horsewoman.

As they proceeded south toward town, Perta came up next to Gandhari and spoke quietly. "I must say, my dear, you're awfully brave, taking a Sn ... excuse me, *Lady Jaratka* ... taking *her* into town. Are you sure it's wise?"

"She is my son's wife," said Gandhari, looking straight ahead. "Why shouldn't she come? The townspeople need to meet her."

"Oh, to be sure. But then, some of the townspeople already have met her, in quite a different context, haven't they? Didn't she and her father once live in the shudra section? Or am I wrong about that? I have such a poor memory for these things."

"You are correct. And her father died at the Lacquer House, where she was taken by your men, where she was rescued by my son. Since that night she has been resident at the palace. All of which you know perfectly well."

"Of course, of course. That horrible fire. So tragic! Still, aren't you worried someone will recognize her? You know how commoners are. They aren't broadminded like us."

The violet veil turned and stared. "Whether anyone recognizes her or not, I know they will be happy to welcome *my* daughter-in-law."

"I see. Well, I'm sure you're right, dear. You always are."

Soon they were entering the town's grid of streets. The day's work being over, most people were at home; they came flooding out of houses or down alleyways with waves, cheers, and shouts of, "Sati! Sati is here!" Arriving in the central square the cortege pulled up next to the well, and as the crowd of several hundred gathered round, jostling in excitement, the queen alighted from her horse and began to distribute the food baskets. Each recipient, after taking a gift from her hands, knelt to kiss the hems of her dhoti. Perta, after a few flustered cries of *oh my* and *isn't this fun*, also dismounted and began to hand out baskets, assisted by her two daughters-in-law, the end of her veil pressed to her nose. Jaratka got down and stood beside Gandhari; she did not, however, touch any of the food.

Once the main crush had subsided, there approached some two dozen of the town's more prosperous vaishya—spice and cloth traders, healers, master builders, and the like—accompanied by their wives. One of the wives was Ani, the girl (you will recall) who had supposedly been attacked by the Pandavas. Her testimony at the trial along with the subsequent favor shown her and her family by the royals had made her quite a star in Hastinapura; despite her reputation as a rape victim, marriage offers had poured in, and she had accepted a position as senior wife to a jeweler, Yashu, with a large house and much influence in town affairs. Now she came forward on her husband's arm, copper beads and bangles clinking, and made a dignified curtsey to the queen. Rising, she caught sight of Jaratka, who was standing back with veil pulled well forward; her eyes lingered for a moment.

Gandhari's maidservant said quietly, "Here are Ani and Yashu, Ma'am."

"Ani, my dear, how lovely to see you," said Gandhari, leaning forward to kiss the young woman's cheek. "And Yashu; you are well?"

Yashu bowed and said, "Your majesty. I am very well, thank you."

Gandhari turned to Jaratka, took her hand, and drew her forward. "Jaratka, come. I want to present my dear friends, Ani and Yashu. Friends—this is my new daughter-in-law, Lady Jaratka. She and the crown prince were married just a few days ago."

Ani and Yashu made obeisance. Jaratka, looking uncertain, made namaste.

Gandhari exchanged more pleasantries with the jeweler and his wife and with other town notables who came up to pay their respects. She introduced them to "Lady Jaratka," allowing Perta to make introductions to her own daughters-in-law. A few of the older folk, apparently remembering the time long ago when Perta had been queen, greeted her as "your majesty"; the younger ones seemed to have only a vague notion of who Perta was.

As twilight descended, the ladies remounted their horses and made their way back through the dusty streets, followed by servants, empty cart, and guardsmen. Townspeople reemerged from the houses, oil lamps in their hands, and lined the way calling out blessings on "Sati … our queen … Queen Sati!" Some tossed flower petals in their path.

When they arrived back at the palace, Duryodhana was waiting in the torch-lit yard. He rushed to his wife, lifted her down from the saddle, and kissed her passionately. The two went inside with arms around each other's waist.

The Pandavas and Krishna emerged from the doorway of the great hall. (The men's meeting had apparently concluded.) As the six of them walked off in close conversation, only Krishna turned to acknowledge the ladies; he made namaste, smiling, but did not stop. Subhadra called out, "Arjunaaaa!" Her husband took no notice.

Stable boys came to take the horses and cart. Draupadi and Subhadra went inside with their maidservants. Gandhari and Perta lingered: Gandhari was having a word with the boy about her mare, while Perta seemed to be having trouble again with the waist tie of her dhoti.

Shakuna came from the great hall. He approached his sister, took her by the arm, and led her to the main entryway. Once within, he moved her to one side and said in a low voice, "They're leaving. Tarashtra gave them some land along the Yamuna."

"So Yudi is out?" said Gandhari. "Duryo remains crown prince?"

"Yes. For now. But I don't like it. Yudi gets to be king of the new territory."

"*Tsk*. That was foolish. Why did Tarashtra agree to that?"

"Krishna was negotiating for them. He was ... smooth. And I think Tarashtra was just happy they'll be somewhere else."

"I imagine so. But still, this is good news: the Pandavas will go, Duryo is married, and he can be crowned king. The succession is safe."

"Yes. I think we've done it, Dhari."

"*We?*"

Shakuna chuckled. "All right, *you*. But I helped!"

Brother and sister went together down the hallway, arm in arm.

Outside, Perta moved away from the entry and called to the boy leading her mare away; he brought the horse back. She mounted and gave a kick to the flanks. The wardens bowed as she cantered through the gate and out into the darkness, heading back toward town.

≈

"Ma'am," said one of the queen's ladies-in-waiting with an air of breathless self-importance, "I'm sorry to wake you, Ma'am, but the steward says there are some men from town requesting an audience with you."

"What in the world?" Gandhari muttered. She rubbed her eyes as she pushed herself to a sitting position. "What time is it?"

"The sun's not been up an hour, Ma'am," said the lady-in-waiting, opening a set of shutters. "The steward says they are eager to see you. *You*—not the king."

"Lord." Gandhari yawned and gave her whole face a vigorous rub. "It's awfully early for petitions. Where are they? You say they're all men?"

"In the council room, my lady."

"The *council room?* I can't go into the council room! What is the steward thinking?"

"I don't know, Ma'am. They said they wanted a private audience with you, so I suppose the steward thought it the best place?"

"A private ... what on earth ..."

Gandhari sat for a moment looking at the humps of her knees under the bedclothes. Then she pushed off the covers, swung her feet down to the floor, and stood up. "All right, Parvati. Send Jaya and Nina in to help me dress. Tell someone I want my honey-lemon water."

"Yes, Ma'am." Parvati turned to go.

"Oh, and Parvati ..."

"Yes, Ma'am?"

"Tell the steward to go wake my brother and ask him to meet me in the council room."

≈

Seated around the council table were the queen, Prince Shakuna, and the six men from town. The latter were highly respectable vaishya, their stature made evident not only by their fat perfumed bodies and richly dyed robes but also by their easy manner in the presence of royalty. Yashu the jeweler, the apparent leader of the delegation, was speaking.

"... and I regret to say, the people simply will not stand for it."

"Don't you mean *you* won't stand for it?" said Shakuna.

"Oh, no, no, your highness; this isn't about us," Yashu said with an oily smile. "We vaishya—that is, we *superior* vaishya—have always been broadminded when it comes to matters of caste, particularly outcastes. No, no; *we* are not the problem. It is the common people of which I speak: the weavers, the oil-pressers; the charioteers and knife-sharpeners; the cruder sorts of artisan. They are intolerant, your highness, very intolerant. And the shudra! They are even more intolerant, are they not?" He looked to his fellows for confirmation; they provided it with puffed cheeks, eye rolls, and rueful chuckles.

"You must realize, your majesty, your highness," said a man whose pouches of herbs strung around his belt proclaimed him to be a healer, "that having a Naga woman as queen would be regarded by the people as a defilement of the entire clan."

"Trade with other clans would be irreparably harmed," said a third man, who had a full beard reddened with henna. "Our goods, especially any foodstuffs, would be seen as suspect. Spices, grain, honey—no one would take them."

"And may I point out," said Yashu, "how demeaning it is to the royal family of Kuru."

"May *I* point out," said Gandhari, "that the entire royal family of Kuru is descended from a fish girl."

"I presume, Ma'am, that you mean Old Queen Satyavati," said Yashu. "Yes. But it was long ago when King Shantanu took her as his wife, and things were different in those days. Besides, everyone knows the old queen is part Goddess. She was *born* of a fish."

"Not to mention," said the henna-bearded man, "her mortal part is shudra. Not outcaste. It is not the same."

There were grunts of "no, indeed," "not the same," "not the same at all."

"I have made my son's wife kshatriya," Gandhari said. "As queen, I have every right to do so. There is plenty of precedent. So, she is no longer outcaste. Where is the difficulty?"

"The difficulty, Ma'am," said Yashu in a tone such as one uses with a slow child, "is that while there is precedent for Arya moving up or down in caste, there is no precedent for transforming an outcaste into an Arya. It is simply not possible."

"The children and grandchildren of indigenes *do* become Arya. It happens all the time!" said Gandhari, her voice rising.

The healer spoke again: "Their children and grandchildren, maybe, but not first-generation indigenes, and *certainly* not Naga. Ask any priest ..." He touched his fist to the table for emphasis. "Snakes are filthy. They eat dung. They worship foul demons. They are impure, and cannot be made Pure."

Gandhari took a breath as if to retort, but Shakuna placed his hand on her shoulder and said, "Gentlemen. You say you will not accept Prince Duryodhana as king so long as Lady Jaratka is his wife. Let me ask you this: Will you accept him as king if he divorces her— perhaps keeping her as a consort?"

The six worthies exchanged doubtful looks.

Yashu shrugged and said, "The king may take whom he pleases to his bed. But if it is a ruse and the Snake woman is queen in all but name, then, no. The *people* will not accept it."

Once the men had gone—their bows, as they filed out, were respectful yet restrained—Gandhari sank down again at the table, flipped the veil back over her head, and dropped her face in her hands.

"We're sunk," she whispered.

Her brother sat down beside her. "Not necessarily. We just have to explain to Duryo that he must divorce this girl. Take another wife. He can always sleep with her on the side. Honestly, he's got to see reason."

Her face, as she raised it to his, was pale and drawn. "Don't you understand, Kuku? He'll never do it."

"Why *not?*"

"Because he loves her."

"But that's insane!"

She sighed and looked away. "Insane or not, we can't do a thing about it."

Oh, yes, Sire, I agree: it was short-sighted of Gandhari not to realize the risk she was running in allowing her son to marry a Naga. I guess she thought that the people's devotion would protect her, and that staging a demonstration of their devotion would deter Perta from talking. She overestimated her influence and underestimated Perta's malice. But even without Perta's help, the story would have gotten out; some former neighbor from the shudra section (Yashu was right that it's the common folk who are most prejudiced when it comes to matters of caste) would have eventually recognized Jaratka and sounded the alarm. I imagine, however, that Gandhari was counting on enough time having passed by then to render the issue moot. Once Duryodhana was on the throne with a son in the cradle, what could anyone really do?

In any event, things went as the queen had predicted. Shakuna put it to his nephew that he must divorce his wife and take another; Duryodhana, in a cold rage, told his uncle that if he ever made such a suggestion again he would rip his head from his shoulders; and Tarashtra, who had of late become occupied with a voluptuous kitchen-maid whose talents included tying the stem of a potentilla berry into a knot using only her tongue, declared that if the boy was going to be that big of an idiot he didn't deserve to be king, and that he, Tarashtra, would just have to go on sacrificing himself for the good of family and clan.

Bhishma, when Shakuna appealed to him for help, also declined to get involved. "Duryodhana has made his choice," he said. "He must live with the consequences. I see no indication that he is not happy to do so."

So the stalemate continued—with Tarashtra as king, Duryodhana as titular crown prince, and Yudi as titular ruler of a patch of land in the western wilderness. Over the next few months, while the Pandavas and Krishna were scouting their new territory, Tarashtra made frequent sarcastic references to "Yudi's forest kingdom." It was clear he saw no further cause for concern, and when his nephews set off on the last day of the third month, with the ten cows plus an elephant he had gifted them and the forty indigenes he had given them leave to round up, he was positively ebullient, joining Perta in waving, sniffling, and calling out good wishes as the train moved out of the yard.

Gandhari stood back, rigid and silent. When the gate was shut and Perta, still sniffling, approached her, she turned away and moved toward the palace door. But Perta clutched her arm and walked with her, saying:

"Oh, my dear, isn't it sad, we shall miss them so much. But they'll be visiting; it isn't so *very* far. And besides," (she glanced around conspiratorially and clutched the arm tighter) "I have some comforting news, you'll never guess what ..." (she leaned in, raising her voice to a loud whisper) "... Subhadra is pregnant! Yes! I'm to have my first grandson. Promise you won't tell anyone. I wanted *you* to be the first to know."

And what do you think, Sire? Subhadra's son, born seven months later, was your grandfather, Abimanyu. With all the plots and maneuvers and battles that were to come, how odd that silly little Subhadra should have been the woman on whom the Kuru line ultimately depended.

But let's not leap ahead. We must turn now to another woman ... No, not Draupadi. Yes, I know you want to hear more about Draupadi. She was the prize, the most desired, every man's ideal; naturally you want to hear more about her, and so you shall.

But first, there is one other family member you must meet;

someone who will play an increasing role as my story continues. Did I say a woman? That's not right. Nor was she boy or man, though some believed she was.

She, if I may call her *she,* was hard to classify.

Shikhandi. She will speak for herself.

Chapter 12

SHIKHANDI

Shikhandi said:
It was my idea, not Ashwattama's, to try and free the elephants. Afterward he tried to get me out of trouble with my grandfather by saying it had been his idea, that he had dared me. That's not how it was. I dared him.

We youngsters, whether of town or palace compound, were supposed to stay away from the elephant paddock. Since it was a good hour's walk from Hastinapura, much of that through thick forest, most of us were happy to comply; I, however, had always loved the wise-eyed, rough-skinned, round-footed beasts and would pay them visits whenever I could, even after I turned eleven and my grandfather had me confined to the women's quarters. Luckily my governesses were even more hopeless than the norm, so I had no great difficulty evading them and going off on my own whenever I wanted. Until the incident, that is.

It was actually Papa-Beesh (funny ... after all this time I still think of him as *Papa-Beesh*) who first took me to see the elephants. That was when I was eight years old and had been less than a week with the Kuru, having been sent from Kashi by my grandmother because my parents were dead, she was dying, and, she said, there would soon be no one in Kashi who wanted me. I could tell there was no one in Hastinapura who wanted me, either, so after a few days of miserable inaction, I escaped the old woman who'd been assigned as my ayah and found my way to the back of the horse barns, where I hunkered down beneath a deodar tree, alternately crying, fuming, and planning my career as a mercenary. I realized *being* a mercenary would be impossible until I was a little older, but I thought I might *find* a mercenary to take me on as his blades-boy, which would be a good first step, providing both training and a close-up look at the life. The fact that I was a girl did not enter my mind as a problem. The only problem was how to get over the compound wall.

As I was wiping my eyes and wondering if it might not work better to impersonate a servant-girl on an errand and simply walk out the main gate, my grandfather came around the corner of the barn. I recognized him because when I'd arrived at the palace a few days back, my escorts had taken me to him; when they delivered my grandmother's message—"Here is your granddaughter, I hope you can find room for her, love, Amba"—he winced. I had shrunk from his obvious disapproval and certainly hadn't expected to see him again, but suddenly, there he was. He caught sight of me and started over to the deodar tree.

"Hey, boy—where are you supposed to be?"

Having torn off my veil when I'd run from the ayah, I had nothing with which to hide my tear-streaked face. I turned my back to him.

"Stand up, boy, when I'm talking to ... wait, it's not a boy." He came up to me, reached down, seized my arm, and lifted me to my feet as if he were lifting a feather. He grabbed my chin and peered into my face. "You're that girl from Kashi. The one Amba sent."

As it didn't seem to be a question, I didn't say anything.

"You've been crying." Still not a question.

He let go my chin, folded his arms, and stood looking down at me, frowning. I wanted to look away; instead, I forced myself to meet his eyes, folded *my* arms, and frowned back.

After a minute his lips twitched. "What's your name again, girl?"

"Shikhandi," I said.

"Shikhandi ... that's right. Aren't you happy here, Shikhandi?"

I did look away then, for I could feel another tear welling up and I wasn't going to give him the satisfaction. "There's nothing to do here. It's boring."

"There are lots of other little girls in the compound. Don't you like playing with them?"

Girls are stupid, I thought. But I just shook my head.

He stood silent for another minute. Then he said: "Do you like elephants?"

My eyes grew wide. "You have elephants here?"

"We do." He held out a brawny hand. "Come. Let's go see them."

≈

He told me I must call him "Lord Bhishma," but after a few weeks—during which time we visited the elephants twice more and started going for a horse ride each morning—he said "Grandpa Bhishma" would be more suitable, and soon after that I hit upon "Papa-Beesh." The first time I called him by the nickname he gave me one of his stern looks, but I had learned by then that the thing to do was to glower right back, beetling my brows just as he did, and wait until he looked as if he were trying not to laugh. Then I knew I had him.

I loved those morning rides. He had arranged for me to have a pony, a stout brown one that I named Miss Chubby. He said that as his granddaughter and a kshatriya I must be taught horsemanship, and that he may as well teach me himself since it didn't make sense to take a horse master away from his duties for the sake of a girl. So each day early we'd set off, he on his tall gray stallion and I on Miss Chubby, sometimes along the river but more often into the forest to take one of the many paths that had been cut or tramped there. It was autumn, and the earth beneath the horses' hooves was cool and damp in the aftermath of the rains. We'd stay out for an hour at least; if my riding was especially good and Papa-Beesh in an especially good humor, we might go all the way to the elephant paddock before heading home.

Ashwattama, Drona's son, came with us sometimes. He was nine, a year older than I. He took riding lessons with the other kshatriya boys, but Papa-Beesh, noticing that I still refused to play with the girls of the compound, decided I ought to have someone my own age as a companion and thought Ashwattama would do. He and I got along right away, and soon we were spending days together (whenever Ashwa's father didn't have duties for him, that is). We swam in the river, played tag, climbed trees, threw rocks, built mud-and-stick forts … oh, we had good times! My ayah, scrubbing the dirt off me each evening, would click her tongue and warn me I'd never find a husband if I looked so wild—which sounded just fine to me.

Ashwa also taught me to fight: wrestling, mostly, but also swordplay. Taking blunt swords from the weapons shed, we'd go to a forest clearing and practice the techniques he was learning on the training grounds. He seemed to relish the chance to be my guru and treated me just like a student of martial arts. Only one afternoon, after what seemed to me a good bout, I asked him if he thought I was ready to join the soldiers' practice sessions. He laughed aloud.

"What? You're a girl! Girls don't fight for real."

I didn't speak to him for a whole day after that.

But I remained his friend. The other choice was to have no friends at all, and at least Ashwa was sensible and liked the things I liked. So for three years I was happy enough: playing with Ashwa, riding with Papa-Beesh, and generally doing as I pleased.

Then one morning in early summer, sometime around my eleventh birthday, the ayah woke me early and told me to hurry and dress because I was moving to my new rooms.

"New rooms? What new rooms?" I asked. "What's wrong with this room?"

"You're to have lady's rooms from now on," she said, dragging a comb through my hair not the least bit gently. "And ladies to wait on you."

"*Ow.* What do you mean, ladies? Why can't you go on waiting on me?"

"I am an ayah. Not a lady's maid." She sounded half-cross, half-relieved.

"Who's decided this?"

"Your grandfather. Lord Bhishma."

On hearing that, I relaxed a little. If this was his doing, it was surely all right. I didn't know why I would need *rooms* or *ladies* (plural), but on the other hand, I'd never much liked the ayah. Maybe this would be an improvement.

She helped me put on my best—that is, least soiled—outfit: a rust-colored set of dhoti, chest-band, and veil. (The veil was actually spotless, having been worn rarely.) We walked through the maze of corridors, alcoves, and courtyards leading from south wing to west wing, finally arriving at a small suite of rooms that looked and smelled as if they'd been freshly plastered. Papa-Beesh was standing just inside the doorway. Four women stood off to the side: two in servants' garb, two in embroidered saris. Everyone was smiling at me.

"Shikhandi," said my grandfather, holding out his arms. I went to him and hugged him. Out of the corner of my eye, I saw the ayah drop a curtsey and leave.

"Papa-Beesh!" I said, laughing. "What's going on?"

"These are your new rooms," he said. "Now that you're eleven, it's time you had proper lady's rooms. These are your new maidservants, Priya and Chhaya, and your new governesses, Lady Amisha and Lady Eswari." They all curtsied at me, tittering.

I threw them a namaste and turned back to him. Seeing some worry in his eyes, I reminded myself that he probably intended this as a nice surprise and that I must not hurt his feelings by seeming ungrateful.

"Papa-Beesh, I love it. Thank you." I gave him another hug. He smiled, and I was glad to have put his mind at ease. "Shall we go for our ride now?"

His smile faded. "Not today, Shikhandi. I'm busy."

"Oh ... well, that's okay. I'll see you tomorrow, then."

"I think from now on you'll be too busy to go for rides with me," he said. I didn't understand why he looked so unhappy. "Of course, you may go with Lady Amisha and Lady Eswari. They are both fine horsewomen; I made sure of that. Oh, and," (his smile returned, but it was strained) "I've arranged for you to have a mare, a real mare of your own—no more fat little pony!" He looked at the two sari-clad women, who tittered some more.

All at once it dawned on me what was happening.

I was to be made a *lady*. A creature who sewed and spun and gossiped and simpered and sat indoors doing absolutely nothing. Who one day would be married off to a man who would do disgusting things to her such as I had seen the he-goats do to the she-goats. A soft, useless blob with shiny jewelry and shiny fingernails who might as well be dead.

"No," I said.

Papa-Beesh folded his arms and looked down at me, his face full of sorrow.

"It must be, Shikhandi," he said.

"No!" I shouted. I threw myself at him and beat his chest with my fists. "*No, no, no!*"

The two governesses rushed forward, gasping in horror, and tried to pull me away. "Lady Shikhandi, Lady Shikhandi," they cried. "Stop it at once!" "Apologize to your grandfather." "This is no way to behave." "My lord, we are so sorry."

It was not their plucking and mewling that made me stop; it was seeing Papa-Beesh turn away from me. He went to the door, put his hand on the lintel, and with his shaggy gray-and-white head bent down said: "I'm sorry."

"I hate you!" I shouted at his back.

"Lady Shikhandi!" the governesses cried.

I rounded on them. "*I am not Lady Shikhandi!*" All four of the women stepped back aghast.

I knew I must control myself. I took a deep breath and placed my hands, with their dirty broken nails, flat on my breast. "I am Shikhandi," I said.

When I turned again to the doorway, Papa-Beesh was gone.

≈

For the rest of the summer I was accompanied everywhere by at least one of my waiting-women. At least that was the theory; as I said, they were such a pathetic bunch that in practice it wasn't hard to escape them whenever I chose. And my grandfather had not forbidden me from seeing Ashwattama. He was allowed to visit me in my rooms, but since playing jacks or dice or twenty questions under female eyes held no more interest for him than it did for me, he simply stayed in the habit of coming once or twice a week on our morning rides. These rides, supervised by Lady Amisha and Lady Eswari, he found a little humiliating, but luckily those so-called horsewomen were incapable of anything more than a gentle trot, so he and I were always able to make a break for it. We'd gallop up the river road or into the forest—at those moments I was, I'll admit, delighted with my new mare—and find a place where we could spend an hour swimming, climbing, or in some other enjoyable activity. I knew my ladies would never tell: they'd be too afraid of my grandfather's wrath should he find out about my illicit adventures.

Occasionally Ashwa and I would go all the way to the elephant paddock, and it was one morning while we were peering through gaps between the sharp-topped fence posts, watching three of the big loggers being fitted with harnesses and drag chains in preparation for a forest-clearing expedition, that I got the idea.

"Poor things," I said. "Chained and beaten and made to drag logs all day. Poor things."

"They don't all drag logs," said Ashwa. "Some are pack elephants. And some are trained for war."

"I *know* that," I said, punching him in the arm. "Anyway, carrying packs is no better. Going to war ... well, maybe that's better."

"If I were an elephant," he said, "I'd be a war elephant. What would you be?"

I thought for a moment. "None of them. I'd be a wild elephant."

"Ha! Then you'd be captured and tamed."

"I wouldn't," I said. I could feel my face getting hot. "There's lots of elephants that aren't captured. They live wild."

"Not around here," he said, waving an arm to indicate the forest pressing thick about the clearing. "If any come around here, they get caught."

"Then I wouldn't come around here. And if I did and I got caught, I'd run away."

"You couldn't. The fence is too tall and strong."

"I could."

"No you couldn't."

"Yes I could."

We pressed our faces to the gaps. Fifteen paces away, some wallahs were shoving a baby cow elephant into the crush, the body-tight rectangular pen where, I knew, she'd barely be able to move and would have a boy in a sling lowered onto her neck while she struggled and squealed, her mother standing by, until finally she'd give in and allow him to sit. Then she'd be fed a treat. Then the process would be repeated many more times. This was elephant education.

"Ashwa!" I said.

"What?"

"Let's set them free!"

"Huh? What do you mean? Right now?"

I rolled my eyes. "No, stupid, not *now*. Tonight. When it's dark."

He looked doubtful. "How would we do it?"

"We'll come back at midnight, when the mahouts and wallahs are asleep. We'll go around and undo their leg chains, the elephants' I mean, then we'll open the gate, and they can run out."

"What if they don't run?"

I rolled my eyes harder. "Of course they'll run. They want to be *free*."

He pressed his face again to the gap and said nothing.

"Dare you," I said.

He didn't look at me as he said, "It's a stupid dare. The mahouts will just round them up again. And if they realize we did it, we'll catch holy hell."

"What, are you afraid? Afraid like a *girl?*"

He looked at me. "I'm not afraid."

"Then let's do it. I dare you twice. I dare you ten times."

He chewed his inner cheek. Then he grinned, his beaky nose curving down over his upper lip. "Okay. Let's do it."

≈

What I hadn't understood was that the elephants were already free.

Oh, not all the time, of course. But every evening they had their fetters removed and, after a dip in the broad stream that ran west of the paddock, were set loose to roam in the forest until morning. If I had thought about it I would have realized it must be so, for elephants eat a *lot*—even a baby can consume a whole banana tree at one meal—and bringing sufficient food to an entire herd would be an impossible task. Instead they must be allowed to forage for themselves. Since they need only two or three hours of sleep, they can work all day and still have most of the night in which to stroll, dine, and socialize. They rarely wander more than a few kosa, either at home or when traveling. At daybreak, each mahout tracks down his own elephant using his knowledge of its footprints and droppings (elephants also produce a *lot* of droppings), summons the beast by calling its name, and rides back to camp.

"They do not come running; they are not dogs," said an old mahout to me, years later when I asked why they would return willingly to chains, packs, and saddles. "They do not want to go to work in the morning any more than you or I want to go to work in the morning. But they know that to be alone is no good. They want to be with their elephant-and-human family who loves them. So they come back, and we go to work together."

At midnight, Ashwa and I set off from the compound. I had long ago found a place where I could get over the wall; he met me there and we walked, the strong moonlight helping us find our way through the trees. Arriving at the paddock, we saw just one elephant: an old cow, long past her prime, whom I had seen that morning having her left hind leg examined by the chief wallah. She was a hulking dark-gray shadow next to a pine tree; we could see her trunk moving from ground to mouth, ground to mouth, and hear her slow munching. There was no sign of the fifteen or so other bulls, cows, and calves that made up the Kuru herd.

Ashwa grasped the situation right away and said we should forget the whole thing. I, I am ashamed to say, was blinded by my zeal and insisted we "free" this poor lone elephant. I taunted my friend for his timidity until at last he said *fine.* He ran around to the open gate; I followed. We went up to the animal—who regarded us with mild surprise in her wrinkled old eyes —undid her fetters, and when she did not move, began prodding her hind legs with sticks, hissing, "*Go! Run!*" She stood still, continuing to munch on the heap of bamboo piled before her and glancing back at us now and then with the same mild look.

I think one of us must have poked her on the wound or abscess for which she was being treated, for suddenly she tossed her head, trumpeted, and charged away across the paddock, scattering the bamboo and dragging her fetters behind her. As she approached the fence line she tried to pull up but stumbled and fell head first into the barrier, shattering the logs like twigs. She struggled to her feet, still trumpeting, and I saw in the moonlight a long dark object sticking straight out of her chest. It was a fencepost. She continued to charge around the enclosure as Ashwa and I clung to the pine tree in terror. Moments later a swarm of men emerged from the huts on the perimeter; the chief wallah saw us, ran to us, grabbed and dragged us out and away to safety. The old elephant (her name, we learned later, was Miss Honey, because she was always so sweet) continued her rampage as the wallahs and mahouts watched helpless, until at last she sank to her knees and keeled over on her side, crying, whereupon they all ran to her, surrounded her, pulled out the post, and stayed with her, stroking her ears and trunk and singing in low voices for the ten more minutes it took her to die.

The next day Ashwa and I were brought before my grandfather. Drona was there, too. As the chief wallah recounted what had happened, I kept my eyes down. Ashwa, as I've said, tried to take the blame, but I could not let him do it; when my grandfather asked me whether Ashwa spoke the truth, I said—softly, with eyes still down— "No. I dared him." We were forbidden to see each other again. I don't know what further punishments Ashwa got. My punishment was to be confined to the compound under twenty-four-hour guard.

"And there will be no more riding," said my grandfather. "Not with anybody."

As Lady Amisha and Lady Eswari were leading me away, I turned back. He was sitting in his tall chair with arms folded.

"Papa-Beesh," I said. "I'm so sorry."

Then—I know it was madness—I folded my own arms, beetled my brows, and frowned at him. I waited for his lips to twitch.

His face was like stone.

≈

Autumn and winter passed in a dull haze. Then two things happened that were to affect my fate: the Pandavas came back, and my monthly bleeding began.

I'd been nine going on ten when the Pandavas were banished. At the time, I'd had only a vague idea of the reason for it; my ayah had whispered about a "rape," but since I didn't know what "rape" was and had barely ever seen my five famous cousins—outside of occasional glimpses of them on the training grounds before being shooed away—the whole affair meant little to me. Their return from exile was the occasion for much gossip and giggling among my women as we sat indoors spinning flax for linen. The general opinion was that Naku was very handsome, Yudi very distinguished, but Arjuna—*Arjuna* was to die for! I stared out the window, spindle in my lap, and fantasized about strangling the four of them with their veils.

As for the onset of my bleeding: no one had warned me, and when Chhaya, exclaiming, pointed to the back of my dhoti and I screwed my head around to see the red stain blooming there, my first thought was that I had contracted a deadly disease. But the women's reaction—a combination of excited squeaks, patronizing smirks, and wrinkled noses—suggested something less dire. I began asking questions. Somehow amidst all the blithering I managed to get out of them that this seepage of blood would happen every month from now on, that there was no medicine to stop it, and that it was, like my growing breasts (another source of dismay), a sign that I was now fertile, hence marriageable. Of course none of this boded much better than a deadly disease, and when I heard I would also need to go to something called the *chaupadi hut* for fourteen days ("Only this

248

first time," said Lady Eswari, seeing my shocked look; "after that, it's just five days") my mortification seemed complete.

Watching them scurry around packing my things, however, I suddenly realized I was going to be *away* for two whole weeks: away, in the forest, without chaperones. The chaupadi hut, they had told me, was for unmarried upper-caste girls only; married women and widows went into monthly seclusion at home, while shudra women, having to continue their work, were exempt. As for guards: no man came anywhere near the place for fear of defilement. So, even if there were other girls in residence ("Girls just your age!" said Lady Eswari. "Won't that be nice?") there would be no one to stop me from run-ning away—if not this time, perhaps next time. At the very least, I'd be able to climb a tree, sit in its branches, and think my own thoughts. As I set off, escorted by Chhaya, I was feeling a little more cheerful.

The hut was northwest of the compound, like the elephant pad-dock but a good deal closer: only a fifteen-minute walk through the woods. It sat on the bank of the stream that ran parallel to the river, and it turned out to be larger than I had expected, a shed big enough to house a dozen, although there were only three others there when I arrived: one brahmin girl, whom I recognized from the palace, and two town girls, both vaishya. They sat in separate corners. We did not speak but exchanged nods as I went to the fourth corner, where Chhaya helped me unroll my sleeping mat and place my food bas-kets on a rickety shelf. Then she curtsied and left, saying she would be back in fourteen days.

I sat down on the mat, feeling uncomfortable in the special undergarment I'd been given to wear: an extra-tight loincloth with a thick pad of cotton stuffed in the crotch. There were more pads in my pack, but not enough to last the five or six days I'd be bleed-ing; Lady Amisha had said I must wash them out every night in the stream and hang them to dry on the beams of the low ceiling. (Hanging them outside might attract wild animals, she said.) There were a dozen of these damp gray cloths already slung up; they were, I assumed, the source of the fish smell pervading the hut's interior. Two tiny windows let in next to no light or air. The dark funk was depressing, so I got up and went outside. The other girls watched me go, but said nothing.

I wandered away and soon found myself in a small clearing

where the sun streamed down on a cluster of banana trees. I was
ambling around the open space, kicking at dirt and twigs, when I
spied on the ground a long, straight stick with two knobs sticking
out a palm's breadth from one end, almost like the hilt of a sword. I
picked it up and swished it a few times. Then I went over to a dangling bunch of bananas, planted my feet, bent my knees, and began
to spar. Left and right, back and forth I danced, lunging and slashing
at the green fruit, all the while trying to remember the techniques
Ashwa had taught me.

I was so absorbed, my breathing so loud, that it must have been
some time before I heard the laughter of the two horsemen who had
entered the clearing behind me. I whipped around, ready to fight if
they came at me. But they just sat there chuckling.

"What do you think, Bima?" said the one on the white horse.
"Should we run for it?"

"I don't know, brother," said the other, a massive man on an
equally massive dapple-gray. "It's looking grim for us. This could be
the end."

They both doubled over, guffawing.

I lowered the stick and said, "Who are you? Declare yourselves!"

They turned to each other with brows raised and mouths open,
then fell into more fits of mirth, slapping their thighs. The big one
sat up straight, put his hand to his breast, bowed low, and said, "We
are Bima and Juna—your humble prisoners, dread lord!" The smaller
one guffawed again, ivory beads jumping on his bare chest.

So these, I realized, must be two of the Pandavas: Prince Arjuna
and Prince Bimasena, out hunting. Of course I knew they were
mocking me, but I decided to play along in hopes they would tire of
the game and go away. I made my own bow and said in the formal
diction I'd heard soldiers use: "Friends, there is no quarrel between
us. You are free to go."

At this, Arjuna stopped laughing. He tilted his head and said,
"Who are you, girl? What are you doing out here?"

"I am Shikhandi," I said. "I'm staying at the chaupadi hut." I
pointed off through the trees. They both glanced in that direction,
lips curling in faint disgust.

Arjuna said, "All right, but who *are* you?"

I lifted my chin in defiance. "I told you. I am Shikhandi." Then,
sensing that defiance would serve no purpose—honestly, when had

it ever served a purpose?—I looked down and said, "I am the grand-daughter of Lord Bhishma. Sir."

"Oh-ho!" said Bimasena. "A calf of the great bull!" He was smiling again, but there was a slight change in his tone: a trace of respect.

I could hear it in Arjuna's voice, too. "Bhishma's granddaughter, eh?" he said, dismounting. He came across the clearing to me and held out a hand for the stick. I gave it to him; it would have been silly not to.

"Where did you learn those skills?" he asked, giving the air a casual slice or two.

"From Ashwattama," I said. "Drona's son."

"Did you hear that, Bima?" He called over his shoulder at his brother, who had also dismounted. "She says Drona's son is her guru."

"He's my friend," I said. "I mean, he *was* my friend. Papa … my grandfather won't let me see him anymore. He taught me a lot. About sword-fighting, I mean."

"Show me," said Arjuna. He gave me back the stick and drew his sword, causing me to step back in alarm. He looked amused. "Don't worry, I won't cut you. I won't even nick you. Just show me what you know."

Slowly, I took up the proper stance and crossed my stick on his sword. We began to spar, very gently at first, then with a little more vigor, until I was bobbing and weaving, thrusting and cross-cutting, just as I used to do with Ashwa. Of course Arjuna was only feinting, putting no force at all behind his moves; even so, as I slashed at his blade my stick grew more and more battered, until finally it snapped in two and I fell back with my hands up. He touched his point to my throat, laughing softly. Bimasena, who had been standing by watching, applauded.

"Not bad!" said Arjuna, re-sheathing his sword. "Really, not bad at all."

I was exhausted, panting. He was barely breathing hard. He was eighteen, in the first flower of his manhood. I wanted to do something with him; what, I did not know.

"She's quite the little warrior," he said to his brother.

"I'm not," I said, still panting. "But I *will* be one, someday."

They both grinned at me. Bima ruffled my hair with his big paw.

"Come on," he said to Arjuna, "I want to get that deer." But Arjuna didn't move; he seemed to be in the grip of an idea.

"Say, Bima," he said, "we ought to give this girl lessons."

"I could teach her to wrestle," said Bima. He poked my arm with a gourd-like finger, and I nearly fell over. Once more, they found this incredibly humorous.

"No, I'm serious," said Arjuna, regaining his composure. "Shikh … what's your name? Shikhandi? Yes, Shikhandi here has been ill-treated. Locked up in the women's quarters, I bet. Is that what happened? Your grandfather had you locked up? Won't let you play anymore?"

I nodded.

"We could train her." He faced his brother, but his eyes slid back to me. "She's got talent. And when the time is right, we'll show the mighty Bhishma what his sweet little granddaughter can do. We'll tell him all about the time we spent alone with her and how we … *trained* her. It'd be a good joke, wouldn't it?"

At the time, I heard neither the malice curdling his voice, nor the words "good joke," nor the odd emphasis he gave to the word *trained*. All I heard was, "She's got talent." I had a vision of myself at the head of an army marching into battle, my golden sword drawn, my golden armor flashing in the sun.

Bima said, "We have to go west soon. That's the agreement."

"Not for three months," said Arjuna. "Krishna bought us more time." He turned and gave me a gorgeous smile. "What do you say, Shikhandi? You want us to teach you to fight? To be a real warrior?"

"Yes. Oh, *yes*," I said.

"Excellent." He laid a hand on my shoulder. "We'll start right away."

≈

In order to understand my actions years later, during my marriage and in the Great War, you must understand that those days with Arjuna and Bima—but mostly Arjuna—were the happiest days of my life. I lived them as if in a dream: a dream of all my dreams coming true.

For the two weeks I was in the chaupadi hut, they returned each afternoon, by arrangement, and gave me lessons in swordplay and wrestling. Arjuna brought an old sword and told me it was mine, though he would have to keep it for me when I returned to the palace. The bronze was green with age, the blade notched and dull. I loved it with a passion. Bima treated the sessions as a lark, "wrestling" me on his knees with one hand tied behind his back and laughing uproariously as I put my spindly shoulder to his gargantuan one and pushed, my feet scrabbling on the loose soil. Arjuna, on the other hand, took me seriously: he gave me drills, taught me technique, chastised me when I was slipshod, and praised me when I did well. He also insisted I practice on my own and noticed when I made progress as a result. This was nothing like my childish tussles with Ashwattama. I was really learning to fight.

In the second week, Bima would arrive in the clearing with his brother but stay only a quarter of an hour, leaning against a tree and watching us spar before heading back into the forest to hunt. Arjuna would continue our exercises for another hour or so and then declare that we needed a break. We'd sit down by a banana tree and he'd tell me about the warrior's code, which is the highest Law for a soldier. I found this almost as exciting as the actual lessons and hung breathless on his every word.

He told me warriors were brothers-in-arms, sworn to protect and help each other in every way—"*every* way," he said. He said a starving soldier would always share what little food he had. He described how on cold nights two soldiers would keep each other warm by huddling together under a blanket, thereby sharing their body heat. He demonstrated by having us both lie down and wrap our arms around each other. "They must get as close as possible," he said. "There must not be a finger's breadth of space between them." I snuggled in tighter. "Very good," he said. "You're going to make a fine warrior, Shikhandi." I glowed with pleasure.

He told me soldiers also tended to each other's injuries. "They are not the least bit squeamish," he said. "They must bind wounds, set broken bones, and suck the venom from snake bites." He pricked his arm with a thorn and had me suck the blood. "And they must be willing to handle all parts of the body, for an injury can occur anywhere. *All* parts, Shikhandi: do you understand?" I nodded firmly. He had me practice by taking a rag and binding up imaginary wounds, first on his ankle, then on his knee, and finally on his upper thigh. For the latter he lowered his dhoti and stood there all but naked. I had to move his male member aside in order to wrap the cloth, and I hesitated; but Arjuna looked off into the distance and said sternly, "I thought you wanted to be a soldier, Shikhandi. Was I wrong about that?" I shook my head, terrified he would cut me off, and proceeded to do as he asked.

When my fortnight in the chaupadi hut came to an end, I was downcast, but Arjuna promised he would meet me again next month. "We can do two more sessions before I leave for the west," he said. I begged him not to forget me. He took my face between his hands, looked deep in my eyes, and said, "How could I forget my brother-in-arms?" Then he held me close for a long time.

We had decided that Chhaya would inform him when next I went to the hut. I had no trouble getting the girl to agree; she was thrilled at the thought of talking to any of the Pandavas, let alone the best Pandava. When she dropped me off the second time, she stayed barely long enough to help me unroll my mat. Then she rushed off, cheeks flushed, to deliver the message.

This time chaupadi was only five days. Bima did not show up at all, but Arjuna was as good as his word. I cannot describe my relief and joy when I saw him riding into the banana grove on his white horse, my sword laid across his lap. During that week, the proportion of exercises shifted a bit: we did a little less sparring, a little more talking and play-acting "soldiers." It did not enter my mind to complain.

The next month, I knew he would be leaving soon and that this would be our final meeting. On our last day in the clearing, my despair was such that even his high praise of my abilities, his insistence that I had "special talent," did not console me. Seeing my misery, he said we should stop early and have one more talk about the soldier's life. We went over to our tree and sat down on the ground. He took my hands in his.

"There is one more thing you must know, Shikhandi, about the warrior's code," he said.

"Yes? What is it?" I wiped a tear while pretending to scratch my cheek.

He ducked his face to look into mine. "You know that warriors must help and support each other in every way."

"Yes, Arjuna," I said.

"And I imagine you know that warriors—men—have physical needs."

"Like eating and staying warm," I said.

"Yes, like that. But also, they need to release tension. Especially when there are no women available."

"I see," I said, trying to look as though I saw.

"It is essential to a warrior's health that he release tension regularly. If he doesn't, he can become very ill. And since there are no women on the battlefield, we warriors must help one another in this way, too. Will you let me show you how we do it?"

I nodded.

He stood, pulling me up with him. He undid the waist tie of his dhoti and dropped it to the ground. He took my hand and placed it on his member. He showed me how to fondle and rub it, and soon it became long and stiff. Closing his eyes he said, "That's it, Shikhandi; that's it, my love; harder, now; help me; you must help me; oh, fuck, that's good, yes, good." He began to moan. He leaned across me, bracing his hand against the tree trunk, and his moans grew louder, and I was growing frightened, but his hand was gripping mine, moving it faster and faster, and I could not have stopped even if I had dared. At last his hips made a violent jerk and from his throat came a strangled bellow. I felt something warm and wet in my hand. He crushed my body to his and ground against me for a while longer, grunting and sighing. Then he released me and stepped back.

He pulled up his dhoti, retied the waistband, and gave me his most approving smile. "Well done, Shikhandi," he said. "Now we're truly brothers." I looked down and saw his discharge smeared on my stomach.

In that moment I understood that he had done to me what the he-goats do to the she-goats, only into my hand rather than into the place where my blood came out. I felt no more fear, however; I felt only pride and pleasure that I had been able to help him. That I, a girl just turned twelve, had been able to do for him what a real warrior does for his brother-in-arms.

There you have the beginning of Shikhandi's story. Next, we will—

What's that, my lord?

You don't believe it? What don't you believe?

Ah ... I see. You don't believe that your great-grandfather—tiger of the battlefield, incarnation of Indra, hero of the age—could have done such a thing. After all, women fell at his feet; he could have anyone he wanted. Not to mention he already possessed the most beautiful princess in the world as his wife, so why would he bother to lure an unattractive little tomboy into lewd activities?

And even if he did, wasn't Shikhandi as much to blame, if not more? She had already shown an astounding lack of modesty: running wild in the forest, defying her grandfather, taking up weapons, breaking the seclusion of chaupadi. Goodness, her behavior caused the death of a valuable elephant! Clearly she had no shame. Does it not seem likely that the foul games with Arjuna were *her* idea? Or, just as likely, that she made it all up for the sake of drama.

That's what you're thinking.

Well, Nephew; you may be right. But I ask you to wait until my tale is done to draw conclusions about Shikhandi, and about Arjuna. I also ask you to consider that all five Pandavas are still alive, while Shikhandi is long dead, which means Arjuna and his brothers have had many years to shape the story. And if you say it is the bards who shape the stories, I must remind you: it is living princes who mostly pay the bards.

But let us return now to Draupadi. In this next part of my story we'll be flying through time as swiftly as celestials, touching down only here and there; for, what with her reluctance to tell me of her married life, I could elicit from her only a few memories of the years between her wedding and the great dice match. You will not blame her for what happened; unlike Shikhandi, women like Draupadi do not get blamed for these things. Nevertheless, she blamed herself. Her anger, she said, and later her laughter, were the sparks that lit the fire of my father's rage.

Chapter 13

DRAUPADI

16–4 YEARS BEFORE THE WAR

S ubhadra put the baby to her breast. *"Look how he sucks! Look, Padi. Isn't he strong? Isn't he greedy?"* She giggled as the infant fell to his task with gusto. *"He's just like his Dada! Arjuna loves my breasts. And so does Baby Abi. Yes he does. Oh, yes he does."* She squeezed Abimanyu rather violently, causing him to unlatch and squawk in protest. *"Oh, no! Oh, nooooo, poor baby! He must have the boobie-doobie, mustn't he? Yes he must! Just like his Dada. Here we go, sweetie, here we go. Just like Dada."*

She eased nipple back into mouth and reclined on the daybed with a triumphant smile at Draupadi, who was seated by the window of the public room they shared.

"Do you think he'll visit us again soon, Padi? I hope so. I love it when he visits. When do you think we'll move out to the new place? Soon, I hope. Except it's hard to give him all the attention he needs, now that I've got Abi. Not that he's hard to satisfy, but he's so" (more giggles) *"so eager, and sometimes I'm like, 'Arjuna, my love! Remember I've just had a baby, please, go easy on me.' And he does, or anyway he tries, but then he forgets and oh! My poor hoo-ha!"* She squirmed on the daybed. *"Oof, it gets sore. But then we married women must put up with these things, mustn't we? And we don't mind. Or anyway, I don't mind. Not with a man like Arjuna. I feel lucky, honestly. Every lady in the palace is jealous of me; you see how they all stare at me. Nasty cats. I don't care. Ha-ha to them!"*

She gazed down at Abimanyu and made kissy sounds.

"I bet Abi will have a little brother before he knows it. Won't you, sweetie-baby? Because Dada just can't keep his hands off Mama. No he can't!"

She looked up again and in a more serious tone said: *"If you* want any tips, Padi, just ask me. I've got *so* many good tips. Now listen to me, here's the main one: *His pleasure comes first.* Remember that and you can't go wrong, you really can't."

Draupadi kept her eyes on the summer-weight cloak she was embroidering for their husband. "Thank you," she said. "I'll try to remember."

≈

With the winter solstice only three weeks past, suppers in hall were dark affairs. Extra oil lamps had been set on the royal table, throwing streaks of light and shadow across the faces there.

"Draupadi, dear, you must eat." Perta, sitting next to her daughter-in-law, spoke with quiet urgency. "You're skin and bone. You'll never get with child like this."

"Yes, Mother," Draupadi whispered. She picked up a bit of roti, crumbling it in her fingers, but made no move to put it in her mouth.

"Look at Jaratka, now!" said Perta, gesturing across the table at Duryodhana and his wife, who knelt side by side, their shoulders touching. "*She* was too thin, but she made an effort to eat nutritious food and it paid off. Remind us of when you're due, Jaratka, dear?"

Jaratka patted her stomach. "Three more months. That is what the midwives say." She turned, smiling, to her husband. Smiling back, he took her hand and gave it a squeeze.

Draupadi's eyes flicked to their hands, to Jaratka's midsection, and down again.

Subhadra, on the other side of Perta, said in a shrill voice, "Ooo, Jaratka, I know! You and I can have baby wars! Just like Mother and Queen Gandhari. First Mother had Yudi, then the queen had Duryo, and—and so on. We could do the same. Cause you know *what* ..." (she leaned over, elbow on the table, and grinned at Draupadi) "I'm definitely pregnant again."

Draupadi said nothing. Her jaw clenched.

"How nice," Perta said with a chilly glance at her son's junior wife. She turned back to Draupadi. "You see, darling? You mustn't let the other girls outdo you. Just look at Jaratka. Look how pretty she is. No wonder Duryo is so fond of her. Men prefer ladies who have a bit of padding." She smiled down at her own large bosom, drawing her veil coyly across.

Subhadra arched her back proudly. "Yes! Men prefer *boobies!*"

Draupadi lifted her head. She was looking at Jaratka, but her eyes were unfocused as she muttered: "As far as I can tell, men prefer sluts. Sluts like you."

Duryodhana flushed red. "*What* did you call my wife?" he growled.

Draupadi did not appear to have heard him. She picked up her knife and began to saw at her hunk of beef.

Duryodhana reached across the table and pulled her plate away. "I *said:* What did you call my wife?!"

With a face of fury, Draupadi pointed the knife at him and hissed: "I didn't call your wife *anything*. I don't speak to *dung-eaters.*" She pushed herself to her feet and ran from the table.

Duryodhana made to rise, too, but Jaratka seized his arm and said, "Sit down, Duryo. Let her go. Let her go. She is just unhappy." He subsided, glowering.

Perta, murmuring "oh my, oh dear," got up and went after her daughter-in-law.

Subhadra applied herself to her beef with a satisfied smirk.

≈

A ray of spring sunshine came through the window of the public room and fell on the curtain over the door of the bedchamber. The groans within had ceased minutes ago; the ladies and maidservants, seated on the floor or on stools, looked at one another with anxious faces.

Draupadi arrived and went over to Karna. He was leaning against a pillar at the back, head bowed, the only man among the watchers.

"Where is Duryodhana?" she asked.

He pointed to the curtain. "With her," he said. "He would not be kept out."

"Has the baby come yet?"

He shook his head. "Not yet."

Draupadi stood still, her head also bowed, waiting with the rest.

There was a prolonged, strangled scream, as of someone making an immense effort, along with the sounds of women crying encouragement. Then: a thin wail.

The ladies and maidservants all said, "Ah!" They exchanged grins and nods. Draupadi caught her breath and touched Karna's shoulder; he looked at her, and they smiled at each other for an instant before she dropped her hand and moved a step away.

Ten more minutes passed. From the bedchamber came a swishing of skirts, a clinking of pottery, and the occasional soft laugh. The infant's wails lessened. A woman's deep voice said, "Now the afterbirth. Hand me that bowl." More bustling and murmuring.

Suddenly, a man's voice came loud through the curtain: "She's b-bleeding!"

For the next half hour, bursts of confused noise from the inner room assailed the tense silence in the outer room. Cries were heard: *Quickly! Harder! Help her sit up!* At one point the woman with the deep voice said, "Please, my lord, you must stay back." The watchers dropped their heads or stared, quiet, at the sunlit doorway; some of them seemed to be praying.

The man's voice came again: "Help her ... p-p-please, help her!"

Then the inner room grew quiet, too.

The quiet stretched on and on: a quiet that would never end.

Duryodhana pushed aside the curtain and stepped out into the sunshine. He put up a hand to block the fiery brightness. He took a step; then another; then another. He dropped his hand, and his eyes were like the eyes of one in a soma daze. The ladies and maidservants all scrambled to their feet and curtsied as he passed.

Karna and Draupadi intercepted him as he reached the outer doorway.

"Duryo," said Karna. "I'm sorry."

Duryodhana did not look at him, but nodded once. "Thank you, Karna," he said.

Draupadi's hands were clasped at her waist. Her posture was erect. "Your highness," she said with formal diction, "please accept my sympathy on the loss of your beloved wife."

His face turned toward her. His eyes narrowed.

"You," he said.

Draupadi took a tiny step back.

"You," he said again. His jaw clenched; his scar flared. "You will not offer me your sympathy. And I will not offer you mine. Ever."

He went out the door and down the corridor.

Draupadi looked at Karna with something like despair. Karna

reached out and touched her cheek, gently. Then he turned and went after his master.

≈

"Hot as hell in that wagon." Perta was looking uncharacteristically rumpled as she took Krishna's hand and clambered down from the covered cart. "Damn baby cried the whole way. *Oof.* Thank you, Krishna."

"Dearest Aunt, welcome to Indraprasta." Krishna bowed and gestured to the main entry. "Your sons are awaiting you. You'll find it wonderfully cool inside."

The palace, now two years in the making, sat a hundred paces back from the riverbank, its façade facing west over the Yamuna. The main house was nearly twice the size of the Hastinapura palace, and with more windows; there was as yet no outer wall and few outbuildings. The trees had been cleared for a half a kosa, creating an expanse of light-green grass, sprinkled with wildflowers, stretching in a semicircle away from the water. Just to the south of the house there was a rough barracks, and beyond that, plots of grain and vegetables. Away to the north, a hundred cows grazed near a cluster of huts. Directly behind the house a path led up a slope to a long flat-topped hillock, beyond which was a round arena with a surface of packed dirt, its circumference marked off by short stakes.

Next to emerge from the cart was Subhadra, carrying fifteen-month-old Abimanyu. (Her second baby, born a few weeks ago, had died; since it had been a girl, no one was unduly upset.) Krishna gave her a perfunctory kiss on the forehead and a light shove toward the door. Ladies and nursemaids came from the uncovered dray and fell in behind her, but unlike with his aunt, Krishna did not wait to see the retinue safely inside. Instead he turned back to the cart and took the slender hand that came through the straw blinds. As Draupadi alighted, he bowed low.

"Your highness," he said, "welcome to your new domain."

Draupadi shook out her light-blue dhoti and made him namaste. Though pale and sweating, she held herself tall. "It's hardly *my* domain, Krishna," she said in a wry tone.

"Have no fear, Madam," Krishna said with another bow. "Here

in Indraprasta, everyone will know who is queen. I will make sure of it."

Draupadi looked around at the mud-plastered house, the wild-flower meadow, the grain fields, and the wide river sparkling in the midsummer sun. She smiled slightly.

"Is my husband within?"

"He is indeed. He is most eager to see you. May I take you to him?"

The princess's women fell in behind her as she walked toward the palace beside Krishna. As she walked, her smile grew more assured; indeed, it became almost hopeful.

≈

Draupadi stood at the window, looking out at the faint gleam of the river under the cloudy night sky. The door curtain did little to muffle the noise from the outer room.

"Boy, more stew here! More beer!" That was Bima.

"And over here, more beer!" That was Mohanu, one of the kshatriya who'd come west with the Pandavas. He'd become quite a favorite, often invited to dine and drink with them.

"Give it up, Mo! You know what happened last time you tried to drink Bima under the table—we had to scrape you off the floor and pour you into bed!" That was Naku. His sally was followed by a pounding of fists on wood and many male voices shouting "drink, drink, drink!" as Mohanu (evidently) rose to the challenge.

In the ensuing brief lull could be heard a light clattering, disappointed groans, and a cry from Yudi: "I win, I win!" He was never as excited as when he was throwing the dice.

Draupadi sighed and went to sit on the mat against the wall by the door. (There were no beds in the palace as yet.) The festivities would end sometime after midnight; until then, attempts at sleep were useless. Krishna and Perta's insistence that Arjuna share rooms with her had resulted in these nightly supper gatherings, which tended to end with the prince staggering into the bedchamber and falling face-down on the mat, there to lie like a dead thing till morning. About once weekly, he went to Subhadra's room instead.

Two voices, not as loud as the rest, began to filter through the curtain; the speakers, it seemed, had come to a corner in order to talk privately. Draupadi cocked her head to listen.

"Darling, you *must* be advised by me on this matter." That was Perta. She was not invited to the supper parties, but she had been known to drop in anyway.

"Mother, believe me. I do sleep with Draupadi most nights. Truly—*hic*—I do."

"No, you don't. You may sleep next to her, but you don't do your duty by her. Don't lie to me, Arjuna, I'm not stupid."

"I sleep with Susu! I gave you a grandson! What more d'you want?"

"Yes, and I love Abimanyu, but one son is not enough. Not a son by that worthless trollop, anyway. Draupadi is your *senior wife,* Arjuna. She is the daughter of the king of Panchala, who is your most important ally. If she does not have children soon, questions will be asked. It will hurt our cause. You must think of your brothers; of your family."

There was a small thud, as if Arjuna had leaned heavily against the wall.

"I know. I know I must. But Mother, she's shuch ... shuch a stuck-up *bitch*. Always looking down her nose at me. At all of us. I don'—*hic*—don' like her."

"Really, dear. You don't have to like a woman to sleep with her."

"Fine, I hate her. Stuck-up bitch."

There was a short pause.

"All right, sweetheart," Perta said. "Let's think creatively about this. Think about your brothers. How long has it been since they had a woman?"

"I dunno. There're some women in the village now. Bima goes pretty often; me and the twins too, sometimes."

"Yes, yes, but indigenous women ... well, they're hardly ... I mean, the *diseases*. They'll do in a pinch, but not as a long-term solution. And you must have seen the way Bima and the twins look at Draupadi. Even Yudi is fond of her, I can tell he is."

"I guess, but ... wait. Mother, what are you saying?"

"I'm saying, Arjuna, that your brothers like your wife very much. So perhaps, seeing as you don't care for her yourself, you could be a little bit generous and *share*."

Another pause. Then Arjuna began to laugh—a long, bubbling laugh.

Finally he stopped laughing and said, "*Share* her. Ha! That'd take her down a peg. If all of us ... wow. Wouldn't that just put Miss High-and-Mighty in her place?!"

Perta said, "Think of it that way if you like. The point is she must have babies. Which one of you begets them, doesn't matter."

"I like the idea, Mother. I really—*hic*—I really really do. Bima and the twins will be up for it, no question. Yudi, though; he might take some convincing."

"Yes, he might. Hmm. Let's think ... oh, I know!"

"What?"

"Tell him there's precedent: precedent for a woman to have several husbands as long as they're brothers. Get your priest—what's his name, Dhaumya?—get him to do a wedding ceremony. Then you'll all be officially married to her, and Yudi will have his excuse."

"Mother, that's brilliant! Ha! This is gonna be fun."

The two moved away from the door. In the bedchamber, Draupadi was sitting on the mat, staring into the darkness, trembling.

≈

The pavilion kept the rain off the fire but did nothing to reduce the mud. There was as yet no Hall of Sacraments, so for all rituals, including this one, Priest Dhaumya made do with a circle of dirt next to the training grounds, in the middle of which was an oiled-silk canopy on bamboo poles, underneath which sat the pyre. During the rains, the place was a slop pit. Draupadi had taken her mother-in-law's advice not to wear shoes, but as she walked around the sacred fire—seven times with each brother, twenty-eight times in all—her sari became soaked and dirty from the knees down. The damp logs smoked dreadfully. Since it had been decided that the ceremony would be kept quiet (being mainly for the benefit of Yudi's conscience), the witnesses consisted only of the bride's attendants plus Perta, Arjuna, and Subhadra. Perta stood to one side, lifting her skirts out of the mire, coughing, and periodically begging the priest to move faster. Subhadra clung to Arjuna's arm, shrieking at every thunderclap. The proceedings having concluded, everyone rushed back to the main house in order to dry off and change clothes.

Krishna was away in Vrishni. He would not learn of the wedding until he returned, in the autumn. When he was told, he showed a flash of surprise—even distaste—but quickly recovered his courteous demeanor, congratulated the brothers, and wished Draupadi joy.

Over the next seven years, she would give birth to five sons.

≈

Suta and Shruta were fussing and squirming against their mother's legs. Baby Nana was asleep in his sling. Draupadi gripped the shoulders of the toddlers and said, "Stand still, you two, or I'm taking you back inside and you won't see Papa Arjuna set the jackal on fire."

Yudi, standing next to her with his hand on her nape, said, "My dear, I don't know why you must always keep the children with you."

Draupadi did not reply. She licked her thumb and used it to wipe a smudge off Suta's cheek. Then she bent down, holding Baby Nana to her side, and kissed the top of each tousled head. Her silver tiara with the light-blue jewels slipped forward a little; she pushed it back in place. Down below in the arena, Arjuna was urging all the children to the front.

"There's no need," said Yudi. "That's what the ayahs are for."

Duryodhana came up, leading his young daughter by the hand. Yudi nodded in friendly fashion: "Ah, Duryo. And little Astika—your first visit? That's right, get a good spot."

The audience included not only palace senior staff and the relatives from Hastinapura, but also some brahmin and kshatriya families (among these were Lady Shikhandi and her husband) who lived in other parts of the doab but were contemplating a move to Indraprasta. A few Vrishni clan members had made the journey at Krishna's special invitation. The guests made a colorful display, all in their best clothes and jewelry.

Naku entered the ring, bronze sword in hand, and crossed to the stake. The jackal lunged, but Naku merely hopped back and wagged his finger *tsk-tsk*, raising chuckles from the crowd. Saku came with the torch. Then Subhadra, wearing her sheerest yellow dhoti, minced her way across, grabbed onto Arjuna, squealed as his bow knocked her in the face, received a kiss on the cheek, lowered herself into her dance pose, and was handed the torch by Saku.

Arjuna made his speech about watching the arrow. The rest went as it always did.

When the jackal was dead and the guests had begun to shuffle their way onto the path back to the palace, Yudi said, "Have you a handkerchief, my dear?" Draupadi drew a square of cotton from her chest-band and handed it over. Yudi took it, coughed into it, blew his nose.

"Fine show, eh, Duryo?" He balled up the handkerchief and mopped the sweat on the back of his neck. It was a hot evening, the monsoons still a few months away.

Duryodhana turned and stared—at Draupadi, who was accepting the soiled cloth back from her husband and tucking it away. "Yes," he said. "F-fine show."

Her eyes met his. It was impossible to tell what each was thinking.

≈

Having had a time rounding up the children, she was among the last to leave the hillock. She was clasping Suta and Shruta's hands in one of hers, grabbing Shata's arm with the other, and shouting at Prata, the eldest, to come *along,* all while trying to shush Baby Nana who had woken up in his sling and begun to whimper—when Karna approached.

"Need some help?" he asked.

Draupadi blew a lock of hair off her brow. "This wretched jackal show. It always gets them overexcited. Arjuna insists they be there."

"Come on, champs! I'll give you all a ride home." Karna knelt down. "Prata, Shata, get on my back. Suta, Shruta, come around front." The six- and five-year-old threw themselves onto his back with delighted yells as he scooped up the toddlers in his arms. Thus burdened—though his tall, muscular frame showed little strain—he headed down the path toward the palace, trotting in zig-zags and neighing now and then, with the boys all shrieking, "Faster, faster!" Draupadi pulled Baby Nana from the sling and walked along with him pressed to her shoulder, singing a song about "elephants all in a row."

When they got to the door, Karna said, "All riders off—bedtime!" This resulted in howls of dismay and frantic clinging.

Draupadi scolded them to no avail. Finally she said, "All right, boys. *If* you stop fussing and promise to be good, then Uncle Karna will come help put you to bed. But if you're the least bit naughty, he's going to leave."

That did the trick. The boys got down and arranged themselves in formation around Karna. As Draupadi led the way into the house, she looked back, smiling up at him, and whispered: "Mothering with threats and bribes."

They all marched down the corridor to the night nursery, where a boisterous bedtime ensued. Draupadi thrilled her sons by proclaiming several times that "Uncle Karna is *just* as naughty and will have to be punished." But at last all faces were washed, all night clothes donned, all stories told, and everyone tucked into bed with the oil lamps extinguished. Baby Nana was handed to the wet nurse. The senior ayah and her two juniors, clearly a little overexcited themselves at the unexpected visitor—Hastinapura's handsome captain of the guard—curtseyed giggling to Madam and Sir Karna as they made their exit.

Draupadi took the route toward the women's quarters. Karna walked beside her. She seemed abstracted and did not prevent him.

"Duryodhana's daughter is growing up very sweet," she said. "How old is she now?"

"She just turned seven," Karna said. "He adores her."

"Why has he not married again? I'm surprised his mother hasn't insisted."

"The queen wants him to, of course. The council has put many names before him. But he won't hear of it."

"I suppose, when you love someone like that ..." Her voice trailed off.

"Yes. There can never be anyone else."

They walked on in silence for a while, their eyes on the ground.

Draupadi arranged her face in a brighter expression. "And how is your wife, Sir Karna? How is Lady Padma?"

"She is very well, thank you. She still attends the queen."

"No children yet?"

"None yet."

"Ah. Well, with the Gods' grace, I am sure they will come."

They arrived at the doorway to her rooms. Women's voices could be heard within, but the corridor outside was empty. Draupadi turned and, with an intake of breath and a courteous smile, said,

"Well, good night, Sir Karna. It was so kind of you to help me with the chil—"

He reached out and seized her wrist. "How do you stand it?"

She frowned, but did not pull away. "Stand what?"

"It. *Them.* It must be … horrible."

She looked down at his hand, holding her wrist, and seemed to reflect for a moment. "It was, at first," she said. "At first, when they all used to … I wanted to die. But now I have the children. And besides," (she gave a wry laugh) "these days, they've rather lost interest in me. It's only Yudi who still feels obliged to do his marital duty."

Karna let go of her wrist. "I only wish … I wish …"

She put out a hand and touched his cheek, gently. "What do you wish, Karna?"

He gathered her to his breast and pressed his lips to her hair. She turned her face upward and placed her hands behind his head, pulling his mouth to hers. They kissed, softly at first and then with more urgency, their lips parting, tongues joining, tasting each other with mutual hunger. He ran his palms down her torso, over her hips and then up again to wrap her waist and upper back; he bent to kiss the hollow of her throat, and she leaned back in his embrace. Their breath came hot and fast. Her silver tiara was knocked askew.

"Is that you, my lady?" The voice was right behind the door curtain. Draupadi stumbled backward into the wall as Karna released her. He turned and strode away down the corridor. The lady pushed the curtain aside and looked out, solicitous: "Ma'am, are you all right?"

Draupadi regained her balance, straightening the tiara with shaky hands. "I'm fine," she said. "I just tripped on my own feet. Silly." She took a deep breath. "I won't be going to hall tonight. Will you see about some supper, please, Harini?" She went through the doorway.

≈

Ten-year-old Prata, fidgeting in his stiffly embroidered vest, collar, and cloak, leaned toward his mother and whispered: "How much longer?"

Draupadi whispered back: "Nearly done. Here comes the high priest."

Dhaumya ascended the dais steps. He and the golden crown he carried were reflected in miniature in the hundred thousand polished tin tiles, each no bigger than a thumbnail, which in the past year had been applied to the ceiling and pillars of the great hall, there to throw myriad sparks of light onto the walls with their elaborate paintings designed to fool the eye. Having reached the center of the platform, the priest turned to face the throng, lifted the crown high, and intoned:

"Blessed be his majesty, King Yudishtira of Indraprasta! May the Gods old and new smile upon him. May Brahma protect him, Vishnu sustain him, and Shiva destroy his enemies. May Indra strengthen his arms; may Brihaspati grant him wisdom; may Agni accept his sacrifices. May the Goddess Kali invigorate his loins so he produces many sons. And may Yama, the God of Law, guide all his judgments and actions from this day forward, until the day he is called to mount the sacred stair to Paradise, there to continue forever his glorious reign."

The old priest turned to Yudi, enthroned and resplendent in a crimson robe thick with gold embroidery, and placed the crown upon his head. He received from one of his juniors a bronze scepter, topped with an orb of garnet, which he placed in the king's hands. Assisted by two other priests, he bowed deeply. Then he rose, with help, and retired to a padded stool at one side of the dais.

With the sacred part of the ceremony over, it was time for the presentation of gifts. Draupadi took Prata down the steps. Earlier the boy had insisted he would stay for the whole thing: "I'm crown prince! It will look bad if I don't." After two uncomfortable hours, however, he did not object to being sent off (although he certainly would have, had it been an ayah instead of a bodyguard waiting there). The queen, of course, could not leave; she went back up the dais and reseated herself beside her five husbands.

The presentations took another two hours, with every family of consequence—from Indraprasta itself, but also from Hastinapura and rural parts of the doab—bringing a gift for the new king and his brothers. As well, there were in attendance quite a few nobles from the neighboring lands of Vrishni, Madrasa, Kashi, and Panchala. The tributes varied in richness: a prince of Madrasa raised oohs and aahs with his teakwood chest filled with silver ingots, while the pair of scruffy-coated hunting dogs brought by Krishna's father, King Vasudeva, elicited only chuckles. Baskets of delicacies, bolts of cloth, caged birds, jewelry, carved statues, weapons, furniture, and all sorts of other treasures piled up on the white marble floor before the dais, and were periodically moved to the side by manservants.

Krishna followed his father. When he knelt to present a bronze sword, its hilt bejeweled with garnets, Yudi rose, descended the steps, and raised him to his feet, saying: "My dear friend: it is we who should be kneeling to you, for all we have is thanks to you. Indraprasta is your work, and the Pandavas are your servants, now and forever." They embraced each other, Yudi in his crimson cloak, Krishna in his royal blue. The people applauded.

Next to present was King Drupada of Panchala. As he walked from the back of the hall the crowd parted, as if by an irresistible force. With him came two kshatriya bearing a long wooden tray on which lay an enormous mace—but of a type few had seen before. It was made of a black metal with a dull sheen, and the spiked ball on top was not tied to the shaft, but seemed to be all of a piece. King Drupada circled the shallow pool at the hall's center and, having arrived at the dais, stepped aside so the men could place the mace at Yudi's feet. Then he turned and spoke to the assembly:

"My friends! Let this weapon, made of the substance called *iron,* be a symbol of the alliance between Indraprasta and Panchala. For like iron—that most virtuous metal, which my sons-in-law discovered and which we now mine and smelt in the far northern fields of Kuru—our alliance is of unprecedented strength. Like iron, our alliance represents the courage to receive new gifts from the Gods, grasp them unflinching, and mold them to our uses. And like iron, this alliance will be to the benefit of our friends, the destruction of our enemies."

He turned to his hosts and bowed. Those on the platform— Yudi, his brothers, their queen, counselors, and priests—rose as one and bowed back. The crowd cheered. The army captains and lieutenants, standing in array down the sides of the great hall, pounded the butts of their spears and shouted approval. A murmur went round: "Iron." "Iron." "Iron."

Finally it was Duryodhana's turn.

He walked down the aisle created by Drupada, around the shallow pool, and up to the dais. With him came a manservant carrying a fruit basket of impressive size. The prince planted his feet wide, put his fists on his hips, and said: "Cousins! I bring you greetings from my father, King Tarashtra of the Kuru, and from my m-mother, Queen Gandhari. I am ... I am ..."

He looked down, giving the smooth hard floor a kick with his toe. "I *am* ..." (he looked up again) "p-pleased to p-present this token of our f-f-f- ... our f-f-f- ..."

A lady in the audience let out a nervous giggle.

"... our *friendship*. And w-we are happy to recognize your establishment as p-p-p- ... prince of Indraprasta."

"*King* of Indraprasta," said Arjuna from the dais.

Yudi waved a silencing hand at his brother. "Thank you, Cousin Duryodhana," he said with a gracious nod. "We appreciate your kind words, and we echo your good wishes for our two countries' ongoing friendship."

"Two ...?" said Duryodhana. He paused, frowning. Then, with a sigh and head shake suggesting weariness with the entire situation and a disinclination to discuss anything further, he gestured to the servant to deposit the very large fruit basket and, after a stiff and shallow bow, turned and began to walk away. The afternoon sun through the west windows glowed on the polished floor like fire and sent sparks dancing from the mirrors on pillars and ceiling, causing him to shield his eyes as he went.

Bimasena said in his booming voice, "Guess we have enough fruit now, eh?" Light laughter rippled round the hall.

Duryodhana wheeled about and glared at his massive cousin. He kept walking backward down the aisle as he said, "It's for you to *share*, Bima. Don't you Pandavas share *everything*?" He stopped, hands again on hips, and looked directly at Draupadi.

Bima and Arjuna stood up. Draupadi clutched the arms of her chair; her eyes widened, then narrowed. There were a few gasps from the spectators.

Yudi's voice was cold: "I don't take your meaning, Prince."

Duryodhana started walking backward again, squinting against the sparks of light. He gesticulated; his voice grew to a shout. "I *mean* that you boys like to hold things in common! Everything in common—your land, your f-food, your horses, your whores ..."

All five Pandavas were standing now, their faces like thunder. Draupadi's face was dead white, her jaw clenched. Duryodhana was still backing up.

"... which is your own business. But when it comes to holding a *wife* in common—"

His left calf struck the rim of the pool. His arms pinwheeled. Over he went, landing on his back with a great splash.

There was a second of frozen silence, and then—the hall erupted in laughter. As he came up, spluttering, the laughter swelled. Men and women alike, nobles and captains and servants alike, laughed and laughed. Over on a side platform, Perta, Subhadra, and their ladies giggled helplessly. On the dais, the Pandavas bent double and howled with glee. Even Yudi could not contain himself; he turned aside, holding one hand to his mouth, and his shoulders shook. Draupadi also laughed, and did not trouble to hide it.

Duryodhana struggled to his feet, climbed out of the pool, and stood there with water streaming off his black clothing, coughing and wiping his face. The people did not seem to find as much humor in this; gradually they stopped laughing. Perhaps they were wondering what he'd do next. Except for a few titters here and there, the hall grew quiet.

Then the queen leaned forward in her chair. She pointed a finger at the bedraggled prince and, with the merriest of smiles, cried:

"The blind son of a blind king!"

Another gale of mirth swept the assembly. The Pandavas, clearly delighted by their wife's quip, laughed anew. Arjuna went and stood behind her, rubbing her shoulders with a look of pride; Draupadi flinched at his touch, but she kept on smiling. The twins sent claps in her direction. Bima roared and slapped his thigh. Yudi, his expression pleased, wagged a finger at her as if to say, "Naughty girl!" All this she acknowledged with smiles.

For a short while Duryodhana stood still, watching the scene on the dais. Then he turned and left the hall. His eyes squinted against the white sparks of light. Water dripped from his clothes onto the white marble. The waves of laughter beat him, and buffeted him, and followed him out the white stone door.

It was Krishna (of course), not the Pandavas, who had discovered the iron-ore field. And it is not even quite accurate to say he had discovered it, for there was a large community of indigenes there already, extracting the ore and smelting it in kiln-like structures they called *bloomeries.*

The field—as you well know, Sire—is some twenty kosa north of Indraprasta, on the western bank of the Yamuna; in recent years the river there has swelled, but at the time it was not much more than a stream and easily fordable. In the Pandavas' tenth year at Indraprasta, Krishna went on an explorative journey up the Yamuna, hoping to find good timber, game, and perhaps a new copper mine. When he and his men spied the tendrils of smoke rising on the far side of the river, they assumed it was the cooking fires of a village. Upon crossing, however, they saw the mine pits: the natives swarming up and down, swinging pickaxes, lugging baskets of ore to the roasting fires; more natives tending the fires, raking out the smoking chunks, carrying them to the chimney-like bloomeries; and still more natives extracting the lumps of sponge iron from the bloomeries and trans-porting them to the forges, there to be reheated and hammered and shaped into all manner of objects. It was a sight, Krishna said, he would never forget.

Fortunately for the Pandavas, the natives were using iron to make tools rather than weapons. Iron axes, cooking pots, plows, even knives—all these they had, but no iron swords, spears, or maces. Even if they had had such things, of course, they wouldn't have known how to use them against kshatriya with horses, chariots, and long training in warfare. It was the work of a few days for Krishna to return to Indraprasta and muster a small force to ride north and take over the area. He kept the natives on as laborers; also as teachers, for they knew how to smelt the new metal, which we Arya, at the time, did not. (Today we have far surpassed them in expertise. I know, Nephew ... it's funny to think that originally, we had to learn all about iron from the indigenes!)

Kurukshetra, as the Pandavas named the field, lay well beyond the agreed boundaries of their territory, so they kept it a secret from King Tarashtra. But they certainly did not keep it a secret from their father-in-law, King Drupada. "Here, at last, is your trump card," Krishna said to the brothers as he set off to Panchala to negotiate the terms of joint ownership of the mine; "here is how you get your army." Drupada eagerly embraced the alliance and, in exchange for rights to half the mine's output, sent a thousand soldiers to Indraprasta to serve under the Pandavas' command, with promise of another hundred each year as long as the mine was in operation. He also sent five hundred head of cattle, a string of horses, and eight elephants. Very soon, Indraprasta's might and wealth surpassed Hastinapura's.

Krishna had been unsure how Drupada would react to his daughter's fivefold marriage. The day before the king was to arrive with the first installment of soldiery and livestock, the prince of Vrishni counseled Draupadi thus:

"I am going to tell your father of a dream I had, a dream in which I saw the five Pandavas as incarnations of Indra and you as Indra's wife, Lakshmi. I will explain that it was a revelation from Indra himself, indicating that you and the Pandavas are destined for each other. I will also remind him of the time when the God Shiva granted a hermit girl five husbands. Should he ask you how you are faring, I advise you to say something happy: modest, but happy."

As it turned out, there was no need for concern. Sitting at supper that evening, Drupada listened politely as Krishna recounted his dream and the story of the hermit girl. But the king was clearly more interested in talking about the iron mine, its prospects for production, and the terms of the deal with his sons-in-law. "Off you go, then, Padi," he said, patting his daughter's hand with a fond but distracted smile. "The men have things to discuss."

Chapter 14

KARNA

Duryodhana *pounded a fist on the council room table.* "They have an army, Father! They are allied with Panchala and will soon be invincible!"

King Tarashtra winced. "My boy, my boy. There's no need to raise your voice. I heard you: they have an army. But *we* have an army, too—and ours is under Lord Karna, so I daresay it's more than a match for theirs. Wouldn't you agree, Lord Karna?" He nodded affably down the table at the commander-in-chief, who occupied the cushion on Duryodhana's right.

"Our soldiers are well-trained and loyal, your majesty," said Karna. "I can vouch for that. As to how our numbers compare, it seems Indraprasta has surpassed us."

"Indeed? How many do they have now?"

Shakuna, on the king's left, scratched his speckled-gray beard. "Reports say nine hundred foot-soldiers, three hundred cavalry, fifty chariots."

The king frowned. "And cattle? How many cattle?"

"Not clear," said Shakuna, "but it looks like at least five thousand."

"*Pff!*" said the king with a wave of a pudgy hand. "Unimpressive. That's half the size of our herd."

Duryodhana leaned forward with elbows propped, pressing his fingertips to his forehead. "More like three-quarters the size of our herd. And they have an iron mine."

"Yes, what about this mine?" said the king, his tone suddenly irritated. "It's far outside the boundaries of the land I gave them; I don't like that, no, I don't like that. Cheating, is what it is. On the other hand … does it really matter? I've heard of this stuff *iron,* and I must say, I don't see what the fuss is about. Shakuna, I think it was you who showed me that thing the other day, that whatchama-callit—*horseshoe*. A shoe for a horse! Ha! Insane! If that's how the Pandavas want to spend their time, digging black metal out of the ground to make shoes for horses, let 'em." He broke off, chuckling.

Bhishma, seated at the center of the long table, said, "Iron is much harder than bronze. Far more durable. Yet it's easier to shape and mold."

Drona said, "We have a few iron spears now in the weapons shed. One sword; couple of shields. Lord Bhishma is right: bronze shatters against iron."

"I would not like to face an army equipped with iron weapons," said Karna. "An iron mace is especially fearsome."

Drona nodded his agreement and said, "It also makes unbreak-able chariot axles." Karna nodded back.

"Yes, yes, all very interesting," said the king, "but as long as they're using it to make *horseshoes,* why worry?"

"They're for the hooves, see," said Shakuna. "They keep the horses' feet protected."

"I thought the hooves *were* the protection," said the king. "Hooves are hard."

"Not as hard as iron."

"Well, but—"

Duryodhana rose to his knees and slammed both hands down. "WILL YOU ALL SHUT UP AND LISTEN TO ME!"

Everyone around the table flinched. The old men, Bhishma and Vyasa; the mature men, Tarashtra, Shakuna, Drona, Vidura; the in-their-prime men, Karna and Dushasana; and the young men—Drona's son Ashwattama, now an army captain and Karna's right hand, and fifteen-year-old Vaishamya, the high priest's heir appar-ent—all ten of them watched open-mouthed as the crown prince pushed himself to his feet and began to stride up and down the room, arms flailing, veins in his thick neck bulging. There was no hint of a stammer as he railed:

"I will not stand for it! Do you hear? It is not to be borne. He calls himself king, not prince, *king* of Indraprasta. He said he welcomed the friendship of our two countries. *Two* countries! Don't you see? That coronation—my Gods, the show they put on! You should have seen the crowd, the gifts, the groveling from the neighboring lords. And their assembly hall—now they've tricked it out with mirrors,

mirrors everywhere. What does it matter how many cows they have? Don't you understand? They're setting themselves up as an equal— no, not an equal, a *superior* power. Drupada said their alliance would destroy their enemies. That means *us*. They mean to destroy *us*. They won't rest until they've wiped us out and the five of them sit on five thrones right here in Hastinapura palace."

He paused, breathing hard. Then he flung out shaking hands, fingers curled as if he wanted to strangle the lot of them. His voice became half snarl, half scream:

"Right here in our great hall: the five Pandavas and their *slut queen!*"

He dropped his hands to his sides and stood there with chest heaving, staring round at the council. Karna looked down at his lap; the others stared back.

Only Bhishma seemed unperturbed. He said, "If this is true—if the Pandavas are indeed preparing for war against us—we must act."

Duryodhana pointed a finger as if to say, "Exactly." He rubbed his scalp hard with both hands, then went and sat down again at the foot of the table. There was silence for a bit.

Karna said, "Do we know they are preparing for war?"

Duryodhana's anger seemed to be spent. His tone was even as he said, "Why else would they hold a coronation? Why amass an army? Why the alliance with Panchala?"

"Maybe they just want to feel secure in their territory," said Karna.

"*Bah.*" The prince flicked a hand. "I'm telling you, if you'd been there, you'd know."

"It's just that ..." Karna hesitated.

"Yes? Go on, Karna, say it, whatever it is."

Karna took a breath. "Sir. You've told us of a big show, in a lavish hall, with lords and gifts and talk of alliances. And yes, they have an army and an iron field, and those things are worrisome. But ... the Pandavas have made no actual *moves*. They have not declared war, or raided our cattle, or threatened us in any way. We still exchange friendly visits several times a year. For the coronation, didn't they send the invitation to you personally, saying they'd be honored to have you attend?"

Although the council room was dim, Duryodhana squinted

suddenly, as if from bright lights in his eyes. "Oh, yes. They invited me, personally."

"I only wonder," said Karna, "whether the threat is real, or whether … whether …"

"Whether *what?*"

Karna took another breath. "Whether you just envy them."

Around the table, more looks of shock. No one had ever heard Karna speak to his master thus.

"*Envy them?*" said Duryodhana. He looked out the window, and his voice grew quieter. "Envy them?" A ray of late-afternoon sunlight fell on his face, but he did not squint.

He turned back to Karna. "Of course I envy them. What kind of a prince would I be if I did not set sights on my rivals, resenting their success and striving to increase mine? What kind of a p-prince does not pursue his advantage and the advantage of his people by fighting to acquire more land, wealth, and p-power at the expense of others? You talk as if it's wrong to envy the Pandavas, to want to bring them down. I ask you, Karna: Why do we kshatriya train with weapons and chariots? Why do we hunt? Why raise cattle and grain beyond what we can consume? All these things are m-meaningless games if they aren't part of an enterprise whose sole purpose is to reduce the enemy."

"But they are not the enemy." That was Vidura, down on the king's right. His face, grown lined in recent years, was at the moment cut with even deeper creases. "They are your cousins. We are on the same side."

Duryodhana regarded the counselor with a sardonic smile. "Ah. The same side. Yet I seem to recall, Uncle, that you once chose a side. And that side did not include me."

Vidura shrank back and said no more.

"My brother is right," said Dushasana, propping his strong fore-arms on the table and glaring round the group. "The Pandavas may be our cousins, but they're not our friends. By holding a corona-tion, accepting tribute from neighboring clans, making a separate alliance with Panchala, taking over the iron mine—which, as the king my father notes, is well outside their original borders—they have announced their intention to be a rival power. They intend to surpass us. Eventually, they'll eliminate us." Duryodhana gave him a nod of approval.

"Forgive me, my lords," said Drona. "But I recall his majesty saying Prince Yudi might rule his new kingdom. Could we not see all they've done as a mere matter of … ruling?"

Duryodhana hit the table again with his fist. "Of course we can! That's the point, Drona. Yudi has declared himself king. Being king is not about sitting all day in a palace with a crown on your head and having all the b-beer and w-women you want." He glanced at his father, who was fiddling with his ring. "It's about *ruling*: expanding your domain, gaining wealth for your clan, winning fame and glory in battle. Yudi wants to be king? Very well. But I will not p-play at kings with him. Let him *be* a king, or let him withdraw from the contest."

More silence. Most of the men sat with heads bowed, as if considering.

"If we move against them now, we'll lose." Karna spoke quietly but with assurance. Duryodhana gave him a sharp look. He said, "I'm sorry, my lord, but it's true. They outnumber us, they have iron weaponry, and they have Panchala for an ally. We wouldn't stand a chance."

"What if …?" That was Ashwattama. All heads swiveled toward the young man, who broke off blushing. His father, seated next to him, appeared displeased by his outburst.

Karna said, "Go on, Captain."

Ashwattama swallowed and said, "I was just thinking … what if we could somehow put their efforts on hold while we took time to build up our strength. If we had just a few years' grace, we could probably match them."

"And how would we do that?" Dushasana's tone was sarcastic. "Put their efforts *on hold* for a few years?"

"I … I don't know," Ashwattama said. "Perhaps my lord Shakuna …" He leaned and looked down the table at the queen's brother.

Shakuna bent one purple-clad knee and rested his forearm on it. "Don't look at me," he said. "I don't have magical powers."

"Now, now," said High Priest Vyasa. The old brahmin's voice had grown still raspier with age, but his black eyes retained their fierce glint and his scalp its wild shock of hair, now pure white. "Don't sell yourself short, my lord Shakuna. We all remember the last time you took care of our little … *Pandava problem,* shall we call it? I'd be surprised, very surprised, if you didn't have some sort of an idea this time."

"Ha. Sorry to disappoint you, but I don't," said Shakuna. He raised his eyes to the ceiling, whistling under his breath. Duryodhana made a move as if to speak, but the high priest (seated on his left) grabbed his wrist and laid a finger to dry, wrinkled lips. The room waited.

Shakuna stopped whistling and said, "Although …" He went on gazing at the ceiling, tapping a finger on his bearded cheek. Outside the window, a couple of parrots squawked.

"… we might hold a Dicing."

"A dicing?" said Dushasana, his lip curled. "How will that do any good?"

Shakuna shrugged, frowning. "It won't. Forget it."

"No," said the high priest. His eyes were aglow, his face stretched in its customary grin. "He's talking about a Sacred Dicing. Aren't you, Lord Shakuna? Please, say more."

Shakuna shrugged again. "Well, as you all know, though I guess" (he looked pointedly at Dushasana) "some of you *don't* know, a Sacred Dicing is an old custom whereby a king is challenged to prove he has the Gods' favor by engaging in a public dice match. There are rituals surrounding it, but the game itself is perfectly standard: it's the pachisi version, the board with the cross-shaped path and the animal pieces. In this case, I believe, the board and pieces are made extra-large so the audience can see. But the thing is: a king thus challenged may not refuse. It's like being called to a duel. Were he to decline, it would show his cowardice and, therefore, his unfitness."

Duryodhana was leaning forward. "I have heard of this custom. What are the stakes?"

"That's the beauty of it," said Shakuna. "There are no limits on the stakes. Jewels, horses, cattle, weapons, servants—whatever the players want to wager, they can."

"A kingdom?"

"Certainly. If they want to."

Duryodhana smiled, wolf-like. "And Yudi will want to."

"Yes. We all know how he loves to gamble. Once he gets going, he can't stop."

Around the table, expressions ranged from excited to doubtful, thoughtful to confused. King Tarashtra was still fiddling with his ring and seemed to be paying no attention at all.

"But look here," said Karna. "This is dangerous. Prince Duryodhana will have to match every stake. What if he loses?"

"Are you suggesting the Gods *won't* take our side?" said the high priest, his black eyes dancing. "Really, Commander. How little faith you have."

Karna did not rise to the bait. He turned to Duryodhana and said earnestly, "It's too risky. You must not do it."

"You mistake me, Karna!" cried Shakuna. "I'm not suggesting the crown prince should be the challenger. You're right: that would be much too risky."

"Who, then?" asked Karna.

Shakuna raised his eyebrows. "Me, of course."

≈

By the end of the meeting it had been agreed that a delegation consisting of Dushasana and several palace priests should be sent to Indraprasta forthwith to issue the challenge. The proposed date of the event would be three months hence, in the middle of the seventh month, for (as Vyasa noted) it was tradition to hold a Sacred Dicing in an outdoor pavilion, making it essential to wait until the monsoons had come and gone.

The young priest Vaishamya begged to be among the delegates. Dushasana grimaced and said it would not look good to send a one-armed man—"as if we were mocking them"—but Vyasa stood up for his adopted son, saying that as he himself was too old to travel, it was only right that his appointed successor should represent him. Dushasana made to continue the argument, but King Tarashtra, suddenly rousing from his stupor, said:

"Oh, let it go, Dusha. So the boy has one arm. He's a priest, isn't he? And a good one, I hear. Even the Gods can have deformities, you know. The God of Love is blind, like me. Some say it's a sign of the Gods' favor when a child is deformed. Anyway it's for your brother to say, not you. Let it go." He turned to his right and said querulously, "Vidu, are we finished? Help me back to my chambers. I'm worn out, I need to lie down."

"Yes, your majesty," said Vidura. He helped his brother to rise.

All the others rose, too. While being led away, the king was mumbling, "Shoes for horses ... did you ever hear such nonsense, Vidu? ... as if the hooves weren't already hard ..."

The others filed out of the council room. At the doorway, Duryodhana looked back and said, "Karna."

"Yes, my lord?"

"Let's go for a ride. I need to clear my head."

They went and collected their horses from the barn and were soon riding north along the river road. The sun was down and the midsummer air not too terribly hot, although the cracked mudflats, dotted with dead fish and strewn with dried clumps of water-weed, gave an impression of nature gasping for breath. Keeping their mounts to a walk, they did not speak for some time. Both seemed lost in their own thoughts.

Finally Karna said, "How is Astika?"

"She's well," said Duryodhana. "She has her own rooms now. Waiting-women and all."

"She's growing up."

"Yes. Eleven years old. *Lady* Astika, we must call her now." He shook his head, smiling. "I asked if she had any thoughts of a husband, and she said ... she said, 'I would like to marry a bard, so I can be a bard's assistant.'"

Karna chuckled. "How did you reply?"

"Oh, I told her that sounded nice and we would have to see. She must be well m-married, to a lord of another clan. But there's lots of time before we need to get into all that."

"You've said she's good at telling stories."

"She is. She is indeed. She always liked to tell *me* stories at bedtime, not the other way around."

They rode on. As they passed into the deeper shade of a double line of banyan trees, Duryodhana said: "Karna, I'm sorry."

"What for?"

"You know what f-for. I'm sorry I said that about ... about her."

Karna shook his head. "It's fine."

"I know how you f-feel about her."

"It doesn't matter. As you say, she's one of them."

"Yes, she's a Pandava, all right. But I know how you f-feel about her."

They emerged from the trees. Duryodhana pulled his horse

around to face the river, and Karna did the same. They sat side by side, looking out over the slow, brown stream.

Duryodhana said, "This is me."

"What?"

"The Ganges. The way it is now, before the rains. Sleepy and slow; drifting. That's how I've been for eleven years, Karna. Ever since … since Astika was born, I've been drifting along. Drifting, and dreaming, and doing nothing."

"You've been grieving."

"It's no excuse. Our herd has dwindled, our crops are not what they were, the compound and the town buildings are not maintained. Our mines and forests are neglected. Trade is anemic. The people no longer trust my f-father's judgments; I hear them, they laugh at him, they call him 'Old Blindey.' Oh, they still respect the queen my m-mother, but there's only so much she can do on her own. Meanwhile, Krishna and the Pandavas have been building a palace, a town, an army—right on our border. And what have I b-been doing all this time? Hunting. Sparring with Drona. Playing with my daughter. Remembering …" He passed a hand over his brow, his stocky shoulders slumped.

After a moment he sat up straight and looked out at the water again, his jaw set. "Things cannot go on like this. I will *not* allow the Kuru to be reduced. And I will not allow those … those *degenerates* to take what is mine."

Karna said, "You must take the throne, then. It's the only way. You must replace your father."

"I know. And for that, I must be m-married."

"Yes."

Duryodhana sat for two more breaths. Then he brought his horse's head around with a jerk and set off back down the river road at a canter, heading for home. Karna followed.

As the commander came up behind him, the prince shouted over his shoulder: "I will tell Uncle Bhishma to get me a bride!"

≈

Midnight. The fifteenth day of the seventh month.

Karna stood on the teakwood platform under the new pavilion

set north of the barns. It was a clear night with no moon. The only light was starlight; the only sound, the chirr of cicadas.

Two roasting pits had been filled and shrubs and grass removed in order to create level ground for the pavilion. The platform, seven paces square, was large enough to hold a giant-sized game board and two players, while wooden benches raised in several tiers on the sides would seat an audience of seven score. The bamboo poles and roof were decorated with streamers, which the morning light would reveal as crimson, violet, royal blue, emerald green, pink, yellow, and saffron. Right now, however, the world was only black and deeper black.

There was a sound of panting, as of a person in haste, and the soft creak of a floorboard. He turned and said, "I'm here." He was no more than a vague shadow, his golden earrings faint glimmers in the starlight. She came toward him with arms outstretched, groping her way. He said again, "Here." He stretched out his hands to meet hers and drew her body to his, holding her tight. Their mouths found each other.

She shrugged off her dressing gown and knelt, pulling him down with her. The teakwood was smooth but hard under their knees. He said, "Wait," and crawled to one side, waving a hand before him. He grabbed a long narrow cushion off a bench and dragged it over to her, saying, "Lie on this." They both began to laugh, softly, as she tried to figure out the cushion's orientation, lying on it catty-corner and banging her head on the boards a couple of times. He said, "Forget it. Here, come on top of me." He rolled on his back, pulling her onto him.

They lay full-length for a time, kissing. Her hair fell across his face; he gathered it back in a bunch and tugged, bringing her chin up and to the side. He planted kisses on her neck, biting the sensitive flesh with gentle bites, causing her to groan with pleasure. She rose to her knees, straddling him, and pulled her shift up and over her head, leaving her body bare. He struggled with his sash, said, "Damn it," and finally managed to unwrap his dhoti. She reached down, gripped his hard member, and guided it inside her. She began to gyrate, but he seized her hips, holding them still; his thumb, after tracing her lower abdomen, found the groove of her sex and the button of flesh within. He started to rub—small, fast circles—and she arched her back and said, "Yes," and thrust her groin forward and said, "Yes,

yes," and spread her legs wider, and her whole body shuddered as her inner passage clenched around him. Then she leaned forward, pressing his shoulders to the boards, and began to ride him, hard and fast, and she kept riding as he thrust back and moaned his joy, until at last, with a great gasping scream that she muffled with a hand clamped over his mouth, he too achieved release.

Afterward, lying on his chest with him caressing her naked back, she said, "Yudi's going to lose, isn't he?"

"Oh, yes," he said. "Shakuna will have it figured out."

"Are the dice loaded?"

"Probably. But the game also takes skill. And luck. Shakuna has both."

She lifted her head, wiggled upward a bit, and kissed his chin. "I suppose if he loses, we'll all have to come back here to live. I'd like that."

He kissed her forehead. "I would like that, too." He pressed her head to his shoulder, stroking her hair.

She sighed. "Poor Yudi. I can't help feeling sorry for him. Like a lamb to the slaughter. I'm glad I won't be there tomorrow to see it."

"What? Why won't you be?"

"Oh … my monthly time is coming on. I expect I'll be in seclusion. They'll have to find some separate rooms for me in the palace."

"Ah. I see."

They lay a while longer on the platform. Then they got up and dressed, fumbling and laughing in the dark. He walked with her as far as the horse barns. With a final kiss and a whispered, "Goodnight, Karna," she slipped away down the alley between the barn and the weapons shed, her hand to the wall to feel her way.

≈

Crouched on one knee, Shakuna shook the dice, alternately blowing on his two cupped hands and muttering what sounded like prayers. The audience of one hundred and forty, seated in tiers on the four sides of the pavilion, held its breath. Shakuna gave the dice one last, vigorous shake and with a "Ha!" let them fly onto the game board. Necks craned to see the result.

"Arrggh!" He let out a scream, leaning back and striking his temples in an attitude of despair. "The Gods were with you this round, Yudi!"

"Yes! Yes!" Yudi sprang to his feet and bounced on his toes, arms raised, acknowledging the applause. Despite the day's cloudiness and the cool breeze ruffling the pavilion's colored streamers, his face was damp with sweat. His crimson cloak lay in a heap on the floor. The gold circlet on his brow was a little askew.

Counselor Vidura (having been accepted by both sides as match referee) was seated on a small rug at the northeast corner of the platform. He said, "Round six to the Pandavas. They have won all jewels belonging to the Kauravas and their ladies."

"And the five previous stakes!" cried Bima, who was seated with his brothers in the front row of the east side. "We win back all we lost in the earlier rounds!"

"That is correct, Prince Bimasena," said Vidura, looking a touch annoyed. "This was explained at the start. In each round, the winner takes all, *including* any stakes he lost in previous rounds. Therefore, the Pandavas win from the Kauravas" (he ticked the items off on his fingers) "one hundred head of cattle, all sheep and goats, all horses, all copper and tin, and all silver and gold. And, as I said, the Kauravas' jewels, which were at stake in this sixth round."

"Arrggh!" Shakuna groaned again, dropping his head in his hands. Then he looked up and said to Yudi, "I don't suppose you'll want to go on now, will you?"

"Oh-ho!" Yudi cried. "You'd like it, wouldn't you, if I quit now. But we're not going to quit, are we?" He glanced at his brothers, who responded with "No!" "Keep going, Yudi!" "Wipe them out!" The spectators—men on the north, east, and south sides, women on the west side—joined in the clamor, waving fists and handkerchiefs: "Go on! Go on!"

Yudi, grinning, acknowledged the cheers. He turned back to Shakuna, thrusting out a finger that trembled with excitement. "*Round seven!*" he shouted.

Shakuna held up his hands as if in surrender. "As you wish," he said. "What are the stakes?"

The audience fell silent as Yudi looked to his brothers for suggestion. Arjuna cupped his hands around his mouth and whispered something. Yudi nodded. He turned to the counselor over in the corner and said, "Our entire herd of cattle."

There were gasps from the benches. But Vidura merely looked to Shakuna and said, "Do you accept the stakes?"

"I do," said Shakuna.

"The stakes for round seven are each side's cattle herd," said Vidura. "Reset the board and begin."

Two manservants came from two other corners and reset the pieces—elephants for Yudi, tigers for Shakuna—in their starting positions. The ivory animals were nearly a foot high; the ivory dice were the size of small apricots. Each round of the game took roughly a quarter of an hour. Including the ceremonies at the start, during which the priests had offered invocations to the Gods and oblations into the fires burning in stone-rimmed pits at the pavilion's four corners, the event had lasted some three hours so far.

King Tarashtra was not present. Queen Gandhari had been there for the ritual portion, but had excused herself immediately thereafter. Perta and Subhadra were there, on the west side with the other women, watching eagerly from the fourth and topmost bench. Duryodhana and his brother were seated next to the Pandavas on the east-side front bench, with Drona, Ashwattama, and Karna directly behind them. Bhishma was not there; he was off in Madrasa, negotiating for a bride for the crown prince. Krishna too was absent; he had fallen ill and was at Indraprasta recuperating. He had wanted Yudi to request a postponement, but Yudi would not hear of it.

Shakuna won the next round. Upon hearing Vidura say, "Round seven to the Kauravas; they have won all the Pandavas' cattle and all prior stakes," Yudi became momentarily distraught and looked as if he might bow out. But his brothers urged him on, insisting that he could not quit now, not while he was behind. Shakuna, too, implored him to continue, for (he said graciously) a guest must be given the opportunity to recoup. So, on they went—through three more rounds, all of which were won by Shakuna. In round eight, Yudi lost the Pandavas' weapons and chariots; in round nine, their maidservants; in round ten, their manservants.

After round ten, Yudi stood with limbs shaking and gold circlet slipped down over one eye, staring at the small gong that stood in the fourth corner of the pavilion, the striking of which would indicate withdrawal from the contest. But Bima rose from his seat, went to his brother, and put a trunk-like arm around his shoulders, speaking soothing words—whereupon Yudi took a deep breath and mopped his forehead with his kerchief. He removed the circlet and tossed it aside, bent down, scooped up the dice, and said to Shakuna: "Round eleven!"

The stakes for round eleven, proposed by Shakuna and eliciting more gasps from the onlookers, were each side's entire army. Yudi grew more and more hesitant as the game progressed; he kept looking over at his brothers, causing Vidura to remind him several times that "coaching from the benches is not allowed." But in this round, Shakuna's luck seemed to desert him. He fell further and further behind, and when Yudi made his final throw, up came double sixes. As the audience cheered, Yudi brought all his elephants home, then stood, threw back his head, and howled in exultation.

"Round eleven to the Pandavas," said Counselor Vidura. "They have won the Kauravas' army, plus all previous stakes."

Now Yudi's brothers were drawing their fingers across their throats and pointing at the gong in the corner, but Yudi himself was gesturing to the servants to come and reset the board. Sweat ran down his face unheeded; his eyes were bright as if with fever. The audience, swept up in the excitement, was pounding the floor with their feet as they chanted, "One more round! One more round!" Shakuna, meanwhile, was standing back examining the nails of his right hand. He glanced at Duryodhana, and the two men exchanged the slightest of smiles.

"Come on, Shakuna!" Yudi shouted. "Round twelve! We will stake the kingdoms!"

Shakuna brought his palm to his chest in a pantomime of shock. "What?!" he said. "The *kingdoms?* Are you *sure?*"

"You are afraid!" cried Yudi, eyes blazing. "You know the kingdom is mine by right! It was always mine, mine and my brothers'. The Gods will prove it! The Gods are with us!"

Shakuna shook his head. "I must ask the crown prince," he said. He went over to the Duryodhana and knelt down before him. The two conferred together. The prince nodded. Shakuna got up and walked back to face Yudi.

"The kingdom it is," he said with a shrug that suggested, *This is crazy, but what can I do?*

The board was reset. The spectators fell silent as the two men began to play.

And now, unaccountably, Shakuna's luck returned in abundance.

Every throw went his way; every move was brilliance itself. His tigers overtook Yudi's elephants, falling back at times only to leap forward, revealing their apparent setbacks to have been merely stratagems to gain a greater advantage. All Yudi's moves, on the other hand, seemed to go awry. As the sun began its descent from the zenith, unseen behind the clouds, Shakuna rolled the dice one last time. The ivory cubes tumbled across the board and came to a stop right on the verge. The spectators craned to see.

"*Won!*" cried Shakuna with a clench of a fist.

As applause from the benches swelled, he rose and stood looking down at his opponent, who was still on one knee, staring in disbelief at his four losing elephants.

"How about that," said Shakuna. "Looks like the Gods aren't with you after all."

"*No!*" It was a strangled scream. The erstwhile king of Indraprasta stood up, weaving a little. His face was bright pink. His lips were flecked with spittle. "*No!* We will play again! You must allow me to recoup my loss!"

Shakuna raised an eyebrow. "Must I? But what will you stake? You have lost your entire kingdom. You own nothing. You have nothing to wager."

Yudi looked around wildly, as if hoping a stake might appear somewhere on the platform. He looked to his brothers; the four of them were sitting stunned, eyes on the ground. "What can I stake?" Yudi said. "Help me, brothers. *What can I stake?*"

There was no reply. The spectators sat frozen in their seats.

Then Arjuna said, his eyes still on the ground: "Draupadi."

"What?" said Yudi. "What? You mean ... our wife?"

"Yes," said Arjuna, looking up at his brother. "*Stake Draupadi.*"

Immediately, the confusion on Yudi's face gave way to relief. "Yes ... yes," he said, rubbing the back of his neck. "Our wife. We can stake her. Yes." He raised his voice as he turned to face Shakuna again. "We will stake Queen Draupadi! She is a princess of Panchala, renowned as the most desirable woman in twenty kingdoms. Her worth is beyond price. Your crown prince once competed for her. Here is his second chance to win her!"

The people turned to one another with shocked murmurs: Had they heard right? Were the Pandavas actually wagering their wife— their queen? Some looked disgusted; others, titillated. Perta, in the back row of the women's section, sat up very straight and stared at her eldest son, her lips in a thin line. Subhadra started to giggle, but stopped with a squeak as Perta clamped a sharp-nailed hand on her thigh.

For the first time, Shakuna appeared genuinely taken aback. He scratched his beard and said, "Uh ... I'm not sure that's legal. What does the referee say?" He looked to Vidura in the corner, but the counselor was sitting with shoulders bent, head down; it was clear he had lost all control of the proceedings and would not render an opinion.

"Why isn't it legal?" Yudi cried. "She's our wife! She belongs to us! Do you accept the stakes or not? If you don't accept, you forfeit the round."

Shakuna threw a glance at Duryodhana. He swallowed and said, "We have nothing equivalent to put up. Our crown prince has no wife."

"Never mind, never mind." Yudi waved his hands frantically. "You don't need to put anything up. If you win, you get Draupadi and everything else. If we win, we get our kingdom back. That's it. Do you accept?"

Shakuna looked again to Duryodhana. He turned his palms outward as if to say: *What about it?*

The crown prince was sitting with legs wide apart, leaning forward with left hand on left hip, right forearm resting on right knee. He was chewing his inner cheek, his eyes flicking from Yudi, to Shakuna, to the game board, to Yudi again. Behind him, Karna was staring at the back of his head as if trying to sway his mind with the power of thought alone.

Duryodhana jerked his chin at Shakuna and said, "Go ahead."

Shakuna responded with a firm nod. He did not wait for the servants but began to reset the board himself, Yudi helping him, and within moments the round had begun. The two players wasted no time, flinging the dice and shoving the pieces as if both wanted only to get the thing over with. Tigers and elephants chased one another up, down, and around the board. First Yudi was ahead, then Shakuna, then Yudi, then Shakuna ... until finally it was Yudi's turn, and all he had to do was avoid a pair of ones and he had the game. Blowing on his two cupped hands, he shook the dice. With a "Ha!" he let them fly. They bounced and tumbled and came to a stop ...

"Snake eyes!" yelled Shakuna. "You lose!"

All five of the Pandavas doubled over, burying their faces in their hands. The audience let out a roar of exhilaration. Duryodhana had not moved a muscle throughout: still he sat with legs wide, hand on hip, forearm on knee. But Dushasana sprang to his feet, fists pumping: "Yes!" he shouted. "Yes, yes!" He wheeled about to face his brother and cried, "Let me go get her! Let me go get the slut queen! I'll bring her here!"

Duryodhana sat up, placing his hands on his black-clad thighs. The wolfish smile flashed. Again he jerked his chin, this time at his brother, and said, "Go ahead."

Dushasana struck one fist hard in the other palm. He turned and strode out of the pavilion, calling to two of his men on the south benches to follow him. The three kshatriya rushed down the slope and disappeared into the alley between barn and weapons shed.

As the spectators continued to murmur and exclaim, Karna leaned forward and grabbed his master's shoulder. Duryodhana, startled, turned to look at him. The following exchange took place in furious whispers.

"Duryo! You must stop this! You must not do it!"

"Must? Must not? You presume too much, Karna. You don't get to tell me what I must and must not do. Now let go of me before I have you thrown out of here."

Karna let go of him. "I'm sorry, my lord. I'm sorry. But you don't understand …"

Duryodhana's scar was turning red. "Oh, I understand. I *understand* she has you wrapped around her little finger. I *understand* you don't want to see her humiliated. Frankly, Karna, I don't give a shit. You said it yourself, she's one of them. She's a f-fucking Pandava. And she's going to get her comeuppance, just like the rest of them."

"No! You *don't* understand. Listen to me, Duryo. She's in seclusion. She's in her monthly seclusion. She can't appear in public. It's forbidden."

The prince looked suspicious. "How do you …? Oh, never mind. What if she is? I'm telling you, Karna, I don't give a shit. I've *won*. I've won their army, their kingdom, *and* their queen. I am the victor. And I want to see them crawl to me. Her, especially. I want to see her kneel and b-beg for mercy. If you don't want to see it, fine. Get the hell out."

He turned around again and planted his feet wide, hands on thighs. Karna sat back, his face a mask of agony. The audience was still buzzing. Yudi, in the meantime, had tottered over to the front bench and collapsed next to Bima.

From the alley between barn and shed, there came a sound of tramping feet. Dushasana emerged, walking with a proud, swinging gait. Behind him came the two kshatriya with Draupadi between them. They had her by the arms and were dragging her along, but her head was high and she did not stumble. She had on only a white cotton shift. Her feet were bare. Her hair hung long and loose. The crowd watched as the trio approached the pavilion and stepped up onto the platform; as the queen was brought to stand at the center of the game board, a small red stain, shaped like a lotus, was visible on the back of her skirt.

Dushasana waved the two kshatriya away. He seized Draupadi under the armpit, hoisting her awkwardly up on her toes, and said in a loud voice: "Take a look! The former queen of Indraprasta—lost in a wager and now our slave!"

There were a few hoots from the men in the crowd. The Pandavas were looking at their feet, their faces ashen. Duryodhana watched: immobile, expressionless.

Dushasana looked around frowning, apparently disappointed at the lack of reaction. "I hear she's up for anything! Can't wait to try her out!" He rubbed his groin lewdly while at the same time gripping her armpit tighter, causing her to wince in pain.

Again a few catcalls—but only a few. On the west benches, the women were like statues.

Dushasana let go the queen's arm and grabbed the front of her shift. His voice rose to a manic pitch: "But we haven't seen the goods yet, have we? Don't you want to see it all? Let's see the quality of our new slave!"

With a series of violent jerks, he tore off the shift.

Gasps and screams came from the audience. Draupadi, as if by reflex, sank into a crouch, wrapping her arms about her shins and dropping her face to her knees. A few of the people covered their eyes, but most stared horrified—or thrilled—at the naked woman huddling on the ground. Dushasana, laughing, tossed the ripped piece of fabric away.

Karna stood up, stepped onto the front bench and down to the platform. He crossed to Yudi's cloak—which was still lying in a heap next to the board—picked it up, knelt down next to Draupadi, and draped it over her.

Perhaps, Sire, you think that was the end of it. Perhaps you think what happened next is that Karna lifted Draupadi in his arms and carried her away, out of the pavilion and back to the palace, with her weeping on his shoulder. Or maybe you've heard the version of the story in which a new skirt magically appears, Dushasana tears it off, another appears, and so on and so on—thanks to some God's intervention. But none of that is what really happened.

Here is what really happened.

As the audience continued to goggle and gasp, Karna remained kneeling beside Draupadi, his arms about her. Slowly, she lifted her head and looked at him; then, in one swift motion, she rose to her feet, flung off the cloak, and pushed him away. He reached for her again, all in anguish, but she held up a hand and said, "*No*. Don't touch me." Her eyes radiated contempt. He fell back to the corner.

She drew back her hair, dropped her arms at her sides, squared her shoulders, and began to turn in place: slowly, very slowly, at the center of the game board, her gaze fixed on the audience. Her thirty-two-year-old body was shapely, her limbs long and strong. Her stomach, a little doughy, bore the marks of her five pregnancies and labors. Her breasts, full but drooping and webbed with blue veins, showed the effects of suckling five infants. The same traceries of blue rose up her calves. Her face was all planes and graceful curves, its youthful fat long gone; her collarbone swept in elegant lines out to her shoulders. The swell of her hips and her muscular arms suggested children hoisted and carried for hours on end. The hair at her crotch was dark and lush. Down the inside of her thighs, there were smears of blood.

As she revolved, tall and silent, it was as if she spoke aloud …

"See me. See me. See the proof of what I have done, not once, not twice, but five times. See the proof of what I can do again, should I choose. See my beauty, my dreadful beauty, which reminds you of your origins in a womb—a place of blood and slime and darkness and infinite power. See the place where each of you emerged. See the breasts where each of you fed, mewling and helpless. See the body that men worship. Dare you laugh at me? Dare you even look at me? Or dare you only fall at my feet and beg for mercy?

"Down on your knees, sad fools, and beg. Beg me to birth you. Beg me to feed you. Beg me to make love to you. Beg me to dance upon you as you lie supine, and I will dance, heedless of your pain and need. My flesh is the earth, my breath the air, my blood the flow of rivers, my passion the fire that connects you to the Gods. Beg me. Beg me. Beg me to dance on your writhing body with my garland of skulls flying upward."

She kept turning. At first the people stared back agog; some of the men, egged on by Dushasana, snickered and jeered. But gradually, gradually, the eyes began to drop. The jeers died away. She kept on turning, back straight, head high. A look of shame and awe came to every face, and soon every eye in the pavilion was cast down.

Except for Duryodhana; he continued to regard her. When she saw this, she stopped turning and walked over to where he sat. She stood before him, quite close, looking down at him. He tilted his head back and met her stare; for a long time they stared at each other. She did not flinch. At last he, too, dropped his gaze.

He rose, stepped around her, went and retrieved the cloak she had thrown off, and returned to where she stood, still facing the benches. He held out the cloak behind her and waited. She, seeming to sense his presence, put her hands back over her shoulders. He placed the top of the cloak in her hands; she took it, draping it so as to cover her nakedness. She turned to face him. He bowed.

He said, "Lord Karna. Please escort the queen back to the palace."

Karna came forward and reached out a hand as if to guide her. But with a sidestep she evaded him and walked away, out of the pavilion and down the slope toward the horse barns, the crimson cloak rippling in the cool breeze. Karna followed a pace behind. He did not attempt to touch her again.

Once Draupadi's seclusion was over, Duryodhana went to see her in her rooms. An hour later he emerged with terms for the Pandavas (who were being kept comfortably, albeit under guard, in the east wing).

The terms were thus: They would depart quietly, go to Panchala, and stay there three years, taking their retainers and the bulk of their army with them and leaving their palace, town, and livestock in the care of Vidura, who would oversee Indraprasta in their absence. Upon their return, they would confine their activities to the territory originally granted them by King Tarashtra, making no attempt to expand their borders. They would limit their soldiery to two hundred and cattle to four thousand. The output of the iron field would still be split equally, but now the equal owners would be the Kuru—that is, the Kauravas—and King Drupada; if the Pandavas could persuade Drupada to share his half portion with them, well and good.

Did they discuss privately the possibility of rejecting the deal, escaping their captors, and going to war? I'm sure they did. One can imagine Arjuna speaking as follows:

"So we're going to turn tail a second time, like stinking curs. After what they did. Stripped our wife in public, leered at her ... treated her like a common whore. I'm telling you, Yudi, I will be revenged. That shit Duryodhana and his shit brother—I'll crush them for what they did to us. It is not to be borne. And then, for him to negotiate with *her!* To go to *her* and ask what terms *she* would accept! That bitch has some nerve, arranging it so she can run home to daddy. Bargaining for how many cattle we're allowed, how many soldiers—*faugh!* I'm telling you, I won't stand for it. We outnumber them. We can fight. I'll kill twenty, a hundred Kauravas for every one of ours they kill. I'll save that stuttering freak for the very last."

But then Krishna arrived, having recovered from his illness, and undoubtedly advised them not to press their luck. The Dicing had been a sacred ritual, after all; to flout its outcome would be to flout the Gods' dictates, inviting bad karma for generations to come. Then there was the matter of Draupadi: by staking her in a wager, something expressly forbidden in every type of lawful marriage, the Pandavas had already risked divine wrath. Moreover, it was thanks to her that Duryodhana had not simply banished the five of them to some far western wilderness and taken everything they had for his, forever—as would have been his right. They owed it to their wife to accept the terms she had negotiated.

So into exile again went the brothers: this time not to the unspoiled forests of Vrishni, but to the bustling capital of Panchala. Duryodhana himself went to supervise their departure and the transfer of Indraprasta to the custody of his uncle. After they'd gone, he did not enter the great hall with its marble and mirrors; he merely glanced around the yard and said to Vidura, "Look after the p-place."

Then he swung himself up on his black horse and went out the compound gate at a thundering gallop, the men of his bodyguard close behind.

Meanwhile, Lord Bhishma had returned with the prince's new bride. She was eldest daughter of the king of Madrasa—and a widow. Her name was Banumati. She was in her thirties and brought little in the way of dowry, but her lineage and character were unimpeachable; she was known to be fertile, having had three children by her former husband; and the alliance she represented, with a wealthy clan whose wealth continued to grow, was of great value.

The day after the wedding, Duryodhana was crowned king of the Kuru.

PART FOUR

THE SKULL
GARLAND

Chapter 15

VIDURA

idura said:

V   When Shakuna came up with the idea for the Dicing, I felt a secret hope, barely acknowledged even to myself, that the rights of the Pandavas would at last be vindicated: purely, cleanly, publicly. I agreed to serve as referee.

Imagine my horror, my sick sense of lifting a rock and staring down into a damp hole teeming with vermin, when Arjuna said, "Stake Draupadi," and Yudi—Yudi did not recoil, but clutched at the abominable notion as a drowning man clutches at a piece of driftwood. As referee I might have disallowed the stake, but by that point the situation was so far gone that I felt the only thing to do was to stand aside and let the Gods take over.

And take over they did; at least, that is what I believed was happening as I watched the naked queen, her thighs dripping blood, revolving at the center of the pavilion. I don't know how else to explain my sudden impression of a man lying beneath her, his arms outstretched, his shaft upright, his face contorted in ecstatic agony as she trampled him. It was clearly a vision of the divine, and judging by the lack of comment from anyone afterward, it was a vision vouchsafed to me alone. I took it as a sign that I, like that supine man, must henceforth abase myself before Ultimate Reality; that I must lie back and let it tread on me, bleed on me, and never think of justice anymore. For what is justice? What is Law? What are the plans and efforts of men—indeed, of the Gods—in the face of such effortless, beautiful, terrible Being?

But then Duryodhana asked me to go as caretaker to Indraprasta, so off I went. Although there was a small staff left there to clean and maintain the palace and compound, I didn't need to concern

myself with them. My main job was to adjudicate the townspeople's disputes, and as this was a task which King Tarashtra had, in
recent years, delegated to me at Hastinapura, I felt confident enough
doing it. I set up a chair in a side room (I had no desire to sit in that
absurdly lavish great hall) and received petitioners three mornings a
week.

Oh, yes; I see the irony. I had sworn to concern myself no longer
with justice, yet there I was, dispensing justice on an endless stream
of the most petty, sordid matters. Stolen chickens. Pilfered rice.
Loud-voiced neighbors. An overflowing sewage drain. Noses broken
in a drunken brawl. A cow that had wandered into the standing crop
of another farmstead. A whore who was suspected of cursing her customers for failing to pay adequately; the aggrieved shrieks of the wife
drilled through my head: "How else do you explain my husband's
lack of vigor? He's as limp as a dead eel! It's all that cunt's fault—just
because he paid her in copper, not silver!"

As I sat there day after day, rubbing my throbbing temples
and urging myself to focus, I could not help but contrast the dis-
solute, grasping, spiteful denizens of Indraprasta with the relatively
hard-working, generous, cooperative people with whom I dealt back
at home. The Arya have a saying: "The horse goes where the head
turns." It seemed to me that King Yudi, with all his reputation for
probity, had done little to guide his people in virtuous ways. Perhaps
he'd spent all his time gambling. Or perhaps the outlandish lux-
ury of the palace dazzled the populace, inflaming their greed and
discontent.

In any case, the complaints and quarrels rolled on in a monot-
onous stream until, three months into my time there, something
surprising happened.

The sun was high and I'd nearly decided to call a halt for the day
when there came a commotion at the doorway. A gray-bearded man
entered, dragging a young man by the elbow and followed by some
fifteen others, men and women, all gabbling with excitement. They
pushed their way through the petitioners waiting their turn (the
receiving room was as crowded as usual) and up before my seat. The
first man threw the second to the ground—whereupon I saw I had
made a mistake: the second man was not a man at all, but a woman
wearing a dhoti, vest, and sword-belt. She was large-boned and lean-
framed. Her straight black hair had been cut to chin-length. She

might have passed for a youth but for the chest-band under her vest, which, despite its tightness, did not flatten her bosom entirely.

The gray-bearded man drew his sword and pointed it at the woman's back as she crouched on all fours, hair hanging over her face, rust-colored dhoti pooling on the ground. "Lord Vidura!" he shouted. "Here is my wife, caught running away again. I demand she be punished! I demand justice!"

"*Counselor* Vidura," I said, passing a hand over my eyes. (They never could remember my proper title.) "Put up your sword, Sir, or I will have you thrown out. Weapons may not be drawn in this chamber."

He complied, glowering. Some of his friends hastened to take the sword's place by aiming curses and gobs of spit at the woman.

"Stop that, all of you!" I snapped. "Now, Sir; give me your name, and your wife's name, and explain the problem. Calmly, if you please."

The man drew himself up and made me a stiff bow. "My lord. I am Biptu, a kshatriya. I have a homestead to the north, one kosa inland along the stream. I live there with my *wife*" (he nudged the woman's backside with the ball of his foot) "and my other wife, and our five children. Four years ago, I moved my family and chattel to Indraprasta. I serve in King Yudi's army, naturally, but having obligations I chose to remain here rather than go with them on their ... ah ... sojourn to Panchala. My homestead is thriving, I have a good crop of barley, flax, also many goats, and I did not want ..."

"Yes, yes, all right," I said, "and what about your wife? What is her name?"

"Shikhandi," he said. "My other wife is called Fani, and ..."

I held up a hand. "Wait," I said. "You say her name is—Shikhandi?"

"Yes, Shikhandi," said Biptu with an impatient nod. "She is my senior wife. We've been married eleven years. The first time she ran away, it was after our first child; the second time, after our third child. We lived in Hastinapura then, and she kept running here, to Indraprasta. She would put on man's clothes and cut off her hair and just ... *leave.* I didn't know what she was thinking; I still don't. I beat her each time, of course, but she wouldn't tell me what was in her mind. Then, as I say, four years ago I decided to move to Indraprasta. When I told her we were going, she seemed happy, very happy. There were no further incidents, until yesterday morning when I woke up to find her gone. Again! One of her women, Tamika, here" (a very fat woman stepped forward, preening) "informed me she was heading for Panchala. So I went after her. She had taken a horse, but I was able to catch her by nightfall and bring her back."

He paused, breathing heavily. His cohort gathered around the corpulent waiting-woman, patting her back in approval and muttering invective at the woman on the ground.

Biptu gripped his sword hilt, seemed to recall he must not, and instead gestured in dramatic fashion. "Now look at her! In man's garb! It's outrageous! What have I done to deserve this? I've given her everything—a good home, children, jewels befitting her station—everything, and this is how I'm repaid. I want it stopped! I demand justice!"

By now everyone in the room was absorbed in the scene. There were murmurs of "Unbelievable!" "The slut!" "Poor man!" and so on.

I held up my hand once more for silence.

"Stand up, Madam," I said. She stood up. She was tall for a woman.

"You are Lord Bhishma's granddaughter," I said.

"Yes," she said. She met my eyes with no sign of fear.

Biptu spoke up again. "That's right. Lord Bhishma arranged the marriage when she was fifteen, I thirty-five. He said she was an 'unusual girl'—those were his exact words, 'unusual girl'—and that he did not want to send her out of the clan. He said she needed an older husband who would steady her and be—'tolerant of her quirks,' he said. I was honored, naturally. She came with a good dowry. And I will say, most of the time she's been docile enough. Fertile, too: she had two girls, and a stillbirth, which was disappointing, but then the boy came, so that's all right. I can't fault her as far as that goes. But this business of dressing up and running off, that's more than a quirk. I ask you, Lord Vidura, what husband would stand for it?"

"*Counselor* Vidura," I said. He looked blank. I gave it up and waved my hand to say *never mind*.

I was not at all sure what to do. If she had been a woman with lesser connections, I would have ordered a public flogging and perhaps the removal of a foot, or half a foot, so she could not run away again. But this was Bhishma's granddaughter. I remembered how he had doted on her when she was a little girl in Hastinapura; then there had been the incident with the elephant, after which he'd had her

confined to her quarters with her women (well, nothing strange in
that) and ceased to speak of her. I believe he blamed himself for having indulged her hoydenish ways. I recall only vaguely her marriage
to Biptu; I do remember how tall she was even then, at fifteen, and
how ill at ease she appeared in her wedding finery. The other thing
that stands out for me was the conclusion of the ceremony, when
Bhishma, taking the place of her father, went to help her into the
going-away cart in the traditional gesture of farewell. She would not
embrace him, would not even look at him, but turned her back and
climbed into the vehicle without a word. Her grandfather stood in
the palace yard looking after the cart as it trundled away, the bridegroom riding beside, and I remember thinking—astounding though
it may seem—that my Uncle Bhishma was on the verge of tears.

All these memories passed through my mind in an instant. I
had learned that the critical thing in handling the townspeople's disputes was decisiveness: always better to give a firm answer, even if
it be the wrong one, than to dither. But dithering is my nature—I
am too aware of the various calls upon me, the various faces of the
Law—and in this case, I truly had no idea what to do. I could feel
my cheeks growing hot and my heart beating faster as I sat looking
at Shikhandi and she stood looking back at me with that unsettlingly
direct gaze. The onlookers grew silent, shifting their feet impatiently,
waiting for me to render judgment. I drummed my fingers on the
arm of the chair and tried to look as though I were deep in reflection.
For some reason there swam before my eyes the image of the naked
queen in the pavilion trampling the supine man, and in my confusion I blurted out:

"Her punishment is to live as a man."

Shikhandi's head jolted as if she'd been struck in the face.

Biptu said, "I'm sorry—what?"

I didn't know why I had said it, but I couldn't take back the
words now. I went on, struggling to keep my voice firm and low:

"She must feel the full weight, the full shame, of what she has
done. If she wishes to impersonate a man, then let her be a man. For
three years, let her take on a man's work and role. Let her wear man's
dress. Let her enjoy none of the privileges afforded women."

"But ... but ... my lord," said Biptu. His mouth open and shut
like a fish. "I can't live with a wife who is a *man.* That would be ... I
mean, how could that be?"

A few nervous chuckles came from the onlookers. I saw the trap I had created for myself. I had to think quickly.

I made a noise of irritation and waved my hand again. "Of course she won't live with *you*, Sir Biptu. I don't wish to punish *you*. Not at all; she will come here to the compound, and live in the barracks with the men." (The Pandavas had been instructed to leave some thirty soldiers behind as palace guards.) "She will train with them, eat with them, do everything they do."

Biptu sucked in his breath. "In the barracks? But won't she ... I mean, won't they ..."

"Take advantage of her?" I said, frowning. If Biptu imagined his wife would be ill-used by the men, he would see that as a far greater humiliation than having a wife who ran away. "I assure you, Sir," I said, "I do not allow immorality or loose living in the compound. Such things may have been tolerated by King Yudi, but they are not tolerated by me. Your wife will be treated with perfect respect. The men will regard her as their brother-in-arms."

Shikhandi had so far remained quiet and expressionless, but at that last remark—"brother-in-arms"—she put her fist to her mouth and made a queer, strangled sound. At first I assumed the enormity of her punishment was sinking in and that she was afraid at the prospect of the hard, comfortless life she was about to lead. But then, as she raised her eyes to mine, her fist still pressed to her mouth, it seemed to me she had the look of someone whose dearest wish, long discounted as no more than a dream, was all at once coming true.

Biptu was exchanging whispers with a few of his friends. Presently he turned to face me again and said, "My lord, forgive me, but ... couldn't she just be flogged?"

At this point I was heartily regretting my mad decree, but there was nothing for it. If I changed my mind, I would lose all credibility. So I merely frowned harder and said, "No. The punishment must fit the crime. My judgment is final. You may go, Sir. Leave your wife here; in three years you will have her back, a woman again." I raised my voice to the room. "Court is adjourned for the day. You may all go."

The guard who stood next to my chair slammed the butt of his spear on the floor and shouted, "You 'eard Lord Vidura! Out! Everybody out!"

Biptu, his friends, and the rest of the petitioners filed out with much murmuring and many a glance back at Shikhandi, who continued to stand before me. She had placed her feet together. Her hands were at her sides, her shoulders back, her gaze aimed at a spot just over my head.

How odd, I thought. *She already looks like a soldier.*

≈

Two months later, as spring neared, I went on my first trip to the iron mine.

There I was to meet Duryodhana—*King* Duryodhana, that is. He was taking a keen interest in the field of Kurukshetra, regarding it as a critical part of the plan for building up Kaurava strength in the Pandavas' absence. In the three years since the mine's discovery, Krishna and the Pandavas had done little more than drive the indigenes to greater efforts and collect their output. Since Duryodhana had taken over, however, he had doubled the number of workers, including unskilled diggers, carriers, and stokers along with the skilled smiths who ran the forges; had set up a system whereby shudra of the clan could volunteer to go and learn smith-work from the indigene experts, thereby raising their status, should they learn well, to vaishya; had deployed two-score men from Hastinapura as a permanent force to guard the mine; and had assigned Drona's son, Ashwattama, to oversee the entire operation. The result of all these improvements was a large increase in production. The finished iron implements went by wagon to Hastinapura. Half the raw iron was still sent to Panchala, where King Drupada had his own forges; they ran, so our scouts informed us, full-blast day and night churning out product. Whether Drupada ever intended to share the wealth with his sons-in-law was unclear.

Kurukshetra is twenty kosa up the Yamuna: two days' journey for a young man, three days for a mature man such as myself. The country up north being uncivilized and bandits (not to mention wild animals) a considerable danger, I took along my personal bodyguard, a group which now included Shikhandi.

Almost from the start, she had fit in remarkably well with the men. True, there had been some stares and snickers when I first took her to the barracks and introduced her as "Shikhandi, the new man," but when I made it clear they were to treat "him" as any other recruit and that anyone approaching "him" unnaturally would be first castrated, then hanged, they averted their eyes and stopped snickering. I expected her to enjoy basic respect; I was surprised, however, when she quickly gained respect on the training grounds, too. She was not much of an archer and declined to take part in the wrestling bouts, but her skill with a sword was impressive (so said the assistant weapons master who had been left in charge of military exercises). Her horsemanship was also exceptional. She took to wearing a loose tunic over her dhoti with the chest-band concealed underneath; in such dress, and with her height, solidity, and total lack of beauty, it was easy to forget she was a woman. I soon decided to make her one of my guards, adding her to the three I had brought with me from Hastinapura.

It was now late afternoon on the third day of our journey upriver. The Yamuna was especially low that year; my four guards and I splashed across at the ford, barely wetting our feet in our iron stirrups, and continued up the forested slope on the other side. As we topped the crest, the trees came to an abrupt end, and Kurukshetra lay before us.

It was a shallow, rectangular valley, like a serving tray, about one-quarter kosa wide and half a kosa long, stretching away to the west. Its surface was reddish brown dirt, dotted here and there with thorn bushes and patches of scrub; only a few trees provided shade, and even now, in late winter, one could feel the heat rising from the sunbaked earth. There were five roughly circular mine-pits, ranging in size from one hundred paces to one hundred fifty paces across and ten to twenty steps deep, arranged in a horseshoe shape (horseshoes were now commonplace), with the largest pit at the bottom of the horseshoe, closest to where we sat atop the crest.

Earth ramps gave access to each pit. Indigene workers swarmed up, down, and around, wielding their picks and shovels, buckets and baskets and rakes. They dug the slag from the pit's sides or bottom—the redness of the earth and rocks signaling the concentration of the ore—then broke it into small chunks and transported the chunks to the roasting fires, where they would spend several hours drying out before the somewhat purified slag was removed and carried to one of the pit's bloomeries. These were hollow chimneys of clay, nearly as tall as a man and twice as thick, heated with a charcoal fire; into them the chunks and more charcoal were packed and left to smelt for seven or eight hours, after which the "bloom"—a porous, glowing-hot lump of black iron, like a giant sponge for the God Yama to use in his bath—was extracted from a door at the bottom. These blooms were then sent to the forges: twelve sets of fire-and-anvil arrayed under a long, open shed situated on a flat stretch of earth between the pits. Each forge was manned by a master smith and his assistants, who reheated, hammered, and wrought the sponge iron into a plethora of tools, appliances, and weapons. But mostly weapons.

The mine-field reached about one-fifth of the way up the valley, with an encampment of soldier's tents situated just beyond. Past the tents, the floor of the valley rose a bit and became a relatively flat plain stretching west and ending in brown hills on the horizon. No doubt there was more iron ore to be dug from this plain; the existing pits, however, were far from exhausted and yielded more than enough to be going on with.

Riding halfway down the steep slope we came to a kind of natural jetty: a flat-topped spur of rock that extended out toward the largest mine-pit. Signaling to the guards to stay back, I dismounted and walked to the edge. It reminded me of the platform on which had sat Princess Draupadi and her ladies for her bridegroom choice—though of course that platform was manmade, with seats and a railing. This open promontory, as I stood on it looking down to the ground fifty feet below, made me feel quite dizzy. Directly below me were the pit's bloomeries: five of them in a tight semicircle around the base of the rock spur. I could see flames and smoke rising from their tops. The central one was flanked by two workers who were packing it with slag and charcoal using long-handled scoops; they bent to their buckets again and again, ladling first slag, then charcoal, then more slag into the fiery chimney. I imagined, briefly, what would happen if I slipped and fell.

I backed away from the edge and said to the guards rather too sharply, "Let's go. The king is waiting."

≈

King Duryodhana, Captain Ashwattama, and I were seated on rugs in the captain's tent. A manservant had brought a tin tray with cups of lassi, setting it on the ground between us. The sounds of the forge shed rang in my ears; through the open tent flap I could see the burly smith of the nearest forge, his soot-smeared brow bound with a rag to keep the sweat from streaming into his eyes, swinging his hammer hard onto an iron blade while his assistant hunkered at the fire, puffing air at its base by means of a contraption called, I'd been told, a *bellows*. Although day was nearly done, the workers showed no signs of stopping, and I wondered if they kept going all night by torchlight. I later learned that the sun's heat on the red-dirt field, augmented by the heat from the roasting fires, bloomeries, and forges, made a long rest in the afternoon necessary; to compensate, the work ran on late into the evening.

We had arrived at the captain's tent half an hour ago. Ashwattama greeted me with respect, but started when he saw Shikhandi. Neither of them said anything; nevertheless, the look of recognition that passed between them was obvious. I had forgotten they were childhood friends. Now, with her and the other guards posted outside, the king and captain were discussing mine operations as I listened and silently cursed myself for doing (as usual) the wrong thing.

"Just three years, Captain," the king was saying. "Not even three years. That's all the time we have to exceed the Pandavas' strength. And I want it *w-well* exceeded. The weapons produced here are critical to the eff … effort."

"Yes, your majesty," Ashwattama said. "I can assure you, production has increased significantly since we took over. In six more months, it will be double what it was."

"Good. Good. And the shudra apprentices? They're learning the craft?"

"Yes, Sire. They're all very eager. Although I must admit, some of the indigene smiths have not responded well to being asked to share their secrets with …" He hesitated, thin lips pressed together under his beaky nose.

"With?" The king raised his brows. His scar, in the heat, was a little inflamed.

"With *whitefish,* Sire," said the captain, looking embarrassed. "That's what they call us. They say we have pale skin and pop-eyes, like a whitefish."

"Ha!" Duryodhana grinned. "Whitefish, eh? I wonder what kind of f-fish they think I am. Surely not a whitefish. What kind of fish would you call me, Uncle Vidu?"

I jumped. "Oh … well … I … I don't think you're any kind of fish, your majesty."

"Hmm. If I *were* a fish, I'd be an odd one. People would catch me, take one look, and throw me back—don't you think?"

"Oh ..." I said. "Well, I ..."

He laughed. "Never mind, Uncle; never mind. We Kuru all come from a fish, do we not? The old queen was b-born of a fish, so they say. But who knows? None of us really knows where we come from or who we are. All we know is ..." He looked out the tent flap, rubbing a spot just below his copper armband, and fell silent.

An enormous *bang* from one of the forges brought him back to himself. He turned to Ashwattama again, his face stern. "The indigene smiths cannot be allowed to hoard their secrets. You must make it clear to them that their jobs are not in danger; quite the contrary. We need more iron and therefore more smiths. The b-better they teach us, the b-better rewarded they will be. Figure out a way to motivate them. Counselor, what do you suggest?"

I had to pull myself together. I thought for a moment, then said: "What the indigenes value most are horses. They don't raise them, and they don't know anything about them, but they covet them. Tell the smiths that for every Arya they train well, they'll receive a horse—even a pair of horses."

The captain looked skeptical. "Do we really want the indigenes owning horses?"

"You think they'll get notions of aggression," I said. "But there's no danger. As long as we have the weapons, chariots, and military training, there's nothing they can really do."

The king nodded. "True. It's a good idea, Uncle."

His praise encouraged me to speak on. "Just make sure," I said to Ashwattama, "that you continue to search them—all the workers— every night before they leave. Any theft of weapons must be severely dealt with."

"Oh, indeed," he said. "We're already very careful about that."

"And if I may, Sire ..." I said. The king flicked two fingers in assent.

"If any of the indigene smiths remain recalcitrant," I said, "I suggest you make an example of them. Beheading, or ..." (I had an inspiration) "you could throw them off that cliff back there; the one that overlooks the pit. That would certainly get their attention!" I laughed in what I hoped was a manly way.

They both looked at me blankly.

The king said, "Yes, well. We can leave such details to the captain."

"Yes, Sir," said the captain.

Duryodhana took a swig of lassi and stared into space, as if once again lost in thought. As he replaced the cup on the tray, his brown face crinkled with amusement.

"Also," he said, "nothing says we have to give them the *best* horses."

Ashwattama chuckled, appreciating the joke.

≈

For the night I was assigned a tent on the far edge of the encampment, facing out to the plain. I lay on the thin sleeping mat, stones poking into my body no matter how often I swept the ground beneath with my hand. My guards took turns to stand watch. Sometime after midnight, a few hours after the noise of the forges had ceased, I heard footsteps approaching and then Shikhandi's voice saying to the man on duty, "Namaste. I'm here."

"Right. Thanks," said the man. I heard him leave.

There was silence for a long time: half an hour, perhaps. I could see Shikhandi's shadow, thrown dim and wavering onto the tent flap by the campfire, as she paced back and forth. Then there came more footsteps, another shadow, and another man's voice, speaking low and soft:

"Shikhandi. I knew it was you. What the hell are you doing?"

"Hello, Ashwa. What am I doing? As you see."

"Yes, I can see all right." I could hear him smiling. "I just can't imagine how it happened. Aren't you married? Does your husband know about this?"

"Oh, yes, I'm married. And my husband does know. I'm being punished."

"What for?"

"For dressing as a man and running away. I've done it a few times. We live near Indraprasta now, so I was brought up before Vidura, and ..." (there were shuffling noises, as if she was moving him a few steps away, but when she spoke again I could still hear just as clearly) "... Vidura is making me be a soldier for three years."

There came another short silence, and then—to my intense irritation—muffled laughter from both of them.

"You don't say!" said Ashwattama. "So in other words, your punishment is you get to do just what you always wanted. Talk about luck!"

"I know! Can you believe it? I live in the barracks, train with the men, everything."

"You kicking their butts in the arena?"

"Ha! You bet. Well … in the sword-fighting, anyway. Not so much the archery."

"Yeah, you always did stink at archery."

Shikhandi's voice rose in indignation. "I didn't *stink* at it. I just thought it was stupid. I still do. Prancing around, shooting at things from a distance. Too girly."

"Girly! Huh. Guess you've never seen Lord Karna with a bow."

"I've seen him. He's no match for Prince Arjuna, though."

Ashwattama scoffed. "Are you nuts? Karna can hit the eye of a kingfisher from a hundred paces."

"Well, Arjuna can hit the eye of a hummingbird from *two* hundred paces."

"No he can't. That's ridiculous."

"Yes he can. I should know."

"No he can't. He … wait. What do you mean, 'I should know'?"

Shikhandi did not reply.

"Khandi … where were you trying to go? Those times you ran away, I mean."

Still no reply.

"You were trying to join the Pandavas' army, weren't you?" he said. "You thought you could fool them into thinking you're a man and letting you join up."

After another hesitation, she said: "All right. Yes. That's what I was doing. I know it was idiotic. But I just …"

"What?"

"I just couldn't bear it, Ashwa. Being forced to marry that old geezer, then having to live in his house, doing nothing. I swear it would have been better to be married to a shudra and have work to do: grinding corn, herding cows, plowing fields, anything. Anything but having to sit and spin and gossip and sit some more, never allowed to use my body or my wits. Then at night, having to let him

come into my bed and flop around on top of me like a dying shark
… *ugh.* I thought the babies might help, but they didn't. Oh, I love
them, of course I do, but Fani—that's his junior wife—she's so much
better with them than I am. And it's her they love. When they're hurt
or sad, it's her they go to, not me. They call her *Mummy;* I'm always
Mother. I knew if I left, they wouldn't … I mean, they might mind
a little, but …"

She broke off. I heard her take a deep breath and let it out.

"Anyway, it makes no difference what I thought. I was always
caught and brought back. Like I said: idiotic."

"Maybe not," said the captain. "Look at you now."

"Yes. I still can't believe it! I prayed to Indra, you know. I'd go to
the shrine near our homestead once a week; I'd take ghee, flowers,
grain, and I'd make my offering and pray and pray. Perhaps he finally
heard me."

"It sure looks that way. And I'm glad for you, Khandi, I really
am. But …"

"But what?"

He paused, then: "You need to be careful."

"What, not to get hurt? *Pfft.* I can look after myself."

"I know that. But if you're still thinking of joining the Pandavas,
you'd better think again. That'd make you a deserter and a traitor. If
you're caught, you'll get no mercy."

"I wouldn't expect mercy."

"Fine words. But listen: you got your wish. You're a man-at-
arms. Why would you risk that to go fight on the other side? Why
do you care so much about the Pandavas?"

"Because I owe them. Arjuna, especially."

"Why? What did he ever do for you?"

Her voice grew dull, almost sullen. "You wouldn't understand."

I heard him sigh. "If this is some sort of girl's crush on Arjuna,
you really need to let it go."

"IT'S NOT …" He must have shushed her somehow, because
her voice dropped to a hiss. "*It's not a girl's crush.* Gods' sake, you
know me better than that! I tell you, I *owe* him. I owe him my loyalty
as a warrior. I can't explain why, but I do. It would be … it would be
dishonorable not to repay my debt. So yes; if it ever comes to war, I
will find a way to join with the Pandavas. And I'll fight on their side."

In an effort to hear better, I shifted on my mat. A sharp

stone jabbed my shoulder, and I cried out. Immediately, footsteps approached. Shikhandi called through the tent flap, "Are you all right, Sir?"

"Yes … yes," I said, thickening my voice as if awakened from a deep sleep. "It was nothing … a nightmare."

"Yes, Sir," she said. I heard her retreat to where Ashwattama stood. "You'd better go," she whispered.

"Yes, I'd better. Look, Khandi: just take care of yourself."

"I will."

There was a pause. I heard a few quick thumps and pictured them embracing as men do, with pats on the back. Then I heard footsteps going away.

"Ashwa …"

The footsteps stopped. "Yes?"

"Thank you for coming to see me."

"Any time, my friend." The footsteps faded into the night.

≈

I must have sunk into sleep after that, because the next thing I remember was hearing the guard arrive to relieve Shikhandi. This one was a big man with big feet, and his loud approach and gruff "Namaste" jolted me awake. I knew I would get no more rest that night, so I got up, pulled on my dhoti and cloak, put on my shoes, and went outside. The guard was surprised. He snapped to attention and asked whether I needed anything.

"No, thanks," I said. "I'm just going to walk a short way. Out there."

"Yes, Sir," he said, and made to accompany me.

"No," I said, "You stay here. Don't worry, I'll not go far."

"Are you sure that's wise, Sir? There may be snakes."

"I'll risk it," I said. He was clearly displeased, but he must have heard something in my tone, for he did not press the matter.

I skirted the campfire and took some thirty steps out onto the plain. I had no intention of going any further; I do not like snakes. The full moon, large as a dinner plate and scarred with shadows, was just sinking down to the hills on the horizon. It cast a cold glow over the landscape, and I knew the guard could see me in its light. Still, I was happy to be more or less alone for once. It is so rare among the Arya that one is ever awake and alone.

I sat down cross-legged on the ground and thought about Shikhandi.

Had she been a man—and she *was* a man, I reminded myself, for I had made her one—her life would now be forfeit. I had overheard her not only expressing support for the enemy, but planning to switch sides and fight for them. Although the allegiance of the soldiers left behind at Indraprasta might be seen as properly lying with the Pandavas, Shikhandi had been appointed by me and was one of my own guards. Coming from her, such statements were blatantly treasonous. And what about Ashwattama? Although Shikhandi was not under his direct command, still it would be the duty of any Kaurava captain, upon hearing such statements from a Kaurava soldier, to report them—something Ashwattama was clearly not going to do.

On the other hand ... what I had overheard had not been an official exchange between captain and subordinate, but rather a private chat between old friends. Had they known I was awake, they would not have spoken. Was it dishonorable for me to have lain there listening without alerting them? Yes, I thought it was. And if my knowledge was dishonorably gained (was that the same as unlawfully gained?), I should take no action based upon it.

And yet ... my awareness of Shikhandi's connections—she was Lord Bhishma's granddaughter and a princess of Kashi in her own right—might be biasing me in her favor. True, the Law for a princess is different from the Law for a soldier, but again, Shikhandi *was* a soldier, made so by me. Therefore, the soldier's Law must be applied. According to that Law, the punishment for a turncoat, whether or not he acts on his plans, is death.

And yet, and yet ... I could not help imagining what Bhishma would do if he found out I had transformed his granddaughter into a man and then had her executed for treason.

I dropped my head in my hands and rubbed my aching temples.

Suddenly I heard a voice, singing in the darkness. Startled, I looked up and around, but saw no one. The voice was very soft; I could barely make out the words, but I knew the song by heart. It was the hymn from the Sunrise Oblation—the one my shudra mother used to sing to me at bedtime—the one Drona had sung with such passion:

> One man with sight has never seen Speech; one man with hearing has never heard her. But to another she shows her beauty as a loving wife, well-dressed, reveals herself to her husband ...

> No part in Speech has he who has abandoned his own dear friend. Even if he hears her, in vain he listens; for he knows nothing of the path of righteous action ...

> All his friends rejoice in the friend who comes in triumph, having won fame and victory in the contest. He is their blame-averter and food-provider. He is fit for deeds of valor; he is worthy to win the prize.

The voice, which had been neither male nor female, faded away as the moon dropped below the western hills.

Another message from the Gods, I supposed. I did wish they would be a little clearer when they spoke. Nevertheless, as I stood up, dusted off my rear, and headed back to the tent, and during the remaining hours before dawn as I lay on my uncomfortable mat, I did my best to reflect upon what I had heard and to discern its meaning. I decided, finally, on a few interpretations.

First, I decided I was being reminded of our limitations when it comes to perceiving the heart of another person, especially a person we don't know well. For what, really, did I know of Shikhandi? Who was she, and how had she spent her life? Why did she want to be a soldier? How had she and Ashwattama grown so close? Why would she not look at Bhishma when he helped her into the going-away cart after her wedding? How had her husband treated her? How had she kept up her training all those years? Did her children really not love her?

And, most perplexing of all: What did she owe to Arjuna?

I did not, and could not, have knowledge of these things; not unless she chose to reveal them to me, "as a loving wife reveals herself to her husband." Without such knowledge, I could not be sure of the meaning, let alone the import, of the statements I had overheard. And without being sure, I could not condemn a woman—or a man—to death.

Second, I decided *I* was the man "who has abandoned his own dear friend." All those years ago at the bridegroom choice, I had essentially thrown Duryodhana off a cliff; yet he had not held it against me, but instead had kept me on as his chief advisor and, with the exception of that one rebuke at the council table, continued to treat me with respect, even affection. It was far more than I deserved. Moreover, hadn't I joined up with the Pandavas hundreds of times, if only in my heart? It was not for me to judge Shikhandi if she did the same.

Finally, I thought about that last bit of the hymn: the bit about "fame and victory in the contest." For I knew the contest was coming. As the gray dawn broke and I emerged once again from my tent, I had yet another vision, this time of two mighty armies about to meet on the plain. I saw captains standing in their chariots in the vanguard, archers lined up behind with bows bent and pointed skyward, infantrymen marching with swords drawn, cavalry swooping around the sides to cut off retreat, war elephants charging forth to break the adversary's front lines. All this I saw in a flash. The overwhelming sight made me reel backward into the tent flap, causing the guard to ask once again with startled concern: "Are you all right, Sir?"

"Yes ... yes. I'm all right," I said, bending over and putting my hands on my knees. "Just stood up too quickly." I asked him to bring water for washing and went back in the tent.

I sat down and thought again about Shikhandi. Where would she be in that great battle to come? Would she be among the infantry? Or riding pell-mell at the head of a cavalry squad, bending low over the neck of her horse, urging her men to more speed? Or would she, perhaps, be one of the captains in the chariots, standing tall and proud, casting her eye on a warrior of the opposing side with whom she desired to duel?

I did not know. But I knew that wherever she was on that field, and whether she lived or died, she would cover herself with glory. And she would have at least one friend, Ashwattama, who would rejoice in her success. I, on the other hand, would meanwhile be sitting on silk cushions in a tent well back from the lines, enjoying a bit of roast partridge as I discussed with the priests the advisability of this or that sacrifice, this or that oblation. I had no valor, no true friends, and no right to make any comment whatsoever on her choices.

She was what I would never be; what so many of us will never be. She was worthy to win the prize.

Chapter 16

KRISHNA

Krishna said:
You might think that when the bride and groom entered the Hall of Sacraments at Kampilya palace, my attention would have been fixed on them: the bride, Uttari, was charming—fourteen years of age, dainty, wide-eyed, and gorgeously dressed in a sari of deep rose with black and gold embroidery—while the groom, Abimanyu, although just fifteen was well-grown and not at all awkward in his finery. Or you might think I'd have been contemplating with satisfaction the benefits of this early marriage: it allied the Pandavas with the powerful clan of Matsya and would, we prayed, soon produce a grandson to ensure the line. But I'm afraid my eyes and mind were, as usual, all for Arjuna: the father of the groom.

At thirty-five he had lost a little of the radiance, the lightning-in-a-jar quality that had enthralled me those many years ago (goodness, could it really be almost twenty?) when the Pandavas first came to us in Vrishni. Still his, however, were that perfect physique, ivory skin, easy carriage, and devastating smile. His martial skills, too, were undiminished; indeed, they were more impressive than ever. Over the past three years of exile, he had taken on the role of commander-in-chief to the combined armies of Indraprasta and Panchala—the army of Matsya would now be added to that alliance—and had put King Drupada's arena to good use as a site for war exercises, scrimmages, and intra-army tournaments. Whenever I was in Kampilya and could get away for an hour or two from the council chamber, I'd go sit on a tier and watch him at work with the men. Sometimes I'd even volunteer to be his charioteer, as in the old days. As we readied to make a circuit, me at the reins, him behind with arrow on the bow, it still set my heart pounding to hear him say: "Now, Krishna! Let's show them how it's done."

I admit I feared for his safety, especially during the scrimmages. He always insisted, at first, on joining the fray and would position himself right out front. Before the fighting began, however, one of his brothers (usually Saku) would go have a word with him, and I knew he was being told that he must not be rash, that he must think of his value to the army and of how terrible it would be if he were injured or even, Gods forbid, killed. From my seat on the third or fourth tier I would see him frowning and shaking his head, clearly rejecting the counsel as craven; I would see Saku leaning in and speaking even more earnestly; and at last I would see Arjuna sigh, nod, and allow himself to be led to the viewing platform at the edge of the field, there to stand with his brothers and oversee the mock battle out of harm's way. I was sure it frustrated him terribly to be thus sidelined. Still, I was relieved.

When he came in the wedding procession on his son's right, splendid in his white-and-silver robes and jewels, I caught my breath. (Subhadra, on the left in glaring yellow-and-gold, was looking as tawdry as ever.) And throughout the ceremony and banquet that followed, hard as I tried to mark the words of Priest Dhaumya, to admire the decorations, or to enjoy the food and music, my thoughts were drawn inexorably back to the man I loved.

King Drupada had, with some reluctance, taken my suggestion and put away the high, round table with the chairs, instead placing the wedding party according to tradition in a semicircle on the great hall's dais, with cushions to sit upon and the dishes placed on trivets—wrought-iron trivets—before us. The hall was brilliantly lit as always, the lamps on the spokes of the wagon-wheel fixtures glittering above. I was on the groom's side, seated between my sister and my aunt. I spoke little with either of them; Subhadra, as usual, was making me wince with her high-pitched babble, while Perta, who I noticed had lost a lot of weight in recent months, was uncharacteristically quiet. Arjuna was on Perta's other side, with Draupadi next to him, followed by the rest of the Pandavas and Prince Tadyu. Draupadi was looking remarkably well, I thought. Her cheeks had a rosy bloom and her hair seemed thicker, more lustrous.

As the dinner progressed, I saw that Arjuna was ignoring her— though not with an air of contempt. He sat rigid, careful not to touch her, as if he were too aware of her presence and a little intimidated by it. He kept leaning across her to talk with Yudi, and finally he got up, stepped around her, and sat down facing his brothers and Tadyu. A moment later Yudi stood and walked behind the semicircle to the bride's side; he bent down to speak some words to the king of Matsya (that is, the bride's father) and King Drupada, who both then rose and followed him back. As Yudi passed behind me, he bent down again and said in my ear, "My friend, will you join us?" I got up, bringing my beer. With many courteous murmurs of *May I?* and *Certainly*, we all seated ourselves in a loose cluster at the end of the dais.

As I sat down, Arjuna was saying to Tadyu: "… and if we'd counted according to the lunar calendar, our time would already be up. But *Krishna*" (he gave me a somewhat surly glance) "said we had to use the solar calendar, so of course, that's what we did."

Ever impatient! I thought with a smile. I settled myself at his side—honestly, it was laughable how much I still always wanted a chance to brush his arm or leg—and said, "Never mind. By the solar calendar, there's only one month to go. Not long."

"Not long until *what?*" said Arjuna, still surly.

"Yes, Krishna," said Yudi, "that is what we wish to discuss with you. And with their majesties." He directed cordial nods at Drupada and the king of Matsya. The latter was a thin man, clean-shaven, with delicate, almost girlish features and a soft, lisping voice. I had been amused to see that a clan renowned for its fierce fighters had such an effeminate king.

Yudi went on: "The time for our return to Indraprasta approaches. You know the terms that were negotiated." He threw a glance at Draupadi with that same diffident air I had noted in Arjuna. "They limit the size of our army and our herd, and prevent us from venturing beyond the boundaries of Tarashtra's original land grant. The question is: Will we abide by those terms? Or will we go to war?"

"*Pfft.* I can't believe we have to ask," said Arjuna.

Tadyu said, "I agree. Why is this even a question? You've been cheated twice now by the Kauravas. Everyone knows the kingdom is yours by right; they've cheated you of what's rightfully yours." His words met with nods from the Pandavas. "And let's not forget what they did to your wife, my sister, at the dice match. It was unforgivable.

War is now a matter of honor, *all* our honor." He looked to his father, who gave no sign of assent or dissent.

"Thank you, Prince Tadyu," said Yudi. "I'm inclined to agree with you."

"What ith the thituation with the Kauravath?" asked the king of Matsya, plumping a cushion and stuffing it behind his tailbone. I must say I found his lisp annoying. If a nobleman can't speak well, he should either practice until he can or give up speaking altogether.

"An excellent question, Sire," I said, striving to keep my annoyance off my face. "In brief, they have grown much stronger. According to our scouts, Kaurava troops number fifteen hundred. They've made alliance with Madrasa. It's Duryodhana, not the Blind King, who now occupies the throne. And they have control of the Kurukshetra mine: that means they have swords, shields, spears, maces, chariot axles—all of iron—enough for their whole army."

"But half the mine's output comes here, to our forges," said Tadyu. "Our armies are equally well-equipped."

There was an awkward silence in which nobody looked at Drupada. It was true: the Panchala army had been fully equipped with iron weapons for some time now. The soldiers of Indraprasta, on the other hand, still wielded a mixture of iron and bronze.

"Yes, well," I said, "however we look at it, the Kauravas' strength now matches or even exceeds our own. Yet that's not what concerns me most."

"Indeed, Krishna?" said Yudi. "What does concern you?"

I hesitated. This was a delicate topic. "What concerns me most is ..."

There was no point beating around the bush.

"What concerns me most is the quality of their commanders and captains."

This drew puzzled looks. Arjuna, after a moment, said, "You mean, their poor quality compared to ours? Why is that a problem?"

"No," I said. "I mean, their captains are better."

Arjuna and Naku gasped in outrage. Tadyu looked baffled. Bimasena simply laughed: "You've had too much beer, Krishna! Better go lie down before you hurt yourself!"

I smiled back at him. "I assure you, Bima, I'm quite in my wits."

"What is this, Krishna?" said Arjuna. That look of angry hurt, the one I always wanted to smooth away, had come to his face. "Whose side are you on?"

Now it was my turn to feel hurt. "I'm on your side," I said. "You know that."

"Of course we know that," said Yudi in a soothing tone. "We will never doubt you, Krishna. Your advice has never failed us. Please, explain: Why do you say their captains are better?"

"Because it's true," I said, taking a breath and blinking quickly to forestall—I am not ashamed to say it—the angry tears that had sprung to my eyes. I looked down, cleared my throat, and went on more firmly. "As war captains they have Karna, Drona, Ashwattama, and King Duryodhana himself. We have only Arjuna. No, forgive me, Sire," (for I had seen a flash of annoyance cross Yudi's brow) "you are the quintessence of reason, diplomacy, and Law, a political ruler beyond compare. But you are not a military captain."

Yudi met my eyes for another moment, frowning. Then he looked away and sighed. "Yes ... yes. It's true. I'm a peacetime leader, not a war leader."

Arjuna's feathers were still ruffled. He said, "Well, what about Bima? He's worth twenty men on a battlefield!"

Bima laughed again and said, "Thanks, Juna, but you know he's right. I can smash heads. I'm no commander."

Tadyu looked as though he were about to say something ... then didn't. He knew I had seen him in the arena, participating in the exercises and scrimmages. He was a capable soldier, but a man who, like his father, would build arenas and stage tournaments, amass wealth and invent new ways to light up a hall; not a man who would win wars.

I let them all ponder for a while.

"And then there's Bhishma," I said.

"Bhishma!" cried Naku. "He's an old man! He's over eighty!"

"Yes, he's old," I said. "And his physical powers may be lessened—though I hear he still cuts an impressive figure. But that doesn't matter. What matters are his abilities as general and strategist, which are as strong as ever they were. We have no one to match him."

"*You* match him," said Arjuna.

I cannot tell you what those words meant to me, coming from him. I wanted to fling my arms about him and kiss him. Of course, I refrained.

"You are kind to say so, Arjuna," I said, "but no, I do not match Bhishma. I am clever in certain ways: I can see beyond what is to what might be. I know what people want, so I can persuade them, sometimes, to a course of action. But I have never planned and executed a cattle raid. I have never led troops into battle. I have not earned the respect of the whole world, friends and foes alike. I have never ruled a clan."

"*He's* never ruled a clan," said Saku. "He's only been regent. Never king."

"All the more reason to fear him," said I. "Whatever he's done, he's done without the Gods' blessing and without a crown on his head. He's done it purely on his own merit. As a leader of men, no man compares."

The servants were bringing out the final course: those same sugar-sweetened little cakes that had been so popular at Draupadi's bridegroom choice nearly eighteen years ago. The group was quiet, reflecting, as the plates were set down.

"I am sorry," I said, "to be a killjoy. But before we go to war, we must think about these things."

King Drupada reclined on his elbow, reached for a cake, and popped it into his mouth. His beard was still black and full; the top of his head, now completely bald, glistened in the lamplight. "Well," he said, "it seems to me we must find a way to even the field a bit."

"How do you mean?" I asked.

"I don't know, exactly," he said, flicking sugar from his fingers. "These things aren't my area. But if their captains are better than ours—and given that we haven't time to grow more captains of our own—I think we must find a way to eliminate one or more of theirs."

"You mean ... assassination?" I said.

Drupada shrugged. "Again, it's really not my area. I'm just saying: if that's their advantage, we must focus on how to reduce that advantage."

The thought was perturbing, but intriguing. I made a mental note to remember what he had said and consider it later.

There was a bustle a short way down the semicircle. Draupadi, I saw, had gotten up. She had one arm around Perta's shoulders and with the other hand was helping an obviously drunk Subhadra to stagger to her feet. Perta seemed to be in pain: she was bent over, gripping her side, and her eyes were squeezed shut. Having hoisted

Subhadra more or less upright, Draupadi turned to her mother-in-law and spoke soft words; then she turned back to Subhadra, said in a firm tone, "Come along, now, bedtime," and began to guide the two women across the dais, passing slowly in front of us.

I was a little dismayed to see her five husbands making no move to assist her. Suddenly they noticed robe collars that needed adjusting, fingernails that needed cleaning, or beers that needed refilling. I nudged Arjuna—after all, those were both of his wives in straits—but he turned his back to me and began to talk animatedly to Naku about something or other.

Draupadi paid them no mind. When she reached the dais steps she hesitated, seeming to ready herself for a difficult descent. Perta was obviously dropping with exhaustion; Subhadra was lurching backward, red-faced, shouting, "Arjunaaa! Lesh go dance! I wanna dansh, come on Arjuna, you wanna dansh ..." Draupadi's hold on her wrist was slipping.

Krishna Vasudeva, I said to myself, *it's up to you.* I got up and seized my sister, pinning her arms and turning her face front. "Off we go," I said, and nodded to Draupadi to indicate she should help Perta. The four of us proceeded down the steps and across the hall.

A gaggle of waiting-women, all tipsy themselves, came up from the lower tables and surged round us, twittering. I rebuked them for not taking better care of their mistresses. Several of them took charge of Perta, several others of Subhadra. As they headed off down the corridor toward the women's quarters, Draupadi waved away her own set, saying, "It's all right, girls. Go back to the banquet. I'm going to bed, I won't need you." After a few *Yes Ma'ams* and *Are you sure Ma'ams,* they went back inside the hall.

Draupadi leaned against the wall of the corridor. She puffed out her cheeks, pushed damp strands of hair off her forehead, and said, "I don't know, Krishna; when I got married, I don't remember bargaining for this!"

But she did not seem upset. She was smiling, her eyes were twinkling, and for the second time that night, I thought how well she looked.

"Your husbands should be more attentive," I said.

She shook her head and laughed. "Believe me, the less attentive they are, the better I like it." Then her face softened. She placed a hand on her midriff and looked down at it, saying, "Although ..."

JOCELYN DAVIS

"Madam," I said, "would I be right to wish you joy?"

"I believe you would," she said, looking up at me again. Her smile was very beautiful.

"May the Gods bless you with a son," I said, using the accepted phrase.

The smile grew contemplative, self-satisfied, like that of a child with a treasure box. "Actually," she said, "I think this one will be a girl."

≈

The following afternoon, I received a summons from my Aunt Perta. I went to her rooms with some trepidation, wondering if she planned a repetition of the scene nearly three years ago, when I had arrived in Hastinapura after the Dicing and she had waylaid me in the palace yard and berated me for a good half hour.

"Draupadi! The queen! *My* daughter-in-law!" she had screamed at me. "Wagered, in a gambling match! Stripped naked! Practically raped! The whole family, humiliated!" She jabbed a finger in my face. "It's *your* fault, Krishna. You know what Yudi's like when he gets his hands on the dice. You should have been there! You should have stopped him!"

I agreed with her, placated her, apologized profusely, and promised I would never desert her boys like that again. After all, she was right: it was my fault. I had just been so ill, and when Yudi came and told me of the challenge, I remember telling him not to go, but in my delirious state I wasn't strong enough to argue, and so …

Well. Enough of my excuses. They went, and they lost. It was indeed my fault.

I'd been told it was actually Arjuna who had wanted to stake Draupadi, but I didn't believe that for a moment. Arjuna would never be so cowardly. Most likely it was one of the Kauravas, Duryodhana or his brother, who had suggested it, and Yudi, driven to desperation, had clutched at the distasteful notion. Yes … I was pretty sure that was what had happened.

At any rate, when Perta asked to see me in her rooms, I was hoping to avoid another harangue. I picked some scarlet flowers in the Kampilya gardens and brought them with me. But when I arrived, I saw immediately there would be no harangue: she was in bed, head propped on pillows, hair in two long braids, eyes closed. Her arms laid atop the covers were roped with indigo veins. The skin on her face was drawn tight. As I approached, handing off the flowers to a maidservant, she opened her eyes and said in voice weak as a kitten's:

"Krishna ... thank you for coming."

I was shocked. Last night at the banquet she had seemed ill, but not as ill as this. I sat down on the stool that someone placed for me and leaned forward.

"Dear Aunt. Are you all right? Shall I send for a healer?"

"No healers. I'm dying, Krishna. There's no healer for death."

I did not know what to say. She was shivering a little, so I pulled off my cloak and laid it gently over her. The deep-blue folds made her emaciated body nearly disappear.

"Krishna ... before I die ... I need to tell you something."

"Hadn't you better rest now, Aunt? Perhaps you'll feel better tomorrow." I felt foolish as soon as I'd said it. Clearly, there might not be a tomorrow.

"No. Listen, Krishna. My sons will be coming here soon, to say good-bye. But first I must tell you something. I don't have the strength to argue, so you must just stay quiet and listen to me."

I nodded. "I understand. Tell me."

She closed her eyes again, as if gathering strength. A waiting-woman came up to the bed and wiped her brow with a damp cloth. Then she opened her eyes, focused them on my face, and spoke as follows:

"I heard you last night, talking about the commanders. About how ours do not measure up to theirs. I heard Drupada saying you must find a way to eliminate one or more of them—one or more of their commanders, I mean—"

"Oh, Aunt Perta," I said, "these are not things for you to be worrying about. I am sorry if I implied your sons are not worthy captains. Of course they are. The Pandavas are the most valorous, the most skillful ..."

Her head jerked on the pillow, as if she were shaking off a fly. "Be *quiet*, Krishna. You *must* listen to me."

I fell silent, and she went on.

"I am going to tell you how ... how to eliminate one of their commanders. To do that, I must tell you a story about me. About the time before I was married. Then you will see.

325

"I grew up in Vrishni, as you know. My father, your grandfather, was king then. Not much ever happens in Vrishni ... it's a backward place." Her lips curved a little. "I don't need to tell *you* that. But it's especially hard for a girl, I think, living in such dull surroundings. You men can get away—go hunting, raid cattle, visit other clans. We can't. My mother died when I was four. My brother Vasudeva and I were close as children, but when he turned seventeen he had to take up the duties of crown prince, and after that I was left alone most of the time. Just me and a couple of maidservants. We weren't rich enough for me to have proper ladies. I was *so* bored.

"But I was pretty; I could tell from the way the boys and men of the palace staff looked at me. I was supposed to be confined to my quarters, of course, but Father thought it healthy for me to get outdoor exercise and had instructed my maids to take me on a walk around the compound each afternoon. I liked throwing glances at the soldiers, the grooms, even the blades-boys, pulling my veil back and adjusting my chest-band just to make them stare.

"Well, as you know, there's no wall and nothing to stop a girl from wandering off. One day I decided I would do just that, thinking it would be a good joke to put my maids in a panic and make them run after me. As we walked out past the barnyard and the two of them were about to circle back, I hiked up my dhoti and took off running as fast as I could into the forest. You know the trees press quite close to the palace, there.

"I ran on and on, laughing at the thrill of it. At first I could hear them crying, 'Lady Perta! Lady Perta! Come back!' But then their voices died away and I realized they weren't chasing me after all, so I slowed to a walk. I kept going, though, because it was all so exciting and new. The trees were thick, with vines all over them, everything green and moist and smelling of earth. Soon I was pushing my way through hanging vines; I remember they had little white flowers like stars sprinkled over them. Just as I was getting tired and thinking of turning back, I pushed through a heavy curtain of vines and came out into a clearing.

"There was a small hut in the middle, made of wood with a thatched roof. In front of the hut's doorway, sitting cross-legged on the ground, was a young man. There was a pile of wooden sticks next to him. He had one of the sticks in his lap and was sharpening its end with a knife. As far as I could tell, he was wearing only a loincloth. A ray of sun, slanting through the trees behind me, fell upon his bare neck and shoulders; he had turned slightly away from the light so it would not dazzle him as he worked. I couldn't see his face.

"As I took a step into the clearing, he looked up. It was then I knew he was a Naga; he had the dark skin, the flattish nose, and the heavy-lidded eyes. We had a few Snake girls and boys in the compound—they did the chamber pots, cleaned the stables—so I knew all about them. I had been told they were dung-eaters, the lowest, dirtiest sort of outcaste, and that I must never, under any circumstances, touch one of them or allow them to touch me.

"But I was still in the grip of my adventure, so I did not retreat (as of course I should have). Instead, I walked forward and stopped just a few paces away from the young man. I smiled at him and made namaste.

"He smiled back at me, laid aside the stick, and stood up, placing his left hand to his breast and making me a small bow. He still had the knife in his right hand, but I was not the least afraid. He was tall and well-muscled, yet he looked to be only a little older than I—perhaps sixteen or seventeen, a boy, really—and his face, as he smiled, had a sweet purity that made me feel as if ... as if I were bathing in honey.

"I remember there were a few squawks of parakeets in the trees around the clearing, but other than that, absolute silence. The sunray was now falling on the boy's torso; his skin was smooth, glowing, like oiled deodarwood. I put out my hand and touched his chest. He did not move for some time, and neither did I. I just stood there with my fingertips grazing his chest, thinking how beautiful he was.

"Suddenly he lifted the knife, and for an instant I *was* afraid— but with a fluid motion, he flung it straight to the ground. It made a *thunk* and stuck point-down in the grass. Then he took my hand and led me to the hut's doorway. We went inside."

She closed her eyes again, and I wondered if she was in too much pain to go on. But she opened them and continued.

"I don't know where his family was that day, or if he even had a family. The whole time I saw no one else, Naga or otherwise, and neither of us spoke a word. When I left the hut, it was growing dark. I had the odd feeling, as I pushed my way through the vine curtain with the white flowers cast over it like stars, that if I turned around and tried to go back to him, I would find no clearing there: only the forest, stretching on forever."

Her eyes moved to the window. Outside, the dusk was closing in.

Her head made that same irritable, jerking motion. "But that's likely just a fancy I constructed for myself to obscure the fact that I had lain, wanton, with a strange man in the woods. A *Snake* man.

"Of course I said nothing to anyone about what had happened. When I got home that evening, my maids were frantic with worry but hadn't yet raised the alarm, being too scared of punishment. I laughed at them and said I'd had a lovely walk in the forest.

"When a few months later it became clear I was pregnant, I thought about claiming I'd been raped: raped by a Snake—or perhaps, more believably, by a town boy. Then I decided my father would be less upset (and my maids less likely to lose their lives) if I told a story about a God coming to me in a dream: yes, it was Surya, the Sun God, who came to me in a dream and carried me off to the forest and made love to me, and I had thought it was just a dream so I hadn't said anything, but now, Father, now I know it was more than a dream …

"He believed me. I spun the story well, and besides, Vrishni is a place where people still think the Gods walk among us. And who am I to say they don't? Maybe he *was* a God, that young man with the sweet smile and the smooth dark skin. When he took my hand and led me into the hut, I certainly felt as if I were being transported to heaven. And when he laid me down on the grass mat and began to caress me, and kiss me … "

I shifted on the stool, scratching the back of my head.

Her eyes came from the window to me. "Sorry, Krishna. Never mind all that." Her lips curved again, mocking me.

"Six months later, the baby arrived: a boy. He was beautiful. Oh, I know all babies are beautiful, but he was—glowing. Like the sun. I would hold him in my arms for hours, gazing at him, drinking in his radiance. I named him Suryana.

"But of course I could not keep him. It would have made me unmarriageable if word had got out. Father found a trader from town who was traveling with his wife and children to Madrasa, and we decided to entrust Suryana to them; although they could not take another baby themselves, they agreed to find some adoptive parents in that northern country. We gave them plenty of silver, for their trouble and to pay the new parents.

"The day when they would depart approached. I knew I would never see my son again, and it made me feel as if a fist were clenching my heart. Then I thought, what if I *did* see him again—someday, somewhere—and not know him? That would be even worse. 'Suppose I mark him with a sign,' I thought, 'a sign that will let me recognize him should I ever see him again.' I summoned a jeweler from town, telling him I wanted some earrings made for myself: 'Golden earrings, with pendants shaped like the sun.' I told him I needed them in three days. He delivered them as promised, and my maids and I pierced Suryana's ears and put them in. He did not cry; not one bit.

"When I handed him to the trader's wife, the fist around my heart clenched so hard I thought I might die. But I did not cry. I thought, if my baby son can manage not to cry when his ears are pierced, I must manage not to cry when he is going to his new mother."

She broke off. Her breathing had become labored. I thought she might be finished, but then she made one hand into a fist, as if to work up a last measure of strength (or perhaps recalling that fist around her heart), and went on:

"Well. You can imagine my surprise when he showed up at a tournament in Hastinapura, twenty-two years later. He won the archery. I was giving out the prizes. I was lifting the garland over his head when I saw the earrings ... it took everything I had to maintain my composure. It turned out he was the son of a palace charioteer and his wife; I guess that trader had unloaded him before ever reaching Madrasa. So he was vaishya, but then Duryodhana took his part and made him kshatriya, and he became a fixture at court. I have been avoiding him ever since.

"But now you see, Krishna. You see how to eliminate one of the Kaurava commanders. Or rather—how to *convert* him."

I did see. I saw very clearly.

"Karna is your son," I said. "In fact, he is your eldest son. By right, he is the king of Indraprasta."

"Yes," she said, "because by Law, 'the son is his who took the hand.' Pandu was my husband, so Karna is Pandu's son as much as mine. Karna is a Pandava."

I looked to the window. Outside, it was now full dark.

I said, "I'm not sure, though. Karna is supremely loyal to Duryodhana. I can't see him breaking faith with his friend and master, just to be king."

"Oh, no. He won't do it just to be king."

"Then …?"

"You've forgotten something," she said. "Or rather, some*one*."

I looked back at her, lying there under my blue cloak, her once-magnificent body wasted away to bones, her once-handsome face haggard and gray with pain.

"The wife of the Pandavas," I said. "Draupadi."

"Yes," she said. "He'll do it for Draupadi."

Chapter 17

KARNA

TWO MONTHS BEFORE THE WAR

T he commander-in-chief arrived in the Hall of Sacraments just as the ceremony was about to begin. The women in the crowd cast him the usual admiring glances as he strode up the aisle, gold-colored cloak flung back to expose his gold-studded leather vest, golden earrings glimmering in the light of fire-pit and torches. He made his way along the front row and bowed to the king, bowed to the queen. Then he bent to the king's ear and said:

"Krishna has arrived. They've put him in the south wing. He'll join you at the feast this evening."

Duryodhana nodded. "Thank you, Karna."

Karna bowed again, went around the side, and found a seat on a bench a few rows back.

High Priest Vyasa—soon to be Old High Priest Vyasa—stood before the altar. His shock of hair, snow-white, sprang up thick as always; his back, however, was bent, and his gnarled hands shook atop his cane. Had he been able to raise his face, one would have seen that his eyes, once black as iron blooms, had grown dull, pink, and rheumy. He would be eighty-two this year.

A gong sounded. The people craned their necks as Ramesha, high priest to be, entered through the doorway, tall and stately in his white robe. He carried in one hand a medallion of onyx, which later would be placed around his neck as his badge of office; in the other, a teakwood staff much stouter than Vyasa's cane. Followed by some twenty priests and acolytes, he processed up the aisle, approached the altar, and bowed to his predecessor.

The ceremony went on from there with the sacrifice of various birds and beasts (the sandy floor soaking up the blood splashes), offerings of flesh and ghee into the fire, and gestures of precise beauty and meaning, all accompanied by the proper incantations. After the first few hymns, Vyasa's part was over; the crowd breathed a sigh of relief as he tottered to a stool and was lowered onto it by helpers. Then Duryodhana came forward and went on to perform his role—a significant one, as the king's always is on such occasions—with assurance. The attending priests, junior and senior, also acquitted themselves well. It was evident that Vyasa, despite his recent decline in health, had kept standards high among his subordinates.

But there was one young priest who, while striking each pose and uttering each verse with exactitude, did it all with a face so grim he might have been presiding at a funeral. His heavy-lidded eyes, fixed constantly on Ramesha, were strained. His high forehead was furrowed. His pale lips, when they were not moving in song, were compressed as if with some fierce pain. And the audience members, who might otherwise have noticed and wondered at the empty sleeve flapping at his side, noticed instead his contorted visage and wondered at that.

At the ceremony's conclusion the crowd stood and made namaste as the new high priest processed around the fire-pit and down the aisle, his colleagues following two by two. The grim-faced priest was at the tail of the line. He was supporting Vyasa with his one arm, matching his pace to the old man's with seemingly tender concern. As they passed the front row, however, he turned and threw the king a look so bitter, so full of hatred, that the curse might have been shouted aloud. Duryodhana did not appear to notice, but Queen Banumati, who was standing beside her husband, half-raised one hand as if to ward off a missile flung in their direction. And in the third row, Karna made a small lurch forward, his hand to his knife hilt.

The moment passed. The one-armed priest continued down the aisle and out the door, Vyasa tottering beside him. The people began to turn to one another with smiles and friendly greetings, buzzing in anticipation of the feast to come.

≈

Dusk was settling over the empty training grounds. Karna put an arrow to the bow and let it fly; it hit the target a thumb's width off the bullseye. He pulled another shaft from the quiver, pulled the bow taut, and released. When that one also went a touch wide, he swore under his breath and looked up at the graying sky, hands on his hips.

"Even you can't shoot in the dark, my f-friend."

Duryodhana was standing alone on the south side of the arena, one foot propped on the low brick wall, forearm resting on knee. Underneath his furred black cloak he was wearing the black vest with the red flames embroidered by his great-grandmother. On his head was the garnet crown of the Kuru kings. He was laughing, lightly.

Karna shrugged, laughing in reply. "In my dreams I can hit it with my eyes closed." He faced the target, closed his eyes, and pointed. "I can feel it. I don't need to see it."

Then he seemed to recall himself. He opened his eyes, turned, and made a correct bow. "Sire. Why are you not at the feast?"

Duryodhana stepped over the wall and came toward him. "I snuck out to visit Astika. She's cross with me for not letting her come to the hall."

"Ah." Karna smiled. "The women are easily crossed. How old is the princess, now?"

"Fourteen, nearly fifteen. 'Old enough!' she says. But she's still unmarried, so of course it's not p-possible. I took her some honey cakes; they're her favorite."

"And was she mollified?"

"Not entirely. She hates to miss the bards." The scarred face stretched in its lopsided grin. "But she was glad of the cakes."

The two men went together to the target. Duryodhana helped Karna pull out the arrows and restock the quiver; Karna retrieved his cloak and slung it over one shoulder. They headed across the grounds toward the weapons shed. Shouts and snatches of song wafted from the great hall as they walked side by side.

"So, tomorrow," said Duryodhana, "Krishna's going to try and negotiate better terms for the Pandavas. That's why he's here."

"Yes," said Karna.

"Whatever he suggests, I'm going to turn him down."

"I see," said Karna. They stepped over the wall on the north side of the square.

"We're strong enough now," said Duryodhana. "We don't have to p-put up with their nonsense. They made a deal—that is," (he chuckled) "their *w-wife* made a deal. In any case, I expect them to stick to it. If not, we go to war."

Karna said nothing.

"I assume you agree?" Duryodhana skirted a small mound of horse dung.

"That we're strong enough?" said Karna. "Yes, certainly. Our forces are more than a match for theirs now."

The other gave him a sharp look. "But you don't agree we should go to war."

Again, Karna said nothing.

They walked along the alley between weapons shed and barn. Karna went around and into the shed. He hung his quiver on a peg, donned his cloak, fastened it across his chest with the gold loops of braid, and slung his bow across his back. He exited the shed to find Duryodhana blocking his path.

"How many times do I have to tell you to speak your damn m-m-mind?"

Karna stopped in his tracks. His shoulders went back, his hands went to his sides, and he fixed his gaze on a spot just over the king's head. "I apologize, my lord. I have offended you."

Duryodhana rolled his eyes. "For Gods' sake. You always act like a sulky girl. Do I have to order you? *Out with it.*"

Karna hesitated. Away north by the roasting pits, the dicing pavilion was a dark outline in the twilight. Some crows came flapping down onto its slatted roof and perched there, croaking.

Karna dropped his eyes to look his friend in the face. "You want to know my mind? All right. I think going to war is insane. I think you're letting your passions rule you, as usual."

Duryodhana's eyes narrowed. "My passions do not rule me."

Karna turned away and laid one hand on the wall of the shed. "Yes, Duryo, they do. *All* your decisions come from passion. Like this decision to make Ramesha high priest instead of Vaishamya. Why would you do that? Vaishamya has been bred to that role, promised it since he was a baby. You took it away from him, and now he's your enemy till the day he dies. What purpose did that serve? And going to war with the Pandavas is the same. What purpose will it serve, except ..." He faced the king again, his eyes distraught. "... except to make more enemies and ... and feed your pride?"

Duryodhana crossed his arms and frowned. "Vaishamya is not

f-fit to be high priest. He has one arm. He's def ... deformed. That's a simple fact."

Karna took a deep breath, let it out, and said quietly:

"It's not because he's deformed. It's because he's Jaratka's son. *Her* son by *your* father. You can't bear to be reminded of that."

Duryodhana's scar flared red. His hand flew to his knife. Karna leaped back and his hand also gripped his knife. For several moments the two men confronted each other, bodies tensed.

Then Duryodhana loosed his hilt, dropping his shoulders. He gave the bottom of the red-flamed vest a tug. His eyes went to a spot on the ground by the wall of the barn.

"You're right. I can't b-bear to see Vaishamya. He reminds me of ..." He put the heel of one hand briefly to each eye. Then he shook his head. "But it's not the only reason. I also see Vaishamya for who he is. He takes after his seed-father; he's Tarashtra's son. He is nothing like his m-mother. He would have made a terrible high priest."

Karna said, "That may be, but by Law he's also your son. The son is his—"

"—who took the hand, yes, yes, I know. I don't care. I will never acknowledge him. I don't trust him."

"Well, you certainly can't trust him now. He's angry. He's been ill-used." Karna turned both palms up, conciliatory. "Duryo, listen. I know how you loved her. Believe me, I know. But you're thinking only of yourself. It's not what a king does."

Duryodhana's jaw clenched. He rounded on Karna and jabbed a stubby finger. "You're a fine one to talk. Who have *you* been thinking of? Eh, Karna? Not your w-wife. Not Lady P-Padma. Don't you think *she's* been ill-used, with you mooning after another woman all these years? Running off every chance you get to cavort with the queen, the p-pretty queen of Indraprasta. Leaving your wife alone and childless. Oh, I'm sure you call it love. It's not. You want to f-fuck Draupadi, she wants to f-fuck you, and that's all there is to it. So you can get off your high horse. You have no idea w-what love is. *No* idea."

Karna drew himself up to his full height. "At least I have some taste. At least I set my sights on a queen, not on a ..." He broke off and looked at the ground.

Duryodhana's face grew hard with contempt. "You're an idiot, Karna. A jumped-up blades-boy, a charioteer's son who's been raised far above his station thanks to—oh, that's right—thanks to *me.* If it weren't for *me,* you'd still be setting up targets and scraping out deer carcasses at Panchala, jerking off at night to thoughts of some b-big-b-breasted court lady. As it is, you're commander-in-chief to the Kuru. The great kshatriya! Friend of the king! Lover of the queen! But I'm telling you, you're not f-fit to kiss the hem of her skirt. She has more courage and grace in her little f-f-f … *finger* than you have in your whole self."

"Who has?" Karna's lip curled. "Jaratka? Or Draupadi?"

Duryodhana took a sharp breath as if to bark a reply, but stopped. He looked again at the spot on the ground by the barn wall; he looked over his shoulder at the pavilion; then he looked back at Karna. He shrugged. "Both, I guess."

A burst of applause, mixed with cheers, came from the great hall; a bard must have just finished a song. All around, the evening shadows were dissolving into night.

Karna took a couple of steps forward. The two men were now standing side by side, one facing north, the other south.

Karna said, "After the Dicing, she told me she didn't want to see me again."

Duryodhana said nothing.

Karna said, "I can handle her being away. But knowing she doesn't want me …" He looked to his friend and said, "Why does she hate me? *You* did it to her. You and Dushasana. I tried to help her."

"She doesn't hate you. She just knows who … who she is."

Karna looked back at the pavilion. Neither man moved or spoke for some time.

Suddenly, and for no apparent reason, the crows on the roof lifted as one and flew off to the west, flapping and cawing. As if pulled by their flight, Karna revolved a quarter turn to face the king. He clapped his hands to his sides, threw back his golden-clad shoulders, and said in a clear voice: "Permission to withdraw, Sire."

Still looking straight ahead, the king gave a slight wave of the hand. "Permission granted."

The commander bowed, took two steps back, spun on his heel, and strode away.

≈

"Your majesty. Gentlemen. I cannot tell you how sorry I am that we've been unable to reach agreement today." Prince Krishna rose from his stool. "Perhaps we might meet again tomorrow? The benefit of a night's sleep ... the perspective a new day brings ..." He laid his fingertips together and smiled round at the men seated in the king's receiving room. His teeth were very white beneath his black mustache.

"Come back tomorrow if you like, Krishna," said the king, beckoning to a serving boy to refill his beer tankard. "You'll get the same answer."

Krishna's smile waned for an instant then waxed again. "Your resoluteness, Sire, is justly famed," he said with a dip of his head. "Might I presume to remind you, however, of another quality for which the Kuru kings have often been lauded? To wit: their *flexibility*. It is a quality held by only the greatest leaders. Take your father, Tarashtra, for example. His unfortunate lack of physical sight never prevented him from seeing all sides of a question. Indeed, he ..."

During this speech, Duryodhana had lifted his mug and drained it, never taking his eyes off the Vrishni prince. He then set the vessel down on the arm of his chair and let out a belch so loud and long it might have been mistaken for a bull breaking wind. Krishna stopped short, wincing as the blatting noise went on, and on ... finally dying away.

"Excuse me," said the king.

Krishna pursed his lips and looked round the company. The Kaurava men—Bhishma, Drona, Dushasana, Shakuna, and Karna—looked back at him blandly.

He inclined his head once more. "Your majesty," he said, "I will deliver your message." With a swish of his royal-blue cloak he turned and left the room, the guards at the door stepping aside to let him pass.

Dushasana and Shakuna, who were seated left and right of the king, broke into guffaws. Dushasana clapped his brother on the shoulder. "Good one, Duryo!" he said. "They won't forget that message in a hurry!" Duryodhana acknowledged the praise with a sideways glance.

There was a brief silence, which Drona broke: "Sire, they won't take this lying down. We must now expect them to go to war."

"Oh, yes," said the king. "That is what I expect."

"Then we need to make plans," said Drona.

The king handed his beer to the boy to take away. "Indeed," he said. "You know the Pandavas well, Drona. How long would you say we have?"

Drona thought for a moment. "Arjuna and Bima will want to move right away, but Yudi will counsel patience, and he'll be backed by Saku, not to mention Krishna. They'll need to muster troops from Matsya—that's their new ally, as you know, the result of Abimanyu's marriage—and that will take time. Then there's King Drupada; he may need convincing to throw his weight in. All in all, I'd say we have two, maybe three months."

"Better assume two," said the king. "Karna: can our troops be ready by then?"

"Yes, my lord," said Karna. "They are ready today."

"Good. But our own sixteen hundred won't be enough. We're going to need Madrasa with us. Lord Bhishma, what's your sense of where they stand?"

The former regent was sitting on Shakuna's right. His broad back was straight as a post, his white-haired chest still swelled with muscle, and the calves below his indigo dhoti were like two gourds. His deep voice had grown somewhat hoarse with age, but his answer came swiftly: "Madrasa won't hesitate if they believe there's wealth to be had. The key will be the iron mine; we'll need to promise them a share."

"Easy enough," said Duryodhana. "When we win, we can give Panchala's half-share to Madrasa. Will that satisfy them?"

Bhishma nodded. "I believe it will."

"Right. So we'll have Madrasa with us, and they've got ... Shakuna, how many troops, would you say?"

Shakuna gave his short-cropped beard a rub. "Only about eight hundred foot soldiers. Their cavalry is strong—four hundred. But chariots are where they really shine: they have more than two hundred."

"Excellent," said the king. "Together, then, we'll have some two thousand foot soldiers, seven hundred cavalry, and three hundred chariots. The Pandavas won't be able to match that, even with Panchala and Matsya joining them. Still, it would be nice to have a cushion." He looked again to Shakuna. "What about Gandaram? Any chance of bringing them in?"

Shakuna looked doubtful. "I don't see my big brother taking much interest in a southern war—as he'd call it. But," (he raised one finger) "he'd probably send horses."

"That's good!" said the king. "See what he'll do. If we've got more horses, we can deploy more chariots and mount more men."

"Where do we expect the fighting to take place?" asked Karna.

"Here, of course," said Dushasana. "They'll march on Hastinapura."

"We'll want to meet them in the western fields," said Karna. "We don't want fighting in or around the town."

Drona said, "There's a case to be made for meeting them at the Ganges. Our men will fight more fiercely with their backs to the water. It's additional motivation."

"It's not good for chariots, though," said Karna. "Chariots need open ground."

"Don't forget the war elephants," said Dushasana. "We have maybe five. How many does Madrasa have?"

Karna, Drona, and Dushasana debated on about the merits of various battle sites and strategies. Shakuna put in a word or two. Bhishma stayed silent, arms folded, looking at the floor.

"Lord Bhishma," said the king at length, "what is your opinion?"

Bhishma's eyes under their bristling white brows rose to meet Duryodhana's. In them was a light the other men hadn't seen in years.

"You're thinking too small," he said.

"Too small? How do you mean?"

Bhishma uncrossed his burly arms and leaned forward. "You're thinking we need to meet them where they come, and you're debating about a few feet left or right. The first rule of warfare is to choose the battlefield. *We* need to choose it. And it should not be here."

Dushasana took a breath to speak, but his brother held out a hand to silence him. "Go on, Uncle," he said.

"Chariots will be our strength," Bhishma continued, "and the commander is right ..." (he gave Karna a nod) "chariots need open ground. Archers, too. We'll want to fight on a wide, flat plain. It must be near water, obviously. And far from here, because if we lose ..."

Dushasana's chin jutted forward. "Lose? We're not *going* to lose!"

Bhishma ignored him and continued: "... if we lose, we don't want their army looting and raping in the town and villages hereabouts. Yes, Yudi would forbid it, but when soldiers have their blood up after a battle, it's often impossible to prevent such things."

The men were silent, listening.

"Finally," said Bhishma, "it should be a place where we know the terrain. A place at least one of our captains knows like the back of his hand."

He paused and looked round the group. "Those are the criteria; any suggestions?" His eyes now held a hint of amusement—or perhaps a challenge.

"Kurukshetra," said the king. "The plain west of the iron mine."

Bhishma nodded. "That's it."

"But," said Karna, "to take our whole army off, leaving Hastinapura undefended ..." He tugged on one of his earrings. "I don't know; isn't that unwise?"

"Not at all," said Bhishma. "As long as the Pandavas are aware of our superior numbers, they'll know they cannot spare even a dozen men to ride on Hastinapura."

"Yes," said Duryodhana, "so we must make them aware, and we must ensure our numbers truly are superior. Again," (his fingers drummed) "I wish we had more of a cushion."

"Kashi," said Bhishma.

"What? What about Kashi?"

"Kashi will come in with us," said Bhishma. "They're a poor clan begging to be swallowed up by a richer one. The only reason they haven't been crushed is the protection supplied by the Kuru. You're the grandson of a Kashi princess. Our alliance with them goes back sixty years, and for that whole time, we—that is to say, I—have honored it. A Pandava regime would be far less likely to honor it. Kashi knows it's in their interest to back us."

Duryodhana was nodding, slowly. "Yes. Yes. But—as you say, they're a p-poor clan, so surely they can't contribute much?"

Bhishma shrugged. "They're numerous enough. For a few generations they haven't been starving, thanks to the cattle I gave them in exchange for Chit's brides. They could muster four hundred sword- and spear-men, I think. That will bring our infantry up to twenty-four hundred."

Duryodhana smiled. "I see that once again, Uncle, your foresight has served us well."

The regent inclined his head.

Duryodhana regarded Bhishma for a moment longer, his fist to his chin. Then he placed both hands on the arms of his chair, looked round the group, and said: "Good. I think we're clear on the overall plan. The only thing left to decide is our captains."

Karna, who had been examining his sword hilt, looked up.

"Lord Karna," said the king, with a nod in his direction, "has been our commander-in-chief for the past several years. Over that time, he and the chief weapons master together have trained our troops to be second to none. In this coming war, I would like you, Drona, to lead the chariots." He paused, looking down at his lap. "Karna: I w-want you in charge of the ar ... archers, naturally."

Karna's brow creased. His mouth fell open.

The king took a breath and went on: "Ashwattama, who as you all know has been supervising the iron field these past few years, I will place at the head of the cavalry; his horsemanship is exceptional, as is his knowledge of the terrain. Shakuna, we will need you for battlefield intelligence. My brother and I will lead the infantry.

"That leaves the question of who is to be our general and supreme commander. Uncle B-Bhishma: I would like it to be you."

Bhishma appeared taken aback. His bristling brows arched; he looked from the king, to Karna, and back again. "Lord Karna is commander-in-chief," he said.

"Indeed, and as I say," said Duryodhana, "we owe him m-much gratitude. However ..." He looked down again, thrusting his head forward. "We must consider whose *capacities* are best suited to the ... to the circumstances. We face a war of unprecedented scope and signif ... significance. I need our b-b-b- ... b-b- ... *best man* in the lead."

His hands gripped the chair arms; his head came up; his eyes went briefly to Karna. Then he twisted his torso, turning his back to the commander and facing the regent full-on.

"Lord Bhishma: Do you accept the position?"

Bhishma still looked perturbed. "I'm eighty-two, Duryo," he said.

"I know that. And I know that with you at the head of our army, we will win."

Bhishma sat for three more beats, one thumb hooked in his bronze-studded leather belt, the other hand resting on his powerful thigh. Then he stood up, bowed low to the king, and said: "It will be my great honor and pleasure, your majesty."

After a little more discussion of strategy and tactics, the meeting broke up. Karna, after making his bow, began to walk out.

"Karna," said the king.

Karna stopped.

"Nothing personal," said the king.

Karna refaced the chair and made a second bow. Upon rising, he met the king's eye and said: "Of course not, Sire. I understand perfectly."

With a swish of his golden cloak, he turned and left the room.

≈

In the long clearing in the forest—the same one where twenty-one years ago the Snake man Ekalavya, still possessed of both thumbs, used to go practice his archery—the arrows flew at the trunk of the babul tree, one after another: *whizz, thunk, whizz, thunk.* Eight of them formed a perfect circle, perfectly spaced; the ninth one flew and hit the exact center of the ring, its tawny-feathered end vibrating. Karna lowered his bow and regarded his work.

"It is as I always say." The cultured voice was pleasant, admiring. "No one, not even Arjuna, can beat the Golden Warrior."

Karna looked to his right as Krishna stepped out of the shadow of the trees.

"Please, don't let me disturb you," said Krishna, smiling. "You don't mind if I watch? I'll be quiet as a fallen leaf." He leaned against a deodar tree, crossing one ankle over the other.

Karna shook his head. "I don't mind," he said. He turned back to the target, plucked the tenth and final arrow from the quiver, fitted it to the bowstring, raised the bow, pulled, and fired. This one hit just a hair above the central arrow, its feathers mingling with its companion's.

"Oh, well done!" cried Krishna, applauding. When Karna glanced at him, he held up both hands and said, "Sorry. Sorry. I promised I'd be quiet."

"It's all right," said Karna. "That's the end of the round, anyway. Got to retrieve the arrows." He started off toward the tree.

"Allow me," said Krishna, hastening over. He beat Karna to the tree and began to pull out the arrows. When Karna came up, he motioned to him to turn around; he refilled the quiver, inserting each shaft with care. "Bit chilly for the end of the year, isn't it?" he said as they started back across the clearing. "I nearly brought my winter cloak. Really, I wish I had."

Karna stopped and said, "Prince Krishna. Why have you come to see me?"

Krishna walked on a few paces then stopped, too. He turned to face Karna, smiling again. "Because," he said, "I have some information for you."

"Information? About what?"

"About you, Karna. About who you are. About who you might become."

The commander frowned. "What are you saying, Krishna? If this is some trick to try and get me to spill Kuru secrets, you can take yourself off. I'm not that stupid."

Krishna's expression turned serious. "Nothing of the kind. Believe me, Karna; I do not think you're stupid. And it's *because* you're not stupid that I think you'll be very interested in what I have to say."

≈

The two men had walked down to the Ganges and now stood on the strand, looking out over the water sparkling in the late-winter sunlight.

"He relies on me," said Karna.

"Not enough to put you in charge, evidently," said Krishna with a twist of the lips. "Doesn't sound like reliance to me."

"He made me kshatriya."

"He didn't *make* you kshatriya. You *are* kshatriya. You are Perta's natural son and Pandu's legal son: their eldest son. That means you're the highest-ranking Pandava. The throne of Indraprasta—nay, of Kuru, the entire clan—is yours by right."

"Yudi won't like it. None of them will like it."

"It doesn't matter whether they like it or not; it's the Law. But in actual fact, I believe Yudi *will* like it." The white-toothed smile flashed. "He doesn't really want to be king, you know. None of them do. They just don't want to be pushed aside."

Karna said nothing.

"And besides," Krishna went on, "Draupadi will like it. She'll like it very much. Isn't that what matters most?"

"She doesn't want me anymore. She said so."

"Tush," said the prince with a flick of his long, slender fingers. "She was just angry after the Dicing. You can hardly blame her. But she's over it now, I know she is. She told me."

Karna looked at him with eyes wide. "She told you? What did she tell you?"

"That she still loves you. That she wishes she could be with you. Oh, yes: she'll dance with joy if it turns out you can be her number-one husband. Trust me."

Karna looked down, chewing his lower lip. "But ..."

"But what, Karna?"

"What will everyone think? If I go over to the Pandava side ... betray Duryodhana, right before we go to war ... I'll be seen as a traitor. What will everyone say?"

"Oh, dear, no. No, no. You've misunderstood me. I'm not suggesting you should do anything *now.* That would be terribly foolish."

"Then what ...?"

"I'm suggesting, Karna, that for now you should say nothing. Keep your counsel. Go along with the king, just as usual. And then, during the battle—at the appropriate time—find a means of swinging things in our direction." He laid a hand on Karna's shoulder. "I won't presume to tell you how. You're so clever; you'll figure out a way. And *then,* you see, once the Pandavas have won, we'll be free to announce who you are and the role you played in their victory. Trust me; you'll be welcomed with cheers and open arms. As for what the Kauravas will say ... well. They'll be defeated. They won't have much to say about anything."

A kingfisher with back and wings of brilliant teal and breast of saffron gold flew up the river from the south. As it drew near them it veered off to the other side of the water and alit on a high branch of a thorn bush, presenting its elongated beak in profile. Karna took a few steps down the strand, drawing an arrow from the quiver as he did so. He lifted his bow and aimed. But he did not fire; instead, after a moment, he lowered bow and arrow and stood gazing at the bird with its tuft of blue-green feathers rising from its head like a crown.

Krishna came up beside him. "Of course," he said, "you should stick with the Kauravas if you think it best. You'll probably win the war. In that case, the Pandavas will be dead, and you can go on being Duryodhana's faithful friend. As for Draupadi ..." He sighed. "I can't predict what she'll do. She's a very strong-minded woman; I don't imagine she'll look kindly on those who denied her sons a kingdom. Then again, it won't really matter what she thinks, will it? She'll be utterly disgraced. She'll have to go into an ashram."

He turned to walk up the strand—then, as if with a sudden afterthought, turned back. "Although, knowing her, I suspect she'll make the noble choice and burn herself on her husbands' pyre."

He pulled his royal-blue cloak across his chest. "Goodness, this chill wind! It's been lovely chatting with you, Karna, but I simply must get back to the palace and warm up. You'll let me know your decision, won't you? No rush." He began to walk away.

"Krishna!" It was a yelp of despair.

The tall prince stopped and turned again, smiling pleasantly. "Yes?"

"I'll do it."

I know, Nephew, I know! Who would have thought that Karna, faithful Karna, would be the one to betray the Kauravas? And yes, you are correct: that is not how the story is told today. In the official version we hear today, Karna refuses the proposal, so blindly loyal is he to his villainous master, Duryodhana.

But by now you no doubt realize that the official version of the story began with our very own Vaishamya: my one-armed half-brother, who when he became high priest changed his name to Vaishampayana since *Vaishamya* means "Lopside" in the common tongue. Oh, yes: he was made high priest to the Kuru quite soon after the war's end. More on that later. For now I'll just note that it was he, as high priest, who first proclaimed my father an incarnation of the demon Kali (not the Goddess Kali), the Pandavas incarnations of various Gods, and our family history a struggle between good and evil, with my father representing the latter. Vaishamya spun that first thread; the bards picked it up and wove the legend from there.

I was in the Hall of Sacraments for Ramesha's installation

ceremony. I saw Vaishamya's face; saw the silent curse he flung at
my father as he walked down the aisle. I remember wondering at it.
I was only fourteen, though, and caught up in my own resentment
that I would not be allowed to go to the feast that evening and would
therefore miss the performance of a famous bard, a woman, who had
traveled in from Vrishni and whom I particularly wanted to hear. I
remember my father bringing me the honey cakes. I was quite rude
to him, as I recall. I would have been nicer had I known he had less
than three months to live.

But no one knows the future, do they, Janamejaya? The future is
dark, obscure. It lies behind us, and until we grow eyes in the back
of our head, it will remain unseen. The past, on the other hand, lies
before us: a flow of people and events we can watch pass by, vivid as a
wedding parade, bright as a river in sunlight, colorful as a kingfisher's
plumage.

There are a few individuals—Vidura may have been one—to
whom are given glimpses of the future as if they were the past.
Vidura said he stepped outside his tent in the dawn and saw two
mighty armies meeting on the plain of Kurukshetra. I think it was
these flashes of foresight, coming more often as he aged, that made
him humble: humbly aware that no matter how he tried it would
not change events to come and that therefore he should not try. He
did believe there were some men (and one woman, dressed as a man)
who could perform world-changing deeds, but he did not believe
he was among them. So he remained at Indraprasta: judging the
people's disputes, keeping the palace roof patched and the sewage
ditches cleared, taking no part in the great discussions and preparations underway at Hastinapura.

On the seventh day of the second month, a messenger arrived
with a summons for Vidura to return. He packed his few belongings
and set out, bringing the three men of his bodyguard with him but
sending Shikhandi to join the regular troops at the iron mine. Upon
arriving home, he found a huge army encamped on the field west of
town: swordsmen and spearmen, archers and cavalry, chariots with
their charioteers. At the far end, a makeshift paddock held several
war elephants. The banners of Kuru, Madrasa, and Kashi fluttered in
the breeze. Approaching the compound, he was overtaken by a scout
galloping up the road; entering the gate, he saw manservants and
stewards, priests and messenger boys hurrying to and fro across the

yard. He went to the council chamber, where Duryodhana, Bhishma, and the other Kaurava men were intent on a map drawn on cowhide, laid across the table.

"Ah, Uncle Vidu," said the king, looking up as he entered. "Come, we need your help. We march for Kurukshetra tomorrow. You know the area well; at this time of year, where is the best place to pitch camp? We'll need w-water, which suggests we should stay by the Yamuna, but then there's this other stream that runs north of the field, behind these hills ..."

So the stage was set for war.

Chapter 18

SHIKHANDI

S hikhandi said:

The nearly full moon slid behind a cloud, leaving the world black as I made my way up the slope through the thick trees. I told myself to slow down; I could do no good for the Pandavas if I arrived at their camp with a sprained ankle—or worse, never arrived, having knocked myself unconscious on a tree branch in the dark.

The war had been going on for five days. Ashwattama, when I'd reported to him thirteen days ago at Kurukshetra, had assigned me to the cavalry under his direct command. I had seen no action as yet, however. He had said he would keep me in the reserves to be deployed "only if needed," and so far the reserves weren't needed, because the Kauravas were doing well. I was a little disappointed, but then fighting for the Kauravas had never been my intent, and sitting out meant I could wait and watch for an opportunity to run—which was what I was doing now.

I had a general idea where the Pandavas' camp was. They—I should say *we,* for as far as I was concerned the Pandavas were now "we" and the Kauravas "they"—*we* the Pandavas were based on the east side of the iron field, in a series of clearings that lay on the broad, heavily wooded slope rising up from the Yamuna river. The Kaurava troops were situated to the north, their tents spread along a tributary stream that also ran through forest, though not such dense forest; they were a little farther away from the battleground, roughly half a kosa, with a line of low hills between them and the fighting. When I left the Kaurava camp an hour after dark, my plan was to follow the stream east until it hit the Yamuna, turn south and follow the main river until I sensed the mine pits were directly to my right, then turn west and make my way up the wooded slope with the expectation of eventually running into the Pandavas. With caution and some luck, I would reach my goal before midnight.

But haste (as usual) did me in. I must have made all the noise of a wounded stag, puffing and snorting as I crashed through the bracken. When I heard a "Halt! Who goes there?" and felt the point of a spear pressing my sternum, I could only think to gasp out, "A friend!" which of course did nothing to reassure the two sentries of my good intentions. Before I knew it my sword was wrenched from my belt, my hands were tied behind my back, and I was being hustled along without respite. *Well,* I thought, *at least I'll get there faster.* Since they did not blindfold me, I made an effort to note, as best I could in the dark, the path we were taking. Observation, unlike stealth, is one of my strong points.

In half an hour we arrived at a clearing with some twenty tents spread around. I was marched to the central one, which had the Indraprasta banner set atop it. "What have you got there?" asked the guard. "A Kaurava spy," said the first sentry. "And a damn shitty one," said the second; "he made enough noise for a whole army." The guard went into the tent. Presently he reemerged and held the flap open for the three of us to go within.

The light given off by many oil lamps hanging from the roof poles blinded me for a minute. As my eyes adjusted, I saw five, six … no, seven lords seated on cushions around a table bearing many supper dishes. I recognized Arjuna and Bima at once. Yudi, Naku, and Saku I could also identify, as I used to glimpse them here and there around Indraprasta. Prince Krishna I recognized, too. The seventh man was unfamiliar to me: slender with dark hair and pale skin, a narrow nose and full lips, almost girlish in his good looks.

They looked at me with mild curiosity as I was pushed down onto my knees.

"These Kaurava spies are the worst," said Naku. "What is this— the third one we've caught?"

"Fourth," said Bima, chewing a large mouthful. "Seriously, they need lessons."

"Take him away," said Yudi with a wave of the hand. "Hang him with the others." They turned back to their food and drink. My captors made to lift me up by the armpits.

"No, wait!" I kept my voice pitched high. "I'm not a spy. I've come to join you. I'm Shikhandi."

They all looked at me again, this time with surprise.

"What on earth?" said Krishna. "Is that a *woman?*" He got up from the table, came over to me, took my chin in his hand, and tilted my face up to the light. "It is!" he said. "A woman, in man's dress!" His black-mustached mouth twisted in disgust. "These Kauravas; they'll stoop to anything. Who are you, girl, and what do you think you're doing?"

"I'm Shikhandi," I said. "Please, my lord. I am no spy. Prince Arjuna ... he knows me." I leaned to one side, trying to catch his eye.

"By Indra!" Arjuna was also leaning sideways, peering at me from his seat. "I can't believe it. Is that the little girl from the chaupadi hut?"

"Yes, my lord. It's me. Shikhandi." I felt dizzy with relief.

"Shikhandi," he said, nodding slowly. "That's right. Hey, Bima, what do you think? Here's our little warrior girl, all grown up. Remember her?"

Bima set down his beer mug. "Can't say that I do. Oh, wait ... wait." He stared hard at me. "Yep, I remember now. The gawky one. Ha! You gave her fight lessons."

Arjuna's nodded again, smiling. "I did ... I did indeed." One finger stroked his clean-shaven chin. The ivory beads on his chest glowed in the light of the oil lamps. I found him as entrancing as I had all those years ago.

"So you're a soldier now, Shikhandi?" he asked.

"Yes, my lord," I said.

"How ... no, never mind. It doesn't matter. You say you've come to join our side?"

"Yes, Sir," I said. "I want to fight for the Pandavas. Please."

He, along with the others, regarded me a few moments longer. Then, "Untie her hands," he said to my captors. They did. "Dismissed," he said. They bowed and left.

"Lads," he said looking round the group, "this is a friend of mine. An old friend. I'll vouch for her." He turned again to me and beckoned with a smile. "You must be hungry, Shikhandi. Come, have some food."

Now that I was no longer in fear of imminent death, I was noticing the aroma of the supper dishes and remembering I hadn't eaten since early that morning. I got up, went to the table, and sat down on the cushion Arjuna indicated. It was next to him, but at one corner and a little in the shadows; I was glad of that, for I was feeling overwhelmed and would just as soon be inconspicuous for a while. I applied myself to the dish that was passed to me: beef stew, vegetables with curds, and roti. None of the men seemed inclined to give me any further attention, and looking back on it, I can see why: once Arjuna had introduced me as an "old friend," they would have assumed I was just one of his many mistresses—an unusual one, to be sure, but of little interest nonetheless.

"Tadyu, please continue." King Yudi turned to the slender, dark-haired man on his left, who I now realized must be Prince Tadyu, twin brother of Queen Draupadi and second-in-command of the Pandava joint forces. "You were giving us your report."

"Yes," said Tadyu, "as I was saying: I'm afraid the news is not good. We did well on the first day, but since then, not so well. Our lesser numbers have been a detriment. Our troops are a match for theirs in skill, and of course in courage, but without the sheer numbers it's difficult to prevail. For example, yesterday morning our cavalry challenged theirs to a head-to-head in the saranam formation, and ..."

He went on at length about the moves and countermoves each side had made in the main battles, with further description of the duels and side skirmishes and their outcomes. As I ate my food and listened, I felt a surge of pride that we were all Arya: Arya, who know what it is to make war with honor—unlike the indigenes, who fight like animals. Indigenes will set ambushes in the forest, make attacks at night, even burn villages and run away. A true kshatriya views that sort of thing as beneath contempt; our battles are conducted according to the warrior's code, with rules of engagement and open, formal challenges. An Arya captain would no more think of flinging his troops at the enemy in some sort of hideous free-for-all, or using low methods to gain an advantage, than he would think of hacking a foe to pieces as he slept in his bed.

Those were my thoughts as Prince Tadyu talked on. I was sopping up gravy with my last bit of roti when I heard him say, "... but for all that, our real problem is that our commander-in-chief ..." He paused.

"Yes?" said Arjuna, looking up from his dish. His voice was soft, almost a whisper. "What about our commander-in-chief?"

Tadyu glanced away. Then he looked back at Arjuna and spoke

firmly. "Our real problem is that our commander-in-chief has been absent from the field."

Arjuna took a swig of beer and dabbed his mouth with his napkin. His voice remained soft and pleasant as he replied:

"We have discussed this, Tadyu. We have decided that at this stage, I am needed for strategic oversight. When I am needed on the field—*if* I am needed—then I will deploy."

Tadyu's eyes remained steady. "I believe you are needed now, Sir."

"Really?" said Arjuna. His voice, still pleasant, went a notch higher in volume. "That's your assessment, is it? That I, the commander-in-chief, should rush down and join the fray? Flail around in the dirt with the rest of the grunts? That's where you think I'm best used?"

"Not at all," said Tadyu. "I would have you in a chariot. The men need to see you. They need your leadership."

"Leadership. Ah. I see. So you're saying that *your* leadership, Tadyu, is insufficient. You're saying that you and all our fine captains are incapable of leading a battle on your own."

"Yes," said Tadyu, "that is what I'm saying. I'm saying we need your help."

"My help!" The voice grew strident. "My *help!* You think you have not had my help? All the direction I provide—you're saying that's not helpful? I see. I see. Since this war began I've done nothing but plan formations, consult with our intelligence officers, construct strategy after strategy. Not to mention provide *you* with guidance— much more guidance, I might add, than would be necessary with a competent second-in-command. I've caught no more than two hours of sleep each night. I have barely taken time to eat. But I see now that none of that is *helpful.*"

Tadyu was looking discomfited. "I ... no, I did not mean that at all. I only meant ..."

"That you want more *help*. Right."

I was feeling a little confused by this exchange. On the one hand, it seemed wrong that Arjuna hadn't been on the field; I knew he was the best and bravest kshatriya of our day and that he, like all great kshatriya, lived for the joy of battle. On the other hand, what he'd said about oversight and strategy made sense to me; after all, those are a general's job.

Yudi leaned forward. His voice was even-toned, soothing: "Arjuna, you're right: we need you as our mastermind. No question. Nevertheless, I must point out that all of us—Bima, Naku, Saku, and I—have also been contributing to the plans, and yet we have all taken the field at appropriate times; why, even Krishna has had a turn or two with the chariots. It's important, if only to inspire the men. And you know none of us can inspire as *you* do."

I was shocked to see Arjuna's face become downright sulky. He slumped, stirring his food with his spoon, and said, "Oh, well, Yudi. If that's what you want, I'm only too happy to oblige. If I had *my* way, I'd be in every skirmish. I was only thinking of what's best for the side." He put down his spoon and rubbed one shoulder. "One thing, just so you know: that old injury of mine has been acting up. I guess it's the lack of sleep. I wasn't going to mention it, because I didn't want to worry you ..." He winced, still rubbing. "But it doesn't matter. I'll do as you say, of course."

The other men glanced at one another with concerned expressions. Naku whispered something to Saku. Bima took a few mouthfuls of stew.

Only Krishna, at the other end of the table, kept on looking at Arjuna. He was sitting up very straight with mouth a little open, brow creased. I wondered what had distressed him. It popped into my mind (strange, these things that pop into our minds) that he looked like a man watching a God transform into a demon. Or a vermin. Something horrible, anyway.

Saku spoke up. "If you can't pull a bow, Juna, you should not be on the field."

Arjuna lunged forward, slamming both hands down. "*I can pull a fucking bow!* Gods! What I *can't* do is deal with the idiots at this table!"

"Arjuna, Arjuna." Krishna's demeanor had undergone a rapid change: he was smiling now, sitting at ease, and his voice was smooth. "I believe I know the *real* problem."

"Oh?" Arjuna sat back, looking wary. "What problem is that?"

"It's your charioteer. What's his name—Pushta? Pushtu?"

"Pushtu."

"Yes, him. He's been with you a long time, and you're too tactful to say anything, but I've seen him at work. What is he: Fifty-five? Sixty?"

Arjuna shrugged.

"In any case," Krishna continued, "he's well past his prime. And you feel loyalty to him, which does you credit; you don't want to push him aside. But you're concerned about taking the field with him at the reins. Not for your own safety, of course; for his. Now, tell the truth, my friend: Isn't that what's holding you back?"

Arjuna's eyes were still wary, but he nodded. "Yes … yes. It's true. I *have* been thinking about Pushtu. He's been with me a long time. He's almost like a father to me. I don't want him hurt. No, I don't want him hurt."

"Indeed, and as I say, your feelings do you credit. But we must not let fine feelings stand in the way of our success. Now, listen, Arjuna: I have a proposal. I want to propose that we retire Pushtu and get you another charioteer."

Arjuna made a scoffing noise. "Who? It's not as if we have charioteers to spare."

"Me," said Krishna. "I'll be your charioteer."

Arjuna's lips shut tight. His eyes shifted to and fro. Another strange thought came to my mind: *He looks,* I thought, *like a man trapped.*

"Just like the old days, eh?" said Krishna, cocking his head and smiling more broadly. "What do you say, my friend? Shall we show them how it's done?"

Arjuna looked down at the table and said nothing.

What I did next … I don't know what came over me, except that I was feeling much better having had some food and was recalling the whole point of my venture: to join up with the Pandavas and fight for them. To help them win—to help *Arjuna* win. I opened my mouth and heard myself say: "Let me do it. I'll drive the chariot."

The men all jumped and stared in my direction. They had surely forgotten I was there.

"Uh … what?" said Tadyu.

"She's had too much to drink," said Saku. Nods and chuckles ensued.

"All right, warrior girl," said Bima, leaning across the table and ruffling my hair with his massive paw. "That's enough beer for you."

"Maybe she feels like entertaining us before we go to bed," said Naku with a grin. "You wouldn't mind, Juna, would you?" This met with more chuckles.

"For Gods' sake, Arjuna," said Yudi, pinching the bridge of his nose. "Get rid of her, would you? We're discussing serious matters, here."

Arjuna, however, had held up one hand to forestall any more comments. He was looking at me with a curious expression. It occurred to me it was the same expression he'd had long ago in the clearing near the chaupadi hut—right before he'd remarked, "We could train her."

"I remember now," he said. "You're Bhishma's granddaughter."

"Yes, my lord," I said.

"Can you actually drive a chariot?"

"Yes, Sir. For the past three years I've trained with the men of Indraprasta. Our weapons master insisted we all learn to drive, just in case we ever had to take the reins. Not that I'm a charioteer," I added, lifting my chin slightly. "I'm kshatriya."

"Yes, I know," said Arjuna. He still had that musing look. "Your grandfather, Lord Bhishma. Is he well? I mean, you've seen him since you were a girl?"

I didn't know what he was getting at, but it was not my place to ask. "Yes, Sir," I said. "I've seen Lord Bhishma now and then at the family gatherings—at Hastinapura and at Indraprasta. I used to go, sometimes, with my husband. That was before …" I looked down at my soldier's garb.

"*Arjuna,*" said Yudi.

"Hold on, brother." Arjuna patted the air with his hand. "I have an idea. It's a good one. Strategic."

"Well? We're all ears."

"I'll tell you in a minute. But right now, I think we're being terribly rude to our guest." He leaned toward me, solicitous. "You must be exhausted, Shikhandi. Look, there's my sleeping mat." He pointed to the last in a line of five mats, heaped with blankets, situated to the left of the tent flap as one came in. "Go on, now. You go lie down and take a nap. We'll all get out of here and leave you alone so you can get some rest. And in the morning …" He smiled his gorgeous smile. "… in the morning, you'll get your chance to help us win this war."

I wanted to protest—curling up on the captain's sleeping mat is certainly not the way of a warrior—but did not dare. Anyway, he was right: I was exhausted, and nothing seemed better to me at that moment than the chance to be horizontal with eyes closed. I got up, went to the mat, lay down on my side, and pulled the blankets up to my neck. Almost at once, I was asleep.

≈

It must have been after moonset but still well before dawn when I awoke. I had been dreaming about chariots: two chariots with two drivers racing in slow motion down a long dark plain that ended in a cliff. I was screaming at them to turn, to stop, but (as is so often the case in dreams) my screams made no sound. Just before they went over the cliff, I opened my eyes. The tent interior was just as dark as the plain in my dream, except for the dim glow of one oil lamp that sat on the table end nearest to me; in its aura I could see the shapes of two men seated with heads close together. They were speaking in low voices. I strained my ears to listen.

"Arjuna, hear me. All you have to do is get yourself onto the battlefield. This fearful mood of yours: it's only a mood. It will pass."

I knew then that the two men were Arjuna and Krishna.

"I don't know how many times I need to tell you." Arjuna's voice was a thin hiss. "*I. Have. No. Fear.* I've simply figured out how to deal a crushing blow to the Kauravas. Why can't you appreciate that?"

"Because the means are contemptible, and you know it. Using a woman as a shield? Good Gods, Arjuna. It's something savages would do."

"I can't imagine a savage doing anything of the sort. They haven't the wits."

"That's not the point. Please, you must listen to me. Have I ever steered you wrong? Have I ever thought of anything but you, you and your brothers, and what's best for you? I'm telling you, this is a mistake. You are kshatriya. A kshatriya does not behave thus. Your reputation is at risk."

"My reputation! What am I, the tawdry third wife of a silk trader? We're trying to win a war, here."

"Your honor, then. Consider your honor."

"Honor comes with victory. Victory is what I care about."

"Fine. Then get on the field. That's all anyone is asking. Use me as your charioteer, use Pushtu, use some other man, it doesn't matter. What matters is that you engage; that you pull yourself together and *fight*. Listen, my friend, my dearest friend," (he laid a hand on

Arjuna's shoulder) "you've worked your whole life for this. All the training with bow and sword and spear—all the hunting, the chariot practice—this is what it's all *for*. And no one is better at it than you. This is your chance to show everyone your mastery! I know it feels strange, the first time you face a real war and death is a possibility, but you'll see, I promise: once you get out there, with an arrow to the bow and the screams of your dying foes resounding in your ears, you'll feel ... immortal. Like a God. *Fear* will be the furthest thing from your mind."

I heard Arjuna's teeth grinding. "I warn you, Krishna. If you say that word one more time, our friendship is at an end. I *warn* you."

Krishna drew his hand back. There was a pause. Then he said:

"Very well. You're the commander-in-chief. If this is what you're set on doing, I can't stop you."

He got to his feet. I shut my eyes, lest he should see the lamp-light reflecting off them as he walked out.

≈

Over breakfast, Arjuna explained to me that he had challenged one of the Kaurava captains to a duel, a chariot duel, and that I would be his charioteer.

"Now this is only if you're willing, Shikhandi," he said, pouring more hot broth into my cup. "You don't have to do it. But I would like you to do it."

"Of course I'll do it, my lord. I am deeply honored." I meant it with all my heart.

"Good, good. I've made enquiries, you know; I hear impressive things of you. And we make a great team, don't we? Remember back in the day—our practice sessions in the clearing? And those talks we used to have, about the warrior's code?"

"Yes, Sir. I remember. I want you to know that ..." (I gulped at my own presumption) "that you can rely on me."

He reached out and gripped my forearm. "I know I can, Shikhandi. You're my brother-in-arms. I've never forgotten."

He did not tell me who our adversary would be, and I did not ask. He did say, however, that the duel would use the parallel joust method, which is when two chariots, starting at one end of a long field, drive toward each other then turn and run side by side, the two kshatriya shooting arrows as they race along. The strategy lies in how close to get to the other chariot; the closer you get, the more likely you are to hit your man, but the more likely he is to hit you, as well. Arjuna said he wanted me to get quite close to our opponent: "Close enough to see the whites of his eyes," he said. When I wondered aloud whether it might be better to stay back, given that he was certainly the superior archer, he shook his head, frowning: "No, soldier. You must leave the tactics to me. You just get us as near as you can." I agreed at once, feeling ashamed to have questioned him.

I had worn my bronze helmet when I'd left the Kaurava camp, but not my bronze breastplate; I'd been worried it might weigh me down. Arjuna supplied me with another and saw that my sword was returned to me. He himself had a splendid helmet and breastplate of silver inlaid with ivory, along with his impressively large bow— he told me its name, *Gandiva*—and his quiver full of long arrows fletched with peacock feathers. Thus equipped, we set off for the battlefield on a couple of utility horses. (The chariots and warhorses were kept in a staging area behind the lines.) Yudi, Naku, and Saku rode with us, along with Arjuna's personal bodyguard, none of whom gave me a second glance. Tadyu and Bima, I was told, had left at dawn for a skirmish between the infantries: Tadyu to oversee the fray, Bima to join it.

It took a quarter of an hour to ride up the long wooded slope from the Yamuna and another half hour to make our way down the steep rocky escarpment to the iron field, past the mine pits with the forge shed amidst them, and along the south side of the vast, treeless plain toward our troops' staging area. As we came near, I could see that the morning's engagement had concluded and that the infantry-men, sweaty and dirt-streaked, were now occupied with collecting the bodies of the dead: some forty on each side, by my rough count. The staging area teemed with men watering horses, polishing swords, tending the wounded, tending cooking fires, calling to their friends, shouting at blades-boys, sitting fanning themselves in the hot sun, eating, drinking, urinating, or hunkering over a dice game. (When the end of the world comes, I believe most men will see it as an opportunity to play dice.) Each had a white cloth band wrapping his bicep, the counterpart to the Kauravas' garnet.

In front of one tent sat Bimasena, his enormous hindquarters overflowing a campstool, his enormous spiked iron mace leaning against his leg as a healer applied a dressing to his side. Arjuna hailed him. He got up and came toward us.

"Been a good morning's work!" he said. "Looks like two score of ours to fifty of theirs. Got a little scratch, though." He clapped a hand to the bandage, grinning.

"Well done!" said Arjuna. "Is everything ready for us?"

"Think so," said Bima. "I know Tadyu delivered the challenge and they accepted." He waved a hand behind him. "Your chariot's been taken to the starting point. I told them to polish it up good."

"Excellent," said Arjuna. "We'll go along, then."

Leaving Yudi and the twins chatting with Bima, we rode on, followed by the bodyguards, and in another ten minutes reached the western end of the plain. Arjuna's chariot was waiting, his two white stallions already hitched; half a dozen grooms were swarming round checking bridles, rubbing rosin on the floorboards, and giving the bronze-inlaid sides a final buff. Prince Tadyu was there, as well; he dipped his head to Arjuna as we rode up.

"Commander," said Arjuna, dismounting and tossing his reins to a groom. I did the same. As with the guards, none of the grooms paid me any mind, and I was glad to be passing as a real charioteer. I thought about what I'd heard Krishna say last night: about how it was dishonorable for Arjuna to shield himself with a woman. *But no one realizes I'm a woman,* I thought. *They take me for a soldier—which I am. So where is the dishonor?*

Tadyu approached us. "We're all set," he said. "We begin at noon." I glanced upward; the sun was nearly at the zenith.

On the north side of the plain, directly across from us, I could just make out another chariot and team, also drawn up facing the field and also surrounded by a milling group of men among which, I assumed, must be our opponent. The distance was too far to see who it was, though. I looked back eastward and saw that the troops, a few thousand on each side, had begun to line up along the field as along a parade route. I could hear a faint buzz rising from the throng. Feeling nervous, I tucked a stray lock of hair under my helmet.

"Come on, Shikhandi," said Arjuna. I went to the chariot, stepped up onto the boards, and put my hands on the ornately carved front ledge, feeling its curls and sweeps. I'd never been in such a fine vehicle; the chariots we had at the Indraprasta training grounds were of plain, uncarved wood, no more than boxes on wheels, with wooden axles that were inclined to snap. I had noted before getting into this one that the axle was made of iron. Arjuna got up behind me and called for his bow and quiver; these were brought to him by one of the guards. Then he called for a water-skin, and we both took a drink.

The sun was now at the top of the sky.

"Ready, Sir?" Tadyu asked.

"Ready," Arjuna said.

Tadyu set out across the plain at a brisk walk. At the same time, a man on the other side set out in the same way. A hundred and fifty paces later the two seconds met in the middle, bowed, and turned to stand side by side facing east.

"All right, Shikhandi," said Arjuna. He placed one hand on my shoulder, his mouth next to my ear. "Take us a little forward and wait for the signal. Now remember what I said: get us close, as close as you can."

"Yes, Sir." I took the reins and gave the horses' backs a light slap. They walked forward at once. They were beautifully trained; Arjuna had said there'd be no need for a whip, and he was right. I pulled up just where the sparse grass gave way to dust and gravel. Across the way, I saw our opponent's chariot pull up on the verge just as we had.

Tadyu and his counterpart, out at the center of the field, unwrapped the kerchiefs from their arms and raised them skyward: Tadyu's white, the other's dark red. The cloths dangled limply in the windless air.

A hush fell over the plain. My nervousness had gone, leaving me with only a keen sense of anticipation. I watched the kerchiefs.

Swoosh. Down they came in wheeling streaks. "*Ha!*" I yelled, slapping the reins down hard, and the white stallions leaped forward, manes flying. We thundered across the field, straight at our adversary. Closer we came, closer, closer … then I saw the other charioteer tug on his left set of reins to bring his team around, and I did the same, pulling my team to the right, bracing my feet and leaning left to take the force of the turn. In a moment we were galloping eastward down the plain on parallel tracks fifty paces apart.

My eyes were fixed between the horses' bobbing heads, on the lookout for obstacles; the plain was admirably flat, but there was the occasional rock or pothole that had the potential to tip the chariot if not avoided. I heard Arjuna say, "Closer! Get closer!" and I pulled

on the left reins to take a slight diagonal. Out of the corner of my
left eye I could see the other chariot holding a straight course. With
the gap narrowed to twenty paces I straightened out, too, but Arjuna
was still not satisfied; he urged me closer, and I complied. The horses
responded to my lightest touch. I was vaguely aware of cheers from
the distant sidelines.

We were about a quarter of the way down the plain and maybe
fifteen paces apart when I heard the whistle of an arrow behind my
shoulders. I realized our opponent had begun to shoot, and I focused
on keeping a steady pace to match his so that Arjuna could shoot
back. But he did not shoot back; instead he said, "Just a little closer,
Shikhandi. Come on, you can do it."

What madness is this, I thought. But I did as he asked, narrowing
the gap even more. A second arrow whistled past, this one just in
front of my chest.

The next moment I felt my helmet come off my head. My loosed
hair whipped my face. *I've been hit,* I thought. But there had been no
thud, no jolt, and now Arjuna was shouting, his voice rising above
the churn of hooves and wheels:

"Bhishma! Hey, Bhishma! Look who's here! Look who it is!"

I turned my head left. There, in the other chariot, was my
grandfather.

The horses still galloped, the wheels still rolled, but suddenly
everything was slow as in my dream. *Of course,* I thought, *of course
it's Bhishma. He's the enemy's commander-in-chief. The two commanders
are dueling. That is only right.*

I craned my neck to look at Arjuna. He had my helmet in his
hand and was waving it back and forth like a flag. Then he tossed it
away, and through my whipping hair I saw it bounce crazily down
the plain behind us.

"Look, Bhishma, it's your granddaughter! It's Shikhandi! Look
at her go!"

Bhishma was standing facing us. His bow was lowered, and he
was leaning forward, gripping the chariot's side with one hand. His
white hair was flying like a horse's mane. His mouth was open. His
eyes were squinting—at me.

Raise your bow, I thought. *Bhishma, raise your bow.*

But the bow stayed lowered as a look of pure bewilderment came
over his old man's face. He straightened up and stood there, swaying

in perfect balance on the bouncing floor of the chariot, staring at me with the same bewildered look as we continued to race down the field, his broad torso completely exposed and no more than seven paces away. A child could have hit that target. Out of the corner of my eye I saw Arjuna raise his bow; I saw his hand reach back over his shoulder to draw an arrow from the quiver; I saw him put the arrow to the string; I saw him pull, and fire. The arrow struck Bhishma full in the chest, the point drilling in deep. He staggered back against the far side of the vehicle.

Everything was still moving very slowly, dreamlike, and as Arjuna drew each arrow from the quiver, set it to the bow, and fired—ten arrows in all, ten shots to the chest—I kept thinking: *Stop this. You must stop this. Stop the chariot.* I leaned back on the reins. The horses, however, seemed possessed by the spirit of the race, or perhaps I was just not pulling hard enough; they galloped on, until at last I saw the other chariot slow and drop back, at which point they did respond to my tugs and cries of "Whoa!" They slowed to a canter, then a trot, then a walk, and finally, finally, came to a halt three-quarters of the way down the plain.

Arjuna and I turned around. The other chariot was stopped a hundred paces back, its horses standing with heads down, breathing hard. The charioteer was slumped forward, a single arrow through his neck; I realized that Arjuna had shot him, too. Fifty paces farther back Bhishma lay supine in the dust, a hedge of arrows sticking up from his torso.

Arjuna threw an arm around my shoulders and hugged me. "Well *done,* Shikhandi! You were fantastic!" He jumped off the back of the chariot and set out at a trot to meet the Pandava troops already surging onto the field with cheers and shouts of "Ar-ju-NA! Ar-ju-NA!"

I took off running toward my grandfather. I'd seen a small group of Kaurava soldiers stride out from the north side, and I wanted to reach him before they did. I passed the slumped-over charioteer and ran on, heart bursting.

When I got to him I fell to my knees. His eyes were open; he still breathed.

"Papa-Beesh!" I cried. "I'm sorry. I'm so sorry."

His eyes met mine. "Shikhandi," he said.

"It's my fault," I said. "All my fault. I should have known." I curled a hand weakly around one of the arrows. I wanted to pull it out, but knew it would only cause him more pain.

"Shikhandi, no. Listen." He took my hand and laid it back on my knee. "I die on the battlefield. It is all I could ask for; all any kshatriya can ask for. There is no cause for sorrow. But listen. You must promise me something. It's very important."

"Yes, I will. Anything." I dashed a tear from my cheek, not wanting to shame myself or him with a woman's weakness.

"You must perform my funeral rites. It is ..." He coughed, and a trickle of blood emerged from the corner of his mouth. "It is essential that a son do it. I cannot pass on from this world otherwise. My soul will not be freed. You know this."

"Yes, Grandfather. I know this. But I am not your son."

"Yes, Shikhandi, you are. You are my son. You are my true and only son."

Now the tears were streaming down my cheeks; I could not stop them. I nodded. "All right. I will perform your funeral rites, Grandfather. I promise."

"Good. Thank you."

He closed his eyes. I clutched his brawny hand in both of mine and said, "Don't die, Papa-Beesh! Don't die. I will miss you so much. I *have* missed you so much."

His eyes remained closed as he said, "I have missed you, too, Shikhandi. I am ... I am sorry. For shutting you away. For not letting you be what you wanted to be. Forgive me."

"I forgive you. What I wanted, it was all ... all stupid, anyway."

He smiled. "Not stupid."

I squeezed his hand tighter. Behind me, I could hear the footsteps of the Kaurava soldiers.

"Shikhandi."

"Yes, Papa-Beesh?"

"I must go now. I'll see you tomorrow, yes? We'll go ... we'll go see the elephants."

His head fell to the side, and he died.

≈

Three days later I found myself standing on a high branch of a pine tree in the hills north of the battle plain, looking down into the sla-vering jaws of an angry mother bear.

Once my grandfather's soul had departed, I had kissed his hand, stood, and backed away, watching as the Kaurava soldiers surrounded and lifted his body. I was afraid they might confront me, but they paid me no mind; I was just a charioteer, and a charioteer was of no importance at such an awe-inspiring moment: the battlefield death of the world-famous regent, last scion of the old Kuru line. They carried him to his vehicle. When they saw the dead driver with the arrow in his neck, a couple of them turned back to regard me with puzzled faces; I knew they were thinking, *Wait—which charioteer is that, and why was he kneeling by our chief?* I didn't give them a chance to ponder the question but set off trotting back the way I'd come, and instead of collecting Arjuna's chariot I simply kept going and soon found myself among the tents west of the forge shed. There it was easy to stay out of sight—not that anyone on the Pandava side would be worrying about me either. They'd be too busy celebrating Arjuna's victory.

The tents were all empty, the iron-field troops having departed days ago for the Kaurava staging area. I was able to scrounge a few provisions: a couple of water skins, which I filled at a nearby tank; a ragged cloak; and a cloth bag into which I stuffed some dried beef, dried fruit, and stale roti. Then I threw myself down inside one of the tents to take a nap. Waking at twilight, I gathered my gear and set off northwestward, heading for the line of low hills that lay between the battle plain and the Kaurava base camp.

My only aim was to disappear for a while. I could not join up again with the Kauravas; I was a deserter, and Ashwattama would have no choice but to treat me as such. As for going back to the Pandavas, that too seemed unwise; at first they'd give me a hero's welcome for the part I had played in the chariot duel, but then in a day or two, I predicted, someone would come across my body in a ravine or washed up on the riverbank or perhaps just lying on the battlefield, whereupon Arjuna would make a great show of grief for his "little warrior girl." The simple truth was that I had seen too much and knew too much. Arjuna would realize that my past love for him was not enough to keep my lips sealed, and he would take action to seal them.

A coward must silence his beholders, I thought as I tramped up the hillside through the trees. I wondered briefly what would happen to Krishna.

Yet I didn't want to disappear permanently. For one thing, I had given my promise to Papa-Beesh about the funeral rites. For another, I was hoping I might find some way, however small, to assist the Kauravas. Oh I know, I know, I was a sorry excuse for a soldier, flipping sides twice in a week. Worse than a mercenary; at least they stick with the side that's paying them. But I could see now that my devotion to the Pandavas had been all along a delusion and a source of evil, and that the only way I could hope to make amends was to return to my friends—my *real* friends—and offer my help. Yes, they might hang me for a traitor. If that was my karma, I should screw up my courage and face it.

It took me only half an hour to make my way along the wooded hills to a small clearing high up and well away from the path on which the Kaurava troops traveled to and from the battlefield. There I settled in to hide, rest, and think. There was a brook for fresh water, some berry bushes to supplement my provisions. For two days I lay undisturbed except for the occasional doe or fawn wandering by. On the late morning of the third day, however, I was sitting with my back against a pine tree eating the last of the dried beef when I heard a scuffling noise, looked around, and saw a small black bear with his nose in my food bag. I snatched up the bag, leaped to my feet, and shouted, flailing my arms to shoo him away—but it was too late. The mother bear lumbered out from the trees, saw me threatening her baby, and stretched her mouth in a furious snarl.

I dropped the bag and jumped for the lowest branch, swinging my legs up and over. I gripped a knothole in the trunk, yanking my body up just before the mother bear, dashing forward and rearing on her hind legs, could snap my skull in her jaws. I got my feet under me, stood on the branch, reached for the next, and kept clambering upward. Bears can climb, but once they're big they don't like to, so if I could get high enough, I thought, I'd probably be safe. Up and up I went, scratched by bark and needles, until I found myself on a branch some twenty-five feet in the air. There I paused and looked down. The bear had her paws on the trunk, still snarling. She cursed me for a minute or two longer, then dropped back on all fours and collected her baby, who had meanwhile eaten the remaining contents of my food bag. The two of them padded off into the woods.

I didn't think it a good idea to descend just yet, so I sat down straddling the branch, which was broad and flat enough to be tolerably comfortable, and looked out over the treetops. I was facing south with a view down the hill to the plain some three hundred paces away. Over the past few days in the clearing I had grown used to the distant sounds of battle; they rose and fell, and I paid them no attention—after all, it didn't matter to me anymore who won—but now it was as if I sat on the topmost tier of a vast arena, the sole witness to a tournament of mouse-sized soldiers. I couldn't help but be drawn in.

Seeing the forces of both sides massing, I counted on my fingers and realized it was the ninth day. The bards' songs tell us that wars (Arya wars, I mean) are fought in segments of three days, with every third day the occasion for a battle between the armies entire—infantry, archers, cavalry, elephants, and chariots—and that the starting time for such a battle is always high noon. I peered down with increasing interest.

The formations appeared standard: the two infantries were spread out in lines with the cavalries clustered on each right flank; the archers were arrayed in front; the elephants, five per side, stood on each far left flank, riders on their backs with spears ready to fling; and the chariots were front and center, some two hundred per side, arranged in two squares facing, their bronze sides flashing in the sun. From this distance it was difficult to pick out individuals, of course, but I could discern the banners of the various clans: on the north side, nearest to me, the banners of Kuru (a cross of white on a garnet ground), Madrasa, and Kashi; on the south side, the banners of Indraprasta (just like Kuru only with colors reversed), Panchala, Matsya, and Vrishni. All the flags fluttered in the day's sharp breeze. I could see that Kauravas still outnumbered Pandavas, at least when it came to chariots and cavalry. I could also see that so far, neither side had lost a too-damaging number of men; each army was, if not as strong as it had been, still strong.

I focused on the Kaurava chariots. The one set a little in front of the phalanx would, I knew, be Bhishma's replacement: the new commander-in-chief, Lord Karna. His chariot flashed brighter than any other, as did his armor, and I remembered he was nicknamed the Golden Warrior—mostly due to the gold-colored clothes and jewels he wore, but also due to the favor that had always been shown him by Prince Duryodhana (now King Duryodhana) and to his shining good looks. There had been some muttering among the troops when it had been announced that Bhishma, not Karna, would be our leader. Karna, it seemed, had been popular with the men, and some thought it unjust that he'd been demoted. But then, we regular soldiers had little to do with generals; we reported to our captains, who discouraged gossip about such things.

I could not tell who was at the head of the Pandava chariots. Likely Prince Tadyu, I thought. I felt sure it would not be Arjuna.

I scooted out a little further on the pine branch, snapping off some bushy twigs that were impeding my view. From my high vantage point I could see what the Pandava army down on the field could not: the areas where the Kauravas' infantry line was weakest. In every general battle (so I recalled from the lessons in military strategy given us by the Indraprasta weapons master), one of the biggest tactical questions was how thin to spread your infantry. You always wanted to outflank the enemy, which meant spreading your line out as long as possible, but this (if the foot soldiers' numbers were roughly equal) meant leaving some sections dangerously thin—maybe only one or two men deep. You could try to mask those sections with chariots or cavalry, but a savvy foe knew that trick, so often it was better not to try. From my perch I could see that the Kauravas had left two, and only two, very weak patches in their line; they lay directly on either side of the chariot square. I supposed this had been Karna's decision. *He must have confidence in his chariots to protect them,* I thought.

For the past quarter of an hour the troops had been moving slowly into place, taking up their positions like pieces on a pachisi board. Now the whole plain became still, waiting for the signal. I held my breath. It was the prerogative of the Pandavas, as challengers, to sound the attack, and presently I saw Tadyu—if it was indeed he in the front chariot—raise a horn to his lips. The blast rang out loud and long, echoing off the hills. The battle was on.

The first thing to happen was that each side's archers rushed forward forty paces, knelt, and fired a volley of arrows. As usual the other types of soldier hung back out of range until the arrows were mostly spent; some brave bowmen, however, having escaped harm in the first round, made a second rush forward, knelt, and fired again, thereby managing to bring down a few of the enemy's infantry. The archers then peeled off to the sides, allowing the rest of the army to take the field. At this point, I knew, some commanders would elect to send their elephants charging at the foe's front line, while others preferred to wait and use elephants more like cavalry, deploying them after the battle was well underway. Either method was understood to be acceptable. I was curious to see what these commanders had decided to do.

The chariots began to roll, the infantries began to march. It looked like the elephants would be reserved for later. A great rumbling roar arose from the plain as boots struck the ground, swords beat upon shields, wheels groaned on their axles, and yells of defiance burst from every throat. Onward the two armies came, picking up the pace as they advanced, closing the distance between them to two hundred paces ... one hundred fifty ... one hundred ...

As if on cue, the entire Pandava army divided fluidly down the middle, formed two columns with a chevron of chariots at the head of each, and drove straight toward the weakest parts of the Kaurava line.

I clapped a hand to my mouth as I saw the columns penetrate with the ease of two spears stabbing two eyeballs. More than twenty-four hundred Pandava warriors poured through the gaps that were immediately opened, then turned either right or left, with a discipline obviously rehearsed, and fanned out behind the Kaurava troops. The Pandava chariots galloped all the way along the back, around the flanks, to the front again, there to join forces with the Pandava cavalry who had meanwhile ridden hard in from the right side and spread out across the battle plain. The entire Kaurava army was now trapped: a wall of Pandava infantry behind them, a wall of Pandava chariots and cavalry before them.

Faced with this unprecedented maneuver, the Kaurava troops had no idea what to do. They turned on their heels, unsure which way to charge or whether to charge at all. The Kaurava archers, clustered in the center, set their backs to one another and raised their bows, but could not fire for fear of hitting their comrades. When the two Pandava columns had first formed, the Kaurava chariots had slowed down, Lord Karna holding them back with the intention, no doubt, of figuring out what was going on—but the result of this hesitation was unfortunate, for now most of the Kaurava chariots were trapped, as well. Only Karna himself and a handful of others had gotten out beyond the ring. They had wheeled around and were now pulled up on the south side of the field, also (it seemed) at a loss. Arrayed in a giant oval, the Pandava troops waited with perfect patience. Once again I thought: *They practiced all this in advance.* I also thought: *How did they know where to aim the columns?* But before I could think anything else, a second horn blast rang out. The Pandavas moved in.

I said I was proud that the Arya do not fight like savages. Having seen the last battle of Kurukshetra, I will never say it again. The slaughter ... it was as if a thousand tigers surrounded a herd of cattle and leaped upon them, rending with tooth and claw. And yet not so, for the Kauravas were not cattle; far from it. If their training had never prepared them for something like this, it had nevertheless prepared them to fight to the death. They battled back bravely, their captains striving to arrange them in formations and impose some type of order. But everything was jumbled—chariots, archers, cavalry, swordsmen, and spearmen rushing wildly here and there, each man striking and slashing and firing wherever and however he could—so that any half-orderly attack soon disintegrated into chaos. The plain churned with mayhem for a long time, the clash of iron and screams of the dying floating up to the cloudless sky.

Only the elephants, five per side, stayed well out of it. I could not tell if their mahouts ever urged them forward or not; if they were so urged, the beasts did not respond. They stood placidly on the sidelines watching the free-for-all, shifting their weight on their big round feet, now and then lifting and waving a snakelike trunk as if to say: *We salute you, Pandavas! We salute you, Kauravas! May your rebirths be fortunate!*

Now I should recount what I saw of Lord Karna's actions. As I mentioned, Karna and a handful of Kaurava chariots were the only ones outside the ring when the Pandava troops closed in; when that happened, although most of those chariots turned at once and drove back into the fray, Karna did not. *He wants to get an overview of the situation,* I thought; *then he'll attack.* But he stayed where he was, fifty paces removed from the fight. Moreover, although he was commander-in-chief and therefore—one would have thought—a prime target for the enemy, not a single Pandava warrior came after him. (At the time I assumed it was because of the chaotic state of the battle; in hindsight, though, it does seem odd how he was left alone.) After a while he began to shoot arrows into the scrum, but not many, and not with much speed. A couple of times I saw his charioteer turn and gesticulate; the distance was too far for me to see Karna's reaction, but if the charioteer had been asking permission to drive either toward or away from the combat, Karna must have refused, for the chariot did not budge.

The battle raged on. It was clear the Kauravas were getting the worst of it. Brave and skilled warriors though they were, they simply could not recover from the shock of the Pandavas' initial trap-and-pounce. The only group having any success was the company of about two hundred swordsmen who had gathered to King Duryodhana's banner on the west side of the plain, to my right; he had managed to get them into formation and was now leading charges in an eastward direction, advancing and falling back with something like discipline. But his troops were too few to make much of an impact on the roiling melee, and when I saw Bimasena—his gargantuan bulk easily recognizable even from that distance—surging toward them at the head of a company of five hundred Matsya infantry, swinging his spiked mace and roaring like a rakshasa, I was sure it was all over for the king and his company.

That was when Karna finally made his move. I don't know whether he saw the king in straits or what he was thinking, but suddenly his chariot began to roll across the plain toward the royal banner, faster and faster, its golden sides flashing in the sun, and as Bima came lumbering toward the king with mace raised to strike, Karna drove his chariot straight between the two men, firing a single arrow as he went. The arrow struck Bima's breastplate, knocking him to the ground, but the big man bounced up almost at once and renewed his attack; meanwhile the Matsya troops had swept down on the Kauravas and were fighting two against one. Karna wheeled around and drove back into the tumult. Men scattered and fell as he laid about him with his sword, his charioteer doing a brilliant job of keeping the horses moving in broad, smooth sweeps, thereby giving Karna control and scope for his slashing blows.

Bima and the king were still fighting man-to-man. The strokes of the great iron mace were fearsome in their power, but Duryodhana's feet were quicker, his sword was quicker, and I thought he was about to prevail when I saw a Matsya spearman come creeping up with weapon poised ready to thrust into his back. "Behind you!" I shouted—insanely, my voice a squeak on the breeze. Thank the Gods, here came Karna in his chariot, driving straight for the spearman, running him down and saving the king from certain death. I exhaled with relief; but an instant later the chariot tipped—perhaps on the spearman's body, perhaps on a pothole—spilling Karna and his charioteer to the ground. The charioteer jumped up and dashed away, but Karna lay sprawled face-down in the dust, unmoving. Both the king and Bima had whipped around when the chariot had capsized, startled enough to pause their fight; now another Matsya soldier rushed in to challenge the king. Taking advantage of his foe's distraction, Bima took two steps forward, raised his mace, and swung it down onto Karna's back. He raised it a second time and swung it down. A third time: down. A fourth: down.

Duryodhana slew his man. As I watched him draw back his sword and turn to look again for Bima, I heard three short, sharp blasts of a horn, followed by three more blasts.

The surrender signal.

I scanned the plain and saw a single chariot sitting atop a small rise on the east side, about a hundred paces from the iron field. The man was too far away for me to identify him with certainty, but based upon the white-on-garnet banner and the two black horses, I guessed that it was Captain Drona, now second-in-command of the Kaurava forces—or *first-in-command*, I thought, *if Karna is dead.* The horn blasts came again, two sets of three, as all across the plain men stayed their hands and lowered their weapons, or pulled up their mounts, or stopped in midflight, gazing around for the source of the sound. Drona blew the horn a third time, and gradually, gradually, everything became still.

The bodies of the dead and wounded strewed the ground. The survivors, maybe a few hundred in all, turned toward the east and stood like statues, their black shadows stretched out before them. Even the sun ceased moving, suspended halfway between the zenith and the western hills. Silence covered the plain. The war was over.

Suddenly, I saw Drona's body stiffen. His hand flew to the nape of his neck. Then his hand dropped, and he collapsed onto the side of the chariot, head and arms hanging down. I could just make out a long thin shaft sticking up between his shoulder blades. At the end of the shaft was a tiny, luminous spot of blue-green.

A peacock-fletched arrow, I thought. *It came from the iron field.*

The charioteer turned and bent to his fallen master. I knew his efforts at revival would do no good.

Only a very great archer, I thought, *could have made such a shot. Only the greatest archer in the world.*

≈

As it turned out, I needn't have worried about being hanged for a traitor. When at dusk I arrived back at the Kaurava base camp and made my way to the tent of Ashwattama—nearly choking with relief upon being told by another returning solider that yes, the cavalry captain was alive—and finding no guard posted, pushed through the tent flap and kneeled before him, he at first merely squinted at me in confusion. He was sitting on a stool, his body caked with dirt and blood, having a long gash on his thigh cleaned and bound by a healer while a standing soldier delivered a casualties report. After a moment he recognized me and said:

"Oh, Shikhandi—it's you. You came back. Are you hurt?"

"No, Sir," I said. "Not hurt."

"I'm glad. I was worried about you. Did you find a safe place to go?"

In that instant I knew the truth: my friend Ashwattama, far from suspecting me of treachery, had simply assumed that when the conflict became hot I had run away and found myself a hiding place, too afraid to fight. *Afraid,* I thought, *afraid like a girl.* He didn't remember my vow to join up with the Pandavas; or if he did remember, had dismissed it as the fanciful product of—what was it he'd called it?—"a girl's crush." His mildly concerned expression was a knife in my guts.

"Yes, Sir," I said. "I was up in the hills overlooking the plain. I saw most of the battle from there. How many did we lose?"

He passed a hand over his dirt-streaked brow. "Easier to say how many survived ... maybe a hundred of ours; five hundred of theirs."

I bowed my head. Six hundred, out of seven thousand.

With a *whap,* the tent flap swept open and King Duryodhana strode in. I jumped to my feet and, along with the other soldier, stood to attention. The king passed us without a glance and went to Ashwattama, motioned him to stay seated as he tried to rise, pulled up a stool for himself, and sat down heavily. The healer, at a gesture from the captain, got up and backed his way bowing out of the tent.

"You've received the reports?" said the king. His face, too, had smears of dirt and blood. He wore only his black dhoti and his sword in its belt. There was a bandage wrapping his left forearm, another wrapping his bare chest.

"Yes, Sire," Ashwattama said. "It's bad."

"Worse than bad," said the king. "The latest count has us with fewer than a hundred survivors. All our captains, except for you, are dead: Rahul, Ishana, Aviral ... all dead. My Uncle Shakuna: he insisted on fighting. They say he killed twenty men before he was speared through the heart. And my brother, Dushasana: they just now b-brought his b-body in." He put his elbows on his knees and rubbed his face hard. "And your father. I'm sorry."

"Yes, Sire. Thank you."

The king ran his hands back over his scalp. "That's not why I grieve. Drona, Dushasana, Shakuna, all the rest ... they died in combat, as kshatriya should; they will go straight to paradise."

"Yes," said Ashwattama.

"I grieve because I survive, and I have lost. I have lost everything."

The two men were quiet for a while, heads bowed.

"Lord Karna?" Ashwattama asked. "Is he also dead?"

"He lives," said the king, "though barely. Bimasena crushed his spine as he lay helpless on the field. I b-brought him back myself. He's in my tent; the healers are doing what they can."

Ashwattama's mouth tightened. "Karna smashed in the back. Drona shot in the back. The Pandavas—they did not fight fair."

"No," said the king. "They did not."

"That maneuver, at the beginning. They knew exactly where our weak spots were. How did they know?"

"I don't know," said the king.

"Someone must have tipped them off. But who? Who would do such a thing?"

"I don't know."

"May he burn in hell," said Ashwattama, clenching a fist. "If he's dead, that is. If he lives, may he suffer agony each day he lives. I curse him. May the Gods hear my curse."

A spasm of something like pain crossed the king's face. "I can ap ... appreciate your curse, Captain. But I doubt there's any need for it."

Ashwattama unclenched his fist, opening his palm upward. "No, you're right. The Gods always punish traitors. Of that we can be sure."

"Yes. Of that we can be sure."

The other soldier coughed, causing the king to look up and for the first time notice our presence. Ashwattama said, "All right, men; dismissed." The other soldier bowed smartly and departed. I did not move. Ashwattama frowned at me and jerked his head toward the exit. I took a step forward.

I've been thoroughly mad so far, I thought. *A little more madness won't hurt.*

"Please, your majesty," I said. "Permission to speak."

"Shikhandi, for Gods' sake." Ashwattama was glaring at me now. "This is not the time."

"What's this?" asked the king. "Who are you, soldier?"

I dropped my shoulders, tilted my head, clasped my hands at my breast, and said:

"Sire, I am Lady Shikhandi. I am Lord Bhishma's granddaughter. Three years ago, Counselor Vidura condemned me to live as a man as punishment for running away from my husband."

The king stared. I clasped my hands tighter and went on.

"For the war, I was assigned to the cavalry. After a few days I deserted to join up with the Pandavas. Arjuna saw how he could use me. He made me his charioteer in the duel. My grandfather lowered his bow when he saw me, and ... and that's how he died."

Now both men were staring at me open-mouthed.

The king turned to the captain. "Explain. Is any of this true? Or is she deranged?" His eyes slid back to me, suspicious.

Ashwattama shrugged. "The first part is true enough. She is Bhishma's granddaughter. And Vidura did make her a soldier; she's been with the troops at Indraprasta the past few years. I don't know about the last part: about her joining up with the Pandavas, or the chariot duel." He sighed and shrugged again. "Knowing her, it's certainly possible."

The king said, "Lady Shikhandi, what are you saying? Are you confessing to treason?"

"No, Sire. I mean, yes, Sire," I said. "Yes, I did desert to the Pandavas. But I came back, because I saw who they are. I saw how ..." (my cheeks grew hot with rage) "how *low* they are. I want to help. I want to help you defeat them."

"If you are a traitor, I don't know why I should trust you," said the king. "But go on."

"Yes, Sire. The thing is: I know the way to the Pandavas' camp. I can lead you there. Tonight."

"Eh? To what purpose?"

"So you can challenge them. Challenge Arjuna! Or Yudi. To a duel."

"Too late for that." The king shook his head. "We surrendered."

"You can retract the surrender," I said. "Drona was wrong to do it. You are the king. You can retract it. You can challenge them. You must! You *must!*"

Ashwattama frowned and said, "Shikhandi!" but the king waved a hand to silence us both. He regarded me with narrowed eyes. I was a little appalled at my outburst and wondered if he was going to throw me out. But after a minute, he shook his head again and said:

"It's no good. If I go to their camp alone, they'll just kill me. And I won't take a bodyguard and risk m-more men. We've lost far too many as it is."

I hadn't considered any such details, but I pressed on. "We can go when they're asleep. I'll go into their tent and wake them. They know me. They won't hurt me. I'll tell them you've come and you want a parley. No men. Just you and them. Then you can issue the challenge."

Suddenly the king squinted, as if from a bright light, though the twilight shadows were creeping in around the tent flap. He brought a hand up to cover his eyes. "When they're asleep," he said. He sat like that, with hand over eyes, for a long moment. Then he dropped the hand and stared at Ashwattama. "W-when they're asleep," he said again.

Ashwa stared back. Then he nodded, slowly. I could not read his expression; it seemed half-excited, half-afraid. I was glad that my idea had met with approval.

"Lady Shikhandi," said the king (but he kept his eyes on Ashwattama), "do you know the Pandavas' *exact* location?"

"Yes, Sire," I said. "Yes. I know which clearing, and I know which tent."

Outside, an owl cried: once, twice.

"I have no more advisors," said the king to the captain, "so you must be my advisor in this, Ashwa. Tell me your m-mind. Would such a … an *action* be lawful?"

Ashwattama looked down at the bandage on his thigh, rubbing it in long strokes. He rubbed five, six, seven times before looking up and replying thus:

"My father always said we were kshatriya, not brahmin. If ever I asked him a question about the Law, he would tell me to hold my tongue and mind my business. So I don't know how to answer your question, Sire. But speaking as a kshatriya, I can say this …"

His fist clenched, and his eyes gleamed though there was no lamplight.

"You may have lost. But the Pandavas have not yet won."

Chapter 19

DRAUPADI

She sat in the tent watching her five husbands sleep.

For several hours she had lain on her mat staring upward, stroking the swell of her belly, listening to the sporadic hoots of an owl in a tree somewhere west of the clearing. Finally, realizing it was useless, she had heaved herself to her feet (*Gods, this baby is a big one*), padded over to the long table and sat down, trying not to breathe too loudly lest she wake the men. The flame of the single oil lamp cast less of a glow than the full moon's light filtering dimly through the thick weave of the tent fabric.

The Pandavas had won the war. Two days ago Arjuna, knowing they would win—how he had known had not been clear to her then—had sent for her and the children to come to the camp at Kurukshetra. Unlike his brothers, Arjuna had always shown a keen interest in the children; from the time they could walk he would insist they attend his after-dinner shows, and as they grew older he would take them hunting and give them rudimentary lessons in archery, swords, and wrestling. Even after they'd been turned over to the chief weapons master for the majority of their education, he would still drop by the training grounds to watch or even to join in an exercise. It was very important, he said, that the boys should have a father's example.

So it did not surprise her, his wanting them there for the victory celebrations. "Come quickly," the messenger had said—repeating the words with exact tone and phrasing as messengers are trained to do—"it will all be over in two days." She had packed the boys up and set out from Indraprasta with only a small escort, everybody on horseback, no cart, not even for her and Baby Nana (*not* Baby *Nana, just* Nana, *he's eight years old for goodness' sake and a fine rider already*), keeping them to double-time as they traveled up the Yamuna.

Prata, aged fourteen, had grumbled the whole way, just as he'd been grumbling every day for the past three months while the war preparations were ongoing.

"But *why* does Abimanyu get to fight and I don't? He's only a few months older."

"Twenty-seven months older," she replied for the umpteenth time.

"Fine. Whatever. But I'm crown prince. And I can beat him at sword-fighting! Papa Arjuna has seen me do it."

"It doesn't matter. Sixteen is the age at which kshatriya men may fight. That's the Law."

"It's fourteen for cattle raids."

"A war is not a cattle raid. Anyway, the war is almost over. Papa Arjuna said so."

Prata groaned and kicked up his horse to ride on ahead of the group. She shook her head, smiling; soon they'd have the same conversation all over again. As the party splashed across a creek, low in the drought of the second month and thick with waterweed, she thought about Abimanyu and stopped smiling. Was he still alive? She prayed so.

Shata, nearly thirteen, seemed content to leave the arguing to his older brother, even though he was growing up to be the better warrior. He was half a head taller than Prata—nearly as tall as Abimanyu—with more lean muscle, and more focus in all his pursuits. He showed a special talent for archery, which pleased Arjuna greatly. Suta and Shruta, aged eleven and ten, were still at the run-wild stage, and inseparable; whatever trouble they got into, which was a lot, they got into together. As for Baby Nana (*just Nana!*), he looked like taking after his Papa Saku: he was quiet for an eight-year-old, serious, and very fond of Arya lore. He had memorized the names of all the clans participating in the conflict and could draw their banners, describe their territories, and recite an astonishing amount of their histories.

The new one was due in a month. A girl; she knew it was a girl, which meant none of her husbands would give it a second thought. But she would. She would love this child, she felt sure, with a love even greater—if it were possible—than the love she bore her five sons. She was riding sidesaddle on this journey, for the midwives said that riding astride, even for a seasoned horsewoman, was not good for a baby in the womb.

Yudi and his entourage met them on the far side of the Yamuna ford just as dusk was falling on the second day. She alighted from her horse and dropped him a curtsey. The young princes followed suit, kneeling to touch the feet of their father the king.

"Welcome, my dear," he said, taking her by the shoulders and planting a dry kiss on her forehead. "Prata; boys." He gave them a nod. He looked clean and well-rested; if there had been a battle that day, he surely had not been in it.

"What news, my lord?" she asked. "Have we won?"

"We have won," said Yudi, "but at some cost. We don't have the exact count yet. On our side, there appear to be five, maybe six hundred survivors. The Kauravas, less than a hundred. You there!" He beckoned to a couple of grooms. "Take the queen's and princes' horses and see them watered. Bring them up to the camp after."

Her eyes widened. "But that's … how many dead?"

He shrugged and took her hand to lead her up the path through the trees. "A few thousand, perhaps. But there's no need to distress yourself, my dear. We are all unhurt, my brothers and I. Krishna, too. Not a scratch on any of us—well, except Bima, of course, but his wounds are minor. And it was a great, great victory."

"Arjuna sent the messenger three days ago," she said, puffing a little as they climbed the hill. "How did he know you'd win?"

Yudi held a low-hanging branch out of the way for her. "Ah. Well … not to take anything away from our brave troops, but we received a bit of help. One of our spies was passed information by a Kaurava captain. I won't say who …" He laid a finger to his lips with a smirk. "… but it was someone high up. Oh, yes, *very* high up. It allowed us to formulate a unique strategy. We all put our heads together and came up with it. Then Arjuna rehearsed it with the men." He chuckled, nodding. "It worked brilliantly."

They continued up the slope, the trees now pressing close around them. Yudi tucked her hand in the crook of his elbow. "But I mustn't bore you with military talk. The important thing is: we have won. And from today, you are queen not only of Indraprasta, but of all Kuru!" He patted her hand. "It was good of you my dear, in your condition, to come so quickly. You're not too tired? The camp is only a little farther."

"No," she said, "I'm not tired."

She looked behind to make sure all five boys were still following.

Reassured they were, she turned back to the king. "What about Abimanyu?"

Yudi knit his brow. "Now, that I don't know. He hasn't shown up yet. I trust he will. He was in Captain Hansa's company of archers; Arjuna thought that safest, and indeed, he came through all the previous skirmishes just fine. Hansa was killed in this last battle, though; they brought his body in a short while ago. No sign of Abimanyu. I do hope he's all right."

"I hope so, too," she said. "His wife, Uttari, has been terribly anxious for him. You know her baby is due in four months."

"Ah, yes. So I hear. Well, that will be a happy event, won't it? Arjuna will be awfully pleased to have a grandson." He patted her hand again. "We'll be thinking about a bride for Prata soon, eh? Fifteen years old. It's high time."

(Fourteen.) She did not correct him.

As twilight descended they arrived at the clearing, where the torches were being lit by blades-boys. This area was for lords and officers, most of whom had come through the battle alive and relatively unscathed, so aside from the occasional horse's whinny or a man's groan coming from the healers' tent, all was calm. The ordinary troops were camped in a string of clearings a little farther south, where, no doubt, there was much more hubbub.

Yudi led her up to a large tent near the center of the clearing. "Here's where we are," he said. "Rough quarters, I'm afraid, but there's plenty of room for you, my dear, and supper will be on in a minute. I've ordered a beer barrel. We'll be having a little pre-celebration. Just a few friends." He gestured to another tent close by, calling over his shoulder, "That one's yours, boys. Go along, now. Your mother needs some rest."

"I'll go help them get settled," she said. "We brought barely any servants."

Yudi looked annoyed. "What about your ladies? Can't they deal with it?"

"I didn't bring any. I knew it would be rough quarters, as you said."

He sighed. "You're a *queen,* Draupadi. I don't know why you always have to ... Oh, never mind. Suit yourself." He pushed open the tent flap and went inside.

She went to the other tent. The boys had rushed to it and were now inside fighting over who would have which sleeping mat. An ayah, a maidservant, and a manservant were starting to unpack their gear. She spent the next two hours sorting out supper for the five of them (Shata hated most vegetables, Shruta had been prescribed a bland diet for his recurring stomach upsets, and these days Nana would eat nothing but rice, oranges, and partridge-wing meat cut into very small pieces); arranging for an additional guard to post outside the tent (Yudi had assigned one, but she thought two were necessary); and last but not least, refereeing the debate over the sleeping mats.

All the boys expressed outrage at being put to bed so early:

"Mother, I am *fourteen*. You're saying I have to go to bed at the same time as these children? It's insulting!"

"Oh, shut it, Prata." (That was Shata.) "It's late enough. I'm tired. And we have to be up early tomorrow for the celebration."

"Shata needs his beauty sleeeeep!" (That was Suta and Shruta, chanting in unison.)

"And you two maggots need a kick in the rear! Which I'll give you right now if you don't shut up!"

"Mama ..." (That was Nana.)

"Yes, darling?"

"Can I have a story first?"

"*May* I have a story first."

"*May* I have a story first?"

"Yes, darling. You may *all* have a story. But not unless you all get onto your mats and lie down before I count five. Otherwise I'm leaving right now, and *no story*. One ... two ..."

That did the trick. It always did.

Half an hour and three stories later, Prata, Shata, and Nana were already fast asleep. Suta and Shruta were struggling mightily to stay awake but losing the struggle. The ayah and the maidservant were curled up on a rug in a corner. She gave each boy's cheek a light kiss, snuffed the lamp, and tiptoed—as best as anyone can tiptoe, eight months pregnant—out of the tent. The guards bowed as she passed them with a quiet "Namaste; good night."

Outside her husbands' tent she paused, listening to the noises within and wincing slightly. There were no guards posted here. Steeling herself, she pushed open the flap and went inside.

As anticipated, the party was in full swing. Not quite such a crowd as usual—perhaps some of the regular guests had been killed or wounded—but still, enough to fill the large space. Men stood, sat, or lounged on rugs or the bare ground, each with a tankard in his hand. The long table was laden with dishes and strewn with legs of mutton, half-chewed bird carcasses, and fragments of roti; a barrel stood nearby, a knot of men pressing around it to fill their vessels. The air was thick with the smells of meat, beer, sweat, and flatulence. Back there was Bima, seated at the table, chugging mightily from his tankard while a small group cheered him on; over here was Naku, supine on a mat, his beautiful face contorted with pleasure as his genitals received the oral ministrations of a whore; next to him was Saku, stark naked and asleep, with another whore draped snoring across his chest; and right in the middle of it all was Yudi, hunkered down (*of course*) over a game of dice.

She was just about to turn and leave with the intention of following the maids' example and curling up on a blanket in the boys' tent, when Arjuna pushed his way through the scrum.

"Padi! Hey, Padi! You—*hic*—you made it!"

He was clearly in great spirits. Before she could curtsey to him, he gripped her cheeks between his two hands and gave her a sloppy kiss on the lips.

"We won! Did you—*hic*—hear? We won! We crushed those shtinking ash-holes!"

She stepped back, clasping her hands on the shelf of her abdomen to help her resist the urge to wipe her mouth. "Yes, my lord. I heard. Allow me to congratulate you on your victory."

"Yeah," he said, grabbing her arm as a passing guest bumped into him, causing him to stumble. "A *great* victory! The greatest ever! And it was all me. All my shtra ... *shtrategies*. Yudi, hey, Yudi!" He dragged her over to where the dice players were squatting and nudged Yudi's backside with his toe. "Look who's here ... it's Padi! She brought the boys!" He turned to her, squeezing her arm. "You brought the boys, right?"

"Yes, I brought the boys."

"Egg—*hic*—eggshellent. I'll see 'em tomorrow. Yudi, tell her how we won! Tell her how it was all my shtrategies!"

Yudi seemed angry at being disturbed midgame, but when he saw her he composed his face, got up, and made her a small bow.

"Ah, there you are, my dear. Boys all settled down? Good, good. Have you had any supper?"

"No, Husband. Thank you. I'm not very hungry."

"Nonsense, nonsense. Your condition … you must eat. Plenty of food on the table, there. Go along now, go get yourself something. Arjuna, go with her. Make sure she eats properly. But no beer, now!" He wagged a finger at her, smiling, and returned to his game.

Arjuna accompanied her to the food table and—oddly—sat with her while she filled a plate and ate. He regaled her with tales of the war, stressing at every point the critical role he and his "shtrategies" had played. After half an hour of this, and feeling a little mischievous after a few swallows of beer (*the midwives say it's fine, so Yudi can go hang*), she said:

"How interesting! And who came up with all those clever ideas? No, no, don't tell me; I can guess it was Krishna. He's the mastermind, isn't he? I know how you rely on him."

A flush of rage suffused Arjuna's face. "What? *Hic* … No! Krishna had nothing to do with it! Nothing! He shpent the whole time changing his fucking clothes an' combing his fucking hair. No mastermind. No ideas. Why would you even shay … say that?" His eyes suddenly narrowed. "Where is he? Have you been talking to him?"

A bit shocked at this change in demeanor, she set about soothing him down:

"No, no, my lord, of course not. I only meant that he's always been a good friend to you. I assumed he had helped you. But I'm only a woman; I know nothing about these things."

"Thash right. You don't. So you can shut up about it."

She bowed her head submissively. "Yes, Husband."

He grabbed a nearby mutton leg and took a bite, seeming mollified. As he chewed, a sly grin stretched his mouth. "But you know what, Padi? You're right. You're absho … absolutely right. Krishna did help in *one* way. He got someone to turn on the Kauravas. You'll never guess." He leaned in, gleeful. "You'll never, never gesh who it was."

She looked back at him warily. "Who?"

He leaned in farther and hissed: "*Your boy Karna.*"

She felt her guts contract, but kept her expression neutral.

"Karna? You mean the Kaurava commander-in-chief? Duryodhana's friend?"

"The very same." He sat back; his eyes were little drops of spite. "No idea why he did it. He and the stuttering freak mus' have had a falling out. But who cares why; he gave us some *eggshellent* information. And we promised in egg ... in exchange, to leave him alone in the last battle. Ha-ha! Yeah ... thash what we promised."

She kept her voice very calm. "And did you keep the promise?"

Arjuna turned to Bima, still sitting at the end of the table with his drinking mates, and shouted: "Hey, Bima! Remind me again what you did to Karna today?"

Bima grinned, raised his tankard high, and brought it down with a crash. "Smashed him like a bug!"

Arjuna turned back to her, laughing. "Bima smashed him like a bug."

"Is he ... is he dead?"

Arjuna shrugged and took another bite of mutton leg. "Pretty sure." He laughed again, spraying bits of meat over the table. "That Karna. What a fucking moron."

For another hour or so she sat at the table, listening to Arjuna describe his various triumphs, watching the crowd of men (and a few whores) drink, eat, sing, dance, screw, throw dice, stagger outside to pee or vomit, and stagger back in again. Much sooner than she had expected, however, the party began to break up. Perhaps it was her presence that put a damper on things; as the night wore on, she noticed men eying her with uneasy frowns before muttering something to their friends and taking their leave. By midnight only the dice players were left, squatting in their circle on the ground, still intent on the game. Suddenly a couple of them looked up, saw they were the last, and began to apologize to the king for overstaying, whereupon Yudi, in rather a frantic voice, begged them not to go, but then seemed to recall himself. He saw them out with many claps on the back and promises of a rematch on the morrow.

Most of the oil lamps had guttered, leaving the interior in shadow. Three of the sleeping mats, lined up to the left of the door, were already occupied: Naku and Saku had long been asleep, their female companions departed, while Bima had a minute ago lurched over and fallen face-first onto his mat like a toppling tree. Yudi looked at the trio, sighed, and went down the line pulling up a blanket over each brother. Then he laid himself down on the first mat by the door. "All right, Juna," he said, yawning. "Let Draupadi go to bed. And you go to bed, too. Big day tomorrow." He rolled over and closed his eyes.

As she got up from the table, Arjuna grabbed her hand. His voice held a note of entreaty as he said: "Hey, Padi ... whuddaboudit, eh? Li'l shelebration?"

She drew her hand back and laid it on her stomach, keeping her eyes modestly down. "I am honored, my lord. But the baby ... we must not risk ..."

"Right. Right. Yeah. Mussen risk it."

"Thank you for understanding." She made him a curtsey and turned away. He grabbed her hand again. (*Gods preserve me.*)

He staggered to his feet, still holding onto her. "Lisshen, Padi," he said to the back of her head. "I wanna shay shumthing. You and I ... you and I ... never zackly gotten along. But I'll shay thish: you've been a good *wife*—to all of ush. Given us shuns. Many ... many fine shuns. Maybe my brothers don't 'ppreciate that, but I do."

She wondered if she could pull her hand away yet. "Thank you, my lord. I have done no more than my duty."

"Yeah, well, I 'ppreciate it. You've been good to Abimanyu, too. Been a ... a good *mother* to him. More than Susu. I don't ..." His voice trailed off. She waited.

He cleared his throat. "Anyway, I wanna give you shumthing."

He let go her hand, and she heard a clicking noise. Then she felt a knobby, loose thing being lowered past her ears and laid upon her breast. She looked down. There, glimmering in the light of the last oil lamp, were Arjuna's ivory beads.

"A token," he said, sounding almost like Yudi, "a token of my 'ppreciation."

She turned to face him and curtsied low. "I am deeply honored. Thank you, my lord."

"You're welcome." He yawned. "Well, I'm off to bed. G'night."

"Good night, Husband. Sleep well."

He grunted, went to the fifth mat in the line, flopped down, and yanked the blanket up over his head.

Leaving the lamp burning, she went to a mat on the other side of the tent, kicked off her shoes, and pulled off her sky-blue riding tunic. Underneath she wore a white dhoti and chest-band; these she left on as she lay down, suddenly conscious of overwhelming exhaustion. She closed her eyes and tried to relax her limbs. But the God of Sleep, never a friend to pregnant women, would not come. As the moon sank toward the horizon, she got up and resumed her seat at the table. It was now some three hours after midnight.

Her husbands were five dark hummocks in the darkness. They all had a tendency to snore, Bima sometimes raucously; tonight, however, they were quiet. She could hear their slow breathing as she sat and watched. Naku (she thought it was Naku) gave a brief snuffle and cough.

She looked down at Arjuna's beads; they were large, nearly as large as garlic heads, and as unevenly shaped. They draped over her banded breasts and naked stomach. She fingered them, counting: twenty-four in all. She lingered on the lowest one, feeling its cool bumpiness.

Outside, the owl hooted.

She started at a cracking sound. A soldier, creeping up on the tent? No … likely just a doe, or maybe a bear, passing through the clearing. Now that spring was far along the female animals would be out at night with their babies, teaching them to forage so they could be weaned from the teat. Yes, just some nocturnal animal about its business. Nevertheless, she did not like that there were no guards at the entry. War victor or not, Yudi should remain vigilant. There were always those who wished a king out of the way.

She thought about Karna. Was he alive or dead? And Abimanyu: alive or dead?

Her mother's ears, attuned to children's voices in the night, heard a faint cry: "*Mama.*" That was Baby Nana, she felt sure, calling out in his sleep. She was not alarmed. Nana was given to night terrors; sometimes he would even sleepwalk. Just a phase he'd grow out of. All the ayahs knew what to do. She contemplated going back to bed.

Then she heard it again: "*Mama.*" And for some reason, a cold hand clenched around her heart. She got up, went to the tent flap, and stood there for a minute, telling herself not to be silly, not to go stomping over and waking the children, waking the servants, causing a needless commotion. She took a deep breath. And another. All at once the baby kicked, hard; she placed a hand on her belly and said, "Shhhh."

She stepped outside and looked toward the children's tent.

It was the one right at the center of the clearing.

The one with the banner of Indraprasta set atop it.

There was a torch outside that tent, and she should have seen the guardsmen silhouetted, but she did not. Instead she saw two black humps with two thin black shafts sticking up from them, and then there was a *whap* and two shadows, one behind the other, with swords in their hands, burst from the tent, leaped over the humps, and bolted away across the clearing. When they were halfway to the trees a third shadow dashed from behind another tent and joined them. Three running figures, visible in the light of the full moon. She froze, watching them; as they disappeared into the woods, she took off running herself.

Her bare feet were stabbed by rocks and twigs, but she felt no pain. Arriving at the tent she grabbed the torch from its holder, registered briefly the bodies of the two guards with arrows through their throats, stepped over them, and pushed through the flap. She held the torch high. In the warm wavering light she saw the ayah and the maid crouched together in a back corner, clutching each other, their eyes huge with terror. She swung the torch left to illuminate the sleeping mats.

What had happened was clear. The assailants had aimed for speed above all. Working in tandem, in the near-pitch dark, and starting with the mat closest to the door, one man had yanked the blanket back; then the other had raised his sword high and brought it down, once, slashing the neck to the bone. Death had been instantaneous. There were no raised hands, no bent limbs, no signs of struggle. The four older boys lay flat in their preferred sleeping positions: Prata on his back, Shata on his side, Suta and Shruta on their stomachs, all with eyes closed, blood welling from their gaping wounds. Only Baby Nana had woken and called out for his mother to save him from this latest night terror, one in which bad men with swords were killing everyone in the world. But he had not sat up or tried to get away; he had lain there with eyes open until his blanket too was pulled back and the blade came down, slicing his eight-year-old neck clean through.

She did not run to the bodies; she did not fall to her knees wailing. The truth was far too lucid, far too immense for that. The truth was a shimmering wave, so high the top could not be seen, sweeping through the universe, sweeping through time, engulfing everything in its path. In front of the wave there was life: forests, towns, palaces, tournaments, maidservants, manservants, horses, dogs, men, sex, spinning, talking, washing, dressing, supper tables, arguments, hugs, kisses, bedtime stories. Behind the wave there was—not death; nothing so sweet as death. Behind the wave there was a vast, vibrating emptiness, ever-bright and ever-pitiless, in which delusions appeared and melted away and appeared again with sickening speed, like the hectic shapes in a fire, and there was nothing to do but stare into that swirling void, alone and aghast, like a soma addict whose hallucinations provide less and less solace even as they increase their mad hold on the mind.

When the sun rose, she knew, she would be behind the wave, floating in that dreadful null. But the dawn would not come for another hour, and until then …

She would ride the wave. She would be the wave. She would become—not death; nothing so kind as death. She would become Truth: the destroyer of worlds.

She looked to the ayah and maid, still huddled in the corner. Her voice was deep and cold. "You will stay here and watch over them," she said. "Do not call out. Do not wake anyone. Stay here until I return." They stared back at her dumbly. "Deeba? Do you understand me?" The ayah nodded.

She stuck the torch in an iron stand and went to the table, on one end of which were piled the boys' swords and bows: full-size for Prata and Shata, still half-size for the younger ones. She pulled Prata's sword from its scabbard and thumbed the blade. It was sharp; she remembered him insisting it be honed before they'd set out up the Yamuna. "They *might* need me to fight," he had said. "I must be ready."

She gripped the weapon in her right hand and hefted it. It would do.

At the exit she turned back, looking down at the five bodies on the mats. After a moment she walked to the last one in the line, stooped, and took a lock of Nana's hair in her fingers. It fell below his shoulders, beautifully dark and wavy, just like his Papa Naku's. He'd never wanted it combed, of course; it would get in a terrible state, for which she had scolded him often. "I'll let *you* comb it, Mama," he would say with his sweet smile. And she would sit down on his bed, take him in her lap, and comb his hair, starting from the bottom and gently teasing out the tangles as she worked her way upward.

With her left hand, she swept the hair into a high bunch and picked up the severed head.

She left the tent and hurried west across the clearing. All was mostly quiet, though a few muffled sounds of late-night carousing wafted here and there. There were no guards anywhere. She plunged into the trees. She knew her quarry had gone uphill and guessed that after topping the rise he would go straight down the escarpment to the iron-ore field and thence northwest across the battle plain, heading for the Kaurava camp. She trusted that, with his start of mere minutes, she'd be able to spot him once she had achieved the crest. Still, with her bulging abdomen, she could not go as fast as he could; that was a simple fact. "Come on," she said to the baby inside her, "we're going to catch him. Help me catch him." She focused on breathing, deep breaths in through the nose and out through the mouth, as she strode along.

At the top there was no gradual thinning of forest; the trees gave out all at once, and she stepped out into the open to see the full moon straight ahead, huge and white, hovering over the western hills beyond the plain. She looked down and to her surprise saw the three men standing not too distant, halfway down the slope, just where the giant spur of rock began thrusting out over the iron field fifty feet below. They were in a tight circle and seemed to be arguing.

"Duryodhana!" she cried.

They looked up, their faces pictures of shock.

She began to walk down the slope. They watched her come. As she drew closer she recognized the second man as Ashwattama, Drona's son; the third man she did not recognize, although it flashed through her mind that he had something of the look of Bhishma, the old regent. When she was twenty paces from them she heard the king say:

"You two go on back to camp. I'll meet you there."

"Sire," said Ashwattama, "hadn't we all better go? They may have sounded the alarm. Or at least, let us stay with you."

"No. Both of you go. I'll follow shortly. That's an order."

The two men turned and headed down the hill as she came to a stop in front of him.

He looked her up and down, taking in her ungainly figure. "Your majesty," he said, "you should not be here. Go back to your camp."

"I have come to kill you," she said.

She raised her sword. He took a step back, but did not draw his. She took a step forward and placed the point on his bare chest. "Defend yourself," she said.

All in one motion, he stepped back, drew his weapon, and batted hers aside with no more effort than if he'd been brushing away a fly.

She lunged for his chest, just above where the bandage wrapped it. He stepped back again and parried. The next stroke she tried was lower, a cross cut aimed at the waistband of his black dhoti; again, he countered it easily. They went on like this, she attacking and he parrying, the two of them moving gradually back, back along the promontory. Had she been a man and a soldier, one might have thought she was driving him backward, but it was clear that he had absolutely no fear of her and her weak assaults; indeed, that he did not want to hurt her and was being especially careful not to strike her pregnant stomach as he fended off her jabs. She began to pant and sweat. He was not even breathing hard.

When they were about three-quarters of the way out along the jetty, he threw a quick look over his shoulder and said: "Stop. We're getting too near the edge."

"I won't stop," she said, aiming a stroke at his left shoulder. He blocked it.

"You must stop," he said. "Please, Draupadi. You will injure yourself."

"I am already injured; injured beyond hope." She lunged again. He took two steps back as he parried.

"I am sorry for your pain. But your husbands got no more than they deserved."

She slashed for his thigh, and this time she actually managed to nick the black cloth of his dhoti before he knocked her blade away. "My husbands?" she said. "Why do you speak of my husbands?"

He planted his feet and, quick as thought, grabbed her right wrist and bent it upward, pinning it to her chest while at the same time pressing the edge of his sword to her throat.

"Listen to me," he said, with his face only a hand's breadth from hers, "I do not want to hurt you. But you must stop this madness."

She laughed: a long, low laugh. The ivory beads jumped on her abdomen. For the first time a look of concern came to his face.

"Madness?" she said. "Am I mad? Yes. I believe I am. I will show you how mad."

She leaned in, pressing against his razor-sharp blade. A drop of blood welled and ran down her throat onto her white chest-band, creating a dark rosette on the fabric.

He released her with a shove and took a few more steps back. Now he was only a pace or two from the edge of the cliff.

"Draupadi!" he cried. "I am sorry for you. I am. But the Pandavas broke the Law. Do you understand? They used a woman to kill Bhishma. They shot Drona in the back. They crushed Karna's spine as he lay helpless. They used treachery as a strategy, with no regard for the rules of war. Thousands are dead because of them! This is their karma, and it is just."

She laughed again: the same long, low laugh, the ivory beads jumping. "Why do you keep talking about the Pandavas?"

He took one more step back, and now he was almost on the verge. He threw another glance over his shoulder. Adopting a gentler, more soothing tone, he said: "Draupadi. Please. I do not want to hurt you, or your baby. Come. Let me take you up the hill. You can find your way back to the camp from there, can't you? Please. You must think of your child."

Her lips stretched in a smile at once beautiful and terrible, then ... slowly, slowly, she raised the object she held in her left hand: the object that had gone unnoticed by him during the mock swordfight along the promontory. She raised it high so the moonbeams would fall upon it and there could be no mistake as to what it was: a young boy's head, dangling by the hair.

"You're right," she said. "I must think of my child."

At first he stared blankly at it, uncomprehending. Then he cast his eyes back to her face and took a breath as if to speak—but did not. Then his eyes slid back to the head. And finally, as the wave of Truth came hurtling toward him—infinitely high, infinitely lucid, infinitely powerful—his face grew tight with horror. He dropped his sword. His legs buckled. He fell to his knees, raising his hands in supplication.

"Draupadi ... Draupadi. No. It's not true. I did not ... I did not ..." His eyes bulged. His hands shook.

She took a step, holding the head up and forward.

"You did. See the truth of what you did."

"No. No. It was the P-P-P- ... the P-P-P ..."

"The Pandavas? No. It was my five sleeping children."

She took another step. He leaned back, cowering, and the glow rising from the bloomeries at the base of the cliff caught the back of his head, creating a livid red halo to match the livid red of his scar. A couple of indigenes slept on the ground down there, ready to tend the smelting ore as needed, for production had not been allowed to stop just because of the war. Clustered around the rock spur, the chimneys blazed: five mouths of fire.

"No. I *saw* them ... the P-P-Pandavas. I *saw* them."

"You were blind. You saw what you wished to see—as all men do." She brought the head down to his eye level. "Now see what you do not wish to see."

"No. Draupadi. I b-b-b-beg you. I did not know. I did not know. I did not m-m-m ... mean to do it. B-b-b-b ... b-b-b ... *believe* me."

"I believe you, Duryodhana. I believe you." The gorgon smile had faded, leaving behind a look of searing sorrow. "You know that changes nothing."

She took one more step and raised her sword. She placed the point against his sternum. He made no move to evade it.

"I salute you, mine enemy! May your rebirth be fortunate."

She thrust the blade. He fell back clawing the air, over the edge and down, down, down, landing with a great *thud* on the center kiln, which collapsed in a heap of burning clay and ore. The flames rose up like a pyre, engulfing his body in a roaring mass of red, orange, gold, and black. The indigenes jumped to their feet and stared dumbfounded at the inferno.

Above on the cliff, she stood for a while looking down. Then she turned to go. As she wheeled about, the full moon over the western hills sent her shadow looming all the way up the escarpment behind her: a gigantic woman with long black limbs and distended belly, a sword in one hand, a severed head in the other, and a garland of skulls flying upward.

Chapter 20

THE WOMEN

Shikhandi said:

Ashwattama and I did not obey the king's order to return to camp. Instead, I allowed my friend to lead me down onto the iron field and over to the forge shed, where we stopped, turned, and looked back up at the escarpment. "No danger from the queen herself," Ashwattama muttered, "but she may have raised the alarm. We can't leave him alone." I stood quiet, unprotesting, still in shock at what he and the king had done. (Thanks to me. Once again, thanks to me.)

We saw the two figures appear on the verge of the cliff and stand, gesturing; we saw the queen raise her left hand with what looked like a round rock dangling from it; we saw Duryodhana drop to his knees; finally we saw him fall over the edge and down onto the bloomery. We ran to the pyre, but by the time we arrived there was nothing to do but stand and watch his body burn. Ashwattama kept his head and said the necessary prayers. I trust the Gods heard and accepted them, even though he was not the king's son.

Ashwa also remembered to tell the indigene stokers to wait until the fire had burned out, then to collect any bones and bring them to him personally. They did so, late the following morning, giving us a few remains to deliver to his mother for casting into the Ganges. The men in camp, exhausted and demoralized, mostly did not comment on the king's absence; to the few who did ask, Ashwattama said that King Duryodhana was engaged in peace talks and no doubt would return soon.

That whole day, Ashwattama and I worked alongside the hundred or so surviving Kaurava troops and several dozen indigenes—pressed into service from the iron mines and necessary for handling corpses—to transport our fallen captains and prepare their bodies for separate funerals. We helped build the enormous bier on which the regular soldiers would be burned together at the center of the plain. Ownerless horses, along with their chariots, had to be rounded up and led back to camp. Meanwhile the enemy's troops were going about the same tasks, also assisted by natives. Occasionally there was a question as to which clan a deceased soldier belonged to, or who owned a particular steed; then a few men from each side would gather and confer, resolving the matter without ado. No princes were present, but no one remarked on it. Cleaning up a battlefield isn't work for the high-born.

That whole day, Ashwattama and I continued in the belief that the Pandavas were dead.

We learned otherwise at sundown when all five of them rode into the Kaurava camp, bannermen in front and bodyguards behind, to receive our formal surrender. Ashwattama, as remaining senior officer, went forward to meet the party. When he saw the princes, he blanched as if he were seeing ghosts. I, though taken aback, was not shocked. All day I'd been thinking about Draupadi coming toward us down the escarpment. I'd been thinking about the scene atop the cliff. And I'd been thinking about the dangling object: the one she'd held in her left hand.

Shaken as he was, Ashwa once again kept his composure (he had always been much better at that than I; I think it was his father's influence). He knelt and offered the surrender in correct fashion. As soon as he'd finished, King Yudi declared him condemned for the murder of the five sons of the Pandavas. He was taken forthwith to a nearby tree and hanged.

After that I stepped forward and confessed my own participation in the murder. But at once Arjuna recognized me and said, "Shit! If it isn't the little warrior girl!"

Whereupon they all started to laugh, Bima slapping his thigh, the twins rolling their eyes, and presently Yudi beckoned to a couple of his men and instructed them to take me into custody, escort me back to the Pandava camp, and find me some women's clothes to put on; "for this," he said, "is the granddaughter of Lord Bhishma, and she is to accompany us to Hastinapura when we go, there to be given a proper establishment as befits her station."

So back I went, to be made a lady once more.

My husband Biptu, it turned out, had fought for the Pandavas and been killed on the first or second day of the war. So I was not only a lady, but a widow. My children remained with Fani; she remarried, I heard, and they are all still living in the town of Indraprasta.

Bhishma's body was brought back to Hastinapura and given a grand state funeral beside the Ganges, with High Priest Ramesha presiding and King Yudi playing the role of eldest son. I was permitted no part in it, not even the water-casting of the bones; I was, however, allowed to attend the ceremony, and I whispered the crucial prayers as Yudi chanted them, once again trusting the Gods to do the right thing and let his soul depart the earth. The funeral was followed by a lavish banquet at which Arjuna stood and gave a lengthy speech about "our noble grandfather," his many virtues, and his brave death. There wasn't a dry eye in the hall.

Who do I blame? Myself, of course. Had I not gone over to the Pandavas and driven the chariot, Bhishma would not have been killed. Karna, not being commander-in-chief, would not have had the opportunity to betray his side. The war would have proceeded honorably, and the Kauravas most likely would have won—or if not, would have surrendered on a strong footing and negotiated terms to divide the kingdom in two, with Duryodhana ruling the eastern half and Yudi the western half. Needless to say, the Pandava children would still be alive.

Of course, if we ask why I was even in a position to join up with the Pandavas, we must admit it was Vidura's doing. He came to see me, you know; just once, a few weeks after I'd been placed in seclusion in a suite of rooms deep in the Hastinapura women's quarters. He sat on a stool, fingers plucking at his brown dhoti, and apologized for making me a man. His remorse seemed genuine enough, but what he said served only to annoy me: he kept talking about the Law and how he had transgressed it, for a woman should never engage in a man's pursuits and vice versa—on and on in that vein. After a while I wanted to jump up and scream at him:

"I care nothing for the Law! I care nothing for men's pursuits, women's pursuits. All I know is I was given the chance to be a warrior, and I failed. It was everything I'd dreamed of, and when it was handed to me, a shining sword with a brilliant edge, I flailed around like a ... like a rampaging elephant. The Pandavas laughed at me, even Ashwa laughed at me, and rightly so, for it was all a delusion born of—yes, I will say it though it burns me to say it—my crush: my girl's crush on a handsome man who paid attention to me and fed my sense of superiority, my superiority to *ladies* with their stupid sewing and stupid giggling and stupid gossip. Yet the stupidest lady in the world has more sense than I: she sees men's faults, laughs at their flattery, and is never, ever fooled by them. I was fooled. I was *the* fool. The Fool Shikhandi."

Of course I said nothing of the kind to Vidura. I thanked him for coming to see me, dropped him a curtsey as he left, and went back to my embroidery: a summer-weight cloak for Prince Arjuna. Arjuna had asked especially that I be the lady to embroider his clothes from now on. It was an honor I could not refuse.

≈

Gandhari said:

When the news came that my two sons and my brother were dead, I changed my violet veil for a black one and announced my retirement. I offered to give up my rooms; they are some of the nicest in the palace, and I thought Draupadi, the new queen, might want them. As it turned out, however, she was to be queen in name only. For reasons I found out a little later, she had lost all favor with her husbands and was to keep seclusion, almost like a widow.

My brother and sons, they said, had died in battle and had therefore been given, if not state funerals like Bhishma, proper kshatriya funerals on the field of Kurukshetra. Yudi himself brought me the charred bones of Shakuna and Dushasana and told me I would be allowed to take them to the Ganges (the water-casting ceremony being the one sacrament in which a female relative properly takes the lead). But he did not bring Duryodhana's bones, and when I asked why, he said Duryodhana had given the order for the deaths of the Pandava children, making him a murderer of innocents, and although he had earned a kshatriya funeral by being killed in battle—smashed in the thigh by Bima's mace, Yudi said—he nevertheless had transgressed the Law and therefore would not have the honor of a water burial for his remains. I thanked his majesty, told him I understood, and made him a deep curtsey as he left the room.

Then I went to the clothes chest, opened it, and laid the two silk-wrapped bundles next to the bones of my elder son.

Lady Shikhandi had brought them to me the day before. After she'd presented them—just a few sticks rattling loose in a rust-colored cotton bag—she told me what had happened on the last night of the war. She told me of the part they had each played: Duryodhana, Ashwattama, and herself. I wasn't surprised that Yudi's version of events was different. The Pandavas naturally did not want it known that it was their wife who had (once again) defeated their nemesis, so they put it about that Bima had mangled Duryodhana's thigh and left him for dead, but that he did not die immediately; rather he lay on the field all night, and it was as he lay dying in agony (they said) that he had given the order to Ashwattama to go kill the little Pandavas: the "Massacre at Night," as it later became known in the bards' songs.

I was glad, very glad, that that version was untrue. I was glad that his death had been quick and, moreover, that he had not merely given an order but had gone himself, right into the enemy's camp, and struck a courageous blow for the honor of the Kauravas. Yes, he had made a terrible mistake, but as I said to Shikhandi: the courage, therefore the honor, was no less.

The next day at sunrise I went down to the Ganges. I had wrapped and tied all the bones together in one bundle. Aided by my ladies, I waded into the water up to my waist. I held up the bundle and chanted the prayers three times: once for each man. I took the ewer handed to me by Lady Padma, filled it in the river, and poured it over the silk wrappings—three times. Then I lowered the bones into the water and let them go. They floated downstream a short way before sinking out of sight.

That evening I went to see Tarashtra in his rooms. Counselor Vidura was sitting with him. Vidura is about the only person besides me whom my husband tolerates these days; he doesn't seem to know who most other people are.

"Who's that, Vidu? Who's just come in?" he said fretfully.

"It is the former queen, your majesty. Your wife."

"Ah, Gandhari! There you are," he said. He gave a random shove to an ivory horse on the pachisi board sitting on the table before him. "Come see me win this game! Vidu tries, but I always beat him." He shoved the piece again, knocking the others helter-skelter. "There! I won again! Didn't I, Vidu?"

"Yes, Sire. You won again."

"Yes. Heh, heh." He drummed his fingers on his large,

crimson-clad belly. "So, Dhari, what's the news? What news of the—you know. The thing. The war."

"The news is good, Husband. Very good."

"Wonderful, wonderful! Duryo's beaten those Pandava brats? Sent them packing?"

"Well, not quite yet. In fact, they're coming back here to live. The Pandavas, I mean."

"What? Here, in the palace? Oh, Duryo won't like that. No, he won't like that."

"Yes, well, you see: Duryo is going to be away for a while."

"Oh. Off to that whatchamacallit, I suppose. That iron mine. He's always running off to that place. Such a lot of nonsense. Shoes for horses! Have you ever heard such nonsense?"

"No, dear. But he does have to be away, so he's asked Yudi and the others to stay here and look after things while he's gone."

"Ah! Seems too generous. Those Pandavas: give 'em a drop, they'll take the whole barrel. But then he's always been too generous, Duryo has. Can't be helped; he gets it from me." He sighed heavily. "Yes ... he gets it from me." He sat back, tipping his blind eyes toward the ceiling and shaking his head at the folly of the world. Then he sat forward, smiling and patting the table. "Well, Vidu, what about it? Ready for another beating?"

"Yes, Sire," said Vidura. "I am ready."

The guards at the door barely bothered to bow as I left the room.

Who do I blame? Myself, of course. If only I had refused to listen to those vaishya worthies when they came to me fifteen years ago and said they would not accept a Naga girl as queen of the Kuru; if only I had told them to go fuck themselves, as Satyavati advised me, and insisted on Duryodhana's right to be crowned, then he would have been king, Jaratka would have been queen, and when she died in childbed—if she died—Duryo would have either married again or not, but in any case, his position would have been secure. The Pandavas would have stayed at Indraprasta, content with their drinking and hunting, their dice and their whores, and never thought to mount a challenge for the realm.

But then ... I am forgetting someone: that dark-haired, smooth-talking, ever-ambitious prince of Vrishni.

Before he came along, the Pandavas had never been much of a threat. Oh, Perta tried to advance their interests, to be sure, but as a woman her power was limited. Once Krishna entered the picture, however, they were driven by him: driven to compete in tournaments, forge alliances, burn forests, build palaces, grab iron fields, and even go to war—to war against their own family. Krishna has no family (just an old father and a drunken sister whom he has always ignored), so how can he know what it means to lose one? How can he know what it feels like to cast away the bones of everyone you have ever loved and watch them sink into the river?

He came to visit me, you know; it was when he was in Hastinapura for Yudi's coronation. He sat on a stool with his blue cloak draped over his tall knees and apologized, with many professions of respect, for ousting me from my position. He seemed a little unnerved (as people tend to be) by my veil, so as he talked on, I remained still and silent, hoping he was imagining the face of a beast, or worse, behind the black silk. When his blitherings finally petered out, I nodded gravely and said:

"Thank you, Prince Krishna. There is no need to apologize. I know you could not help it; it was your unnatural attraction for Prince Arjuna, combined with your weakness for weak people. Yes, the Pandavas and their weakness drew you in, like a moth to a lamp. It was not your fault—any more than it is the moth's fault when it immolates itself in the flame and drops to the ground, a blackened, shriveled corpse."

His pallid face, as he took his leave, gave me some satisfaction.

≈

Draupadi said:

My girl-child was born one week after Yudi's coronation. I named her Chandra, for the full moon. She did not live long; I had not expected it. "Failure to thrive," the midwives called it, and put it down to the fast, stressful journey up the Yamuna when I'd been eight months along. "Failure to thrive," I repeated. "Yes, that sounds right."

After that I had the idea of starving myself. *I, too, will fail to thrive,* I thought. I did not eat for ten days; only sips of water and some betel nut to chew. My ladies were most distressed. But on the eleventh day, as I was lying on my settee staring up at the ceiling as

usual, I heard a commotion in the hallway and in came two guardsmen with ... Subhadra.

"What is this?" I asked, struggling to sit up. "What are you
doing with Lady Susu?"

They shoved her roughly, and she fell to the floor. She was red-
faced, crying. Her hair was a rat's nest. Her breasts sagged in their
threadbare yellow chest-band.

"Prince Arjuna's orders, Ma'am," said the taller of the two guards.
"She's been causing trouble. Prince Arjuna says she is to stay with you
from now on. He says you are to keep her under control, or ... or
..." He broke off and looked to his colleague.

"*Ashram*," the other hissed.

"... or she will be sent to the ashram!"

They turned without bowing and stomped out. I got up—shak-
ily, to be sure, but I could still manage to stand—and crossed to the
bedraggled, sniffling heap. I put my arms around her. She laid her
face on my shoulder and continued to bawl, wetting my veil with her
tears and snot and gasping out, "Abi ... Abi ... my baby Abi."

I shushed her and rocked her, saying, "Don't cry, Susu, don't
cry. It will be all right. You'll see. Everything's going to be all right."
Eventually she stopped crying, and I beckoned to a couple of maidservants. "Take her to the chamber and help her wash," I said. "Find
her some clean clothes. Fix her hair. Then you can bring us both
some food."

From then on, I no longer thought of killing myself. I had to
look after her, you see.

You might have assumed that the Pandavas, fresh off a victory
and with both their old wives disgraced, would have quickly set about
finding new wives. There was initially some talk of Yudi's marrying
Banumati, Duryodhana's widow and the former queen; perhaps Yudi
didn't like her, but in any case, nothing came of it. She was sent back
to her father the king of Madrasa (who had survived the war after
losing three sons on the battlefield). Then there was talk of a princess
from Naimisha, and one from Panchala (she was a cousin of mine),
and even one from far-off Mundra by the sea. No negotiators, however, were sent—Krishna seemed the obvious man for the job, but
he was spending less and less time in Hastinapura—so those plans
fizzled out, too. Then there were the Kuru war widows, a thousand or
more, any of whom would have given their back teeth to marry one

of the Pandavas. Many of these women were invited to the nightly parties (which had continued apace), and there were always one or two of them creeping out of a prince's room at dawn; but again, no marriages were proposed.

In those early months the queen-by-default was Uttari, Abimanyu's young widow. She, as you may recall, had been five months pregnant when the war began. The Pandavas made much of her, seating her (so I heard) at the royal table and even on the queen's throne for some of their audiences. As her time approached, they professed great anxiety. Midwives were summoned; special foods and medicines were ordered. When she was delivered of a boy, the celebrations were lavish. Then, after a month, invitations went out for the naming ceremony to be held in the great hall. Susu and I were allowed to attend, heavily veiled and seated behind a screen with the other court ladies, in conformance with the new practice of segregating men from women at public events. Uttari, also veiled, sat on a stool at one side of the dais, holding the baby in her lap; the five proud grandfathers sat on their five thrones at the center. "His name is Parikshit!" said Yudi, and the hall erupted in cheers. Yudi went on to declare him the heir and crown prince, and a grand banquet followed.

Who do I blame? Myself, of course. I don't say I was wrong to choose Arjuna instead of Duryodhana at my bridegroom choice; it seemed the right thing at the time, and in any case I had to follow my father's wishes. But I was wrong, later, to hate those two: Duryodhana and Jaratka.

I hated *him* for so obviously not caring that I had chosen another man. I hated *her* for having a husband who adored her, who made love to her, who gave her a child. Oh, I hated Subhadra, too, but only in a half-hearted way; Susu was so pathetic, her jabs at me so crude, that it was hard to work up much ire toward her. No, it was Jaratka and Duryo I truly hated, for their radiant, self-contained happiness: a happiness I knew would never be mine.

Even after she died, I went on hating him. He hated me, too, and our hatreds fed on each other, until his finally boiled over at the Dicing. Had I knelt to him then, weeping and begging as he wanted me to, that would have been the end of it; and I probably would have, had Karna not made that histrionic display, rushing over and covering me with the cloak like some lovesick cowherd. That enraged me so ... Well. You're aware of what I did.

I went to see Karna, you know. It was a few weeks after Susu had moved in and I'd started eating again. He had been given a small room just off the soldiers' barracks, where of course I am not allowed to go, but I dressed myself like an upper maidservant, veiled my face, and walked across the compound with the confidence of a message-bearer. His wife, Lady Padma, was there when I arrived; it is her prerogative to care for him now that he's bedridden. There is also an outcaste man to roll him over, wipe him down, change the bed-clothes, and so forth. When I entered, pulling back my veil, Padma recognized me. She greeted me kindly and brought a stool up to the bed. Then she apologized, saying she needed to attend the dowager queen; "I mean, the dowager queen that was." She curtsied to me and left. The outcaste man stayed, squatting in a corner.

"Hello, Karna," I said, seating myself on the stool.

"Hello ... your grace." He was much thinner, but still hand-some. His bare chest above the saffron blanket was unblemished; his mop of brown hair, just a few threads of gray, fanned out on the saf-fron pillow on which his head was propped; his worn leather satchel lay at his side. He pressed his palms together in namaste: "I am sorry I cannot rise to greet you."

"How are you, Karna? Are you in any pain?"

"A little. In my shoulders and neck sometimes. Below the waist, there's nothing."

"I see."

We talked of this and that. He said he was sorry about my brother Tadyu; I thanked him. I asked him how his mother did; he said she was well, still living in town, and came often to visit.

We fell silent awhile, listening to the coos of pigeons in a tree outside the small window. Then he looked down at his hands and said: "The thing is, when you love someone, and you do something terrible for their sake, it kills the love."

"I suppose that's true," I said.

He raised his eyes to mine: wide, brown eyes. "Do you think he forgives me?"

I paused, reflecting. "I think he is in paradise. And I think every-one in paradise forgives everyone on earth. Why would they not?"

He looked down at his hands again. "Yes. Why would they not?"

I told him I must get back, for Lady Subhadra would be missing me. He thanked me for coming and hoped I would come again soon. I said it had been my pleasure. As I went out the door I cast a glance back over my shoulder: he was looking out the window, and the sun was glinting off his golden earrings.

≈

Satyavati said:

Oof. Ouch. Gods, it's hard, being this old. Everything always hurts.

No, Sisi, *not* like that. Get up and let Astika do it. Come here, child; you rub my legs for me. You do it much better than anyone else. Just like your mother, Jaratka ... she was the only one of my maidservants who ever knew how to give a really good massage.

Aah. That's right. *Ooh.* Keep going, child. That's good.

So, we were talking about that bard, the new one who performs after dinner every night. What's his name again? No, don't tell me, I won't remember it anyway. You were saying how he's been telling our family story: "the great story of the Bharata"—is that what he calls it? Yes. It's an apt enough title; King Bharata was the first Arya king in these parts, and all the clans are descended from him, so the name of our people—taking in Kuru, Panchala, Vrishni, Kashi, Madrasa, Naimisha, all the rest—is Bharata.

I suppose you have to sneak into the great hall to hear him, seeing as you're still unmarried. *Tsk!* Such a shame. Nearly sixteen, aren't you? I know a lot of men were killed in the war, that ridiculous war, but that's no excuse. Your grandmother, Gandhari, now: she really ought to see to it. You mention it to her, dear, the next time you have a talk with her. If she won't do anything, you let me know and *I'll* talk to Yudi about it. Honestly, these young generations ... never a thought for anyone but themselves! Back in my day, you would have been married two years already, with a baby in the cradle and another on the way.

But you were saying: about the bard, and how you have to sneak into the hall to hear him. Ha! I would have done the same at your age. I never let silly rules stop me from doing as I pleased. Seems there are a lot more rules, these days ... for women, anyway ... all those screens and veils and stricter chaupadi and telling us when we're allowed to speak and not speak and who knows what else ... the priests seem to come up with new rules every week.

I guess they do have one advantage—the screens and veils, I mean. They make it easier for a woman to go unnoticed. I imagine you could drop a blanket over your head, slip in behind a screen, and sit listening the whole night if you wanted to. Heh. I wouldn't mind giving it a try myself. But then, I haven't walked anywhere in years.

The Mahabharata. Hmm. It's not a bad title, not a bad title at all. And it begins with me as a fish girl, you say? I like that. Of course it's complete nonsense, all that about the great sage Parashara appearing to me on my ferry boat in a magical mist and telling me not to worry because he'd use his divine powers to restore my virginity, and me joyfully accepting his love. Ha! Absolute horseshit. Parashara was a grimy, lustful, bloody-minded ascetic who used to prowl the riverbank looking for young girls to rape. He raped me. I became pregnant. When I gave birth, I tried to drown the baby ... then took him to the ashram instead. That was Vyasa, my son, whom I made high priest; he died recently, you know ... was it last month? I can't recall. He took after his father in many ways. Then Tarashtra took after *him,* and I must say it seems that Vaishampayana (Lopside, I still call him) is taking after *his* father.

Parashara, Vyasa, Tarashtra, Lopside: a long line of fairly disgusting men.

You're shocked to hear me call our new high priest disgusting. But he is; oh yes, he is. The whole reason the Pandavas promoted him is that he started going to their parties, bringing whores with him: very young whores. (How do I know these things? My girls tell me.) He joined in the drinking and the dice games, taking good care to lose. And *then* he started making statements about Yudi and the rest being Gods—I forget which ones, exactly—and your father being the demon Kali, and saying Goddess Kali and demon Kali are the same, which they certainly are not, but the Pandavas lapped it up. Before long the court was repeating it, the bards began spinning the tale, and, well ... here we are.

It *was* foolish of your father to pass over Vaishampayana; it's never wise to make an enemy if one can help it. But then you know what they say: "The seed of a rapist will find a way down." I suspect our little Lopside would have ended up siding with the Pandavas in any case.

Who do I blame? *Tush,* child; what a silly question! There is no one to blame. Sometimes the wrong side wins, and that's all there is to it.

Suppose I hadn't driven that hard bargain with King Shantanu, making him put Bhishma out of the line of succession in favor of my own children. Oh, I know what people are saying: that was the start of all the strife, they say, the root of the poison tree. Makes it look like the whole thing was my fault. But mark my words: Bhishma had plenty of chances to put himself back in the line. He could have done it when Amba begged him to marry her and make her queen; he could have done it when Chit died and I begged him to sire sons on the widows; he could have done it when Pandu died and the question of an heir was thrown open again.

Who would ever have stood in his way? What could any of us have done, had he simply declared his intent to take the throne? The people were always with him. His reputation was unassailable, his competence undeniable. Even Perta, even Gandhari, would have had to admit that Bhishma was fitter to rule than either of their husbands—and fitter to select the next king, should he have had no sons himself. So why did he hang back? Why did he always refer to his "vow": that vow he had uttered as a four-year-old, a vow that no tribunal, secular or sacred, would ever have enforced?

Here's the truth: Bhishma did not want to be king. He feared the power of the kingship. So he clung to his so-called vow like a talisman, using it as an excuse to turn away from power—like a nervous bridegroom on his wedding night, turning away from his sweet bride as she unwinds her sari and holds out loving arms.

He was a good man, though, Bhishma. I miss him. I miss talking with him. I miss your father, too ... he always made time to visit me, even after he became king.

Oof. All right, child, that's enough. I'm getting sleepy ... I think I'll take a little nap.

Sisi! Where are you, Sisi? ... Oh, there you are. Must I always scream myself hoarse? Bring me the blanket, there's a good girl.

Now, Astika: just pull it up over me and tuck it in a bit. That's right. Goodness, your face is so like your mother's: those heavy-lidded eyes.

She was very beautiful, you know. And brave. I never knew a braver girl.

The townsmen said she could not be queen because she was an outcaste. I told Gandhari it was all nonsense. "Nonsense," I said. "Caste means nothing to women. We make our own way in the world. Kshatriya, shudra, Snake ... what does it matter? We're our own caste ..."

Epilogue

ASTIKA

nd that, Nephew, is the end of my story.

Forty years later, it's amazing to see how the other story—that is, the false one—has taken hold. Bards sing it in the halls; soldiers tell it around campfires; ladies use it to while away their idle hours. Why, even the priests have picked it up, inserting some of its verses right into the sacraments! Old High Priest Vyasa would have been aghast.

The false story has its appeal, of course, what with its clear heroes (the Pandavas) and clear villain (Duryodhana). Bards and their listeners prefer clarity. But it's funny: despite all the condemnations and maledictions they heap on my father, they still haven't worked out a way to send him to hell in the end. Since he was a kshatriya who was killed (supposedly) in battle, he has to go straight to paradise, and since the Pandavas in their pride will never allow the real circumstances of his death to come out, that version stands. I find that amusing.

The Pandavas … the Pandavas. When *they* finally die, what will happen to them? They won't have met their end on a battlefield, so a sojourn in Yama's kingdom seems likely. I wonder how the God of Death and Law will judge them.

I wonder the same thing about my seven storytellers. How were their cases judged? And where are they now? The first to go was Satyavati, at the age of ninety-eight. Karna died a year later from complications of his war wounds. Vidura, Draupadi, and Shikhandi succumbed to the bloody flux that swept the palace the summer six years after the war. (Poor Susu lived only a month longer.)

The following winter, Krishna died. His visits to Hastinapura after the war had grown increasingly rare; being Parikshit's godfather, however, he was expected to be there for certain occasions, and that time he had traveled in for the boy's First Purification. After the ceremony he went hunting in the forest with Arjuna. A poacher, we were told, mistook the flutter of his blue cloak for a bird and shot him dead. Arjuna was distraught; he personally tracked down the poacher and had him executed.

Last to go was Queen Gandhari. She had always said that once her husband's wits were completely addled she would walk with him into the Ganges, and that is exactly what she did, on the ninth anniversary of the war's end.

Parikshit grew up, married, and was crowned king. The Pandavas moved back to their palace at Indraprasta. And you, Janamejaya: you came along soon after that.

Now you are king. And you must decide the fate of those six hundred Naga, locked in your horse barns.

For three weeks they have been held captive while the rains continued. With the rains ended, earth and air are drying out. It would be quite easy to build a bonfire, bind their hands and feet, and throw them in. "A fit punishment for savage murderers," says the high priest. "It is what the Law prescribes."

Well. He is a brahmin, and a man, so he knows more about the Law than I do. And yes, an ambush killing is an evil act, devoid of honor, full of savagery, something only a filthy dung-eater would be capable of. Perhaps, having killed your father in such a horrible way, the Snakes deserve an equally horrible death.

I fear that after all, Janamejaya, I cannot advise you. You must decide for yourself.

I will just say this: Whatever your decision, whatever your choice, don't think you can escape it. Don't think you can disguise the deed, or cast the blame on another, or say it was the fulfillment of someone else's fate in which you had no part. Don't imagine (as men often do) that if you act disinterestedly, merely following the Law as it's given, the fruits of your action will not sprout, the fire of your action will not catch.

I tell you, Janamejaya: The fire will catch. It may stay suppressed for a long, long time, just the tiny flame of an oil lamp deep in the women's quarters, its weak glow barely enough to light a mother's face as she murmurs a bedtime story. But one day that flame will touch a scrap of linen, or a piece of wood, or a chunk of lacquer; it will become a small blaze, then a large one, then a bonfire, a house fire, a forest fire … a vast, unstoppable wave of fire. It will sweep through time, sweep through realms, burning away lies and smelting out truth like a bloom of pure iron. In its searing light, the world will see all you did, all you were. The world will know your story. And the world will judge.

But listen to me rattling on! You must be awfully bored with your old Auntie Tika and her family gossip. It was good of you to visit me these past few weeks; now that you're king, you won't have much time for visits, I know. Off with you, now, Janamejaya. They'll be waiting for you in the council chamber. You'll need to talk about the Snakes.

Nagira, dear, fetch his majesty's cloak. Quickly, now.

Better wrap it over your chest, Sire; there's quite a chill in the air this morning …

What's that? You'll be back this afternoon?

Yes, of *course* you may come, Nephew. My girls and I are always happy to see you.

Don't make it too late, though; Nagira goes home at sundown.

But then I don't need to tell *you* that. Do I?

THE END

Acknowledgments

My material is the Mahabharata, the longest poem in the world, which famously says of itself: "What is here is also found elsewhere, but what is not here is nowhere else." I first encountered this massive Sanskrit work in the St. John's College Program in Eastern Classics, which confers Master's degrees in the classic philosophy and literature of India, China, and Japan. My thanks go to Julie Reahard, who led our study of the epic, and to all the students in that class; especially A. Rose Rickhoff, whose comment about the turtles in the Kandhava Forest sparked the train of thought that led, ultimately, to this book. My thanks also go to Anupam Choudhury, whose editing resulted in not only improved writing but also greater historical and cultural accuracy; to Phil LeCuyer of Respondeo Books, for his sponsorship and encouragement; to Adam Robinson, for his expert design and production assistance; and to Krishnan Venkatesh, whose advice was, as always, invaluable. Finally, I thank my husband, Matt, without whose unstinting support this work would not have been possible.

About the Author

Author photograph © Melanie West

Jocelyn Davis is an internationally known author and speaker and the former head of R&D for a global leadership development consultancy. Her previous books include *Strategic Speed, The Greats on Leadership,* and *The Art of Quiet Influence.* She holds Master's degrees in philosophy and Eastern classics. She grew up in a foreign-service family and has lived in many regions of the world, including Southeast Asia, East Africa, and the Caribbean. Currently she lives in Santa Fe, New Mexico. *The Age of Kali* is her first novel.

Visit her website at JocelynRDavis.com.